THE BLACKWOOD CURSE

T STEDMAN

THE BLACKWOOD CURSE

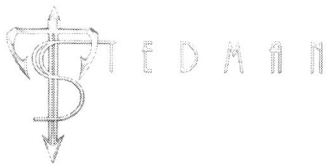

STEDMAN

ACKNOWLEDGEMENTS

This is my first foray into the world of Young Adult fiction. I hope you enjoy it as much as I did writing it and find it as exciting as my adult worlds.
As always, a special thank you to my team: Nicky Lovick, my new artist, Daniela Owergoor, Jane Harrison and, of course, my wonderful readers.

CHAPTER 1

The only thing that made any sense to me was death. It was final and there was no arguing with it, or so I thought. It was strange how naive I was back then. I guess we all are.

The rain was already thrashing the window of the plane as it landed at Heathrow. It seemed fitting. Whether I was in the US or the UK, life would be a dark existence for me from now on. My brother Pete was gone, there was no bringing him back, and the car wreck that had taken him had also taken what little relationship I'd had with my parents for ever.

We filed off the plane and I got swept along with the crowd through corridors, down escalators, Passport Control and Baggage Reclaim. It held none of the excitement travelling with Pete had in the past. Every destination had been an adventure.

My mood remained in its default position of flat line, even when a cheerful man with a Cockney accent held up a board with Rebecca Whitely on it. It didn't seem like my name, written out in full. Everyone called me Beccah at home.

''ello, Miss. I'm Burt. Nice to meet you.' He took my bags from the trolley and nodded his head in the direction he was already walking. 'Car's not far. Good job, its bitter out.'

I quickly caught on that he liked to talk and didn't necessarily need an answer. So I followed as he walked faster than me, even with the bags. He was right about the car park; ten minutes and we were loaded up and pulling out of the parking lot. He continued to chatter, 'Get much sleep on the plane?'

I shrugged.

'I work for your aunt – bit of this and that, you know? Driving and maintenance, mainly.' I tuned out. His voice flowed over me as I watched the grey buildings and traffic pass by.

It seemed a very long time until everything got greener and wilder. The road became thin, squashed between the stone walls on either side. Hills rolled and bare trees looked like they were hugging themselves in the cold. It had stopped raining at least. Although the biting, inhospitable wind appeared to cut deeper, willing me to go home. *Well, newsflash, life was just as wintery at home, even in a seventy-five degrees Fahrenheit California.*

The car eventually turned off the lane onto a driveway that appeared to go on forever. Trees overhung it, making it a green tunnel, framing a huge grey house at the end. It was ancient, all gargoyles and turrets.

The driveway ended in a wide shingle circle for turning, where the driver slowed to a stop right outside a huge oak door. I checked my phone quickly before I got out. Just to make sure there were no messages from Mom and Dad. Stupid, really. Since Pete, they were completely lost to their own grief. I had come to realise there was nothing as selfish as loss. It consumed a person so there was no room for anything else.

The driver walked around the car, opened the trunk and held open the door. After a brief hesitation as I took a deep breath, I got out of the car. I wobbled a bit while the driver passed my crutches. He grabbed my bags just as the door opened. A lady in tweed, who looked in her fifties, beckoned me in. I guessed she wasn't my great-aunt; too young. There was no greeting. Just: 'I'll arrange for your things to be taken up to your room.'

The inside was unusual. A large hexagon-shaped hall with doors on nearly every facet and a huge staircase leading up from the centre. It was overwhelmingly dark – even with a window halfway up. It was because the decor was a deep maroon that appeared to absorb the light. The pictures were dark oils of landscapes and racehorses. They had black ornate frames around them, almost as if they were deliberately chosen for Gothic gloom. The ceiling was the same colour as the walls and heavily moulded. A huge black chandelier, that looked low enough to touch, matched the frames and hung in the stairwell.

I wasn't absolutely sure, but the lamps on the walls looked like real flames – maybe even gas. The only nod to the twenty-first century appeared to be a huge ancient-looking iron radiator that gave out very little warmth. The floor was tiled; red and black in a geometric pattern.

'Your aunt is in the drawing room if you want to say hello.' She gave me no time to respond and pointed to one of the doors that looked identical to all the others. I panicked. I was expecting some sort of proper introduction, but she was already walking away.

'Wait. What's your name?' I asked, a little too loudly. 'Sorry … what do I call you?'

'Gertrude,' the woman said without turning around. 'I'll

bring some tea.' She disappeared on the other side of the staircase.

I looked at the maroon door she'd pointed at. A grandfather clock chimed four times behind me, as a nudge to move forward. I knocked.

'Come in.'

I balanced on my good leg, juggling the crutch as I turned the weighty brass handle. It occurred to me how old the voice sounded and it filled me with gloom. *It was going to be a laugh a minute here.* I opened the door and slipped inside.

At first I couldn't see her. I was greeted with another large, dark room, the colour of moss. It did feel a little more homely with the temperature a good couple of degrees warmer than the hallway. It was grander too. The chandelier was gold and so were the frames around the paintings that seemed to be brighter and more full of flowers.

I still couldn't see her so I walked further into the room, passing a wall crammed with faded photographs.

'Come closer, child,' the voice said, coming from a wing-backed armchair with its back to me. It faced the carved, lit fireplace and mirror above, so tall it almost reached the ceiling.

I approached cautiously. I'd never met my grandmother's sister. I came to a stop, close to the fire where I could see her face and feel the flames' warmth on my face.

'Ah, Christina's girl. What's wrong with your leg? Not a cripple, are you? Can't be doing with a cripple.'

Shocked at her rudeness, I quickly answered, 'No, it was the car accident, remember? Didn't Mom tell you in her letter? It should be fine in a few weeks.'

'Mmm,' she said, not sounding convinced at all.

I wasn't sure I'd ever met anyone so old. Her skin looked translucent, like white tissue paper, with thin blue lines threaded across her forehead and the backs of her hands. I was horrified when she put one out for me to take. I got over myself quickly. 'How do you do … Rebecca,' I said, barely touching the tips of her fingers.

'You may call me aunt, even though I should be dead by now.' Her eyes wandered off, as if she could see something in the air around her. 'You have my sister's eyes,' she said, looking straight back at me again with hers, a glassy light grey. 'Sit with me a while,' she said, her expression now speculative.

I looked around and found an upholstered footstool to sit on, near enough to see her, but just out of reach. I couldn't help checking out the room. She looked mildly amused watching me. 'There was great wealth in the family once … once.' She laughed.

The room fitted her perfectly, all doilies and lace; straight out of a Jane Austen novel. *Well, not exactly.* More like a living museum that was unloved and a little worn out.

The door opened and Gertrude came in carrying a tray of tea. I couldn't take my eyes off the dainty floral cups and teapot. It appeared to have a beany hat on top with holes for the handle and spout. My aunt must have read my expression because she said, 'You'll have to get used to taking your tea hot here, girl, out of a proper pot with real tea leaves. None of that iced, tea-bagged tosh here.'

I smiled weakly. I didn't have a clue what she was going on about. I mainly drank juice or coke at home. I guessed there was a lot of stuff to get used to in a new country. With the hole now in my chest, I didn't think it was possible to fill it with anything.

'Shall I pour, Sarah?' Gertrude said.

I was surprised she called my aunt by her first name. It was probably because of the setting that I expected her to curtsy and call her ma'am, or something. She poured the tea and offered me sugar in little cubes with pincers. I took three which made her shake her head, so I put one back.

'When you've settled in, Gerty's girl – what's her name?'

'Tallulah,' Gertrude immediately said, as if it was a regular occurrence.

'Tallulah … will come and show you about the place. It's not too big; we don't use the entire house. I'm just too damn old to get around these days. You're enrolled in the same school, so at least you'll know someone in your class. You start Monday. Can't have you mooning about the place doing nothing.'

I realised as my aunt spoke that she asked no questions because she rarely listened. I smiled weakly. Again. Being in the background was familiar territory. I took in the important things like a good little girl: *school, Monday. Got it.*

It wasn't long before she started repeating everything she'd said all over again. So I was pretty relieved when Gertrude showed up and interrupted the monologue. 'Right then … your room is ready. Don't want to tire out your aunt too much.'

I stood up immediately, grateful to escape.

'You fuss too much, Gerty,' my aunt said, but Gerty was passing her a bottle of what looked like pills. 'Time already?'

'Yes, Sarah. An hour before food, remember?'

Despite her sour-faced exterior, she did seem to genuinely care for my aunt.

After she saw to it that my aunt swallowed the tablets, I followed her out and up the huge curved staircase, slowly, one step at a time. The only concession she gave to my use of crutches was to pause every ten or so steps. Luckily, the staircase shape meant they weren't steep and had a wider space on the outside edge. It allowed me time to balance and study the gloomy faces staring out from the paintings going up.

'Your ancestors,' Gertrude said, by way of explanation. I had no idea I had anyone so grand in the family worth painting, let alone know who they were. My mother had said nothing and now I wondered why.

Each portrait looked stiff and proper. No one had been captured in a natural pose and every single one of them looked unhappy. Perhaps it was the curse of the family. It struck me then that my mother's name was now Whitely. 'What's Sarah's family name?'

Gertrude actually stopped and looked around at me. 'Blackwood.' Then, after a stern glare as if I should have known better, she resumed walking up the stairs.

I followed glumly. As I heaved myself onto the final, arm-trembling steps, the last of the portraits caught my eye.

This one was different. The subject appeared to have been painted in the same style as the others, but this girl had laughter in her eyes – more than that; they held mischief.

I paused to look more closely. Underneath, embedded in the frame, was a small brass plaque that read: Lila Blackwood Dunn. 1839–1857. *Eighteen*. She was exactly the same age as me. Such a short life and yet those eyes seemed to say she'd seen it all.

'The black sheep of Blackwood,' Gertrude said, in a tone of utter disapproval. I'd begun to think she was good at that. Unbeknown to her, she'd just made Lila the most interesting person in the house.

MY BAGS WERE ALREADY in my room when I got there. The two red cases and grey holdall were in a waist-high pile in the centre of a once-expensive rug. The room was large and carried on the dark theme in a faded turquoise, but the ceiling was darker, with silver stars dotted all over. Otherwise, it reminded me of a dolls house. There was actually one in the corner set on a low table near the window seat. That window seat was the only thing I liked about the room. It would be a good place to read. I stroked the coarse mane of an old rocking horse that had seen better days and decided it must have been a nursery.

I ran a finger over the iron mantelpiece in the corner. The turquoise-painted surface was chipped, but someone had dusted at least. It was painted the same shade as everything else. Only the frilly white oval cloths on just about every available surface contrasted with the gloom. They were on the dressing table, the chest of drawers and the nightstand with the ruched green lamp. I sat down on the green counterpane and decided nothing could have changed since the 1800s.

I unpacked and tried out the window seat. It was perfect for comfort and the view. The garden looked even less loved than the house; completely forgotten. I guess that's what winter did; cut everything to the quick. Even what was meant to stay green looked dipped in white or brown. The grass had given up growing at different lengths and the ramshackle outbuildings looked half up or down. They were probably stables once.

Then I spotted a building, standing alone, at the far end of the garden. Hidden, almost. It was perfectly circular and looked more derelict than the rest. It had green-stained arched windows that went all the way around and holes where the glass had once been. The curvy roof was still beautiful in shape, although it had a hole in the only bit not covered in moss. The bare branches of an elm, petrified by lightning, rested on top and threatened to cave it in.

I wondered what it had once been, stuck out there all alone. I imagined the ornate windows when they were white and nestled between the trees in full leaf, like Hansel and Gretel's cottage. Balls and garden parties would have spilled onto the once-manicured lawns. Smart gentlemen escorting ladies in long dresses, would stroll and discover the path to the little house. Perhaps that's what it was meant for; a secret meeting place for lovers. How perfect it must have been with the scent of the flowers and elaborate harmonies of a string quartet carried there by the gentle breeze of a balmy evening.

I shivered. I blinked and looked around me, suddenly remembering where I was. It had been the weirdest sensation, like I'd been transported in a dream. And yet it had felt so real. A little unnerved, I turned away.

The door knock was a welcome distraction. 'Come in,' I said, not bothering to get up.

The girl, who could only be Tallulah, marched straight in. 'Hi!' she said, without hiding the head-to-toe, one-second visual assessment she gave me.

She was tall, pale and blonde and wore too much black eyeliner. It wasn't what I'd expected prim old Gertrude's daughter to look like. She reminded me of a Day of the Dead tattoo; minus the stitch marks, of course. 'Alright?' she said. 'Mum said I had to show you about the place. What's your name?'

'Beccah.'

'Not sure if there's much to see. Dead boring, really. I hate coming here.'

Great. I held in a sigh. It was hard enough trying to look enthusiastic as it was, without someone else putting me on a downer. I couldn't help looking back out of the window. 'I wouldn't mind seeing what's out there,' I said, knowing exactly where I wanted to go.

Tallulah came and stood next to me as if I might have spotted something new. 'What?'

I pointed.

'What, that old shed?' She rolled her eyes. 'Come on then. I should have asked for more than a tenner for this.'

She noticed my leg when I picked up my crutches and tried to stand on one leg while I arranged them. 'What's wrong with your leg?' she asked, with a face like it was contagious.

Guess I'd gone down even lower on her coolness barometer. 'Fracture. Three places. From a car accident.' I didn't wait for her reaction and started to move towards the door. I was quite quick once I got going.

She skipped ahead and opened it for me as if I'd suddenly got interesting. 'Wow. Was it a big crash? Anyone die? Who was driving?'

I closed my eyes while she stood in front of me, barring my way. She clearly wasn't going to let it go until I told her. I opened my eyes and looked at her as icily as I could. I only wanted to say this once. 'It was a side impact on an intersection. My brother died and I was driving.' I looked down and moved forward. She moved out of my way.

'Shit.'

CHAPTER 2

*G*oing down the stairs on crutches was a lot easier than going up. Thankfully, they weren't too steep.

Tallulah didn't ask any more questions about the crash, probably sensing the wall of frost when she got near the subject. At the bottom of the stairs I followed as she turned right, doubling back around them, then through a doorway underneath. I'd completely lost my sense of direction. We went through a hallway that eventually came out into a huge kitchen.

The room was full of a delicious smell of cooking; reminding me that it had been ages since I'd eaten. Gerty was stirring a large pot on an old-fashioned stove. 'Don't go far, girls, supper won't be long.'

'Like there's anywhere to go, Mum,' Tallulah said, rolling her eyes.

We walked right through the kitchen, past the battered rectangular pine table in the middle, to a door that opened to the outside.

Tallulah went straight on, but I paused. The biting chill mixed with the fresh air hitting my nostrils made it tingle. It smelled of earth and leaves and faintly of a bonfire some-where. It literally smelled of autumn here. Everything was different, particularly after the warmth of California, but it felt good to be outside. The daylight lightened something inside me after the oppressive darkness of the house. The sky was dismally grey but oddly comforting.

'It'll be dark soon,' Tallulah said. 'So we'd better hurry up.'

There were several old buildings off to the left but I headed in the direction of the little round house. I sensed Tallulah's zero attention span and didn't want to waste valu-able time on looking at anything else. She seemed oblivious to me steering her there.

It was tricky terrain on my crutches. The path mean-dered, almost overgrown through what had once been mani-cured lawns. Now they were more like shrubland that made me stumble a couple of times.

Tallulah walked on regardless. 'So, Mum said you're starting school on Monday?'

'I think so,' I said.

'What made you come to this God-awful place? You live in California, don't you?'

I wanted to just say: I did. But that would have sparked off a whole other line of questioning that would probably end up in car crash territory and I didn't want to talk about that, ever. 'Mom and Dad are just busy with stuff, you know? They thought me and Aunt Sarah could get to know each other for a while.'

Tallulah studied my face, not sure whether to believe me. It was a stretch, but, in all honesty, I didn't care if she believed me or not, so long as she didn't ask me any more questions.

We got to the little round house and, this close up, I could see it was almost derelict. Tallulah's phone rang and she livened up immediately. I was forgotten to whatever drama was in her life. Recounting some story and gesturing with her spare hand, she walked off.

I was glad of the solitude; for some reason I wanted to be in this place alone. I didn't know why. All I knew was that it made me feel an overwhelming sense of sadness. Not in a grief type way, but in the way of the deep nostalgia a person got when they went back to somewhere they'd loved and not seen in a very long time. It was the strangest feeling.

I pulled away the planks obscuring the little white carved door. The arch-shaped holes had once been filled with glass that had long since broken. It was tricky negotiating the rubble with crutches, so I leaned them against the wall outside and hopped in on one foot. I steadied myself by holding pieces of fallen wood that had once been part of the roof.

Inside, I realized that it wasn't circular at all but an octagon, with a seat and a window almost up to the ceiling on every side. Many of the seats had rotted and much of the white paint gone, but I could imagine the hanging baskets and pots, now disintegrating on the floor, in their former glory. The pastel-coloured flowers would have looked stunning against the white. A stone angel perched on top of a pedestal sat in the middle of it all.

I turned a slow circle, hopping on my good leg. It must have been a heavenly place once. A place of peace, full of floral scent and warmth from the many little windows filling it with shards of light. How I would have loved to see it then. I couldn't understand why my aunt had let it fall into such disrepair. In its heyday, surely she would have enjoyed a place like this.

My leg ached, so I sat on the only window seat that hadn't caved in. The paint had almost all flaked off, but it was sturdy enough to hold me. The wind rustled in the trees and a bird squawked somewhere. How peaceful it was; deathly quiet.

Night was coming and it was getting dark. The wind had finally dropped, meaning the air didn't have quite so much bite. Greying clouds were obscuring the light and a white mist was slowly descending over the trees of the garden. Birds and small creatures seemed to be waking up and calling to their friends. Maybe they were warning them about me sitting there amongst them all.

I'm not sure how long I sat there for, but when Tallulah came back it was almost dark. I stood and she was clearly glad I'd had enough. Gerty's call for supper meant she was completely off the hook, having showed me very little.

I didn't care. She wittered on about something, but I wasn't listening. I grabbed my crutches from outside and headed back towards the grey old house. It didn't look nearly as imposing from the back – even with the black windows peering down like soulless eyes. I had a strange feeling of elation. I'd made a real discovery. No one wanted the little house, so I would claim it as mine.

TALLULAH ATE supper with me in the kitchen. Gerty said it saved her cooking again when she got home, but I suspected it was some sort of charm offensive to get me a friend before I started school. They needn't have bothered. She mainly looked at her phone while we ate, which suited me just fine.

Gerty had said my aunt went to bed very early and had her supper in her room. I thought it very strange. Still, at least I wasn't expected to be sociable around her. I was used to being a loner.

The food wasn't half bad; a thick vegetable and indiscernible meat broth and some crusty bread.

'What were you two doing all that time?' Gert said,

loading pots into a dishwasher. A mod-con that looked weirdly out of place.

'I was showing Beccah the old building at the far side of the gardens,' Tallulah said, not meeting my eyes.

Gerty nodded in understanding. 'Oh, the old orangery. Be careful. No one has used that for years. Should be pulled down really.'

'What's an orangery? I kind of like it. I was thinking of fixing it up … if that's OK?'

Gerty eyed me suspiciously. 'Orangeries were popular in Victorian times for protecting fruit trees in winter; like a greenhouse or conservatory.' She continued to watch me while I ate. 'I'll have a word with Burt. See if he can make it safe for you.'

I smiled. 'Thanks.' I was beginning to think her school ma'am exterior concealed a softer centre.

A berry pudding followed that reminded me of Mom's cobbler. Gerty called it a crumble and drowned it in custard. It was sweet and warming.

'I expect you're tired,' Gerty said, clearing away our dishes.

I was and nodded. With the time difference and travelling, it had been an endless day. It occurred to me then that I hadn't seen a single TV. For a moment I panicked at being completely cut off. Thankfully, I had data on my phone but I wasn't sure how long that would last. 'Do you have Wi-Fi?' I said, not holding out much hope.

'You must be joking,' Tallulah said, laughing.

Gerty shot her a scathing look. 'I explained to your aunt that you would need a computer for your homework. She doesn't much care for technology, you see. Has no use for it. But once I explained and your mother offered to pay for it, I believe it's going to be installed on Monday.'

I was relieved and a little sad. I was glad I would have

contact with the outside world, but Mom throwing money at something to keep me quiet was nothing new. She hadn't even told me she'd had that kind of conversation. 'Thanks.'

'You need to make a list of what you need. Tallulah will go with you into town tomorrow.'

I nodded. 'I have a laptop, but I need to get a British phone.'

'Tomorrow then. And anything you may need for school.'

School. The thought of mixing with new kids filled me with dread. I knew the set-up was different in the UK. They didn't have high schools. Eighteen year olds like me went to sixth form. The accident had pretty much obliterated my last school year, so I wasn't sure how I would fit in. I might even have to repeat the year. I'd have to find out when I got there.

'You'll need some smart clothes. It's business dress at St Bart's and they're pretty anal about it,' Tallulah said.

I needed to buy a lot then. Baggy tops and jeans, mainly in black, had pretty much been my thing. It would take an overhaul for me to pass as remotely presentable. I wasn't sure how I felt about that exactly. I'd just had no interest in clothes since Pete went. It was my way of grieving.

There were no dress codes at my old school, just cliques that you found yourself in without choosing. Mine was the skaters. Then Pete went and I was soon on my own in the cafeteria. I was just too quiet, too brooding, too morose for anyone to handle being around. I was a walking buzz kill. I wasn't expecting a new school to be any different.

Suddenly, I felt overwhelmingly tired. I had Saturday and Sunday to ease myself in. Then, hopefully, I'd feel better about the whole thing. 'I think I'll take a shower and go to bed,' I said.

Tallulah laughed and shook her head.

I shot her a look.

'It'll have to be a bath, I'm afraid,' Gerty said.

I wondered how on earth I'd wash my hair. It was literally the only thing I liked about myself. It was pure white, poker-straight and shiny. I had my particular shampoo, and, with a little coconut oil and loads of straightening, I achieved my deathly pale look. It was no mean feat coming from Southern California.

Gerty must have read my thoughts because she went to one of her cupboards and came back with a large grey earthenware jug and plonked it on the table in front of me.

Tallulah watched, finding it all highly amusing. 'I'm going,' she said, rising from her seat. 'I'll be back around lunchtime.'

Gerty tutted.

'It's Saturday, Mum. It's bad enough I have to babysit – no offence,' she said, turning her head to me.

I just raised my eyebrows and she carried on regardless.

'So I at least want a lie-in.'

She picked up her bag and Gerty followed her out, 'Make sure Burt gives you a lift. It's too dark to ride your bike. Pick it up tomorrow.' Then, speaking in more hushed tones, she said something about making sure she came back at twelve to give me enough time to get what I needed. Then she was out of range.

Gerty came back and I thanked her for supper. Then, as I stood up, it occurred to me. 'Do you stay here at night?' Otherwise I'd be left here with just an old lady in this big, creepy house.

Gerty smiled, seeming to understand. Guess she did have a teenage daughter of her own. 'I'm normally away by six, but I can stay a little later tonight.'

I smiled. It was nice of her, but it didn't help my misgivings. She turned away to get on with her clearing up and I left her to go in search of the bathroom.

I checked out all the paintings again on my way upstairs,

pausing at the last one. I wondered what the secret in her eyes was. Then I retrieved my washbag and towels from my room and found the bathroom at the very end of the hallway.

The room was huge, as they all seemed to be; probably the same size as my bedroom. The fact there wasn't much in it made it look even bigger; just a toilet with a cistern right up near the ceiling and a basin with brass taps the size of my fist.

The bath was going to be a problem. For a start it was on a raised platform and, second, it was tall. I had my water-proof sock, but I would need to get onto the platform, put my bad leg over the side and rest my weight on it so I could get in.

I assessed the height I needed the water to be without getting my plaster wet. It was fiberglass, but I hated getting it soggy. At least the bath wasn't very long. If I positioned myself just right, I could maybe put my leg up over the side. I decided to try.

It looked pretty comfortable – the enamel type I'd seen in films where you had to bend your knees. The lip that rolled over the top would make a good headrest.

The wind whistled and interrupted my thoughts; a creepy sound that fitted the house perfectly. The bathroom must be at the corner of the building. I ignored it and turned the large faucets and, after much coughing and spluttering and knocking of pipes, murky brown water came out. It smelled metallic and made me jump back for a bit, until eventually the water ran hot and clear. There was a rubber stopper on a chain that I plugged into the hole in the bottom.

While the bath filled, I took a closer look at the room. It was decorated in dusky-pink tiles that went halfway up the walls. The top bit was covered in a plum-coloured wallpaper in the design of climbing vines. It was a good colour to hide the bubbling mould appearing in the corners near the ceiling.

A big gold oval mirror hung above the sink and a corner cabinet in dark wood stood to its left.

I leaned one of my crutches against the wall and opened it, turning my nose up at the dusty old bottles. Some didn't look like they'd been used for twenty years. I got the impression that this bathroom was the same.

The words Bath Salts caught my eye on a clear bottle with blue crystals inside. *Soak those aching muscles* was the tagline. I'd give it a go. Bubbles would have been better, but I guessed that was a bit too 'twenty-first century' for this place. It would do the job though, even if just to colour the water.

Abandoning my other crutch, I sprinkled some of the contents into the already half-filled bath. The water instantly frothed and became clouded.

My face cloth and shampoo were in my washbag and I placed them next to the bath, along with the jug. I undressed, then sat on the raised step and pulled the plastic sock all the way up my leg. It had to completely cover my plaster right up over my knee and the elastic had to be tight enough at the top to stop any water that might go in.

The faucets were so large that the bath was deep enough by the time I'd finished. I daren't let it get too full.

Steam came off the surface so I took my weight on my left, good leg and held onto both sides. Then I dipped my right, bad one in. It felt a little hot but I didn't mind. I hadn't felt properly warm since I got here. I put it down, turned and prayed my leg held. As soon as I was in, I swapped my weight and sunk slowly in, hissing, until I got used to the temperature. My legs had to bend to my chest so it was easy to put my bad leg up over the side. The elastic was more likely to hold too, due to gravity. When I eased back with a sigh, resting my head on the curved top, the water was almost over my shoulders.

I lay there looking up at the ceiling and listening to the

19

drips and loud sloshes of water as I scooped it over myself. It was the same dark-berry colour as the wallpaper. The brass light fitting had an opaque glass shade that buzzed and flickered slightly. It made me wonder how safe the electrics were here.

A low moan of wind wailed around the building and rain started to lash against the small window over the bath. It was a lonely, desolate sound and would have scared the hell out of me if I hadn't already worked out it was the wind. It made me feel truly isolated, something I'd only ever felt emotionally at home. The room felt warm now at least.

I picked up my shower gel from the floor and lathered it in my hands, rubbing it over my arms and doing the same with my good foot up out of the water.

The wind moaned again, louder, as if to protest. The lights flickered again. They buzzed and then went off completely.

Crap. I froze.

The drips of the tap and the raindrops rapping on the window were almost drowned out by the sound of my heart, pounding so loud I thought it would beat right out of my ears.

The wind hissed and moaned as if it were saying the words *'Lila ... Lila.'*

The lights buzzed and flickered again. Then came on. The relief was so great I let out a breath I hadn't realized I'd been holding and I sagged back against the bath. My temples were throbbing.

As soon as I'd got a grip on myself, I climbed out – almost stumbling off the dais in my rush to hop onto my bad leg. I wasn't going to hang around for it to go off again. I dried myself quickly, pulled on my nightshirt and hobbled out into the hallway. The contrast after leaving the warmth of the bathroom hit me immediately.

The flames in the wall lamps flickered in a draft and I blessed them for not being electric. Trying not to run and fall over, I reached my room. Gerty must have been in as the lamp by my bed, with the frilly lampshade, was switched on. The curtains were drawn and flames now licked around a log in the grate. After my scare, it didn't really feel that much cosier.

There was no lock on my door so I dragged the surprisingly heavy, old rocking horse, to block it. I figured it would act as an alarm, even though it wouldn't probably stop intruders.

The cheeriest thing was the fire. I stared into the flames and a tear ran down my cheek. I didn't like it here. I was trapped and there was literally no one else who would have me.

The people I'd just met weren't exactly horrible, but they weren't overly friendly either. It felt like I'd travelled back a hundred and fifty years in time. I wiped my eyes with the back of my hand. I don't think I'd ever felt so alone.

I sniffed back more tears and pulled back the old-fashioned blankets to get into bed. I immediately jumped back. Inching forward, I sagged in relief. There, in the middle, was a flat orange bear. I picked it up by the ear assuming it was Tallulah's idea of a joke and it gurgled. I shook it next to my ear. It was hot and full of water.

I instantly brightened. Gerty must have put it there. I put it back, climbed in bed and sighed into the warmth it had created. I was tired and overwrought. Maybe once I'd had enough sleep things wouldn't seem so bad.

I leaned down and pulled my laptop out of the bottom drawer of the nightstand. It was my link with the twenty-first century. It was impossible to be alone with technology. The familiar green light came on and I waited for it to fire up. But nothing happened. I tried again. 'No ... no. Don't break on me now.' All I got was the blue screen of death. Then it buzzed with grey fuzz like an untuned TV. Nothing.

I continued to stare at it for a full minute waiting for something to happen, but nothing did. I fell back against the pillows. The silver stars looked down on me from the ceiling as if painted to brighten up some poor child's life.

I hated it here. *Hate, hate, hate it!*

Then I sobbed.

CRYING WAS the best way to fall asleep. I'd learned that lesson a very long time ago. The next thing I knew, the grey light of a new day was peeping through the gaps between the heavy velvet drapes.

The room air was cold against my face. The fire had long since gone out. I checked my phone: nothing. I sent a message to Mom, anyway, letting her know I'd got here OK. The time was 8.50 a.m.

I loathed the idea of getting up into the cold but I remembered I had about three hours until Tallulah came to collect me for our shopping trip. That meant I had time to spend in the orangery before she got here.

I washed and dressed in extra baggy jeans and the warmest sweater I could find. More sweaters and a pair of boots definitely had to be on the shopping list today. Then I grabbed my phone to read on and went down through the kitchen in search of breakfast before I went outside.

The kitchen was warm and filled with the delicious smell of baking. Gerty was there, beating some mixture in a bowl by hand. 'Fresh muffins cooling. Tea?'

I had to get used to that, but for now I shook my head. 'No thanks. Any juice?'

Without so much as a deviation from the rhythm of her beating, she nodded to a fruit bowl on the side. 'Oranges are over there.' And, with a flick of her eyes: 'You'll find a squeezer in the drawer.'

I picked up a large orange and looked at it quizzically. I'd seen machines do this in a shop.

Gerty tutted, which I realized was a habit of hers when she became impatient. She put down her bowl and took the orange from my hand. Then she took out a sharp knife, cut it in half and began pushing one half down over a conical glass dish. She tipped the contents into a glass and did the same with the other half. I never knew it could be done like that. It barely made half a glass, but when she passed it to me and I tried it, I'd never tasted anything so nice.

'You won't get fresher than that,' Gerty said. Then she picked up her bowl and resumed beating her mixture. The rate she kept up, she must have muscles of steel. 'So, where are you off to this early?'

I picked up a muffin in a paper towel and put it in my bag. Then I arranged my crutches and moved towards the back door. 'I thought I'd read in the round house for a while.'

Gerty stopped beating and studied me for a long moment, as if I'd said something that struck a chord for her. Then she smiled as if she'd swept it away. 'You mean the old orangery.'

'Yeah, it's peaceful there.'

'Well, be careful. Bert will see to it this week.'

I gave her a small smile and left through the back door. Going to the special place I'd claimed as my own filled me with excitement. When I got there, I propped my crutches against the wall outside and hopped in like I did the last time. I held onto the fallen rafters to get closer to the pedestal with the angel. Because against all the faded white paint and rotten wood, in one of the angel's hands was a single, perfect rose – the colour of blood.

CHAPTER 3

*T*he rose played on my mind all morning after that. I tried to read in the round house but my eyes would drift to the rose before the end of every paragraph. *Who was it for? Was it for me or in memorial for someone? Or was it simply to pay respect to a place that once was?* I couldn't help it; it made me wistful.

In the end, I gave up reading, grabbed my crutches and went to get ready for Tallulah's arrival. Something told me I was going to get judged today.

I opted for ripped black jeans that I'd ripped further down the sides to accommodate my cast, a laced-up flat boot for the other foot and an oversized Marilyn Manson t-shirt. It was kind of my signature uniform back home. I scraped my white hair back into a ponytail and left two strands on either side of my temples.

My skin was pale and clear, so I had no need to cover it. I coal-blacked my eyes and just used a little lip-gloss to emphasize my pale look.

My jacket was woefully inadequate here. That had to be first on my list after a new laptop and phone. I'd put my old one in to be fixed. My whole life was on that hard drive – memories of Pete, photos, music, everything, but I didn't hold out much hope.

Tallulah was already in Burt's car when she texted for me to come down. Burt got out to stow my crutches away and she gave me a quick smile and went back to texting when I got in the back seat. In fact, she texted the whole journey.

Burt went on about making the roof safe on the round house. 'I might 'ave some greenhouse glass in one of the sheds somewhere. I'll start putting some glass in … but at a time, you know? Once the roof's done, of course.'

I thanked him. He hadn't once hinted about the rose, although I'd already discounted him. 'Does anyone else go in there?' I said.

Tallulah ignored me or didn't hear.

'Don't believe so, miss. Her ladyship would need me to wheel her out there and she's never asked for that.'

I wondered if Sarah really was a lady, or whether Burt was just having a joke at his employer's expense.

Before long, we drove through an endless car park to a retail outlet with barn-like buildings. Each had huge signs for retailers I'd never heard of. We pulled up in front of one called PC Planet.

''ere we are,' Burt said. 'It's a short walk to the shopping centre over there,' and he bobbed his head to the right, away from the building.

'I know where it is,' Tallulah said, finally putting her phone in her bag.

'Call me fifteen minutes before you want to come home and I'll pick you up at the entrance.'

Tallulah rudely got out while he was still talking.

'Thank you, Burt.'

He smiled and winked, then got out to get my crutches.

As we walked in through the wall of glass doors, it lived

up to its name. Rows, the length of the building and all the way around the outside, of computers, monitors, laptops and phones. This was exactly the place I needed.

All the staff looked under the age of twenty and wore headsets, blue polo shirts and black pants.

Tallulah waved at some guy behind the desk and went to go and speak to him. A pretty young girl came up and asked me if she could help. She had honey-blonde hair in a pony-tail, too much makeup and only came up to my chest. At first glance she looked about twelve until you took in the size of her boobs and ass. She was friendly enough though, so I went to tell her what I needed.

A peal of laughter interrupted my thoughts and I turned around to see Tallulah and the boy laughing together at the service desk. It was too far away to hear what they were saying, but Tallulah sure found whatever it was funny.

'I need an iPhone and a MacBook. It was the most expen-sive, and the least that Mommy and Daddy could do. The girl's eyes widened, but she wasn't going to argue a sale and spoke the order into her headset. She beamed a smile at me and told me to meet her at the desk where Tallulah was. 'Wait!' I said, before she could run off. I got my old cumber-some laptop out of my bag. 'Is there someone that can take a look at this? It just blue screened and won't turn on. I need it to work or get my stuff off it or something.' She turned it over in her hands as if the outside would reveal something to her. Then she passed it back to me. 'Yeah, give it in at the desk. They'll write you out a ticket.'

Tallulah was still laughing with the boy when I went over to join them. I wasn't expecting him to be as nearly as cool or good-looking. I don't know what I expected of English boys, exactly.

His hair was dark, almost black, and swept forward in wisps to frame his face. It was a style a lot of the metal boys wore back home. Except his face was young and angelic-looking with long dark lashes around mahogany eyes. He couldn't be that young because he had several piercings in his ears and one in his nose. He had a navy sports jacket on over his polo shirt but I could clearly see the tattoos on the backs of his hands. 'And who do we have here, Tallulah?'

His accent was very cute on him but the way his eyes raked the length of my body spoke of way too much confidence. It reminded me instantly of the popular boys back home, who would shout for me to show them my jugs – hence the baggy t-shirts. I'd always been well developed for my age and hated it.

'Beccah, Ollie. Ollie, Beccah,' Tallulah said, by way of introduction. 'He's at the same sixth form as us.' His name badge said Ollie Black.

I smiled, a little surprised. He didn't exactly fit the Hogwarts image I had in my mind of St Barts.

'You start Monday?' he said.

I nodded. 'My laptop died on me.' I frowned the minute the lame comment left my mouth. At least I had the old one in my hands so I didn't look such an idiot. 'She said you'd write up a ticket, or something.'

He nodded, took out a pad and started writing without asking me anything further about it. 'Well, you came to the right place. It's your life, right?' He stuck a label on it and put it on a shelf behind him. Then he accepted the boxes of my new stuff handed to him by a runner to put through the register. He beeped them and I handed over my credit card.

He looked at Tallulah with a smirk. 'Loaded!'

She laughed.

I wasn't exactly sure what they meant, but I had a good idea. It irritated me. My brother Pete and I both had trust funds. His reverted to me on his death, and of course there was my parent's guilt money. It had become a game to see how much I could spend before they actually spoke up to tell me, enough. It hadn't happened yet. Ollie seemed oblivious to my annoyance with them, put the boxes into a large carrier bag and pushed them towards me across the counter.

I adjusted my bag on my shoulder to accommodate my crutches. He hadn't even remarked on my leg so I knew Tallulah had filled him in. It made my face flush with anger, even more. 'Bye,' I said, flatly, and went to turn away, but he stopped me.

'Wait! Listen. I'm having a few friends over to my house next Saturday. It's Halloween and we thought it'd be fun. You know, dress up and that. You should come.'

I looked at Tallulah, a little unsure. She shrugged. 'Yeah, you should.'

I was still not convinced.

'It's up to you, but your aunt goes to bed at, like, five o'clock. She won't even know,' Tallulah said with another shrug.

She was right. After Gerty went home of an evening I had literally no adult supervision.

I looked at Ollie, who waggled his eyebrows at me playfully. *Oh, what the hell.* He seemed fun.

'Wait … your aunt?'

'Oh yeah, I almost forgot. She's the long-lost Blackwood niece from America,' she said, giggling.

He raised his eyebrows and nodded slowly in understanding. Then he laughed and said, shaking his head, 'Maybe you shouldn't come.' But he still seemed playful.

Tallulah laughed loudly at some 'in' joke. I suspected she fancied him as she laughed at literally everything he said. Then she stopped and looked puzzled. He continued to stare at her, widening his eyes as if she should know. Then he rolled them when she finally caught on with an, 'Oh, yeah! I forgot … the Blackwood Curse.'

They both laughed.

I was completely confused and convinced they were hazing me. Seeing the look on my face, he seemed to relent and tried to stop himself laughing. 'It's just some silly story between our families, that's all. You're from the Blackwoods and I'm from the Waxley-Blacks. There's some history that goes way back.'

My eyes dropped to his name badge. 'My brother and I drop the double-barrelled bit. 'It's a mouthful, you know?' He waggled his eyebrows again, laughing. He actually made me laugh that time.

'Do some bloody work, Ollie,' an older guy called out from the opposite end of the desk. A queue had formed behind us and Ollie was about to get into trouble.

We said our goodbyes and I decided he seemed OK. 'Tarts and Vicars!' he called after us with a wink, making Tallulah shriek with laughter.

I looked at Tallulah for an explanation.

'The theme,' she said, as if I was stupid. 'For next week … Halloween,' she added, when my face stayed blank.

She tutted when I frowned, kind of getting it but not the two things together. She huffed, taking out her phone again. 'Look, girls dress as tarts and boys like vicars. It's kind of a British thing.'

My mind was racing for the translation.

'Bloody hell, Becks,' she said, rolling her eyes. 'Prostitutes and priests!'

'Oh.' I said, nodding, still not actually getting the link to Halloween. Guess it was a bit *Rocky Horror Show*.

She went straight back to her texting; I'd lost her. I ran over the conversation we'd just had. At least there were two people I'd know when I started school on Monday.

The rest of the afternoon passed pretty uneventfully. I got a warm coat from GAP, next on my list. It was black, quilted and almost down to my knees. I also got some dark-coloured sweaters that I found out were actually called jumpers over here (no idea why). 'They just are,' was Tallulah's explanation. Secretly, I'm sure, she had no idea herself.

We went to several girly shops after that, with booming dance music. Tallulah reminded me that they had to be sensible business clothes for school. I got a couple of skirts and dresses and some slacks for colder days, all in black, navy or grey. I found some low-heeled court shoes that Tallulah said were hideous. I lived in sneakers or boots at home, so I had no idea if they were or not. It was weird trying them only on one foot. I hoped they'd still fit when I finally got my cast off.

Next, we went for stationery, which was always my favourite part of the new school year and a bag to carry my books in. Girls seemed to carry huge shoulder bags here rather than backpacks. Then, lastly, we ended up in a sexy lingerie shop, which I'd never stepped foot in in my entire life before. I was embarrassed, but I had to admit curious too. My underwear was normally bought for me by my mother from Walmart.

'Tarts and Vicars, remember?' Tallulah said loudly, making me look around anxiously.

'Oh,' I mouthed in understanding.

Tallulah got a call and went and sat on a chaise lounge in the corner; she was proving absolutely no help at all. I wandered the racks until an assistant approached me; she was so beautiful, she was probably a model. I shrugged hopelessly when she asked if she could help me. 'Tarts and Vicars?' I said, hoping that was enough to explain what was needed.

She asked me to follow her. I found it fascinating how she seemed to elongate all the vowels at the ends of her words. It wasn't easy with my crutches squeezing between the tightly packed clothes rails. We came to a stop in the furthest corner of the shop. I had to make a conscious effort not to stare at some of the R-rated stuff there. She held up two costumes, both ridiculously short. One was meant to be a nurse's uniform made of some shiny plastic and the other was a maid's outfit. I tried the nurse one on first and felt ridiculous. The maid one was better. It was mainly a black dress with a frilly underskirt and tiny white apron. The bodice laced up under my chest making my boobs look enormous. I guess that was the general idea. I could put one of the cardigans I'd bought for school over the top. It all seemed silly with my ugly, fat plaster cast, anyway.

Tallulah poked her head through the curtain. 'Yes!' she said, laughing. 'You have to get that. You look hot.'

I blushed but agreed, figuring I wasn't going to find anything better. I insisted on over-the-knee socks, not fishnets, though. After all, it was only going to be on one leg. Tallulah seemed unperturbed and just nodded. 'That'll work.'

'Aren't you getting anything?' I asked as I handed over my credit card at the till. Again.

She just shrugged. 'I've already got mine.'

I thought no more of it as she yanked me along by the arm. 'You need killer heels to go with that.' So we went back to the shoe shop we'd already been in earlier. 'On one foot?' I said. 'Really?'

She shrugged it off with: 'The overall effect will be there.' At first I was reluctant to spend money on something I would only wear one of and probably never wear again, but I had to admit the patent black leather three-inch heels would go much better with my outfit than my sensible school shoes.

Tallulah messaged Burt while I was paying. By the time we got out to the front of the building, Burt pulled up. We stuffed everything in the trunk, which was now 'the boot'. There were so many new things and meanings to remember.

I got in the car, exhausted, after what had proved to be quite a productive day. My leg was fine; it was my shoulders that killed. Using crutches to take my weight for the best part of a day had taken its toll on them.

My mind went back to PC Planet. I hoped they could fix my old laptop. All my memories of Pete were on there; the great summer we had last year, the music we both listened to.

Meeting Ollie had been a highlight and an eye-opener. I wondered if he took the curse seriously at all, or whether he just made the whole thing up.

'Did you have a good day? Got everything you needed?' Burt said as we drove along. I nodded and looked over at Tallulah. Then I realized that she hadn't bought a single thing. 'Yes, thank you,' I said, settling back into the seat. I felt a bit bad hogging the whole entire day. She seemed untroubled so I let it go, assuming she already had her stuff for the new school year as they'd started a month ago.

It was dark when we got home. Tallulah said, 'Bye,' with her head down, still looking at her phone and Gerty had her coat on to leave as I came in. I supposed it made sense to take Tallulah home with her.

'Your dinner is in the Aga. Don't burn yourself. Your aunt has gone to bed. I don't work Sundays, but don't worry; the nurse comes in first thing in the morning and at teatime for your aunt. I've left instructions.'

It was a bit bewildering taking it all in but I nodded, hoping she'd written it all down. She turned back just as she was about to go out of the door. 'Oh, and Burt will take you to school on Monday. Be ready at eight.'

'OK, thanks,' I said and she left.

The kitchen was warm, dimly lit and filled with the delicious smells of cooked meat and baking. I guessed the big iron thing in the corner was the Aga. The stove baffled me until I managed to undo one of the doors with a clang. A dish with a cover on it was inside, so I grabbed the oven gloves from the hook, took it out and put it on the table. I nearly dropped the top dish taking it off and whistled at the close call. It was some kind of pie with vegetables and gravy. It made me instantly hungry. I'd only had a coke and a muffin at the mall.

I searched the many drawers for cutlery and sat down with a scrape of the chair. I think the pie was beef, but I couldn't be sure. It was nice though and I cleared my plate. The piece of paper in the middle of the table was Gerty's list of instructions. I skimmed it and found it was mainly to do with food for tomorrow. There was a telephone number at the bottom, which I tapped straight into my phone to transfer later.

I put the note down with a sigh. I was going to be alone a lot. Not too dissimilar to home. My eyes rested on my many bags of shopping. At least I still had data and could spend the evening setting up my phone and MacBook. That cheered me up a bit.

There was still no message from Mom and Dad. Maybe the time difference had confused them. Deep in my heart, I knew that wasn't it. Talking to me was just too painful, which was why I'd been sent here in the first place. I was a living reminder of their dead son that should have been me.

After putting my dirty dishes into the empty dishwasher, I struggled up the stairs with my many bags. I paused at Lila's portrait. It was weird as I always felt the need to acknowledge her. I wondered if she knew of the Blackwood curse. Maybe she had something to do with it and that's why the secret smile. I'd probably never know.

I dumped the whole lot on my bed. Gerty had left the lamp on and the fire lit. I was grateful. It made the lonely room kind of cosy. Plus, I still hadn't got used to the layout of the room to negotiate it in the dark.

I went over to the window and peeped out from the closed curtains. The garden was in blackness. I wondered about the rose for the hundredth time that day. *Who cared enough about the place, or someone, to put something so beautiful there for no one to see?* I was sure it wasn't for me.

Then my mind went back to the conversation with Ollie and the Blackwood curse. It was intriguing. But first I needed to make sure it was a thing and not made up. Although he did say that my family was old and so was his. I made up my mind to spend my Sunday exploring and finding out more about it.

For once I was grateful for the solitude. After all, the round house was out there in the darkness, waiting for me to go back.

CHAPTER 4

I woke up late on Sunday. I'd stayed up until 1 a.m. setting up my MacBook and iPhone with all my apps and numbers. I washed and dressed and finally came downstairs at around noon.

The house was quiet. The only sound was the grandfather clock ticking loudly, amplified by the high ceilings in the hall. I made my way around the staircase to the kitchen, parked my crutches and picked up Gerty's note listing what there was to eat.

Bacon and eggs in the fridge for breakfast.

OK, that wasn't too hard. I switched on an old transistor radio on the windowsill, found a frying pan on a wall rack and soon had weird, fat slabs of bacon on the go. Delicious smells filled the air along with some old rock 'n' roll from a band I'd never heard of.

After throwing in my eggs and going for scrambled, I demolished my breakfast in seconds. I could never see the point in all that effort cooking and cleaning up when it took precisely ten seconds to eat. I loaded the dishwasher, determined for it to take as little of my time as possible. I had plans.

I pulled a sneaker on my good foot and an old sock over my plaster cast. Then, grabbing my crutches, I headed straight out of the back door in the direction of the round house.

I couldn't wait to get there. It occurred to me that the round house and its secrets was the last thought I had before I went to sleep and my first when I woke up. It was strange that a ramshackle old building could rouse me so much after feeling dead for so long.

When I was almost there something made me pause. Unease began to tingle up my spine. I got the distinct impression that I wasn't alone. It was too quiet, and a weird feeling of anticipation hung in the air. Someone else was around.

My heart pumped. 'Hello?' My voice cracked so I coughed and said it again, more loudly this time.

Instead of a reply, I heard what sounded like rocks falling. I moved closer, dropped one of my sticks and shoved open the door. 'Hey!' I shouted.

At first, all I could see was dust. When it cleared, no one was there. Part of the roof had caved in above the one seat that hadn't rotted and had completely flattened it. There wasn't that much rubble, just a roof beam and some plaster.

Thankfully, it hadn't hit the angel. She didn't appear to have been damaged at all. She stood resplendent, even in the dust, and left me spellbound; just as she always did. Her hand held a perfect rose just like last time, but it was very definitely fresh. This one had barely opened and was covered in droplets of morning dew. The dust was settling on top, giving it a light sprinkling of snow. She was now facing a different direction; the hand holding the rose was pointing directly at the damaged seat.

Before I ventured in, I looked up. There didn't appear to be any danger of more falling wood. I leaned one of my crutches against the doorframe and hobbled in. I hated that the building seemed to be disintegrating before Burt had time to fix it. I hoped he'd hurry up now the weather would be getting in.

One large piece of timber had crushed the seat. I stooped to see if I could lift it. It wasn't that heavy, so I moved it about a foot to the side and let it go with a clunk.

I looked down and sifted through the rubble with my crutch. The seat must have been hollow and hadn't stood a chance with the force of the beam hitting it. Maybe Burt would be able to fix it or put something else in its place.

I was just about to turn away when my cast clinked against something metallic. I bent down and ran my hand through the dust and plaster fragments. I only just saw it. I thought it was an old washer at first; it was so dusty and old. I picked it up and gave it a rub on my jeans. It quickly shined up to a gold ring with a magnificent half pearl in a stunning circular setting. It was beautiful and antique-looking.

I gave the inside another clean with the corner of my shirt: *LB, my heart I will follow, JWB.*

Did the couple still meet here? Maybe they made a hasty exit when they heard me coming, or when the roof started to give. I looked around. I'd thought I'd heard something but I was in front of the only door. Although the large floor-to-ceiling windows held barely any glass; someone could easily have climbed through one of the window frames. A small piece of plaster fell to the floor to prove a point. It wasn't safe so I decided to go back to the house.

I CAME out from under the stairs into the hallway to the sound of a loud clanging bell. I followed the sound to the drawing room where I'd met my aunt for the first time. Maybe she needed help.

I turned the knob and went inside. 'Hello?' The fire was alight at the far end, just like it was last time and the heat drew me to it.

'About time. Come here, girl,' my aunt said. I'd seen so little of her I'd forgotten she actually lived there. I approached the chair with its back to the room and smiled when I came face to face with her.

She reminded me of a Dickens' character sitting there, so stiff and straight in her lace collar. 'Sit and talk to me a while, girl,' she said, pointing to the upholstered footstool nearby. She reached over to a table next to her and picked up an old Thermos flask and unscrewed it with her gnarly hands. 'It will have to be this bloody gnat's pee today. Gerty will have to teach you how to make a fresh pot if she's going to go off gallivanting on a Sunday.' She poured milky tea into the two plastic beaker parts of the lid, while I tried to hide my amusement at the thought of Gerty gallivanting anywhere.

'Thank you,' I said, taking a sip and trying to conceal my grimace. 'I guess I could give it a try.' Surely no attempt I made could taste any worse than this.

'Sugar's there,' Aunt Sarah said, pointing at the small china bowl on the tray.

I dropped in two lumps and gave it a stir but still wasn't sure if even sugar improved it.

'So, tell me what you have been up to since you arrived?'

I skimmed over what I'd bought at the shops yesterday and seized my chance to mention the interesting conversation I'd had with Ollie Black – minus Tarts and Vicars, of course. 'We met a boy there, in PC Planet. Tallulah knows him from school. He said his family had been close to ours for generations, or something.'

I watched my aunt carefully, hoping that she could keep a

thought in her head for longer than three seconds before she forgot it again.

She frowned as if she was thinking very hard who that might be.

'He said his name was Ollie Black but had dropped half of it. I forgot exactly how he put it,' I said.

My aunt nodded slowly as if she was just realizing who it must be. 'Young Waxley-Black. Calls himself Black now, does he? Well, he'll have to work a damn sight harder than that to get rid of the cloud over that family,' she scoffed.

Her reaction was so lucid and quick, I could only assume it was true. It appeared there was an ongoing feud between the two families rather than them being close. I was glad I asked as I fully intended to go to the party next weekend, so I made no mention of it. 'He's in my sixth form, apparently. Tallulah knows him quite well, I think.'

'Yes, well she would. She's nothing but a fly-by-night, that one. She'll get herself in all sorts of trouble if Gerty doesn't rein her in. Stay away from that boy and that family, if you know what's good for you.'

She really was getting herself worked up about it. I couldn't take my eyes off the blue vein protruding down the middle of her forehead. I was seriously worried she'd give herself some kind of seizure so I nodded vigorously, although, I did want to seize the chance to get more information out of her. 'Yes, Aunt. Of course. More tea?' I asked, reaching for the flask. 'I totally got the same impression. To be honest, Aunt, I didn't like him much. I thought him a bit arrogant.'

It did the trick. My aunt chuckled and relaxed back into her chair, taking the cup I offered with her. She nodded slowly. 'You're a wise girl. Boys like that have been the ruin of many a good family.'

'Oh, really?' I said in my most conversational tone. I don't think I'd uttered so many words out loud since Pete died. I was surprising myself. 'He mentioned something about a Blackwood curse. What's that all about? Is it a real thing?'

My aunt looked at me so shrewdly that I wondered if all the forgetfulness was an act. Maybe there were times when her brain was sharp. 'So they say. Best stay away from the boys of that house to be on the safe side,' she said with narrowed eyes.

It didn't sound as though there were any daughters. It made me wonder about Ollie's brother and whether he was an older, hotter version of him. 'What is it, then?' I tried to modify the excitement in my voice. 'You know, if it won't affect me anyway.'

My aunt reflected for a moment. 'My mother told me stories – many years ago. The curse started way before I was born; about a hundred and fifty years ago. Lila Blackwood – in the portrait at the top of the stairs – struck up a friendship with the eldest of the Waxley-Blacks. Jedediah, I believe he was called. It was an age-old tale of forbidden love. Jedediah's father forbade him to marry or even to have anything to do with Lila. Born the wrong side of the blanket, you see. We Blackwoods had a somewhat chequered past,' she said with a wink. 'Her mother was a low-born scullery maid; they said she was a witch. She'd died of consumption, so could no longer defend herself. Needless to say, it was easier to blame her and say the master of the house was bewitched, rather than a weak-willed old reprobate. It was, of course, a lousy excuse. Her dowry was simply not big enough to smooth over her low birth. Marriages were transactions back then. Money or power were how marriages were made.

'Anyway, the Waxley-Blacks' fortune was almost depleted owing to the old man's excessive gambling and so their love was doomed. They were forced to continue to see each other in secret.'

My heart pounded. I knew what she was going to say before she even said it.

'In the old orangery, I believe – That is, until his new wife's family put a stop to it. His father threatened to cut him off if he messed up the marriage deal. Lila disappeared after that. Some said she ran away to be on the stage – not a reputable business back then, but most believed she'd committed suicide because of a broken heart. The truth was, no one ever really knew what happened to her. However, the night before she disappeared, the servants reported she'd gone berserk with grief; saying all manner of wild things, like they were out to get her and that if she died she'd come back and haunt them. She cursed them all: neither the Waxley-Blacks nor the Blackwoods would ever find love or happiness unless they avenged her death. And an alliance between the families would mean certain death.

'Whisperings had always abounded about her mother being a witch and so she could very well have the where-withal to make such a curse.

'Well, true to her word, she disappeared the next day. No one would use the orangery, saying it was haunted and there has been a long catalogue of deaths and divorces in both families ever since. So you could say the curse came true.' Then she winked.

I was left open-mouthed, unable to work out whether she was being serious or not. It was corny and out there, but it was compelling and romantic too. However outlandish it was, I couldn't shake it off. The round house had lured me from the beginning. There were the roses, the fallen beam and this morning the ring, still in my pocket. The inscription by *JWB*, which had to be Jedediah Waxley-Black, and *LB, Lila Blackwood*. I wanted it to be true, but I wasn't entirely sure why. Maybe it was just a Heaven-sent distraction from everything else that was heart breaking and hopeless in my life. 'Star-crossed lovers,' I said, more to myself. 'Do you know who leaves the flowers?'

'What flowers?' my aunt said with a frown.

'Someone left a beautiful red rose yesterday and today in the round house – orangery,' I corrected.

My aunt looked exasperated and a little uncomfortable, as if the information had disturbed her. Then she looked reflective again. 'Then we are too late. It's already started again.'

'What's started?' I asked, desperately trying to steer her back on track.

'More tea, dear? Only got this blasted old thing. Never keeps the tea hot enough.'

I stared at her for a full minute while she went on about the tea. I was so disappointed. She'd forgotten the whole conversation and started right back at the beginning again. There was nothing else for it but to ask her something completely different. 'Aunt Sarah, if there was anything I needed to find out about my family, the Blackwoods, where would I go?'

My aunt looked at me as if I'd gone mad. 'Why, the library, dear child. Every family of substance keeps a good library.' Then she dismissed me with a sigh and a roll of her eyes. 'Directly across the hall. Journals, family trees, everything. Historic papers going back generations. I'm not really sure. I'm tired now. It was all such a very long time ago. Can you leave?' I was shocked at her rudeness, then I remembered that she was suffering from dementia. Her eyelids looked heavy already.

I took the half-full cup from her so she didn't drop it and put it on the table next to her. Then I tucked the blanket around her knees and quietly left the room.

The library wasn't that big, but there were floor-to-ceiling racks filled with books. A desk was next to the window and a pair of brown sofas faced each other in the middle. I rested my crutches against one and turned a circle.

Where to start?

I began with the desk and soon found that what I was looking for would be far too old to be in there. I did, however, find a bunch of old keys on a large ring.

Next, I checked out the books. Beautifully bound, but there was nothing out of the ordinary. Running my hand along the rows, I came to a cabinet with a locked glass door. I could see it was filled with racks of journals and parchment scrolls. This could be something. My mind scrambled for a moment on how to get in, then I remembered the keys. I hopped back to the desk, grabbed them and tried three before one finally fit. I opened the glass door, guessing if I was going to find anything useful at all, it'd be in here.

There were many ledgers of accounts and binders containing birth and death certificates. I pulled out one of the scrolls and was thrilled to see it was a beautifully hand-drawn family tree. It only went back to 1903, so I took another. I took it over to the desk and laid it out using two heavy paperweights to hold down the top corners.

My finger traced the many branches looking for the familiar name. There were many children. Some had very short lives. A lot never even got to marry.

I was about three-quarters up the page when I came to Lord Byron Horatio Blackwood, who married Matilda Letitia Grey. They had a son and two daughters and there, on a limb all on her own, was Lila Mirabella Blackwood Dunn. There she was, the object of my fascination since the time I'd first arrived. Somehow, seeing her there made her more real. And even though it represented the reality of her situation, I felt sad for her; there all alone. She was on the same line as the other three but not joined to the tree. It made me angry for her that she was so conspicuously different. I'd found the object of my search, treated like an adopted member of the family. I couldn't help feeling the parallel to me. I was stuck out on a limb and ignored; we were kindred spirits.

I put the scroll back and went through the binder of birth and death certificates next. Both were in a plastic wallet together, one for each person. Now I knew the name of her father, Lila was easy to find. Everyone's was the same; birth on the front, death on the back. All that is, except Lila. There was only one, recording her birth. Lord Byron was recorded as her father and Florence Dunn her mother. I guessed it was pretty lucky that she appeared there at all.

It all pointed to the theory my aunt had spoken of earlier, that no one actually knew where she went and, therefore, when and where she'd died. There wasn't anything else of interest in the cabinet after that. I locked it and put back the keys.

I browsed the books again. This was going to be my favourite place after the round house. The collection was amazing. Many of them belonged in a museum. They were leather-bound and some were even first editions.

Eventually I came to a battered, well-thumbed copy of *Wuthering Heights*. It was so worn and well-loved that I adored it instantly. I took it with me to sit on one of the sofas. When I opened the cover and heard the comforting crackle of the spine, my mouth went dry and I could barely breathe. The elaborate looped handwriting on the title page said:

LB,
   your eternal rock,
   JWB

        .   .   .

THEN, underneath, a quote from the book:

IF ALL ELSE PERISHED, *and he remained, I should still continue to be, and if all else remained and he were annihilated, the universe would turn to a mighty stranger.*

WOW! It felt like the author was speaking to me just as she'd spoken to Lila all those years ago. It felt like a promise – the promise to live on to find the other. Then something fluttered out of the pages onto my lap. It was a note scrawled with another quote:

HONEST MEN DON'T HIDE *their deeds.*

THEN, underneath:

BUT INDEED I MUST.
  Let me send words as arrows to your heart, that they may be sure and true. A rose shot by the bow of an angel as my life's blood.
  JWB

IT SOUNDED like some kind of riddle and I had no idea what it meant. I looked at it and looked at it again, hoping the note would tell me something new.

On the surface it was poetic and romantic, but I couldn't help thinking it held some hidden meaning. I folded the note carefully and put it back inside the book, then tucked it into the waistband of my pants.

I left the library, the words of the letter going round in my head. Over and over. I went back to the kitchen where I made a ham sandwich for lunch. I took the note out again, read it and reread it. *What was it trying to tell me?*

I went back to my room and tried to read the old, worn book to see if there were any other hidden scribbles or notes to be found, but there were none. Always, I ended up rereading the note.

Dusk came. Then nightfall, and the round house disappeared from view of my window seat. With a deep sigh I took out and read the note, yet again. Then, as if the words were highlighted to me, three words jumped out of the page:

Words

Angel

Rose

I almost stopped breathing. *Could it be?*

'The orangery!' I said aloud, looking out into the blackness. If only there was enough light. In the morning, as soon as I woke up, I would go back.

JBW had left something else in the round house and I had to find it.

CHAPTER 5

*T*he kiss woke me up with a start. It was deep, with tongues and his weight was sublime on top of me. It was so real; I could see the pink of his skin and his dark lashes through my barely open eyes, but they were a veil hiding who he was. He felt so familiar in my arms. Even his smell attracted me and wasn't overshadowed by the scent of roses all around us.

Open ... open your eyes.

When I did, instead of seeing him, my eyes opened to the stars and the small glass chandelier on the ceiling of my room. I couldn't help feeling disappointed. The brightness was replaced by grey; that grey of early morning. My body still tingled from the kiss and the feel of him, so close to me. It made me feel hot and in need of a shower.

I wiped my brow with the back of my hand and reached for the glass of water on the nightstand. The clock said 7 a.m. I might as well get up. I threw the covers back and my legs over the side of the bed, forgetting my cast. Feeling stiff, I hopped over to the window. The curtains scraped on the metal pole as I pulled the curtains back. I remembered it was the first day of school today, then I froze at the sight of the garden below me. Everywhere, as far as the eye could see, was a blanket of untouched snow. *Oh my God.* I couldn't believe it. I thought England's climate was warmer than this in October.

I switched my clock over to the radio to hear the news and all it told me was what I already knew: *Snow, snow, snow.* My mobile said flat battery and so did my MacBook.

I frowned. I'd had extraordinary bad luck with my tech stuff lately. It was weird.

I decided to get dressed and see if Burt or Gerty were around. 'Hello, anyone home?' I called over the banisters. There was no answer.

Then I began to worry about my aunt. With Gerty not here, perhaps she was stuck in bed. I knocked on the master bedroom door and couldn't hear a sound. The house was silent.

I pushed open the door a little and listened. I could hear the indiscernible talking of women's voices. It could be the TV, so I went further in.

A lady I didn't recognise turned around. I could see my aunt sitting in the chair in front of her. She was giving her a wash, a towel in hand. 'Sorry,' I said. 'It's just no one else is around and it's snowed.'

'Yes, it's bad, miss. I had to walk here today,' the woman said. 'I'm Rose, your aunt's nurse.'

I smiled. 'I'm Beccah. Do you know if I'm still going to school today?'

My aunt's face took on a faraway expression. She didn't seem very lucid this morning. 'It won't stop now,' she said. No one's going anywhere until you meet him.'

'Meet who?' I said. I wasn't sure if she was talking about me or lost in a memory.

'The Waxley-Black boy.' She sighed deeply. 'It's happening again, and no one can escape it.'

'Shush now,' Rose said, rolling her eyes and shaking her head.

I found my aunt really disturbing like this, so I made my excuses to go. 'I think I'll get ready and wait, just in case.'

'There's no point ... no point,' my aunt said over and over. Rose gave me a sympathetic smile.

I TOOK a quick bath and dressed as warmly as I could. I decided on one of my new sweaters and a long skirt I'd got for school. I pulled on some long socks, stretching one over my cast.

I knew exactly where I was going first. Without even a drink or breakfast, I shot out of the back door, finding the snow pretty heavy going with my crutches. The cold was already seeping in through my sock; the soft powder impossible to keep out.

My heart beat faster as it always did as I neared the round house. I just never knew what I'd find. When I got there, it looked like a fairy-tale cottage with icicles glittering in the sunlight. I peered in through one of the broken windows. Snow had come in through the hole in the roof. I propped my crutch in the door jamb as usual and pushed open the door. It was more difficult to move over all the snow that lay like fluff on the floor.

I managed it with a couple of hefty shoves, hopped in and scanned the room for change. Apart from the snow, everything appeared to be the same. The angel was in the same place and she still held the rose, only it had opened a little more today. My eyes followed where she was pointing at the crushed seat. It was where there was the most snow, as the hole in the roof was directly above it. I hopped over and crouched down, scooping up the snow in my hands and putting it aside. I wanted to look more carefully this time. There had to be something I'd missed. Some message. But I found nothing. All I found were six red rose petals amongst the snow that reminded me of drops of blood. I wondered if this was the message but dismissed it. The note I'd found in the library was written over a hundred years ago. Still, it did look like spilled blood.

I was bitterly disappointed. I'd been convinced I'd find something – a hidden note or personal keepsake. I couldn't help feeling that the snow had been sent to keep me there for a reason, however silly that sounded, even to me.

I went back into the warmth of the house and was surprised to find Gerty there, stirring a huge pot. 'Porridge?' she said.

'Oh, you got here. Yes please. Do you know if the school is open today?' I said.

'No, it won't be. No one will be going anywhere today unless it's in a four-wheel drive or on foot. That's why I was late. Burt will be here in a while, I expect. He'll probably get on and start fixing the orangery. At least patch it up against the weather.'

I sat down at the table with my bowl of oatmeal, not sure if I liked the idea of Burt fixing the round house or not. I didn't want him unknowingly destroying anything hidden there. 'Do you think he'd mind if I helped him?'

Gerty looked at me as if I'd sprouted wings, or something. 'You'll have to ask him.'

'What's Tallulah doing today?' I asked. On her phone, I guessed, with endless rounds of 'he said this, and she said that'.

'Well, when I last saw her, she whooped with delight and announced she was going back to bed.'

Her impression of her daughter made me laugh. I could so imagine her doing that.

Gerty switched the old transistor radio on; it was the size of a small clutch bag on top of the windowsill. It kept on about the freak weather for October that had closed schools and roads and even affected the power supply for some people. Guess I had my answer confirmed about going to school. Then I asked, without holding out much hope, 'Will they still install the Wi-Fi today?'

Gerty widened her eyes as if I'd reminded her of something she'd totally forgotten about. 'I doubt they will come out. They said the router will be posted. That might come today, if the postman can get here on his rounds. I'll give the telephone people a ring this afternoon.'

I sighed, not sure what I'd do with myself.

Just then, the back door opened, and Burt came in after banging his boots on the step. 'Mornin', ladies … bloody weather. In October … have you ever heard of it?'

I certainly hadn't. Gerty tutted. 'It's inconvenient, that's what it is.' She put a cup of tea down on the table for Burt and said, 'I've got things to do.'

'Gerty said you might work on the orangery today?'

Burt picked up his tea and pushed back his flat cap a little while he thought. 'Yeah, should do really. Get the roof done at least. We don't want more snow to ruin the inside, do we?' He smiled and took a large gulp of tea.

I scraped the last of my oatmeal into the bin and said, 'Can you be careful? I mean, if you find anything weird, or interesting, can you save it for me?' I didn't look him in the eye. I sounded too much like a weirdo.

'Will do,' he said. 'Can't say as I think there'll be much to find. Specially now the only love seat left was squashed flat.'

My eyes widened. 'Love seat?'

'Yeah, that's what they used to call 'em. Courting couples

would sit and talk. They could look out over the gardens and that, while their chaperone waited not too far away, outside,' he said with a wink, which made my cheeks go red. 'So, what you gonna do with yourself today, then?'

I shrugged and was about to say something when Burt interrupted. 'Oh! I almost forgot.' He bent down and took something flat and heavy from the bag by his feet.

'My old laptop?' I said with a frown. I recognised it because it was ancient and covered in stickers of bands.

'Yeah, I bumped into young Ollie Black yesterday and he gave it to me to give back to you. Said, when they switched it on to test it before they sent it off, it worked fine. So, he said try it and see how it goes. No charge or anything.'

I took it from him, thrilled to have it back. I'd already prepared myself for the worst and apparently I needn't have worried. I'd have to thank him when I saw him next. My MacBook wasn't working either today. Maybe something was interfering with everything electrical round here. I'd try it again later.

'Do you need any help today?' I said. 'I'm going to be bored.'

Burt laughed and rolled his eyes. 'No, love, why don't you go off for a nice walk? The snow makes it look like a Christmas card out there and there's some lovely country-side. You can take Brutus with you if you want?'

I stared at him, slightly wary at who the hell Brutus was.

He laughed. 'He's my little Jack Russell with severe 'little guy' issues. He's in the Land Rover. Gerty won't have him indoors. Says he upsets your aunt. More likely because of her spotless floors,' he said, with another of his characteristic winks.

'Ok,' I said, not convinced. I guess it could be fun.

'Come on, I'll introduce you. Wrap up and I'll meet you out front.'

I put my bowl and Burt's cup in the dishwasher and went back up to my room to put on a few more layers. I put a boot on my good foot and another thick sock over my cast. Then I put on a hat and gloves. I was lucky, I'd only just got them.

In the end I wasn't sure if I could move very far at all with all the padding, let alone through the snow. If I fell over, I was sure I would never get back up. I went down the stairs and straight out of the front door.

Burt was already there, letting out an impatient-looking black, white and brown terrier from the back of his Land Rover. He had the cutest brown eyebrows, brown muzzle and black button nose that scooted near the ground, sniffing, and headed straight for me as soon as he saw me.

'Down, Brutus!' Burt shouted when he jumped up at my legs.

I had to laugh at the most inappropriate name I'd ever heard.

'Take this,' Burt said, passing me a leash. 'You won't need it unless another dog comes along. Then put it on, because he thinks he's a German Shepherd at times.'

The dog was already sitting, looking up at me expectantly; clearly recognising the lead. His tongue was comically hanging out the side of his mouth as he panted.

'Don't go too far. It won't be easy on crutches.' Burt pointed to a footpath that led off through the trees. 'Follow the path. There'll be less snow there. You'll come to a fork eventually. Take the left one. It'll bring you in a loop back here.'

I wasn't sure and looked up the drive to where I knew was a road.

'The snow is deep on the road,' he said, bobbing his head at my bad leg.

'Where does the other fork go in case I get lost?' I took my phone out of my pocket and there was still no signal.

53

'If you come out at the Waxley-Black place then you've gone too far.'

I tried to hide the surprise and interest from my face. Suddenly, the idea of a walk had become a whole lot more appealing. My sense of curiosity completely overtook the downside of an arduous walk. I just wished I hadn't got the darn plaster cast on my leg. It was going to slow me up a lot.

I said a goodbye to Burt, making him promise again to keep anything interesting he found in the orangery, called Brutus, and assured him I wouldn't stray from the path.

The dog, eager to get going, bounded past me and straight into the woods at the opposite side of the drive. At least he seemed to know where he was going.

Burt was right. Everything did look like a winter wonderland out here. The sun was now out, reflecting off the snow, making it glitter like diamonds. I took out my phone and took some amazing scenic photos and a cute selfie with Brutus, panting with his tongue out the side of his mouth. We continued on the path with him criss-crossing in front of me wherever the scent took him. It felt like we went on like this for ages.

My hands and shoulders began to ache, and I had to take frequent stops. It occurred to me then, that apart from the path, everywhere looked the same in all directions. If it snowed anymore it would be easy to get lost. The melting ice crackled around me sounding eerie, like everything was moving, and a bird called in the distance making a bleak and lonely sound. I quickened my pace.

When I finally came to the fork in the path, I wish I could say that I forgot Burt's advice, but I didn't. The truth was I was intrigued to see what the Waxley-Black place looked like.

I walked on for about ten more minutes, until the snow-laden trees began to thin out. The path led to a circular drive in front of a large old house, very similar to my aunt's. Brutus ran on, eager to investigate, just as the front door slammed and a young man came out to a grey van parked just outside. Brutus barked to say hello.

'Brutus!' I hissed, hoping I could call him back and remain unnoticed at the same time. But he ignored me, like the traitor he was, and jumped up at the guy's legs. He turned and looked down at Brutus in surprise. Then he looked up and quickly found me hovering at the edge of the trees. He stooped and fussed the little dog and straightened, looking at me the whole time.

At first, I thought it was Ollie, there was such a strong family resemblance. He had the same dark, unruly hair under his grey beanie hat. But he was too tall and filled out in his large black woollen overcoat. And after first thinking he had on a high-necked sweater, I realised that his neck was covered with tattoos right up to his jawline. *The older one.*

He hadn't said a word, just stood and watched me. It was so uncomfortable that I put up a hand in the end and said, 'Hi!'

He totally ignored it, turned and slammed the van door. I watched him, open-mouthed, as he walked back to the house. With one last look over his shoulder on the doorstep, confirming he'd definitely seen me, he went inside.

I was completely stunned. *How rude.* I called Brutus to me, who'd sniffed everything in the vicinity and made my way, retracing my steps, back down the track. I was moving fast in anger. He was so up himself to ignore me like that. My cheeks burned with the humiliation.

When I came to the fork, I made sure I took the right one, all the while my mind went over the strange meeting and why he would have ignored me like that. It made me angry that I remembered every detail of him; how his hair was almost black, how his jeans were ripped and cool and tapered into logger-type boots. I bet he was covered in those tattoos. There was no denying that the guy was hot. I had not expected to meet a guy like that out here in rural England. Someone who was so arrogant that he didn't even see fit to say hello to me.

The downside of fuming all the way home was that I took no notice of the view, the good thing was, it seemed to take no time at all. However, by the time I reached the house it was lunchtime. My arms and shoulders killed and my toes had gone numb with the cold – particularly my plastered foot.

I headed straight for the warmth of the kitchen and forgot Gerty's Brutus ban. She tutted, immediately complaining, 'That dog's brought wet snow in right through the house.'

'Sorry,' I said. 'I think he needs a drink.'

She tutted again, but I suspected she didn't hate him that much, as she found an old bowl under the sink, filled it with water and set it down for him.

After glugging down a pint of squash myself, I headed straight out to find Burt before I peeled all my layers off and thawed out. He was just closing the door to the orangery as I got there.

'Roof's patched up. Did you have a nice walk?'

'Yes,' I said, watching Brutus greet his master with a wagging tail. 'He was a good boy, but Gerty doesn't think so.'

He laughed. 'Gerty's bark is worse than her bite – oh, I almost forgot. I found this.' He rummaged in his pocket and pulled out what looked like a length of cane or bamboo about as thick as my thumb.

'What is it?'

'Not sure, but I didn't want to just chuck it before you saw it.'

He passed it to me, and I turned it over in my hands. 'Where did you find it?'

'Under where the roof went. I guess it was under or part of the love seat.'

I looked at him and smiled. 'Thanks.'

'Best be off.'

I thanked him again, too distracted by the object to see him go. In the end, I tucked it away in my pocket and went inside to take off my boot and wet socks. After a warming bowl of chicken soup, I went up to my room to check out the wooden tube.

It was about six inches long and about an inch wide. I took out my phone and switched on the torch to look inside it. It was then I saw it. All the way round the inside was what appeared to be black writing.

My heart flipped. It was a concealed note. This was the secret message I'd been expecting, and I'd been right. I could whoop for joy.

I hurriedly rummaged in my makeup bag for tweezers. Then, slowing down my breathing so I didn't shake, I pushed the tweezers down the side of the tube, careful to get one prong between the paper and the edge. After a couple of attempts, I managed it. I very slowly pulled the paper out.

I was surprised to find it wasn't that long; just a few lines:

LILA,

I won't be coming here again.
I can see now that it was a mistake.
I could never love someone as low in station.
Please don't contact me or ever speak to me again.
Jedediah

. . .

57

I WAS STUNNED. The tone was so different. No LB and JWB, as before. As if all pretence had gone. I was expecting a love note, as I was sure Lila was too. She must have been devastated. Now the rumours of her suicide began to ring true. I wondered what terrible things happened that night.

Although, whatever way I thought about it, it didn't make sense. I couldn't understand what could have happened between the note in the library declaring undying love and this one, to make such a dramatic turnaround.

I'd had all these wonderful scenarios in my head where they'd planned to elope. Maybe she ran away in grief. Deep down, I didn't think so. Someone was trying to tell me something: the roses, the petals. The round house itself was calling me, I was sure of it.

My eyes fell on my old laptop, left on my bed from earlier. I found my old charger and switched it on. I sagged in defeat when only the blue screen of death greeted me. *Ollie!* I wanted to scream in frustration. Now I'd have to take it all the way back to the shop.

I hit the escape button over and over and it started loading some random gibberish that looked like code. It went on for a few seconds until it stopped.

Then one word came up.

'Hello?

CHAPTER 6

*H*ello. *I know you're there. You may as well talk to me.*

I stared at the screen. Just one of those nerdy things coders did for their kicks. *Wasn't it?* Then it did it again.

I looked around for the hidden camera. Creepy. My fingers tapped, lightning fast. *OK, quit freaking me out. Who is this?* My mind was racing all the while, trying to come up with a likely culprit from my old friendship circle, but I came up with no one. The friends I had were not techy enough for this, even if they still bothered with me – which they didn't.

I leaned back against the headboard with my laptop across my thighs. When nothing came back, I let out a blast of air in relief. It had me going for a minute.

It's Wax, and you plagued me!

My mind shot to the only person I knew by that name: Waxley-Black, but I couldn't be sure. The one thing I knew, was that they were speaking to me in real time. I wanted to say something back, but I didn't want to give anything away yet. *Call me Pearl – Pearl White,* I shot back on impulse. It was the first thing that came to mind close to my surname of Whitely.

Three crying with laughter emojis came up. Then: *Like a CB radio call sign or something?*

It felt weird. Whoever it was, they were chatting to me like we'd met at school or a party or something. I had to remember I had no idea who this person was. *Yeah, I guess... you never know what weirdoes are on the internet. Is that what yours is?*

Erm... There was another gap, as if whoever it was was having to think a great deal. *Black Wax, as in candle.*

My mind was racing. Black Wax – Waxley-Black? I needed to keep them talking: *I thought church candles were white?*

Who said anything about church? Not mine ... they're black. It's the only way I sleep.

Every word was a step further into weirdo country and yet I was drawn to speak to him. Yes, him. I don't know how I knew, but I did. It was the most interesting conversation I'd had in days. *How old are you?* It felt essential to ask, even though he could say literally anything.

Twenty!

My fingers hovered over the keyboard while I processed the information. I was beginning to wonder if – maybe even hope – this was the guy I'd seen earlier.

Why? How old are you?

For a moment I warred with what to say. I decided on honesty; after all, I wanted honesty in return. *Eighteen! Are you a guy?* Even though I was already convinced, I held my breath.

Hahahaha! littered across the page. It conveyed laughter much more than his emojis of earlier. *Yes, I'm a guy. 6'2', 180 lbs. Why, you'd prefer a butch girl???*

I burst out laughing at that. I couldn't believe I was

batting to and fro with a guy I had never met, and one that was sounding more appealing by the minute. *Jock?*

Yank?

It was my turn to write: *laughing.* To which he replied: *hahahaha.* Followed by: *I can't believe you wrote the actual word.*

I hadn't laughed in such a long time. It was a good feeling. *Oh and I'm a girl, in case you wondered. Unless you prefer a boy?* I said in panic, then felt stupid immediately after. It felt like flirting and I didn't think it was appropriate. My cheeks blasted red. Especially when he replied with a simple: *???.*

After I literally died, he sent a smiley face and: *I knew you were a girl. I've heard your voice.*

My heart stalled. *How?* I shot back. Did he mean this morning when I called 'Hi' and he ignored me?

I dunno. I see you in my mind.

I wasn't sure why I liked that but I did. I should really be freaked out, but I was becoming more and more convinced he was the older one of the two Waxley-Black brothers. I had to know more. Maybe he was just imagining what I looked like. The dream I'd woken up with this morning gave me a warm feeling in my stomach. *How do you see me?* I said, hedging, but my heart was beating hard in my chest.

Blonde. You're very blonde. Pale. Then he left quite a gap. *And cute!*

Maybe I should have been creeped out, but, the truth was, I was glowing. I couldn't remember the last interaction I'd had with a hot guy – well apart from Ollie, and I couldn't really count a guy that had to talk to me in a shop.

That kind of narrowed it down. It could only be one of them. How else could he have got me so right? I had to find out more about him. *All from your mind's eye, eh? So what about you? What do you look like? You could be a little nerdy troll who sits in his room all day eating candy bars.*

Again *hahahahah* covered the page. *Well, I guess* one *of those things could be right.*

It wasn't the answer I was expecting and my heart stopped with fright. I could be talking to a spotty thirteen-year-old with raging hormones, grounded to his room. Although I soon relaxed; there was something about his easy tone that was too confident to ever be that. I frowned and clicked hesitantly. *Well, which one was right?* I held my breath and waited.

After a long moment: *The sitting in my room part.*

I let out a long breath of relief.

I don't go out much – not in the day, anyway. Re the rest. Tall, dark – I promise – no spots.

I hitched in a breath at how he'd read me so right again. There was something in that promise that quickened my heart, but there was an undercurrent of sadness too in just a few short words. *Are you sick then?* I was already praying that he wasn't.

Some might say. Then another smiley face appeared. I got the impression that it was to cover up for something he wasn't ready to tell.

So, where do you live, vampire boy? It was the only thing I could think of to lighten the mood; even though I'd pretty much guessed already. I sent a smiley face of my own.

His laughter came back with: *Vampire boy? Wax isn't dark enough? You have to imagine me drawing the blood from young virgins?*

I almost wrote back: 'Who said anything about virgins?' but stopped just in time and backspaced. We'd only spoken for ten minutes and it seemed too flirty and could send the wrong message. I sent an embarrassed emoji with a red face and *Sorry* instead. *I guess never going out in the day would make you pale like a Goth,* I said, trying to remember the guy from that morning, but he had a beanie hat on and was a long way off.

A thinking emoji came back. *Maybe a bit. I'm just not really a people person.*

I absorbed that for a moment, trying to decipher what he meant.

So, tell me a bit about you, Blondie. You're a little pale yourself.

There was the familiarity. *Do you know me or something?* He must have seen me. There weren't many people with hair as white as mine.

Again he sent over laughter. *Sorry, didn't mean to freak you out. No, I don't know you but, like I said, I have a knack of seeing people and that's how I see you when I close my eyes. I'm dark, you're light, I'm black and you're white.*

I frowned and looked closely at the words. They were strange and compelling. Quite poetic, really. I knew I should be careful, but I felt drawn to him. Maybe there was something magical about this place. The way it had snowed, and everything felt cut off from the outside world. *What colour are your eyes?* I said, feeling swept up in it.

Blue!

Somehow, I just knew he was going to say that, even though Ollie's had been dark brown. Then an idea occurred to me. *OK then, wise guy, if you can see me, what colour are mine?*

The gap was long enough, so I thought I had him. *Mind's eye not working???* I said, but I felt a little disappointed.

You're hiding. You've got to want to be seen, Pearl.

I smirked, but he intrigued me. *What do you suggest I do, smile for the camera?* I zoomed my face into the screen, convinced there must be something he could see through.

Just think open thoughts. I told you, I see things that other people don't. Just think to yourself: 'See me, Wax.'

I half laughed and half frowned. This boy was definitely strange. *OK, OK, right, I'm doing it* I sent back. Then I don't know what made me try, but I said it to myself: 'See me, Wax.' I said it out loud and felt silly after.

Blue, but paler than mine. Yours are the colour of an Arctic glacier.

My heart was pounding, and I had to quickly reason with myself. It wasn't just that he had got it so right, but the way it came across. As if he was whispering next to my cheek. It was utterly unnerving. *Clever. Are you David Copperfield or something?* I swallowed hard, hoping my joking would come across. It certainly felt like he was weaving a spell around me. *You're good.* It was all I could say. I felt out of breath.

There was no reply for several minutes. I panicked that my joke had come across as mocking him. In the end I had to cave and say: *Are you there?*

Nothing. I stared and stared, until eventually the screen flickered and my username and password prompt came up. I suppose I should have been glad that my computer appeared to now be working, but all I could say was, 'Shit!'

I clicked all the keys frantically to get the blue screen back, but it had gone as if I'd imagined the whole thing. All I could think of was: How on earth would I get to speak to him now?

It was no good, I was going to have to go back to his house.

THE WAIT WAS as frustrating as hell. It was too late to go back today. It would be dark soon and covering that distance on crutches in the snow once today had taken its toll on my shoulders. However, the more I thought about it, the more confused and angry I became. First, he blatantly ignores me this morning and then goes to all the trouble of talking to me on some weird non-internet link, only to get offended and leave without so much as a goodbye.

That's the way my thoughts went for the rest of the day. Luckily, Gerty pulled me out of them for an early supper so she could get a lift home with Burt. I ate my stew and dumplings at the kitchen table, silently churning over the day and not even noticing the taste of what I was eating. It wasn't even just the Waxley-Blacks, but the note Burt found as well. That wasn't sitting right with me either and I couldn't understand why. It bothered me.

'You're very quiet this evening,' Gerty said as she finished loading the dishwasher.

I shrugged and put a huge spoonful in my mouth so I couldn't talk.

'You're bored senseless, I suspect,' Gerty said with a sigh.

I averted my eyes, letting her draw her own conclusions.

'Shall I get Tallulah to come tomorrow if the snow is still bad? If we have more there'll be no school.'

I shrugged again and then a thought struck me. She was my way into the Waxley-Black house. I instantly brightened. 'Yes, that'd be good. I'm going stir crazy here.'

She smiled. 'That settles it then. I'm finished for the evening. Just switch the dishwasher on when you've finished. 'I'll see you tomorrow.'

I nodded. 'Thanks. See you tomorrow.'

The moment Gerty went, the quiet in the room became oppressive. Every scrape of my spoon was deafening. I shovelled the last of my stew into my mouth, stood and put the empty bowl in the dishwasher, remembering to switch it on like she said. I grabbed a couple of cookies from the jar and went upstairs on my crutches. I glanced at Lila as I reached the top. I could swear she was smirking at me. It always felt like she was watching my life and finding it very entertaining.

I started running my bath. Then I went to my room to collect my robe, nightshirt and wash things. I couldn't help a last look out of the window. The light was going, and the roundhouse was a dark outline in the gloom. It hadn't snowed again all day but it only served to add to the feeling, it was waiting. My plans would have to change if school was open tomorrow. Somehow I doubted it would be. Everything in me was driving me to that house.

I drew the heavy curtains and grabbed my old laptop to listen to music in the tub. Everything echoed in this old house. The wind groaned and pipes knocked, long after the taps were turned off and I wanted to block it out. Before I left, I couldn't resist a last try on the laptop, but the password prompt came up straight away.

Leaving the crutches behind, I hobbled along to the bathroom carrying my laptop, night clothes and sponge bag. The bath was at the right depth by the time I got there, so I put my laptop down and clicked play on Linkin Park. Then I turned off the huge taps and sloshed the water around, adding shower gel for bubbles.

I straightened up at the sound of the wind whistling again. The wind always howled around this part of the house, even when it didn't appear to be windy outside. I undressed, careful not to topple over when I pulled off my socks. Then I hopped over to the sink and looked into the mirror.

I *was* pale.

Deathly pale.

How did vampire boy know that?

I had dark circles under my eyes that seemed worse lately. With a deep, resigned sigh, I picked up my toothbrush and squeezed out a line across the bristles. I started brushing automatically, spat, and looked back in the mirror. A face was next to mine. Pale with large eyes, in varying shades of sepia like an old photograph.

I screamed and, in shock, tripped over my own plastered

foot and fell backwards, landing on my backside. Hard. It took me a full minute to calm my breathing to gather myself to get up. I retrieved my fluff-covered toothbrush from the floor next to me and managed to get up by grabbing the sink.

After swallowing several gulps of air, I risked another look but there was nothing there except my own reflection. I really was going mad. I rinsed my toothbrush with shaking hands and began again. My heart was still beating erratically. Tomorrow I had to make an effort to make friends; too much time on my own was doing me no good.

I turned up the music and hopped into the bath, which was an acrobatic feat in itself. I managed it without getting my cast too wet and sank deep into the soothing warm water. I breathed out on a sigh. It was the best medicine for my nerves. The steam rose all around me against the cold of the room and I began to relax. I must have been over-wrought. It had been an exhausting day both physically and emotionally. Lila's painting was the last thing I saw, and my mind was clearly playing tricks with it.

Linkin Park's 'Numb' aptly filled the space and drowned out the howls of the wind trying to get in. Somewhere during the chorus, I must have fallen asleep. I was back in the wonderful dream of this morning. Instead of the warmth of the water, the heavenly weight of his body held me down as his lips came next to mine. I could even smell the faint smell of mint from his breath and the sandalwood soap on his skin. 'Don't!' he whispered. 'Don't let's start this again.'

I felt myself frown, even in my sleep. It was said so angrily I could feel the sharpness of his breath through his teeth. I couldn't help myself; I nipped at his lips and he kissed me for one incendiary moment. I couldn't breathe.

No, I really couldn't breathe.

His weight had pushed me below the water line and no matter how hard I scratched and pushed at his shoulders, I couldn't get him off. His lips were gone, and I gurgled, choked and spat. Until, as suddenly as it came, the weight lifted off me and I sat up, sloshing water over the sides. 'Shit!' I spat, taking huge gulps of air. I must have fallen asleep and had one hell of a nightmare. *God!* It felt so real.

I wasted no more time and flopped out over the side, landing in an undignified heap. I was just relieved to be out. I barely dried myself before dragging my nightshirt and robe on. Snatching up my laptop, I limped back to my room with my head pounding now the oxygen was rushing into it.

I crawled straight onto the bed and scrambled under the covers. It took me a few minutes to calm down. I pulled over my laptop, turned the volume down and stared at the screen. I willed it to do something. Anything. Instead, all I could see was the screensaver of Pete and me. We looked so happy; both laughing with my arms looped around his neck. He was giving me a piggy-back through the shallows of the ocean, so I didn't get wet. I missed him so much. In that moment, I was the most alone I'd ever been in my life. I wiped away a solitary tear. I had no one.

I SLEPT AFTER TEARS. I always did. It seemed part of my sleep regime these days. My dreams were filled with disturbing visions of Pete laughing at an angry dark-haired boy with blue eyes, shaking his head in disappointment. Every time I got near enough to ask him why, he'd just put his hands up, defensively, to keep me away. All the while, Lila smirked from the shadows.

I woke up sweating more than once. In the end, I sat up more exhausted than before I went to sleep. I dragged my sorry bruised ass out of bed at 7.30 and hopped over to the window. I didn't know what I'd rather see: the snow gone so I could go to the unfriendly, strange environment of a new school, or a thick blanket of the stuff, forcing me to face my fears and knock on the door of the Waxley-Blacks.

I whipped the curtain back with jingle across the pole, and there it was. My answer: a thick covering of snow, as far as the eye could see.

I jumped at a loud knock at my door. Followed by: 'Open up, Becks. It's Tallulah. If I've had to get up to come all the way over here, you have to bloody get up too.'

I sagged in relief. Her rudeness was oddly comforting. I went to the door and yanked it open.

'Ew ... you look like shit!'

I ignored the insult and got straight to business. 'Good! I'm glad you're here. I want you to take me over to the Waxley-Black place.'

Her eyes immediately glittered with mischief. 'Oooh, why? What's happened?'

'Nothing, just meet me downstairs.'

For once, she had no wisecrack comeback, just nodded animatedly. Then she literally skipped off down the hallway. It was the most enthusiasm I'd seen her show in anything so far.

I dressed warmly, grabbed my hat and gloves and, using my crutches, made my way down to the kitchen after her. The warm smell of toast hit me as soon as I got there. Tallulah was already slathering butter on a slice and taking a huge bite out of it when she saw me. Gerty was stirring a cup of tea and put it down on the table.

I'd never much liked toast, but I sat down and took it gratefully. I was a woman on a mission today and, I had to admit, I was getting used to the taste.

'You gonna tell me what's up?' Tallulah said with her mouth full.

I glared at her and flicked my eyes at Gerty so she understood that I didn't want it broadcast. 'I just needed to get out today to be around some people, that's all,' I said to smooth over her comment.

Gerty soon excused herself to go and do some dusting, telling us to not get into any trouble before she went.

'You going to tell me what this is all about?' Tallulah said, her eyes bright, then looked down at her nails in fake boredom.

I had to think fast and decided to stick as much as I could with the truth. It would get me faster results. 'Look, I've been getting these weird messages on my laptop and I think they're coming from one of the Waxley-Blacks.' I straightened my back and put my chin up. 'And I want to go over there today and confront them.'

Her eyes widened in understanding and she half smiled and looked amazed all at the same time. 'Why, what on earth did it say?' she said, conspiratorially. 'Show me!'

'That's just it. I can't. It wasn't on any social media, just on the front screen before I'd even logged on. Remember Ollie took it to get it fixed? At the mall? He sent it back saying there was nothing wrong with it. Then I got the messages and then they just disappeared.'

Tallulah stared at me for ages, her expression changing as she ran over everything I'd just told her. 'I guess it could be Ollie playing tricks. He would do that. Like, what did it say?'

'That's the weird part. We were having a real conversation. Like getting to know each other.' I was shaking my head while I was speaking. 'I don't think it was Ollie.' Then I looked Tallulah dead in the eye. 'I think it was the other one.'

She blanched and frowned dramatically. 'Who, Bret?' Then she shook her head emphatically and laughed derisively. 'No way. He's a sod, but it couldn't be him.'

I didn't understand why she was so sure and told her about my walk with the dog in the morning. 'He was rude to me, so I just want to go over there and clear this up.'

Tallulah shrugged. 'Well, that definitely sounds like him. OK,' she said, like she had nothing better to do today. 'It's your funeral. You really don't know Bret.'

I'd got her to agree so I didn't want to argue with her further. I drank the last of my tea and thought about what she'd said: *How bad could it be?*

Ollie was a friendly enough guy. Surely they couldn't be so different. The other one was probably just a more anti-social version of him.

We finally left the house at around nine and set off through the forest. My unease grew with the sense of Tallulah's barely contained excitement all the way there. She was acting like she was anticipating something – and thrilled to have a front row seat.

CHAPTER 7

*T*he front door was huge and intimidating. I stood partly behind Tallulah so whoever came would see her first. 'Knock again,' I said.

Tallulah rolled her eyes at me over her shoulder and whacked the door knocker again, loudly, twice. We waited while I held my breath. Looking around me, I noticed the snow was thick, with ruts in the driveway, proving the older brother's van had moved and come back since it had last snowed.

It seemed like forever before the clunk of the latch sounded. I was surprised to see it was Ollie – and not looking as happy as I remembered him. He looked anxiously over his shoulder. 'Now's not a good time, girls.'

Just as he said it, there was a loud thump as if something had hit a wooden floor from a great height. Then an almighty crash of glass and a roar of rage that sounded like a wild animal.

I jumped behind the shelter of Tallulah's body in case something ran out. It sounded like an ogre on the rampage in there.

I couldn't believe my ears when Tallulah said, 'Is it Wax?'

For a moment I actually forgot my fear and stepped out to look at her. She just tutted. 'Ollie's brother Bret ...'

She was interrupted again by another crash and something rolling along the wooden floor. A round silver tray whisked past Ollie's leg, then mine, like a hub cap.

There were other raised voices now, shouting orders as if to corner or trap something. 'What's wrong with him?' I said in horror.

There followed the sound of some doors slamming and Ollie stepped back quickly to look. 'Quickly, come into the library,' he said in a loud whisper, ushering us in with his arm.

I hesitated, trying to decide whether I wanted to go or not, but Tallulah yanked me in by the arm, forgetting I was on crutches. I almost toppled over.

The house was even bigger and scarier than my aunt's. It was darker too, if that were possible. This was the set of a horror movie for sure. All the wood in the large vaulted hallway was intricately carved and black, right up the large staircase. The walls were an ugly dark green. I didn't have time to take in any more as there was another loud crash from the floor above, and Ollie pulled us into the room on the left.

I watched in alarm as Ollie pulled over a chair to prop up against it. Then he looked at Tallulah for help. They locked eyes and communicated something. 'It's OK, we'll explain,' She pulled me away from the door to follow Ollie, already flopping into a chair by the fire.

'Come and sit down. I'll get you something to drink when they quieten him down,' he said, waving an arm at the sofa next to him.

I went with Tallulah over to the red velvet Chesterfield, next to Ollie's chair and cautiously sat down. I was still listening out for violence outside as I lay my crutches on the floor.

I sat and tried to calm down. It was then I realized properly where I was. It was as dark as the hallway. There were black velvet curtains over the windows, but I could see row upon row of black shelves filled with books, even more than were in my aunt's library. There were hundreds. A black glass chandelier was on above us and several smaller lamps dotted sideboards with black or maroon shades. The only cheery light appeared to come from the fire.

Ollie was chewing the corners of his fingernails, staring into the flames. No one was saying anything – as if they were in shock. In the end I had to break the silence. 'What's with the chair? Is he dangerous?' I looked nervously behind me at the flimsy barrier pushed under the door handle.

'It's his brother, Bret,' Tallulah said. 'Well, we don't call him that. His real name is Archie. His parents call him Bret. It's a middle name. We all call him Wax …' Tallulah rambled.

Ollie rolled his eyes, clearly having heard enough and cut across her. 'Let's just say my brother has issues.'

'What happened?' Tallulah asked with her eyebrows drawn together in concern. She sounded the most bothered about anything I'd ever seen her. It confirmed what I first thought, that she definitely more than liked Ollie.

Ollie looked drained when he shrugged. 'He came home this morning more drunk than usual. He's been bad all week; just getting worse and worse.' He put his hand to his forehead.

Tallulah reached over the arm of the chair and held his hand.

'Who are all those other voices?' I said.

'My uncle and the servants,' Ollie said, but he didn't look over at me.

I felt my theory of the identity of the mystery hacker quickly dissolving. Even if it was the same name, it sounded like his brother was very ill.

Then Ollie seemed to drag himself out of his thoughts. 'What were you even doing here, anyway?'

'Oh, yeah,' Tallulah giggled, as if she'd forgotten herself. 'Becks thinks one of you has been hacking into her computer.'

I went crimson and could have killed Tallulah for saying it like that. I wasn't accusing anyone, I just wanted to get to the bottom of a mystery.

Ollie's face brightened. 'It's working OK, then?'

I frowned. 'Well, yeah. Eventually. I had some messages come up even before the password request – well, I had a whole conversation, actually.'

His eyebrows popped and he looked thoughtful for a moment. 'That is weird. Did it look like code at all?'

I shook my head. 'No, just a flashing curser and then the words came up.'

He looked surprised. 'Old school. What did it say?'

Tallulah kicked him in the foot. 'It wasn't you, was it?' She was half laughing as if it was totally something he would do.

He laughed and immediately put his hands up in defence. 'No, I swear. It's a great wind-up. I wish I'd thought of it. Did he or she give you a name?'

I took a moment to look at Tallulah before I answered, not sure if I should say it at all. I swallowed, then went ahead. 'He just said people call him Wax.'

Ollies face dropped and he immediately looked at Tallulah. She looked just as shocked back. 'Would he have that kind of know-how?'

Ollie flashed his eyes angrily. 'Of course. It's all he bloody does. He's cleverer at it than anyone.' Then he shook his head as if he just couldn't believe it was him. 'What sort of thing did he say?'

I shrugged. 'What normal people say when you get to know someone online.'

Ollie rolled his eyes and laughed derisively. 'That couldn't be him. Tell her, Tallulah,' he said, nudging her arm.

She laughed. 'I already told her.'

'But why?'

'He doesn't talk to anyone!' they both said at exactly the same time.

I found it hard to believe that a person could live their whole life without talking to anyone at all. My thoughts must have been on my face because Ollie's features softened. 'He barely talks to me, and he blanks new people completely.'

It made me think of the boy standing on his porch yesterday morning, blatantly ignoring me. It certainly fit the profile. I sank back into the chair. *Well, someone had to have done it.*

I looked up. Tallulah was giggling and flirting with Ollie. 'So, is the Halloween party still going ahead with everything … you know?' she said, tipping her head towards the door to indicate the morning's events.

'Yeah, course. He'll be gone long before you all get here. As soon as it's dark, he can't wait to get out of here.'

'What, you let him out alone?' I said in horror.

They both looked at me and laughed. 'It's pretty hard to stop Wax from doing anything,' Ollie said with a wry look on his face.

All seemed to have gone quiet for a while outside. Ollie got up and walked towards the door and put his ear to it. Then he took the chair away.

'Is Wax violent?' I said, feeling nervous again. 'Like with people, I mean?'

Tallulah nodded animatedly, as if it was the most exciting

thing ever. 'Sometimes, I think. Everyone in the village is scared of him, but he only ever smashes stuff at home.'

Oh, that's OK then. That's made me feel better. I was amazed at how matter of fact she was able to be over all this.

'Do you want a drink? The coast is clear now.' Ollie was already opening the door.

'Yeah, I'll have a coke,' Tallulah called.

I nodded. 'Same … Actually, do you think it would be safe to use your restroom?'

Olly laughed like he was back to his old self. 'There's one just down the hall on the left.'

Tallulah took out her phone and started texting. She'd actually stayed off it for a remarkably long time this morning. I picked up my crutches and took the opportunity to slip out of the room.

Ollie had already disappeared off to the kitchen somewhere, so I made my way slowly down the hall. My crutches sank into the huge old fashioned red rug and then conspicuously sounded on the polished floorboards. Whatever mess had been there had already been cleared up.

There were large dark paintings everywhere. A lot of ancient-looking landscapes or pictures of horses and dogs, but as I reached the foot of the staircase portraits went all the way up. *What is it with these old houses?* I couldn't help myself, I just had to take a closer look. I quickly checked around me for witnesses and slowly climbed the stairs.

High above me, there was a huge bank of stained-glass arched windows, where the staircase changed direction. It was a welcome bit of cheer, leaving little dancing lights on the grim faces looking out of the walls.

It occurred to me then that most of the portraits were men. The ones at my aunt's were mainly women. *How odd.*

Finally I reached the top of the stairs and a long hallway that went in both directions. It looked like a hotel, there were so many doors on either side. The house was certainly big enough.

There was a loud clomp and then a moan that made me freeze. I looked behind me and debated whether to go back down, but something made me want to go on. I could say I was lost looking for the toilet, if someone challenged me.

I pushed on slowly to the right, thankful for the thin strip of rug that ran the length of the corridor to mask my footsteps. Every black carved door was closed, and I moved steadily onto the next. I was beginning to think it would be the case for all of them, when the next one opened and a woman in a black dress and white apron came out and went left without seeing me.

It happened so quickly, I barely had time to flatten myself against the wall. She didn't see me though and disappeared through a door further down. I took some breaths, composed myself and straightened up. I wanted to see in the room she just came out of.

I inched closer and carefully peeked around the doorpost. I intended just to take a quick look and then go, but my feet froze, and the sight rendered me useless. I simply stood there, unable to move. There, in the room, completely decorated in black, was the boy I knew I'd come to see. He was lying in a huge carved bed with black curtains draped from above it and a coat of arms like something out of a fairy tale.

Those brilliant-blue eyes met and held mine. I felt mesmerized and was no longer hiding at all. I just stood there helplessly looking and he appeared to do the same. He didn't say a word and neither did I. His black hair was an overlong mess around his face and his skin was pale. A nurse was bending over his wrist administering something. He was propped up on black pillows and covered in blankets to his waist. What I could see of his body was entirely covered in ink; from the knuckles of his hands to his arms and his neck.

His stomach was covered the same, with the design on his chest morphing into wings along his collar bone and feathers and flames up to his jawline. I couldn't quite make it out what they were, but I was sure there were smaller tattoos around his eye.

I just knew, without doubt, it was to ward people off. It had nothing to do with fashion. I would bet good money it was to scare people, to make them form a bad opinion and keep them away. It didn't scare me. All it made me think was, *why?*

His eyes looked directly at me as if he were lazily mapping me in the same way. Then I saw his eyelids lower and I realised he was too relaxed. He'd been drugged. The nurse straightened up and it was clear what she'd been doing; a syringe was in her hand.

It was then I saw the pain in his eyes. His lips parted as if he was going to say something, but then his eyes slowly closed.

A man appeared from behind the door in front of me. He was slim, in a black suit and had greying hair. *The uncle.* I was about to blabber some sort of an apology, but, without uttering so much as a word, he looked right through me as if I wasn't there, and slowly closed the door in my face.

I stood there, stunned, and blinked. He was rude, but I'd been trespassing where I didn't belong, so I could hardly complain. I prayed that he didn't either.

I turned quickly and retraced my steps down the stairs as quickly as I could on my crutches. I used the loo to calm my nerves and cover my tracks and then went back to find the others.

My hands were still shaking when I entered the room. I paused when I saw Tallulah sitting across Ollie's lap. His arms were circled around her. I coughed to announce I was there. They turned their heads and smiled, but neither jumped up. In fact, it was me who went red for them. 'You've got some great old paintings out there,' I said as the first thing that came into my head. 'All quiet now,' hearing myself sounding more ridiculous by the minute. They didn't seem bothered at all. I wanted to question Ollie about why his brother needed to be sedated but knew I couldn't.

Ollie smiled in his easy-going, laid-back way. 'Yeah, the old ancestors. I expect you have them too.'

I nodded and sat down, a little more at ease now. 'But did you know that yours are all men and the ones at my aunt's are mainly women?'

His eyes widened. 'I've never been in your place, but I guess that is strange.'

'Maybe it's the curse,' Tallulah said, wide-eyed, putting on her best scary film voice.

I looked straight at Ollie to gauge his reaction. He just laughed and shrugged. 'Maybe. The guy who started it is the one at the top of the stairs.'

My heart stalled. The ones at home were labelled. I had no idea who was who here. 'Who? Jedediah Waxley-Black?'

Ollie blanched as if he was confused for a moment. Then he shook his head. 'No, it was his brother Ainsley.'

My heart stopped completely at that. 'But I thought Lila Blackwood was marrying Jedediah?'

Ollie shook his head again. 'No, the story was, she was in love with Jed but meant to marry Ainsley.'

I was stunned. I needed to think about this and what it meant with all the clues I'd already found.

Tallulah was already bored with the subject and blurted, 'Becks has got her costume for Saturday, haven't you, Becks?'

It pulled me out of my thoughts. 'Yeah, if it's still on with everything.' I said, immediately blasting red at drawing the attention back to poor Ollie's family situation, but he didn't seem perturbed.

'Great! I can't wait for you to meet everyone,' he said. 'I think they'll think you're a right laugh.'

Tallulah giggled.

I felt uneasy about it. It wasn't an ideal way to meet new people dressed as a tart and I remembered the haunted look in his brother's eyes. It felt wrong planning a party in the middle of all that.

There were three cans of coke on the table, so I guessed one was for me and took one. I cracked it open and took a huge gulp. 'Are your parents cool with it?' It was a bit daunting after having just met the uncle.

'Yeah, they travel a lot. My dad's business takes him away and my mum prefers London. My uncle stays here most of the time to keep an eye on things while I'm at school.'

'I thought all you Brits went to boarding school.' Although Ollie at Hogwarts didn't compute somehow.

Ollie and Tallulah both laughed at that.

'Only the posh ones,' Tallulah said, looking lovingly down at him.

'Well, we did,' Ollie said, a little more seriously. 'But Wax got expelled and I refused to stay after that. So we came to St Bart's and I met this one,' he said, tickling Tallulah in the ribs.

I smiled, deciding I liked Ollie. He was obviously devoted to his brother and, despite his fun-loving personality, apparently the more responsible of the two of them.

'And Wax is older?'

'Yeah, twenty.' He was still cavorting with Tallulah and speaking absently, but the age was very relevant to me. It was exactly what the mystery guy had told me on my computer. It had to be the same person.

'Where does he go now?' I was genuinely intrigued after today's events.

'He doesn't. He's one of those brooding geniuses. He does his degree online.'

The vampire boy who never came out of his room. It made up my mind more than ever. That drugged, tattooed, wild boy upstairs was the one I'd chatted to, I just knew it. Today had been a success in more ways than one.

Wax, Jedediah, Ainsley. I couldn't shake the growing feeling that everything was connected.

CHAPTER 8

*I*t was late afternoon by the time we walked back and the sun was leaving an orange blast on the horizon before it went down.

Tallulah chattered on, but I tuned out for most of it, answering with a 'Mmn' and a 'yeah' in the appropriate places.

As soon as we walked into the kitchen, she launched into an exciting blow-by-blow account to her mom, Gerty, about Wax's meltdown. I kept quiet. It wasn't something I felt comfortable gossiping about. Gerty just tutted and shook her head, listening, while she dished up our supper.

I ate the stew ravenously with huge chunks of bread while they talked.

'Those boys have no real parental supervision. No wonder they run wild,' Gerty said.

It made me frown when I thought about my own situation, which she seemed to have missed.

I demolished my food in less than five minutes, so I helped load the dishwasher and clear away. Gerty said they were going and she'd see me in the morning.

'Will there be school, do you think?' I said.

Gerty shrugged. 'It's so out of season, there's no telling. We'll have to wait and see.'

Tallulah said, 'Later,' while she was looking at her phone and they bustled out the door with Gerty's various bags. It left me sitting at the kitchen table in absolute silence. I looked around and wondered, *what now?* I was tired and it was too dark to check on the round house so, grabbing a water from the fridge, I decided to go up to my room. Downstairs seemed too big to be all on my own.

I climbed the echoey staircase slowly on my crutches, saying hello to all the grim faces on the way. It took my mind off the wind groaning up in the rafters. It had been an exhausting day and I couldn't handle any more excitement.

I decided on a strip wash after my last experience in the bath. The bathroom was creepy and it felt too unsettling to spend any time in there. I put on my PJs, clomped along the landing double-time and slid into bed with my old laptop on my knees.

My heart was already beating fast as my finger hovered over the power button. My thoughts raced. I knew if it was the boy I'd seen this afternoon, there was no way he would be awake to message me, but I still really hoped for one anyway.

I switched it on, and the curser flickered. I held my breath, knowing the message would come before the Welcome screen. Then I sagged with disappointment when the laptop prompted me for my username and password. I gave myself a mental slap. This just meant I was right; Wax probably was my mystery messenger, and that thrilled and terrified me at the same time. He was dangerous, attractive and fascinating; all rolled into one.

After that, I played some music for a while with my earphones on, but it reminded me too much of Pete. There was nothing as emotive as music to remind you what you'd lost. We'd loved those songs. It wasn't a good idea to do this when I was tired; I'd be bawling in a minute. It made me decide that I had to get some new songs and start to associate them with new experiences. Perhaps I'd get to like some UK bands.

Next, I checked the weather forecast for the morning, which seemed non-committal about more snow. Somewhere between that and checking my Instagram account, I must have fallen asleep.

I awoke with a start.

My head and heart went straight into overdrive when the noise happened again.

Three slow knocks on my door.

My heart was in my mouth, strangling my voice when I called out timidly, 'Who's there?'

No one answered.

Then I'm sure I heard some whispering.

'Tallulah?' I called, a bit louder.

There seemed a lot of whispers until they all came together in what sounded like a female voice saying something very much like, 'Shade … Shade … Come with me, Shade.'

It made no sense; I couldn't figure it out at all. I was terrified, trying to sit up and pull myself together enough to answer. 'My name is Beccah. Who is it, please?'

When I got no answer, I leaned over to turn on my lamp, but nothing happened. The power was out.

'Shaaade,' came like a moan from the other side of the door. I swallowed, but all the spit had gone from my mouth. I slowly put my legs out over the side of the bed and slipped down. I grabbed one of my crutches and stood up, a little wobbly at first. I was too shaky to go without. I needed a free hand with a crutch that could act as a weapon.

I went to the window first and pulled the curtains to let in some light. A full moon helped me see the room in shades of grey. Then I slowly approached the door and held out my hand to grab hold of the round brass doorknob. I turned it, holding my breath. It felt icy in my hand. I pulled the door open and took a step back all at the same time.

There was nothing there but a huge rectangle of blackness to the hallway. I couldn't see anyone or anything because there was zero light.

Then the voice sliced through the air and repeated the words again from a little way off. 'Shade … Shade … come with me.' It sounded like it was singing a melody to a song.

My heart was still thrashing in my chest, making me swallow with a sandpaper-dry mouth. Whoever she was, she wanted me to follow, but my mind was lurching all over the place, working quickly for a logical explanation of who it must be. But there simply wasn't one and a grim suspicion crept up my spine. I was scared stiff. I'd seen enough horror films to know following something into the dark was the last thing I should do; I shouldn't step into the blackness of that hall.

Then a thought occurred to me. I remembered my phone on charge next to the bed. I retraced my steps to the nightstand and pulled the charger out from the phone. The power must have been out for a while as it was only half charged. I hoped it was enough for what I was going to do.

I switched on the torch, arranged my crutch under my arm and headed back to the open doorway. 'Hello!' I said before I stepped into the darkness.

I edged out, stopped and looked left into the black. All I could see was the landing going off into the dark. When I heard no more sounds I began to walk slowly along, careful not to scuff the rug and trip. My chest was heaving up and down as if I was out of breath and I could only see a few feet in front of me. 'Where are you?' I said, my voice sounding weak and choked.

I stopped dead when it said, 'Shaaade,' again in a long, drawn-out whisper. I couldn't see it anywhere and yet all my senses said it was a little way ahead of me. 'I don't understand. Who are you? What do you want?' It began to feel like it was waiting for me, so I started to walk again, very slowly along the landing in the smallest steps. I was very conscious of feeling more exposed the further I got from my room. It felt like the darkness was circling and surrounding me.

I finally came to a dead end; a wall with wood panelling. It took me a moment to get my bearings, but I realised I was right next to the bathroom at the top of the stairs.

'Shaade,' the voice said again, but she sounded distorted.

I moved to the left and quickly checked inside the bathroom by throwing open the door and pointing the torch at every corner, but the room was empty. The whispering noises definitely sounded like they were coming from behind the panelled wall.

A loud bang made me jump backwards in fright. I only just grabbed hold of my crutch, so I didn't fall, but I'd dropped my phone and was plunged into ink-black darkness. I squealed and looked down all around me and found it had fallen face down. I had to bend down shakily to grab it, which wasn't easy balancing on one leg. When I stood back up, I was barely breathing. My heart was beating so fast, I felt sick. The noise was definitely coming from the other side of the wall. At first, I wondered if it was a trapped animal, like a bird or a rat but, deep down, I knew that it wasn't.

I tried to breathe while I strained my ears to listen. Whatever it was appeared to be still. I edged forward, slowly, holding out my shaking hands to touch the wood. Then I ran them over the surface.

I almost missed it: a small keyhole tucked right next to

the raised edging of the panel. I wondered if it was just a small cupboard at first, but someone had gone to a great deal of effort to conceal the keyhole, making me suspect it was a secret door. I ran my hands over the wood in case there was a hidden handle, but I couldn't find anything. *I need a key.*

I stood up straighter. The only bunch of keys I'd found were the ones in the library. *I wonder?* It was a long shot, but I had to check. Despite being terrified of what was behind it, I knew I wouldn't sleep until I found out.

I crept down the creaky staircase as fast and as quietly as hobbling on one crutch would allow. Sliding my free hand down the banister holding my phone, I prayed the battery wouldn't die on me.

The library was the same as I'd left it, so I went straight over to the desk and opened the drawer. The keys were in exactly the same place. I put my finger through the ring so I could hold my phone and not drop them and made my way back up the stairs. It was harder going up on one crutch, so my progress was slower.

It was totally quiet when I came back to stop in front of the secret door. No more bangs or whispering voices. I leant my crutch against the wall and angled my phone on a small pedestal while I examined the bunch of keys. I tried a few but they were all too big. Then I came to the last one. It was brass, narrow but long, and had a small loop at the end. It looked much older than the others. It had to be the one.

I held my breath as I gently put it to the keyhole and pushed it inside. It went in, so I gently turned it, hearing the satisfying click. The door didn't move. I gripped the raised part of the panel and pulled. At first it wouldn't budge, as if it hadn't been opened for centuries. Then it scraped a fraction and dust spilled out of the tiny gap. I could just about get my fingers inside for a better grip and yanked it all the way.

Strangely, I wasn't as scared as I should be. Excitement was slowly overcoming my fear.

Dust was everywhere and took some time to settle. Eventually, I could see it was far smaller than an ordinary door: about three feet high by about eighteen inches wide. It had to be an unused cupboard or a door to secret passage. All these old places were supposed to have them.

I shone my torch inside. The whisper had completely gone, making me wonder if I'd actually heard it in the first place. Maybe I'd imagined it, half asleep. But then I paused. Something had led me to this place.

The ceiling was low and sides were narrow; not much bigger than the door itself. It appeared to go on further than the beam from my torch, making me think it had to be a passage. I listened for any noises, dipped my head and ventured inside. It was such a confined space it was difficult to use my crutch, but it did help me balance having to crouch forward.

It smelled musty and dirty; as if it hadn't been opened up for a very long time. The ceiling felt like it was bearing down on me as I made slow progress. My neck ached already with my head bent over and not being able to stand up straight. I tried not to dwell on my fear of coming across anything alive in here with nowhere to run. Still, I pushed on through; curiosity winning over fear.

It went on for some time, turning left then right; a long tunnel going into the bowels of the house. The tendrils of claustrophobia were just starting to creep over me at being so far from the entrance – the place had no air – when I finally came out into a tiny room. It was no bigger than about six by six feet. I'd read about priest holes in History at school. Catholic families hid priests in them when their worship was banned.

At first glance, the room appeared to contain a few

bundles of something; a couple of boxes and an old trunk. I checked my phone and my battery was almost empty. I didn't have much time. I went closer and saw there was some sort of old-fashioned Holdall full of old clothes. I took the lid off one of the boxes and it was filled with trinkets: silver boxes, jewellery and bottles in various colours. I was conscious of the time to examine them too closely.

Then I came to the trunk, dusted off the brass plaque above the handle and my heart stopped. I closed in with my torch, just to make sure. *L. Blackwood* was engraved into the metal.

I stood back and took it all in. My heart thumped while my mind raced. I couldn't believe it. With renewed energy, I pulled at the catch. It was stiff at first. Then it came loose with a hefty pull and fell open. I peered in, terrified at what I would find.

There in front of me was everything a young Victorian woman would need in life. Boots, corsets, dresses, everything. All that she'd take with her if she was travelling somewhere.

An icy chill began to crawl up my spine. It was also everything a person would need to hide to make it look like someone was leaving. I hoped I was wrong. But why else would someone take the trouble to put it all the way in here? If it was packed and she didn't go, or even if she became ill, it wouldn't explain why it was hidden here. It was becoming more and more clear that she didn't make it anywhere. I remembered the whispers that woke me up. The orangery, the house, maybe even Lila herself; someone – something – was trying to tell me something terrible had happened. It was starting to feel like I was brought here for a reason. Then my battery ran out.

. . .

I WAS THROWN INTO DARKNESS. My good knee howled in complaint as I landed on it, heavily. A huge gust of wind had sucked the air from my lungs and the words, 'Get out … get out … GET OUT!' shrieked loud enough to rattle my teeth. Running completely on instinct, with no time to think, I scrambled in the dust on the floor, unable to get my balance to stand. In the end I crawled, dragging my crutch behind me and crushing my knuckles into the floor where I refused to let go of my phone.

I reached the dim light of the doorway, noticeable only because of the blackness threatening to swallow me up. I struggled out sweating, grimy with dirt and my breaths hacking in and out of my lungs. My throat was sore, but I ignored it in my effort to finally stand. I almost fell again in my rush to hop with one crutch along the landing back to my room.

As soon as I got there, I closed the door and pulled the rocking horse in the way. I let go of my crutch and clambered onto the bed. Then I dragged my quilt over me. I pulled it right up under my chin while my chest rose and fell like I'd just run a sprint. For a few seconds I waited for my heart and thoughts to catch up with the rest of me.

Oh my god! What was that? There had definitely been something in there with me; something not female – I wasn't sure it was even human.

I continued to lie there, trying to calm myself down; I was shaking violently. I noticed a bottle of water I'd left on my nightstand, grabbed it and guzzled it down. I hadn't realised just how thirsty I was. I felt a little better and reached over for my old laptop in the hope of distracting myself for a while. I wasn't going to sleep any time soon. It said 4.35 a.m. on my clock radio, which brightened me instantly as it meant the power was back on.

I switched on the lamp and relief flooded me. Every part

of me breathed a sigh and relaxed. It was amazing what a little golden light could do for the spirit.

I wasn't even really taking any notice as I switched my computer on, but when I did there it was; the message I'd waited for and dreaded:

What the hell do you think you were doing?

CHAPTER 9

I stared at the six words on the screen for a full minute, until I had to write, *who are you?*

You know who I am. Just stay the hell away from my house.

My mind scattered. I naturally assumed it was to do with the ordeal I'd just gone through, as I hadn't fully recovered, but it was to do with earlier today. *Wax.* It was him. It had to be him.

Don't think just because you're a Shade you can go wherever the hell you like.

OK, he'd freaked me out now. He'd used the very name that the ghost, or whatever, had scared me half to death with earlier. I tapped furiously: *Wait! I don't understand. What are you talking about?* But there was no reply. *Hey! ... Hey! You can't say something like that and just go!*

The screen flashed and the ID and password prompt came up. I pulled at the roots of my hair and screamed;

'Arghhh!' I wanted to throw the laptop across the room, he was so frustrating, but then how would I tell him what an asshole he was being. Him cutting me off before I even had a chance to say anything had infuriated me so much that it almost eclipsed my terrifying experience in the secret room. He'd called me Shade and so had the ghost. It had to mean something.

I slid out of bed and pulled a chair in front of the door as well as the rocking horse – I was taking no chances. Then I hopped back in and pulled my laptop back over my knees. I Googled the definition of Shade. The answers were unsurprising. Could he mean shady, like untrustworthy? I couldn't believe he meant that as it wasn't true for a start, and he didn't know me at all.

It made me angry that he had this effect on me already. It was obvious he didn't like me, which was really unfair and kind of hurt. I kept telling myself that I didn't care, but I did. Deep down, I wanted that strange, damaged boy to like me.

I logged out and shimmied down in the bed, leaving my lamp on. I was exhausted and couldn't think about anything anymore.

I WOKE up the next morning at seven, surprised that I'd slept so well. I guess exhaustion won out in the end. I sat up to check my barricade was still in front of the door, then flopped back down, the events of last night tumbling through my head. It was weird how different everything felt in the light of day.

I got up, hopped to the window and drew back the curtains. Another layer of snow. As far as the eye could see, white blanketed everything. Like a layer of foam, it protected and soundproofed the world. I was starting to feel cut off and isolated.

I needed to be around people, so I washed and dressed and made my way down the staircase. The whiteness of outside seemed to pierce through the stained-glass windows high in the hall and washed the walls in multicoloured light. The faces on the paintings looked less amused than usual. Even Lila.

I found Gerty already busy in the kitchen. 'Porridge?' she asked as she stirred a huge saucepan.

I was becoming accustomed to the new word for oatmeal, shrugged and nodded. 'Thanks.' Then I sat at the table and she put the steaming bowl in front of me. I sprinkled sugar over the top and stirred it. 'Is Tallulah coming over today?' The snow would mean no school again and boredom would soon set in.

'Probably this afternoon,' Gerty said. 'She wouldn't get up this morning.'

I could imagine and was a little glad. Tallulah could be overbearing if you spent too much time with her. I decided to probe Gerty while I had the chance. 'Do you know anything about the history of this place?'

Gerty frowned like she didn't know where I was going with the conversation. 'It depends on what you want to know?' she said, eying me curiously.

I shrugged, blowing over my spoon. 'Not sure. Just interested in general, I guess.'

'Like what period of history were you after?' she asked, loading the dishwasher.

I decided to just go ahead and say it. 'My aunt told me about Lila Blackwood – you know, the one at the top of the stairs – and Jedediah Waxley-Black. And Ollie told me that it was Ainsley – his brother – she was supposed to marry.'

'My, you have been busy.' She stood up straighter while she thought about it. 'Yes,' she said absently. 'Most people around here know something about it. It was one of those stories that go into folklore. They used to meet in the old orangery I think.'

'Who did she meet?' I asked, heart pumping as I already knew the answer.

She looked around her as if she wanted to get her answer straight. 'Jedediah, so the rumours went,' she said with an emphatic nod. 'I think he was the oldest and had to marry someone higher on the social scale. It was the norm back then,' she said ruefully. 'He would have been the head of the family one day and had to bring in the money, you know? Ainsley was the second son and thought a better match for Isla – not that anyone marrying between the two families has ever been happy. Not then and not since.'

That sparked off a whole other line of questions in my mind. 'Was it common for the two families to be drawn together, then?' My mind pinged straight to Wax and I had no idea why.

Gerty bobbed her head. 'I suppose so. They were the only well-to-do families around here.'

I suddenly felt foolish thinking there was something magical attracting the two of us. Of course, in those days you had to marry within your own class.

It did start to make a horrible kind of sense though. Lila had been seeing Jedediah in secret and Ainsley had put a stop to it. The thought of what had probably happened to Lila made me shudder. It made me wonder what happened to Jedediah after she disappeared. 'Do you know anything about the secret room?'

Gerty froze with what she was doing and looked at me curiously.

'There's a small door to a secret passage in the wood panelling next to the bathroom. I followed it last night. It leads to a small room full of stuff – you know, personal things. I think they belonged to Lila.'

Gerty's raised her eyebrows but remained silent. She continued to look at me as if I'd lost my mind as I blurted, 'Is this place haunted?'

She smiled a little and went back to wiping over the countertop. 'Well, they say a lot of these old places are. Anyway, be careful going off and doing daft things like that. Sounds like you've got yourself quite a mystery.'

She wasn't looking at me and she had an insincere, pained smile while she worked. It irritated me. She wasn't taking me seriously. Nevertheless, I had a gut feeling that there was a lot more she wasn't saying.

'So, you're going over to Ollie's place on Saturday for Halloween, Tallulah tells me.'

I nodded at the obvious subject change and got up and put my bowl in the dishwasher.

'Be careful of the older boy, OK?'

I stared at her, shocked. It made me angry and want to stand up for him. It was ridiculous considering what he'd said to me only a few hours before. All I managed to say was a strangled, 'Why?' The truth was, I wanted to talk to him. He was a grumpy, antisocial asshole from what I'd gathered so far, but I was hopelessly drawn to him. I remembered the nurse injecting him and the stern face of the uncle closing the door on my face and knew I had to see him again.

'He has behavioural issues, that one. Just be careful.'

WHEN TALLULAH CAME over that afternoon, I kept quiet about Wax's message. It felt personal and I didn't want her ratting to Ollie about it. Instead I told her about the secret passage. She couldn't contain her excitement and wanted me to show her straight away.

It was weird going there in the daytime. It kind of lost all its spookiness and made my terror last night seem a little irrational. But the memory was real enough. The key fitted and the small door opened easily this time as if to prove a point.

Tallulah ooh'd and ah'd all along the low-ceilinged passage, until we came out into the room. I showed her all Lila's stuff. When she picked up a corset out of the trunk, I whispered, 'I think she was murdered.' It was out before I could think more deeply about it.

Tallulah dropped it as if it had stung her. Her eyes went wide in the torchlight, but not with fear; excitement. This was just the kind of adventure she lived for. She wasn't here with me last night when I was scared half to death. I looked around me, feeling uneasy all over again. 'And something or someone doesn't want me to know. It knocked me over in here last night.'

Tallulah looked shocked for a moment, then sceptical. 'Well if it doesn't like us in here, then we should take the stuff out.'

I just looked at her, amazed as to why I hadn't thought of something as simple as that. She smiled, knowing full well she was a genius.

We spent the next half an hour dragging the trunk, boxes and bags out through the passage, along the hallway and into the safety of my room. It meant we could go through all the boxes in proper light and without the fear of the ghost of Christmas past disturbing us.

Seeing all Lila's personal things made me feel uncomfortable and a bit sad. It felt like an invasion of her privacy. A young girl's life summed up in a few boxes of trinkets. She'd once had dreams and ambitions, just like me, that had been tragically cut short. There was no grave. No one had laid down flowers. She hadn't been mourned. Rumours had circulated and everyone had contented themselves with the idea that she'd run away.

My mind went straight to the single rose held by the angel and I thought, ruefully, *not everyone*. 'This proves the story that Isla ran away was lies,' I said.

Tallulah looked at me as if she was trying to find an argument against it but couldn't. 'So you think someone killed her?'

I nodded. 'Yeah. I do. And I think they hid her stuff to make it look like she'd run away.' I didn't want to voice my suspicions as to who was responsible until I was sure.

Tallulah shook her head in amazement and surveyed all the stuff. 'So I guess we need to find out what happened to the Waxley-Black brothers after she disappeared,' she said, with air quotes.

She was right. Clues for that wouldn't be in this house, but over at Wax's. The very place from which he'd warned me to stay away. 'How is Wax?' came out before I could check myself.

Tallulah didn't seem to notice my cheeks blast red. She was busy going through Lila's jewellery box. 'Ollie texted me last night and said Wax was out as if nothing had happened.'

My mind went immediately to the nurse injecting him with something to knock him out. I guess that cinched it then. Wax was definitely my mystery messenger.

Her phone buzzed, she took it out of her back pocket and her attention was gone. 'Gotta go,' she said, already walking away. She stopped and turned. 'Look, don't do anything daft. It could be dangerous. We'll talk about it on Saturday at Ollie's, OK?'

I let out a breath and nodded. It was a plan at least. I couldn't help remembering Wax's hostility though. He didn't want me in his house.

'Don't forget to wear your killer outfit,' she said, eyes wide with mischief.

It made me smile. There was no way she was going to let

me get out of it. Besides, Ollie had invited me. Wax would have to just put up with it. 'OK, I promise not to get into any trouble and, yes, I'll wear my tart's outfit.'

Tallulah laughed and left with a loud, 'Laters.'

AFTER TALLULAH LEFT, I went through all the things thoroughly. There was nothing of note except a locket with a man's face painted in it. I hadn't had a good-enough look at the Waxley-Black paintings to see if it matched. Although I was betting it was Jed's.

There was another bundle of love letters, all in a similar tone and handwriting to the others I'd found in the library and the round house. There had definitely been a love affair going on between them, of that there was no doubt, but what was strange was that there wasn't a shred of evidence of Ainsley at all. Even though the pair were supposed to be getting married.

I was slowly becoming more and more convinced I knew what had happened all those years ago. Ainsley had found out about Lila's affair with Jed and in a fit of jealous rage killed her and made it look as if she'd run away with a broken heart.

The day passed and dusk came with the grey light making shadows creep across my room. Everything in the world seemed to be quiet, so before I went down in search of supper, I took out my laptop. It was as frustrating as hell as there was nothing there. Everything was on his terms as he made sure I could only speak to him when he wanted to talk.

I wanted to rail at him; it wasn't fair that he hadn't given me a chance. I didn't want to care. I put my ID in the box but, instead of just putting in my password, I typed furiously:

.   .   .

Everything's not up to you. I don't care how angry and moody you are. Ollie invited me on Saturday and I'm coming. So if you don't want to see me then I suggest you go out.

Then I put my password in and hit return. Of course the spinning wheel whirred for a good minute before it told me my password was incorrect. It made me feel better though; that my anger was somewhere out there in the cyber ether.

I bent down, pushed my laptop under my bed and got up. I went to close my curtains before I went downstairs.

I froze.

There was a subtle warm glow coming from the round house. At first I thought it had to be a reflection, but it was too far away from the house. *Was it Burt?*

Someone was definitely out there.

I grabbed my crutches and rushed downstairs as fast as they would carry me. I was definitely getting faster negotiating the staircase. I went through the kitchen while Gerty was at the sink. 'Is Burt here today?' I demanded a little harshly, out of breath.

'What's the rush? No, I haven't seen him.'

I didn't wait to answer. I flung open the back door and hopped out as fast as I could. The snow was heavy and slowed me down. All my muscles screamed in protest as I cut a path through, almost falling over a couple of times.

At last I reached the line of trees that sheltered the orangery. I slowed my pace and went through, then stopped a few feet away. The cosy orange glow spilled out of all the small panes of glass and glittered gold on the snow around it.

I edged forward, still unable to see any movements inside. I got to the door, placed my crutches down gently on the floor and reached for the doorknob. I turned it and pulled the door open as slowly and quietly as I could.

The snow made a ridge and it wouldn't move more than a couple of inches. In the end I could do nothing else but yank it open.

Before I could see a thing, the wind rushed past me and took away my breath.

Burning pain seared me. A sandstorm blast hit my face and neck and flayed my bare arms. All I could do was scream as a million needle-like shards of glass pierced my skin.

CHAPTER 10

*I*t seemed like the world fell silent for ages, until voices eventually stirred me from my stupor. I felt strong arms and then a sensation of floating. The next thing I knew I was in my bed and the sun was streaming into my room in a bright head-splitting light.

A vaguely familiar woman was bending over me, smiling. 'Ah, there we are. She's awake.'

I remembered her then. She was my aunt's nurse. Then the memories hit me like a sledgehammer, and I struggled to sit up.

'Sshh!' the nurse said, holding my shoulders and pushing me back down. 'You've had quite an accident, young lady. You need to stay in bed today, at least.'

I blinked at her in confusion. I remembered the round house, going to open the door and then nothing but pain. I couldn't remember anything after that. 'What happened?' I said.

'You don't remember?'

Before I could answer, there was a knock at my door.

'Come in,' the nurse said.

Gerty came straight in, thanked the nurse and looked at me with a rueful smile. 'I think you should stay away from the orangery for a while – at least until Burt has had time to fix it up. Your aunt is very upset. You need to go and see her when you're up and about.'

She was shaking her head before I could even say, 'But…' My memories were fuzzy, but I didn't remember doing anything actually dangerous.

'Burt found you. Said you must have pulled the door too hard and loose panes fell out and hit you.'

I put my hands up to my face that felt irritated and tight and hissed at the pain in my arms. They were both bandaged and throbbing.

'Be careful!' Gerty said, quickly. 'You have a lot of cuts. All superficial, but they'll be sore for a while. The doctor said you were a lucky girl and they should heal pretty quickly. The top road is completely blocked by snow if you'd needed the hospital.'

I pointed at my dressing table. 'Can you pass me the mirror, please?'

She passed the small hand mirror immediately. 'It looks worse than it is.'

I stared at the face looking back at me. It was very shiny with some kind of ointment and covered in hundreds of tiny red angry pits and scratches. It went down my neck and looked horrendous.

Gerty smiled weakly. 'It will heal in a couple of weeks. The deeper ones will take a little longer, but you'll hardly notice it in a month or two.'

My heart sank and, strangely, my first thought was Wax. Why I should care if he saw me like this, I had no idea. I passed the mirror back to Gerty and lay back down in the bed.

She placed the mirror on the dressing table and picked up

an empty cup and glass off the nightstand. Then, after whispering something, she left with the nurse.

I thought about what she said. I had been very lucky. My memories were patchy, but I didn't think it had been loose panes that had given me these injuries. They were simply too small and too many.

I must have dozed.

Gerty brought me up a cup of tea and some toast some time later and said Tallulah was coming over at some point. Then, after plumping up my pillows, she left me alone.

My face stung and I felt miserable. Actually, it was the most unhappy I'd felt since I'd left home. My thoughts inevitably took a darker turn into memories of Pete. A place I seldom went for fear I'd spiral down and not come out. I wasn't sure how long it was, or when the tears came, but there was a knock at the door.

'It's me!' the familiar voice said.

Tallulah. I quickly dabbed my eyes on my sheet. 'Come in,' I said, more grateful for the interruption than she'd know.

'Yuk!' she said as soon as she saw me.

I smiled. 'I know, right.'

'What happened? Mum said the orangery collapsed on you, or something.'

I frowned while my mind went back to the moments before it happened, and I shook my head. 'No, that's not what happened.' The pieces seemed to come together in my mind. 'I saw a light in there.' I looked over at my window and remembered looking out and seeing it. I looked back at Tallulah, who was hanging on my every word. 'So I went out to see who it was.' I frowned, when the memories became as clear as day. 'I pulled open the door and the glass …' I stopped, knowing how weird it was going to all sound.

Tallulah waited expectantly for me to finish. 'What?'

I swallowed and took a breath. There was no other explanation for what had happened. 'The glass just flew at me in the wind.'

Tallulah frowned and half laughed. 'The wind did it,' she repeated flatly.

I knew it sounded stupid. 'Well, not a wind exactly.' I took another breath. 'I think it was the ghost out to get me.' My eyes dropped guiltily away from Tallulah's, but I'd said it. I looked at her again when she hadn't said a word.

'Shit!' was all she said after a full minute. It was very difficult for me to gauge her reaction. I wasn't sure if she thought I'd lost my mind or was expressing the gravity of the situation. Her eyes went wide and she sat on the edge of the bed.

I felt a little braver. 'Think about it. It's like a warning.' When she still hadn't said anything, 'My face looks like it's been sand blasted. Surely if the place had collapsed on me, I'd have some deeper cuts?'

Her eyes widened at that as if she was just falling in with what I was saying. 'What are you going to do?' she said, eventually.

It was a good question. One I hadn't thought about yet. I had no idea what I was going to do. I was scared now. What had started off as an adventure to pass the time had quickly evolved into something a lot more serious and very dangerous.

'You still have to come on Saturday,' Tallulah said, as if it was now the most obvious thing in the world.

I looked at her as if she'd gone mad. The thought of meeting new people looking like this horrified me.

'We can help you. You won't get any answers here. You owe it to yourself now to get to the bottom of all this, Becks.'

I continued to stare at her way after she'd finished speaking. Not only was she right, but I was surprised by how strong and sensible she sounded. Somewhere along the line she'd become my friend. A real one. I had to swallow down a lump in my throat.

'Of course I'll get Mum to patch you up good, put you on some intensive healing regime, or something. I'll stress that it's urgent and that you need to go because you'll go mad if you stay cooped up in here much longer.'

By the end I was grinning. Her enthusiasm was infectious. There was no way I couldn't go. 'OK, but if I still look like this by Saturday, you'll have to get me a Freddy Krueger mask or something.'

She laughed. 'Becks, if you still look like that you won't need one.'

I laughed in spite of myself. She was right though. I would go mad if I stayed here much longer. I needed answers: what happened to me and what the hell was going on.

DESPITE THE LIVELY conversation that followed, when Tallulah left, doubts crowded in and my confidence ebbed away. The enormity of what had happened slowly sank into my bones. Someone or something had given me one hell of a warning to stay away and it had scared me. Real fear set in, and because of it the furthest I ventured was to the bathroom. Even then I hurried past the secret door and washed as quickly as I could to hurry back. In the bathroom, memories echoed of the very real occurrences there like ghosts.

Back in my room, I wedged a chair against the door and peered out of my window. It was dusk again and the snow glittered from the reflected light from the windows of the house.

The orangery looked dark now. *Who had been in there? If it was a ghost, then who? Was it Lila walking around because she'd been murdered, Jed having lost his great love, or Ainsley, having had the two closest people to him in the world betray him? The* jumbling thoughts made my head ache. Whoever it was, they hated me getting close to finding out, and that didn't tally with the whole idea of being a ghost; they stayed around so their injustices were solved.

I hopped over and got back into bed. I was feeling tired again. Everything swirled around in my head till I dropped off. All I seemed to do was sleep these days.

My routine of recuperation continued: sleep and bathroom breaks with Gerty bringing me my meals in bed. 'You sure you won't come downstairs today?' she said, when I had lost all idea of what day it was.

'Not yet,' I said, pulling a pained face. 'I'm so tired … Maybe tomorrow.' I didn't want to admit that I wasn't ready to leave my cocoon just yet.

Tallulah Facetimed me while playing a games console at the same time. It was pretty typical for her only to give me half of her attention, so I settled back against my pillows and accepted it as normal. 'So, Mum says you won't get out of bed.' She flicked her eyes away from the screen at me for a second, pulling faces and twisting as if she was turning a corner in the game. 'You're coming to Ollie's on Saturday, Becks.'

Before I could whine an excuse, she said, 'I'll come for you at 6.30. Bye then!' And she clicked off before I could open my mouth.

I let out an exhausted breath. It was going to be harder to get out of this than I thought. Still, tomorrow was Friday then I had all day Saturday; I was bound to think of a way out by then.

I slid down into the bed feeling sad and empty. I rolled over and reached for my laptop on the floor. Whenever I sunk low, I missed Pete the most. I needed to play some music to connect me to him, even though I knew it would be painful.

I flipped open the lid and pushed down the power button. The curser flashed for a full minute making me shout, 'Come on!' Then the words crawled across the page and took my breath away.

OLLIE SAID YOU GOT HURT. *Are you OK? Look, I'm sorry I lost my temper and was hard on you, but you need to go. You need to leave this place while you still can. The snow is already trying to trap you. If you don't go soon, you'll never get away.*

MY HEART THUMPED in my chest making me out of breath. It was fear, excitement and disbelief that he was actually talking to me again, all rolled into one. I needed to talk to him so badly, it didn't make sense. I tapped back: *I'm OK, I'm healing. Do you know what's going on here?* I hit Send. It was a huge risk asking him a question like that. He could disappear, never to be heard of again. But I was getting desperate and needed some help. I waited, holding my breath and chewing my nails, praying for an answer.

YES – *please go. I can't stand it. I can't look after everyone. Shades. What is it with you? You all think you're invincible.*

I COULDN'T BELIEVE what I was reading. *What? I never asked you to look after me. Just a civil word would be nice. And anyway, I can't go home. You don't understand.*

THERE WAS a long gap before he answered as if he was thinking about what I said. *Is it to do with your leg?*

. . .

KIND OF.

ANOTHER LONG SPACE. *Is it true you're coming here on Saturday?*

I THOUGHT CAREFULLY before I answered. It was strange as I'd been looking for a way out up until then. Now it seemed that wild horses couldn't keep me away from that house on Saturday night. *Yes!* I replied.

WELL, I'll be out!

IT DIDN'T TAKE LONG for the bad mood to come back. *Good then. Sounds perfect!* He was making me more and more furious with every exchange.

DON'T SAY I didn't warn you.

IT WAS obvious that he was going and I couldn't bear it. *Wait! Can you at least tell me what a Shade is?*

I THOUGHT he'd gone for sure when he sent: *You don't know?*

No ... how would I?

. . .

THE CURSOR FLASHED a long time again, so long I almost gave up. Then it came just like the killer blow: *Dead person walking.*

I STARED AT THE SCREEN, then I clicked frantically, *Wait ... what?* But the password prompt came up signalling, as usual, that the conversation was over.

My mind went into freefall. He'd talked to me, apologised for his previous behaviour, warned me off and then insulted me again. How dare he try and scare me like that? He was saying I was as good as dead. That was an awful thing to say.

I was so unsettled after that that my heart kept on speeding up every five minutes as I kept getting upset and angry all over again. I put my earphones in and eventually fell asleep listening to Pete's favourite music.

He entered my dreams and I was so pleased to see him. I was ecstatic, but he wasn't. He was worried and upset. He kept warning me over and over to go back, that I was in a no man's land, but he of all people should know how it was with Mum and Dad. He was crying, telling me that death would be at the end of it. 'Go back ... go back,' he said. 'I love you, Beccah. Please, it wasn't your fault, I don't blame you. There's more that you don't know.'

In the end I was crying so hard in my sleep that it woke me up.

It was a dream born out of anxiety and wishful thinking. There was no doubt about it. I was driving that day and I killed my brother. My parents were right to hate me. I killed their little boy.

I DRESSED THE NEXT DAY. After Wax's message and the dreams of my brother, there seemed little point hiding away. I even ventured out in the snow and found myself at the round house – the source of my anxiety and worries. However Burt had boarded it all up so no one could get in. I stood outside and looked at it, soaking up the feelings of gloom it radiated.

Now I wasn't even sure I wanted Burt to fix it up. Maybe everyone would be better off if it was demolished.

AT LAST SATURDAY EVENING CAME. Nerves meant I could scarcely eat a thing. I stood in front of my mirror and wondered what the hell I was doing in going. Here I was, standing in my tarty maid's outfit with my boobs pushed up, my face like it'd been scrubbed with barbed wire, my arms like I'd self-harmed for a year with a razorblade, and my leg in plaster past the knee. *Good grief, what did I look like?* Well, it did look Halloween, I guess. I could be a tarty zombie. At least I had one good shoe on. If I stood sideways, I looked kind of cute.

I heard Tallulah's loud voice downstairs in the hall. I smoothed down the short skirt of my dress and put on my coat to cover myself a bit. Then I picked up my crutches and headed towards the stairs to join her.

When I saw her standing in the middle of the hall, she grinned her approval. She'd had the same idea as me and had a long coat covering what she was wearing. I guessed Gerty wouldn't be impressed, so I paused and did my coat up properly too.

'Come on, you look great. I knew you would.' Then she linked her arm through mine and we walked out of the front door into the snowy night for the maddest night of my life. One thing I knew for sure, good or bad, nothing was ever going to be the same again.

CHAPTER 11

*J*t was the first time I'd noticed that the path had been lit up between the two houses, through the woods. Another thing that pointed to a connection. A lantern had been hung in the trees every ten feet or so, making seeing either side of the path impossible and scary. Despite feeling like bait in a horror film, I felt exhilarated to be out at night. I'd been cooped up for so long, grieving.

The snow glittered on the path in front of us as we chatted animatedly. Tallulah was walking so fast, I had to tell her to slow down a couple of times because of my leg. 'Who will be there?' I asked. The nearer we got, the more nervous I became. I hadn't mixed with people for ages.

'Obviously Ollie,' Tallulah said. 'Then Nicola and Archie – they're a cute couple. Samantha, Joe and Josh. You'll like them; they're all great fun.'

'But will they like me?' It was terrifying. Hearing faceless names didn't make me feel any better. Then, on a whole other level of scary was Wax. I couldn't make up my mind if I wanted him to be there or not.

'Don't be silly,' Tallulah said, bumping shoulders with me, almost pushing me in a ditch. 'Of course they will.'

The trees began to thin out and lights from the house came into view. My heart started to thump so hard I could hear it in my ears. We came out into the circular driveway in front of the house. Wax's van was gone, leaving deep ruts in the snow. A pang of disappointment hit me, not just that he wasn't there, but that he'd meant what he'd said.

The impressive front door opened and Ollie stood bathed in the yellow light. It spilled out a path onto the snow. 'Come on,' Tallulah said, sensing me slowing down. She ran up the steps and gave Ollie a huge hug. I came more slowly on my crutches.

Two others were with him as he came forward and kissed my cheek. 'Ouch!' he said, when he took in all the scratches on my face. 'Thanks for coming. Tally said you'd been in the wars.' A wonderful cologne wrapped itself around me as he hugged me. I looked over his shoulder at the two boys with him. He seemed to remember them and pulled apart. 'This is Joe and Josh. This is Beccah Whitely from the Blackwood place.' Their eyes widened in recognition and they both leant in for kisses. It was a European thing I still couldn't get used to. Joe was a redhead with green eyes, a little plumper of the two. Josh was tall and muscular like an athlete and had blond hair and hazel eyes, hidden under a baseball cap. They were both dressed casually but Josh even more so; in running sweats. 'Come on in,' Ollie said, indicating for me to follow.

We went through the huge hall I remembered from the time Wax had been trashing the place. Until we came out into a huge modern kitchen which completely surprised me. I guess I was expecting a similar living museum to my aunt's place. Instead it was all exposed brick, black tiles, chrome fittings and light oak cupboards. There was a huge American fridge and a sweeping bar-like island with breakfast stools on one side and a sink and work surface on the other. The lighting was warm and inviting from tiny little spotlights in the ceiling.

A girl sitting at the island took a chug of beer before she said, 'Hi. I'm Samantha. Call me Sam. Everyone else does.' I shook her hand and decided she was friendly enough. Her brown eyes seemed kind, framed by all the curls of her dark brown hair.

The last to be introduced were Archie and Nicola. They were sitting holding hands on a small tan leather sofa placed underneath a huge window. Both smiled and held up a hand. The girl was stunning with poker-straight black hair. She reminded me of a goth. The guy had black hair too, spiked up, but his skin was dark with eyes the colour of coal.

'Beer?' Ollie asked, already popping one open on a bottle opener fixed to the countertop.

I looked around. Everyone seemed to be drinking. 'I'm not old enough.'

Ollie grinned, draping an arm around Tallulah's shoulder and looking across the bar at the boys. 'The legal age is eighteen here,' Tallulah said, putting a bottle down on the countertop. 'You're almost eighteen, we all are.'

I looked at the beer, cautiously. 'So you all go to St Barts?'

They all nodded and I realised that they must be some of my classmates.

'Take your coat off, Becks,' Tallulah said, with a giggle.

My heart sank. I should have realised earlier but I hadn't because I'd been too damned nervous and had my coat on. None of the others had dressed up. I looked into Tallulah's eyes, alive with mischief. 'You tricked me.'

Tallulah creased over with laughter.

Ollie half laughed and looked between them. 'You went

through with it?' he said trying to get Tallulah to stop laughing and chuckling along with her. She began to undo her own coat, only to reveal a cute little black skirt and a red sweater. I looked around the room at the other two girls, who wore something similar. My heart sunk lower with each face who couldn't look me in the eye with guilt and suppressed laughter.

'Come on, Becks, let's see what she got you to wear,' Ollie said.

I felt utterly ridiculous. I'd walked headlong into their trap. My face was horrendous, my leg was in plaster and I was dressed in something out of the Rocky Horror Show.

I had a choice; hop out of the house crying, looking even more ridiculous than I did already, or accept the hazing for what it was. I looked down, closed my eyes and began to undo my buttons. There was absolutely no way out of this to save my pride. I'd been tricked and made to look a fool in front of people who didn't know me and would judge me on this moment for ever.

The buttons seemed to go on forever, made worse by the silence in the room. I swear you could actually hear people breathing. At last I opened the coat and let it fall to the floor from my shoulders.

There was a deathly hush, then a snigger and I opened my eyes. Ollie was staring at me wide-eyed and open-mouthed. Then he coughed. I was fully aware that my boobs looked like a fourteenth-century bar wench. 'Are you going to give me that beer or does a girl have to die of thirst around here?'

The two boys laughed at the bar, followed by everyone else. Tallulah clapped. 'Well done!' she said, and everyone joined in with the clapping.

My blush turned from humiliation to pure joy. I'd managed to turn it around.

Ollie, now back in charge, snapped the top off a bottle of beer and handed it to me. 'Where are my manners?'

I took it, grateful for something to do with my hands. Tallulah bumped shoulders with him. 'See, I told you she was OK.'

Archie and Nicola came over and introduced themselves properly this time by kissing my cheek. 'You look amazing,' Nicola said, and Archie agreed. The two at the bar called over their agreement too.

I didn't think I'd felt so happy in ages. I guess it was being accepted and feeling cool for the first time in, well, ever.

Everyone chatted effortlessly after that. I sat at the bar next to the boys and quietly drank my beer. They moaned about the snow and wondered if they'd have a load of work to catch up on at school. Then they told stories of people I was yet to meet. It was easy conversation.

'What brings you to England?' Josh said.

'She was in a massive car crash that killed her brother,' Tallulah said.

It was typical Tallulah but, nevertheless, I gave her a black look. I supposed it would have come out eventually. There seemed to be a collective intake of breath as if it was the last thing they were expecting. I guess it wasn't the usual.

All she said was, 'What?' as if I was being touchy. 'It's true, isn't it?'

I could strangle her at times. I just stared at her and took a huge gulp of my beer, which was going down very well.

The room had got suddenly quiet. I looked around. I didn't mean to make everyone uncomfortable. Then I saw him standing just inside the room. 'Wax,' I breathed. My heart had stopped dead at exactly the moment his eyes found me. I smiled cautiously and his look blackened, sapping all my confidence. He walked to the fridge in long, purposeful strides. I couldn't help taking in his long black-jeaned legs, heavy boots and sweatshirt with the words Likely Dead and a skull on it in dripping blood. His tattoos looked even more menacing close up. He pulled his beanie off, letting loose his messy over-long black hair and opened his beer.

'I thought you were going out?' Ollie said, clearly trying to sound upbeat. It was the most uncomfortable that I'd ever seen him.

'I did. Now I'm back,' Wax said, sipping his beer and not taking his eyes off me.

'We'll go into the sitting room,' Ollie said, already moving to the door; widening his eyes at me and tipping his head to follow. The others didn't need telling twice and I went to slide off my stool.

'Not you!' Wax said, directly to me.

My face blasted red at him singling me out and, if I was honest, I was genuinely scared. I looked to Ollie, waiting at the door, to save me. He understood instantly. 'She came to meet some friends, Wax, that's all,' Ollie said, coming back into the room. In the end he stopped and went to put a defensive hand on Wax's chest to stop him, but Wax simply leaned into it and looked menacingly at his brother. I felt really sorry for him. He was sticking up for me and Wax was terrifying. 'I just want to talk, then she can come and join your little tea party.'

Ollie looked at me and I looked back at him in shock. I was scared, but I didn't want to get him into trouble. Hadn't half of me yearned to see Wax face to face? Well, here he was. Everything I knew about him told me to run, but I needed to hear what he had to say. 'It's OK.' I looked back at Wax, whose gaze hadn't moved from me. 'I don't think he's giving me a choice.'

Ollie slowly moved back and followed the others out of the room. Wax went after them and closed the door. My heart thumped as he stalked back towards me, stopping only when he was a few inches away.

We assessed each other up close for the first time. His eyes were a deep blue and lined with enviable dark lashes. He and Ollie were very alike, but Ollie's were brown and Wax had another six or seven inches in height. I put him at about six three. And where Ollie was warm, everything about Wax scared people off. This close, his coloured tats could be clearly seen right up to his jawline. There were even small stars inked into his temple and corner of his eye.

He made a visual sweep of me all the way down to the floor and back again. It was then I remembered how ridiculous I looked and wanted to die. He widened his eyes and almost cracked a smile. 'What on earth do you look like?'

I frowned and wanted to shove him in the chest, although I didn't dare. 'They tricked me into dressing up.'

The corners of his mouth twitched like he was trying not to smile. His eyes dropped to my pushed-up boobs and back again. 'I was talking about your face.'

He was annoying me now. I hopped away from him and scrambled onto a stool. Wishing for once that I could do something that came off cool – apart from taking cruel jokes, that is. I grabbed another beer from across the island. I needed it. His hand came from nowhere and took it. 'No more beer for you.'

I swung round to look him in the eye; he was much closer than I thought. I had to take a breath as my eyes dropped to his mouth, dangerously close. 'Who the hell do you think you are?' came out as a husky whisper, while my eyes stayed glued to his lips. I swallowed. 'I don't know you. You're horrible to me. You insult me –' Before I could finish, his mouth covered mine, smothering words I'd already forgotten. My hands came up but didn't push him away. His arms came around me, pulling me to face him. So close, my chest felt crushed and every inch of me screamed to be closer.

His mouth was closed first of all and I revelled in the softness of it. I couldn't believe it had gone from us fighting to this, but my thoughts scrambled as he moved his mouth over mine and it felt so good. He was so good at it, teasing and tempting me to give in and let my anger drain away. All that was left was a burning in my lower stomach. It was as if the minute we touched, my body remembered him. I moved my hands up from his chest to his shoulders and gripped them. His mouth opened and mine matched his, meeting his tongue, swirling and tasting the first proper kiss of my life.

All too soon it was over. He was looking down at me as if something miraculous had just happened. I couldn't believe it either. This guy had scared, frustrated and upset me since the day I first saw him outside and now he'd just kissed me. And I'd liked it – really liked it. 'Hello,' I said, still looking him in the eyes.

He laughed a little and his face transformed so beautifully. 'I told you not to come here,' he said, narrowing his eyes.

It shocked me that he was determined to carry it on. I narrowed my eyes to match his. 'I'm not that great at following orders.'

His grin widened. 'Your face is a mess.'

A breath of laughter left me in disbelief. I didn't know if he was determined to insult me or whether this was his weird British way of joking. I decided he just couldn't help himself. 'It's better than it was.'

He nodded and rubbed his thumb across my lower lip. 'Your mouth is in working order, I see.'

I smiled a little. He had a sense of humour that I wasn't expecting. Then my smile drained away as I remembered the guy of the other day that had to be tranquilised and put to bed. I frowned. 'It was mean calling me a Shade.' My thoughts went straight to the ghost who'd called me it as well.

He cocked his head at an angle as if he didn't understand something and picked up my hand. He rubbed the top of it gently and his expression deepened. 'You feel so real,' he whispered almost to himself. 'But it's what you are.' Then he frowned and looked back into my eyes. 'And you don't know.'

Before I could ask him to explain what he was talking about, he pulled me gently off the stool. 'Come on, you need to know.'

I went with him, grabbing one of my crutches on the way. He led me across the hall to a smaller room filled with various sofas and armchairs that didn't match. The light was a warm glow from several lamps and there were a couple bookcases and sideboards around the walls. A small piano was in the corner.

I spotted the others. They were lounging around, listening to music from a laptop.

They all stopped talking and looked at us standing in the doorway. Ollie's eyes went straight to Wax's hand that held mine. 'What's up?' he said, looking at Wax cautiously.

'You need to tell her what you all are – what she is. She doesn't know.'

I watched them all look at each other nervously. 'She's not exactly like us,' Tallulah said. 'Not really.'

Wax gripped my hand hard. 'But she is,' he said angrily. 'Because I can see her.' He picked my hand up, studied it and ran his hand across it. 'I can feel her.'

I watched them all look at each other nervously. Ollie looked at Tallulah and nodded. 'We aren't your normal seventeen-year-olds. We're different.'

Wax's face was blank and unreadable.

'We aren't alive,' said Tallulah.

I stared at her; my face already creased in disbelief. I'd had enough of jokes for one day.

'Not properly,' Ollie added.

My eyes widened, amazed that they all wanted to persist in this. I looked around. There was no laughter any more. A huge lump had appeared in my throat that I couldn't swallow down.

'I hung myself,' Archie said.

'I took my mum's pills. I couldn't stand it without him,' Nicola said.

Tears were brimming.

'There was a crash. The school minibus,' Ollie said, pointing between Tallulah and himself.

'Us too,' Joe said.

'But we died in hospital, later,' Josh said.

'I don't know what happened to me,' Samantha said, sadly. 'I just woke up with them.'

I was looking between them all now with tears streaming down my face. I was waiting for the laughter, but none came. Even Wax's face remained calm.

'But I'm not dead. I know I'm not.' I was beginning to cry properly now which made no sense if they were joking. Maybe it was because on some level I believed them. 'My aunt!' I said, in a bolt of inspiration.

'She was born in 1901,' Tallulah said, in the kindest tone I'd ever heard her use.

'Your mum, Gerty?'

'Cancer, when I was a little girl. She never left me.'

I sunk to the floor and stared ahead of me. 'Stop it, stop it.'

Wax pulled me up and held me to him. 'You said there was a car crash.'

I nodded into his chest, conscious of the trail of very real snot I was leaving on him. 'I lived and Pete died.' I sobbed anew at the memory.

I pulled apart to look up into Wax's face. 'I'm real. They're real,' I said, pointing at the others.

Wax nodded, the most sympathetic I'd ever known him. 'You can feel them because you're one of them.'

'But you can—'

He looked sad once again, cutting me off. 'I have been cursed my whole life. I see the dead. And now, evidently, I can feel them too.' He shook his head and frowned as if he couldn't quite believe it himself.

It started to make a horrible kind of sense. He was so troubled. It was enough to send anyone mad. 'Your uncle?'

He smiled a little. 'Alive.'

I thought instantly of the unseeing eyes as he closed Wax's door in my face. 'My god! He can't see me?'

'He can't see any of us,' Ollie said. 'Wax is the only one.' He looked at his brother sadly. 'He sees all Shades, spirits and ghosts. Sometimes it's hard for him to stand.'

'So I'm dead,' I said, watching him closely.

He nodded. 'I knew from the time you walked here with the little dog.'

My mind went back to the day I'd walked Burt's dog and first seen him. 'But how do you know the difference between a Shade and a living person?'

'You come in a bright light, like a halo.'

'And ghosts and spirits?'

He shrugged. 'Ghosts are like a transparent impression and mostly benign.'

'Spirits are something else entirely. They are energy that you can hear and feel but not see.' My mind was already on what had tried to harm me.

Tallulah nodded, following my train of thought. 'Yeah, they're usually hostile.'

123

I looked at Wax. 'They're something different – something evil.'

'It's gone for her a couple of times,' Tallulah said.

'We need to find out what it wants from you. Something only you can give.'

*W*ax pulled me over to sit with him on the floor with our backs against the dark leather settee. Everyone else seemed to relax and Ollie put the music back on.

I was in a weird kind of numbed shock. The kind I'd had only one other time: when Pete died. I couldn't get beyond the fact that Wax was the only live person here. I don't think he fully believed it either; he hadn't let go of my hand since we left the kitchen. He looked into my eyes.

'You said I'm a Shade, but I still don't really know what that is … I went to the mall.' Then I pointed at Ollie. 'He works there, for God's sake.' I frowned as the points came to me. 'Then there's school … and you don't even like me.' With that final realisation, it was too much and I burst into tears.

Tears that were real. Stinging the scratches on my face.

Wax immediately put his arm around me and pulled me to him. It was the second time I'd cried into his chest. 'Shh,' he said into my hair. 'It's OK … it's OK. The jury's still out on that one.'

I stopped crying and looked up at him. He was almost

smiling. I hiccupped a single blast of laughter and hugged into him again. I wasn't ready to let go of him yet.

'Someone's got to look after you,' he said, into my hair so no one else could hear.

I looked at the others from my shelter of Wax's arms and they were looking amazed. Ollie looked the most shocked of all, and then he looked plain worried.

'Wax is teasing,' Tallulah said with a giggle. Her hand went to her mouth as if she'd uttered a profanity. It was then I realised that it was obviously something Wax didn't do.

I reluctantly pulled apart to look into his eyes. He ran his finger down the side of my face. 'OK now?'

I nodded.

'You need to explain it to her,' Tallulah said. 'But I meant it, Wax, she is different to us.'

I glared at her. Trust her to point out I was weird even for a Shade.

'Look!' She crawled forward from her sitting position on the floor next to Ollie and pinched my hand. I immediately pulled away. It hurt. Then she went to do the same to Wax and her fingers went through.

Wax let go of my hand and went to grab Tallulah and it did the same. She appeared solid but Wax's hand passed right through. I did the same and held her fast. She moved to go back to sit next to Ollie and I let her go.

'See,' she said. 'She is and she isn't.'

'Like halfway,' Sam said.

Ollie nodded.

Wax frowned. 'She's right.' He ran his finger across the top of my hand. 'Maybe that's why the spirit has chosen her. Because she has a foot in both camps.'

I don't get it. 'My leg even itches, for God's sake,' I whined.

Tallulah giggled. 'We seem to keep certain things from our old life.'

'It keeps us grounded,' Archie said.

'Keeps us tied here,' Nicola said, bumping shoulders with him.

'Like my job, for instance,' Ollie said. 'And school. It's not a bad life.'

'Death,' Tallulah said, laughing.

'What's the point, though?' I asked. 'I thought that ghosts were the dead people.'

I looked up at Wax, who was thinking about what everyone said. 'It's a good question. Ghosts are like an impression left here, like an intense emotion. That's why they don't seem to have any real solid form. Shades seem to stay because they won't leave,' he said, grinning and kicking his brother's foot and passing right through it. 'No matter how hard you try to get rid of them.'

It was nice seeing the two brothers acting just like any other siblings in the world. 'So Shades are the ones with unfinished business?'

Wax shrugged and looked at his brother, who did the same. 'I don't really feel anything like that,' Ollie said. 'I just didn't want to leave him all on his own,' he said, kicking Wax back.

'Nor me ... No great mystery for me either,' Tallulah said.

The others just shrugged and looked at each other. Only Sam said, 'I wouldn't mind finding out what happened to me. I have no recollection of it.'

Wax looked at me as if he understood it explained very little. 'I think something else called and brought you here. I think you might be here for a reason.'

'So someone, say the ghost, or spirit, or whatever, of Lila, wants me to solve the mystery of her death, and then what? I cross over to the other side?' By then I was shouting and tears were streaming again. It was made so much worse by the looks of pity on everyone's faces.

'We don't know,' Tallulah said. 'We're just here.'

I dissolved into sobs again. Tallulah came over and put her arm around me. Wax just watched but still held my hand. 'I didn't tell you before because I knew that you were different to us.'

I stopped crying to listen.

'She's right,' Ollie added. 'But we're your friends, even if you don't decide to stay.'

I looked at him and sniffed. He made it sound like I had a choice in all this. 'The snow is keeping me here,' I said eventually.

Wax gave my hand a squeeze. 'For a reason ... I'm sure it's part of the curse. Whenever the two families threaten to join together, this all starts again.'

Everyone looked at Wax curiously as if they weren't used to hearing him talk like this.

'Tell me what's happened so far?' Wax said.

Tallulah sat back. Everyone seemed to have dropped onto the floor and formed a circle to hear better. It all held so much more meaning now. 'It was the round house that first called me.'

'The orangery,' Tallulah translated for everyone.

'It just called me and I felt ... I felt. It sounds silly, but it felt familiar, almost nostalgic to me. There was a rose left there in the hand of the angel and then the roof caved in and Burt found a note hidden under the love seat. There were rose petals in the snow inside. Stuff like that. I found a book in the library that was obviously a gift from Jedediah to Lila. I also found her birth certificate but no death certificate. And then we found all her belongings in a secret room. It points to her death and someone trying to cover it up.' It made me shudder just thinking about it all.

'You have to remember that a spirit can only scare you if you're already dead,' Wax said. 'No real harm can come to you.'

'That's just it though, Wax. Can you be sure of that if she's different?' Tallulah said.

I looked up at Wax next to me. He looked worried. 'I think she is,' he said. There was a long moment where we just looked at each other. It went on so long that someone had to cough. 'I think she's been drawn here for that reason. I think she's been sent here to me.'

'Perhaps you both have to break the Blackwood curse,' Ollie said.

Wax nodded while not taking his eyes off me. My heart skipped. 'Maybe that's what the spirit is trying to stop?' Wax said.

I wasn't so sure. 'I think it doesn't like me delving into what happened to Lila.'

'Maybe there's two.'

We all looked at Archie. 'What?' he said. 'One might want Beccah here and the other one is scaring her away.'

I looked at Wax. He was thinking it through. 'Two spirits,' he said to himself.

'It makes sense.' It totally did. The dreams and feelings were something totally different to the violence I'd experienced. 'Think about it. The flowers appearing. The round house roof breaking the love seat, so I can find the note. It's trying to tell me something.'

'Or drawing you in,' Sam said. When I looked at her, she had a faraway look on her face, like she'd seen something terrifying. I remembered the ghost that called me out of my room, the time I found Lila's stuff, and then when I got there, something screamed at me to go and knocked me over. The dream in the bath where I almost drowned. I wondered now whether that was a serious attempt on my life. 'There's been loads of things, the last was this,' I said, pointing at my face.

'What if one brought you here to solve something and another doesn't want you to,' Nicola said.

I faced her. 'Like the killer, you mean.' It was a terrifying thought.

She looked sympathetically back.

'Or it brought you here to free something,' Archie said.

'Yeah, and I reckon you need Wax to do it. Maybe it needs a Waxley Black and a Blackwood to do it,' Tallulah said. She was actually quite clever when she wanted to be.

Wax bobbed his head. 'Any one of those things could be true. What do you think?' he said directly to me.

I guess it was what I'd always thought. 'I think Lila loved Jed and was engaged to Ainsley, and he killed her in a fit of jealousy. Then he hid her stuff and started the rumour about her running away.' Then I remembered something my aunt had said. 'But my aunt said it was Jed's wife-to-be's family that put a stop to them seeing each other in secret. Not sure how they would have done that?' I glanced at everyone to see if they could shed any light on it and they all looked blank. Then we all turned to Wax for the answer. He shook his head slowly as if he was as stumped as we were. 'All I know is that spirits can tamper and affect things in this plane. They are almost always malevolent. We need to find out more about Jed and Ainsley.'

'Yeah, and what happened between them. What about the newspapers at the time?' I said with a bolt of inspiration.

It was a good idea, but Wax shook his head. 'What would there be? Ainsley's engagement broken off, that's all.'

I looked over at Tallulah. 'I think it's worth a look. You never know. A clue, or something.'

Everyone seemed to agree. It was somewhere to start, at

least. 'How would we get to that sort of information? Won't all the public libraries be shut?'

Ollie smirked. 'You are in the presence of computer nerd greatness. Not one but two Waxley Black brothers to help you.'

He made me laugh. I almost forgot that no more than a half hour ago I found out I was dead. I swallowed down a lump. 'Lead the way then, tech wizard.' I laughed again and we trooped out of the sitting room to the large staircase.

'Be quiet,' Wax hissed and picked up my hand again. 'Otherwise you'll wake my uncle.'

It seemed a bizarre thing to say to dead people, but I shrugged and went along. I slowed us up a bit with my leg, but Wax was surprisingly patient. It made a warm glow in my stomach how he seemed to want to look after me.

We went along the landing to the door I knew was to his room. We all traipsed in and my eyes lingered on the bed Wax had been tranquilised in only a few days before. Then I saw his impressive bank of computers I hadn't seen previously because they'd been behind the door. It looked like something from Wall Street. Numbers and code were running through sequences over most of his six screens.

He let go of my hand to sit in his seat. I stood one side of him and Ollie the other. Everyone else crowded behind. 'Are you going to hack into somewhere?' I said.

Wax didn't look up while his fingers tapped away. 'No need, there are loads of places online where you can search their archives for free.' He found a newspaper archive in seconds and clicked on the date range. His fingers typed lightning fast. I tried not to think of him sitting here alone, messaging me in the same way.

'Here,' he said. 'We need the year she disappeared to narrow it down or we'll be here all night.'

I wracked my brains. Then I remembered her portrait:

1839 –1857. I remembered it distinctly because she was my age. However, there was no death certificate, so they must have used the day she disappeared. Then my heart stalled, unless someone knew she was dead to put that. '1857,' I blurted.

Wax looked up at me and bobbed his head in appreciation. My heart swelled. He seemed to make me feel like that a lot.

He went straight to that year and zoomed in as the print was very small. It was the local paper for the area and was weekly. Then he clicked on the summer dates. 'Just a hunch,' he explained. 'I don't want to waste time.'

He began to scroll through each paper. 'Look for all the headings. Shout if you see anything relating to Blackwood or Waxley Black.'

We all did as he said. I narrowed my eyes and tried to keep my concentration on the screen, but my eyes often strayed to the hair touching his neck in soft curls. I had an almost irresistible urge to run my fingers through them.

I had to get a hold on myself. This was important. My eyes went back to the screen and I saw it. A few of us did, as we all shouted, 'There!'

Wax scrolled back a bit as he'd gone past it. The heading said, *Waxley-Black brothers join forces to start new business venture.* We all skimmed the article saying something about excavating a silver mine somewhere I'd never heard of. Wax hadn't said anything but was just staring at the screen. 'What is it?' I said. It was like he'd seen something none of us did.

He spun around on his chair to look at us all. 'Don't you see it?'

I frowned. 'There was no mention of Lila or either of their engagements.'

'You're right!' he said. 'Going into business isn't something a man is likely to do with a brother who he'd just caught shagging his wife-to-be.'

My cheeks went pink, but he was right.

'What if this was before he found out?' Ollie said. It was a good point.

Wax swivelled back around in his chair. 'OK. I'll check the rest of the year. If there's nothing, then we know something's up.'

By the end, my eyes felt like they'd been filled with grit and I couldn't focus on another word. There was nothing, not one thing about the Waxley Blacks or Blackwoods – not even about Lila's disappearance, which I found informative. It showed how little she was valued.

'That's it then,' Wax said.

'What about the earlier part of the year?' Sam said.

Wax bobbed his head. 'I'll check it later. I don't sleep at night anyway. But I think it safe to say that the brothers far from hated each other, which kind of throws your theory into question,' he said, finishing with his eyes on me.

'What, then?' I asked with a shrug. He was right, but that left me more confused than ever.

'Pizza?' Ollie said.

'Yeah, and a beer,' Archie said, and they all moved towards the door. I stayed riveted to Wax. I knew he wouldn't come down and join in. 'Can I stay with you for a bit?' I said. 'I'm too tired to go down there.'

He paused before he spoke, as if he was going to say something and decided against it. Then he nodded towards his bed. 'Go and lie down. I'll be checking through this for a while.'

I glanced at his grand bed and remembered again the last time I'd seen it. Wax was already scrolling through the newspapers, so I went over to it. I leaned my crutch against the wall and eased myself down onto the soft black quilt. I was immediately hit with his scent and I snuggled down, allowing it to wrap around me. When I opened my eyes, Wax hadn't moved. 'Why do you call it a curse … to see dead people, I mean?'

He took in a deep breath and stretched out his arms and back. 'I hear them, hundreds of them, all the time. They all want something. They don't leave me alone.'

I thought about what he said. It must me like having tinnitus but with guilt. It sounded awful. No wonder he needed to be sedated sometimes. 'And it helps when you go out?'

He shook his head, still gazing intently at his screen. 'No, it's worse. But I can drink and that drowns it out.'

'Shades?'

'Yeah, they're the ones that usually want something.' He looked briefly over at me and then back at his screen.

So he was bombarded day and night. 'I can see why you hated me, then.'

'I didn't hate you. Far from it.' He stood, walked over and sat on the bed next to me. 'You quieten it down, Becks.' He pushed back a strand of my hair that had fallen into my face. 'You've been coming to me in dreams for months. I guess seeing you … it just freaked me out. I didn't know what it meant at first.'

'And you do now?' My heart was beating so hard in my chest I felt sure he must feel it, but he continued running his fingers through my hair.

'When I touch you, I can't hear anyone else,' he said, like he was miles away.

'Wax! What do you know now?'

He stood up and walked towards the window, but it was pitch-black outside and he couldn't see a thing. He just stood there and put his hands in his pockets as if he saw everything there. 'That we're meant to break the Blackwood curse and we're going to have to fight, otherwise it could end up destroying us both.'

I was scared. The thought of going back there tonight, alone, terrified me.

'They're all staying over,' he said, nodding his head towards the door.

I swallowed, not sure what he was really saying.

'Stay!'

My mind shot to my Aunt, Gerty and what he really meant. I was all too aware that he was a red-blooded, hot boy and I was in his room.

He came and sat with me on the edge of the bed again and searched my face. 'You don't have to follow the rules of the living any more, Pearl White. You can do whatever you want.'

I looked into Wax's eyes a full minute before I could answer. He was trying not to smile. Then he gave in. 'You can stay there quite safely. I don't sleep, remember.'

I suddenly felt foolish at jumping to *that* in my mind. My cheeks ignited and I pushed the quilt off, pretending I was hot. He didn't seem to notice and went back to his computer. 'Give me an hour to finish this and I'll show you the house,' he said as he sat down. 'If you want.' He looked over his shoulder with mischievous eyes.

He was playing with me, but my cheeks flushed just the same. 'Sure.' I had to cough to disguise how confused he made me feel. He seemed to control the butterflies in my stomach and he knew it; it was utterly disconcerting. I had to remember how much older and experienced in these things he was than me.

I didn't feel like going down with the others to face their questions about me and Wax. I didn't understand it myself. So I got out of bed, pulled a rolling stool over and sat next to him.

He scrolled the screen like a seasoned pro, far faster than

I could have done. 'It's how I keep busy all night when I can't sleep,' he explained, reading my mind.

He was unbelievably perceptive, I was beginning to realise. I wondered again what it must be like having to sift through hundreds of voices to think inside your own head. 'Are there so many?' I said, needing to say 'of us', but still feeling it was too strange. 'Why are they all here? In this area, I mean?'

Wax stopped scrolling and thought about it. 'That's true. I don't know why … interesting.' He went back to checking the newspapers for a while and then rolled backwards on his chair. 'Come on, let's go down.'

He took my hand and I went with him, bewildered. I mean, I liked it and all, but I was still getting used to the closeness and, at the same time, not really knowing him. It was weird. Not that I would have given it up. *No*. I couldn't.

Everyone was congregated in the kitchen again. I discovered that, despite being dead, they loved their food and alcohol. Plus, as Wax explained, 'It's the furthest room from my uncle's bedroom. They're noisy assholes.'

They seemed to think of the uncle as some sort of ogre and yet he was the one person there to look after Wax. My mind went straight to the meltdown of the other day. I had to constantly remind myself it was the same boy.

'What do you want?' Wax asked, taking a loaf of bread from a box and a cooked chicken from the fridge.

'Yes please,' Joe said.

'Not you,' Wax said, and the boy put his hands up in surrender, looking genuinely scared. I got the impression that many of them were no more used to interacting with Wax than I was.

I was starving and nodded. 'A sandwich would be great.'

I looked around at the others and they were openly staring, as if I'd sprouted another head or something. Tallulah was sitting on Ollie's lap with her arms still around his neck. Then, as if the spell had been broken and I wasn't going to enlighten them, they returned to their conversations and swigging beer.

I couldn't comprehend what it was to be a Shade. I mean, I was there. I ate and drank real food and drink.

Wax passed me a sandwich bulging with lettuce and tomatoes. My stomach even rumbled.

Wax must have seen my expression. 'You feel pretty real, I guess.' He took a bite of his huge sandwich and shrugged. 'For all intents and purposes, you are,' he said, chewing. 'It's just not everyone can see you.'

I took a bite of my sandwich. 'It's pretty good,' I said, trying not to grin with my mouth so full. It tasted wonderful.

He passed me a bottle of coke and grinned wider. I took a sip and marvelled at how good it tasted. 'So, if your uncle came in here now, all he'd see is you, a bottle and a floating sandwich?'

Wax burst out laughing. 'Yeah. I guess he would. Hey! Next time he tries to lock me up I want you to do just that. I want to see his face.' He seemed to laugh harder with every thought and it was lovely to see. It did something to my butterflies knowing that he wanted me there with him.

It briefly struck me that he wasn't fond of his uncle, when I noticed everyone staring open-mouthed again.

'What are you all looking at? Never seen a girl eat a sand-wich before?'

They all looked around them exaggeratedly, like it was all still part of a silly joke. I'd have to weasel it out of Tallulah later.

Wax just rolled his eyes and didn't seem angry at all.

We finished our sandwiches and I put my plate in the sink. 'Come on,' he said. 'I'll show you about the place.' We started to walk towards the door.

'Where you going?' Ollie called.

'Guided tour,' Wax said, without turning around.

Ollie pushed Tallulah off his lap. 'We'll come.'

Wax shook his head wearily and picked up my hand. 'Be quiet then. If you wake him up there'll be hell to pay.'

I worried for the first time then. As Shades, we'd be safe. It would be Wax who'd have to face him.

The house seemed huge – even after my aunt's place. However, despite the large modern kitchen, it was just as antique-looking everywhere else. There were a lot of creaky floorboards that someone managed to continually set off. There would then follow a loud 'Shh!' every time.

'I wonder whether you've got any secret rooms here?' I said as I dragged my plastered leg slowly up the stairs; I'd left one of my crutches at the bottom. Wax held my other arm.

We relaxed when we reached the landing. Wax just pointed and said, 'There're another three bedrooms and a bathroom that way and the same on the other,' he said, turning. 'My uncle's is the furthest one,' he finished, turning back, pointing in the original direction.

'What's the other one?' I could just see a door squashed into the corner next to his uncle's room.'

'That's nothing. Just the stairs to the attic. We shouldn't risk waking him going up there.'

I nodded, seeing the sense in that.

'Hey, let's check out my room,' Ollie said, pulling Tallulah to the door next to Wax's.

It was a little smaller than Wax's and not as grand. It was decorated in blue, with posters of Chelsea football team and various bands on the walls. It looked surprisingly lived in but, conversely, frozen in time, which was exactly what it was. It made me feel sad for Ollie. He was here, but, to the world, he'd gone.

It made me think of my own parents then, for the first

139

time in ages. Now their lack of interest in me made sense. They didn't ignore me because they were mourning Pete, they didn't see me. I was gone too. I quickly wiped a stray tear before anyone saw.

I looked at Wax, who watched me knowingly.

'So when did you … you know?' I said to Ollie, not able to bring myself to finish the sentence.

'About a year and a half,' he said, understanding completely.

I looked at the others, who all nodded. 'About the same,' Joe said.

It made me frown. It was a little odd. I mean, a school trip accident I got, but not the others as well. Something about it wasn't right, but I couldn't work out what yet.

I looked at the neatly made bed. 'Do you still sleep here?' I asked.

'Not really. I don't get tired. I watch TV and go on the internet mainly.'

The others all nodded, as if it was a familiar story for them too. I looked at the small TV and computer that was more dated than Wax's. Then I noticed Wax looked uncomfortable. I guessed then that he must get in trouble a lot with all the antics going on with everyone here. 'Where next?' I said.

'Downstairs,' he said, smiling, clearly a little relieved.

He helped me down as he had going up and then he showed me to two similar reception rooms. One decorated blue and the other green. It was all dark wood with velvet upholstery that seemed the theme in these old houses. One had a piano in though.

There was the library that Ollie had smuggled us in when Wax had trashed the place and a locked room that Wax said was his uncle's study. Then there was just the little sitting room we'd listened to music in earlier and we were back in the kitchen. All pretty mundane really – except maybe the study. I wanted to take a peek in there.

Ollie grabbed something from the fridge, and I noticed there was a narrow door next to it. 'Where does that go?'

'Oh, that's the pantry,' Ollie said. 'It goes down to the cellar, I think.'

I looked at Wax. 'Can I see it?' I needed to check everything out in this house. So far, nothing had helped.

Wax shrugged. 'I guess so. My uncle just keeps his wine down there, though.'

'I'd like to see anyway.'

Wax walked over, opened the door and flicked a switch just inside. We all followed him into the room that was no more than about six by six feet in size. It was dingy and smelly with shelves filled with tins and jars of food. There were wooden boxes containing fruit and vegetables which gave the room its dusty greengrocer's smell.

There, on the far side, was a door smaller and more rickety than the first. Wax opened it and it scraped the floor where it had swollen with damp. A wall of blackness waited on the other side until Wax got out his mobile phone for its torch. 'Shit,' he muttered. He ducked under a huge cobweb and pulled a cord. A lightbulb came on, barely illuminating the top few wooden steps leading downwards to the inky blackness below. 'Be careful,' Wax said, leading me down by the arm. 'Leave that there.'

I saw what he meant. The stairs would be easier to negotiate without my crutch. 'Can we die again?' I asked, seeing how dark it was down there.

Ollie laughed from behind me as we descended. 'I dunno. We've never tested it.'

I held onto Wax, tightly, and he hugged me even closer. I liked it, revelling in the heat of him. The lower we got, the more it smelled of earth and dampness. I was sorry when he released me at the bottom. It was weird how I sought any excuse to touch him.

Wax found another pull-string at the bottom, pulled it and an old florescent strip light flashed on and off, with a glass ringing sound, until it finally came on with a soft hum. The others came down the steps and crowded around us. We looked around. There didn't seem to be anything out of the ordinary. Just a rack on one wall filled with wine, a large chest freezer, boiler, mop and other cleaning equipment. Basically, everything you'd expect to find in a basement in a house like this.

Except Wax looked troubled. 'What's the matter?' I asked. 'Is something wrong?' My heart was already speeding up in anticipation of something bad.

He frowned. 'I'm not sure. I don't come down here that much.'

Ollie came up to his other shoulder to see if he could see what it was.

'But my uncle does. All the time,' Wax said to himself as if he was working something out in his mind.

Then I got what he meant. Unless he was an alcoholic, there was absolutely no reason to come down here.

Tallulah pointed at the freezer. 'Maybe there's a dead body in there.'

Everyone groaned. Ollie chuckled. 'You're not serious?'

Tallulah pulled a face. 'What? It's always in the films.'

Ollie sighed, shaking his head and going over to it. He took the handle and pulled, but it wouldn't budge.

'Is it locked?' Wax said.

Ollie shrugged, then gave it one final heft. It flew open, Ollie leaned over and suddenly yelled as if someone were pulling him in. We all shouted and ran to him.

He immediately dissolved into laughter. Wax checked the chest was empty; it wasn't even switched on. He clipped his brother round the head with his hand and the wind ruffled his hair. 'Asshole,' he said. 'You'll wake Uncle.'

It felt like we all let out a collective breath to relax and my heart went back to normal. 'Let's look around for anything out of the ordinary,' I said.

We split up, even picking up pots and old boxes to look inside, but nothing seemed weird or out of place.

I turned a slow circle, trying to take everything in. Then it came to me and literally stopped my heart for a couple of beats. 'It's small,' I said.

'Not as big as yours, eh, Miss Lah-di-dah,' Ollie said, sashaying over to me.

'No, what I mean is, in comparison to the size of the house.'

Wax nodded, immediately getting my drift. 'This is less than half the floor space above.'

Tallulah continued to look blank.

'This can't be all of it,' I said, looking into all their faces. Their eyes widened with sudden understanding. 'Look for a secret door or panel, however small.'

Tallulah immediately caught on and began tapping on the wall. I went over to the furthest wall, where I knew the house continued above. I was right; it sounded hollow. Wax followed me and did the same.

Ollie started pulling out dusty wine bottles, looking behind for a hidden switch. There were a lot of bottles, so Tallulah and a couple of the others helped.

Wax stood with me, watching. 'Wait!' he said, taking a step forward.

Ollie and the others immediately stopped what they were doing and looked at him. 'What?'

'They're all dirty, except one,' Wax said, pointing to one in the top left-hand corner.

He was right. It looked clean and new. Wax tried to pull it, but it wouldn't budge. I came forward to try, but I couldn't reach up that high.

I hitched a breath when I felt Wax's large hands grip my waist and lift me easily. Instead of pulling, I pushed in and then downwards. There was a loud clank, then a cranking sound. A huge panel in the wall next to it slowly slid to the side. Wax put me down on my feet and we all turned to look at the huge room it revealed.

It was deepest red and illuminated by tens of thick white candles. There was a huge sideboard on the far side with mounds of melted wax where candles had burned in the same place for a very long time. It reminded me of an altar.

We all crept forward as one unit. Something made us pause at the boundary of the room. It was as though we sensed something evil there; an invisible barrier. I took a breath and continued on. When I went to take another step, already looking around the room, Wax shouted, 'Stop!' He pointed to the floor.

There was a perfectly drawn white circle made of some sort of powder with a five-pointed star inside. In each compartment there was a symbol in the same powder. Then there was some sort of artefact at each point of the star: a human skull, a metal chalice, a lit candle, some sort of herbs in a metal bowl. The last one had nothing at all. It was very curious.

'What is it?' Nicola whispered.

'It's witchcraft, I think,' I said.

'Black magic,' Wax said, so quietly I could barely hear.

I had no idea how he could possibly know that. I was about to open my mouth to ask when there was a click and the sound of a door closing coming from the top of the stairs. 'Someone's coming,' I whispered, panicking.

Everyone started to run in every direction, looking for

anywhere to hide themselves. Only Wax didn't move. 'Stand still! Don't make a sound,' he hissed.

We did as we were told and froze. Then I watched in absolute terror as he walked over to the wall and closed the panel by smacking a button and went behind a red velvet curtain. While we stood rooted to the spot, my insides went to liquid. My mind had lost all thought except to run and I was hyperventilating. Ollie grounded me with his eyes, put a finger to his lips and we stood like statues as the panel clanked and slowly opened.

CHAPTER 14

*M*y hands flew to my mouth to stop my involuntary whimper and I tried to stay glued to Ollie's eyes as I lost my balance for a moment. My knee started to shake with the effort and sweat trickled down my neck. Terror at the clonk and crank of the mechanism held me still and stopped me breathing.

The wall slowly opened.

I swear my blood froze in my veins and yet sounded like a train in my ears. I closed my eyes and felt Wax's uncle stalk into the room. I cracked them open a little to see the tall, brittle-looking frame turn and look around.

Ollie widened his eyes to keep me focussed on him.

'I know you're in here,' the uncle said. As if he'd been really clever, finding us in a game of hide and seek. 'You left the lights on out there.'

I closed my eyes. *Of course.* Wax didn't have enough time to turn them off when we heard him coming. I took a small swallow and turned to look at the others, but they kept their positions. The uncle began a stroll around the room.

'Bret!' he said, making me jump. He was so close it was

hard to believe he couldn't see us at all. 'I know you're in here so you may as well come out.'

I wanted to shout 'No!', but Ollie clamped his hand over my mouth as he shook his head.

I was forced to watch helplessly as the red curtain moved and Wax stepped out from his hiding place. My heart broke as he came and stood next to me and took my hand secretly, next to his leg. I could feel him shaking.

Tears prickled my eyes when I looked up to see him looking intently at his uncle. It was clear to me then. The years of fear and reprisals. His uncle was his abuser and his jailer. He knew exactly what Wax could do and medicated him anyway. He didn't care that the world thought Wax was unstable.

I studied his blank, unreadable face in disgust. The memory of Wax in bed with the nurse bent over him was burning a hole in my heart. How I hated his uncle then. I knew in that moment, that Wax was as trapped as we were and his uncle wanted it that way.

'What is this place?' Wax demanded.

I gripped his hand tighter.

'What are you doing down here?' his uncle threw right back.

Wax's eyes narrowed. There was no love lost between them; it was clear to see. 'I came down for a bottle to drown them out.' Then he smirked and shifted his weight to his hip. 'Then I remembered one of them whispering about secret rooms and that the cellar was too small for a house of this size.' He shrugged. 'Didn't take much to find it.'

My heart skipped. However, he worried me. His handsome, hard face, the punching pulse at his neck and the tight grip he had on my hand belied the bravado he was showing his uncle.

His uncle nodded and half-smiled while he began a slow

pace of the room. 'Clever boy. I can see I underestimated you.' He was complimenting him, but even I could tell it was fake and that Wax shouldn't trust him for a moment. 'No matter. To the world you are a paranoid schizophrenic in my care, so no harm done.'

My hatred for the man took great long roots as I felt Wax's discomfort. Embarrassment initially, then as if he was readying himself for something. I was so proud as he didn't cower before his uncle.

'But we know the truth, don't we? You still haven't answered my question.' He let go of my hand and stepped forward. His uncle whirled round and came up in his face. Any joy I held in Wax standing up to him quickly evaporated.

I stayed behind him and felt the others join me in formation. It felt like we were an army on his side. Just for a moment, it felt like we were strong. Then his uncle spoke and broke the illusion. 'Tough boy, eh? A few tattoos might scare the teenagers in the village, but this is me.' They were a similar height, but his uncle began to bear down on him, pushing him backwards, menacingly, against the wall. 'This room and everything you see here is for her. Do you understand?'

I didn't.

He jabbed a finger into Wax's temple. 'You are just a cog in the wheel that helps me get to my goal.'

His uncle was clearly completely unaware of us all swarming around him. I didn't understand what the hell was going on. Wax flicked his eyes and shook his head very slightly for me to do nothing. 'Why do you need black magic?' Wax asked. I was sure it was to stop his uncle realising someone else was there with him.

His uncle renewed his grip on his shirt. 'It's too much for you to understand,' he said, pushing off him and letting him go.

Wax straightened up and rearranged his clothes. 'It's a beacon, isn't it? You're trying to call someone.' Then Wax frowned, as if he was thinking it all through and it was making an awful kind of sense to him. 'Except instead of getting a particular person, you're getting anyone and everyone in a radius around us.'

His uncle turned and smiled genuinely then, looking more than a little surprised. He slow-clapped his hands. It was the first time I really noticed how smartly dressed he was. He reminded me of a Victorian gentleman with his style of clothing. 'Well done, Master Waxley Black. Bravo.'

'But why? It's creating havoc in the spirit world.' Then he looked at me as if something saddened him. 'They are people that aren't meant to be here.' I knew he was thinking of me directly.

Wax looked down at the pentagon in a circle, marked out on the floor. I followed his line of vision. He was taking in the objects. 'What's missing?'

His uncle came up to him and put his arm round his shoulders. Wax stiffened as he looked into his face. 'Why, a Blackwood of course. And I think she's already here. Isn't she, Bret?'

He grinned and looked around the room. It was an eerie feeling having his eyes look right through you but not see you or any of the seven with you at all. I clung onto that; he couldn't see us.

'I dunno what you mean?' Wax said, half-laughing as if he was ridiculous. He pointed at his own head. 'I mean. There're so many. How can I decipher between them?'

His uncle knew he was being smart and narrowed his eyes. 'Maybe. But if she hasn't already, she'll make contact with you soon. She won't be able to help herself. You can feel the curse at work already. The snow is keeping us all here. All the key players are in place.'

I felt my blood run to ice. He knew too much for it not to be true. Everything was making a horrible kind of sense.

Wax shrugged. 'How do you know it'll be a girl?' He went to walk off as if it didn't matter at all to him.

His uncle shot him a scathing look and shook his head. 'Don't act dumb, boy. It doesn't suit you.' He whirled him round by the arm and pointed in his face. 'It's always a Blackwood girl and a Waxley-Black male.'

We were all in shock, absorbing the information, but I didn't want to let this opportunity to question his uncle to slip us by. I pulled Wax down to my mouth and whispered, 'Ask him how long he's been calling everyone.' I had a hunch I needed confirming.

The uncle perked up as if he heard something. 'What did you say?'

Wax quickly straightened and the rest of us huddled together. 'How long have you been doing all this?' Wax said, holding out his arm to encompass the whole room.

His uncle shrugged. 'In part … study, research and such forth, pretty much my whole life. I learned of the curse as a small boy. But this—' He turned a circle to take in the markings on the floor and the altar. 'The magic that you see here … a year maybe – a year and a half.'

My heart sped up. It was what I suspected. Wax looked down at me and I knew he got it too. It was because of his uncle that we hadn't passed over. *He* was creating Shades.

Just for a moment, I saw a flicker of regret in Wax's eyes. It was there and it was gone. It left me wondering if he felt as I did. Disappointment that we weren't the main players in all this. Fate and the curse hadn't seen to bring us together.

Wax looked back at his uncle and I could see the indecision. He wanted to ask more questions but didn't want to give anything away that might reveal us. In the end, he just said, 'What now? … You know, now I know.'

Wax's uncle came over and put his arm around his shoulders. He began steering him out to the normal part of the cellar. 'Go to bed, Bret. We will talk later this evening. It's almost dawn.'

At the boundary, his uncle smacked his palm against the button, stepped back and the wall began to crank and close in front of him. I had wandered after the two of them, preoccupied with what I'd learned, when I was swept up in everyone shooting past me. No one wanted to be left behind. I soon joined them in a gallop to hop over the line. Ollie made a last-minute grab and literally yanked me over the last three feet of space before the wall closed.

I righted myself from almost falling flat on the floor, just in time to see Wax's uncle, hands behind his back, eyelids lowered as his blank face disappeared behind the panel. My heart was still beating wildly at the close call, when Wax picked up my hand and looked into my eyes. They were calming and unsettling at the same time. In that brief look they said, 'I got you', but left me with an unease about what all this meant for us. All I could do was smile weakly. At least we'd escaped unscathed. However, as I let Wax lead me out of the cellar and away to safety, it was with a troubled heart.

Everyone talked at once as soon as we got to the kitchen. 'Shut up!' Wax hissed, shutting the pantry door. 'He'll hear you. Grab what you need and we'll go up to my room.'

Wax pulled a pack of beers from the fridge while I picked up my crutch. I wondered then whether it was invisible as it was with me when I came. Otherwise, Wax's uncle would have seen it leaning against the wall. We made our way back up the stairs, me slowly at the back with Wax helping. I wondered if it was deliberate. When we reached the top, he allowed the others to disappear into his room. 'Wait,' he whispered. 'You OK?'

. I nodded, not entirely sure which bit he was referring to, exactly. 'I think so … he explained a lot,' I said, looking up and searching his eyes for clues. 'So, he made us.' I shrugged as if that was it.

Wax frowned. 'He didn't make you. He brought you here, robbing you of your afterlife.' He looked angry, but not in a way that made me scared. The kind that made you swallow at how handsome he looked when he was passionate about something.

I had mixed emotions. I didn't want to talk about my disappointment at us not being the centre of the curse. It seemed over-presumptuous of me. I mean, I knew he fancied me, but I didn't know how deeply his feelings ran yet. We'd only just met. The fact that he was alive and I was dead was weirdly beside the point. My mind was still sifting through it all. But one thing I was certain of hit me. 'I'm not sorry, Wax. I'm glad I came here. Otherwise I wouldn't have met everyone.' I looked over my shoulder at the door to his room, left ajar. 'I wouldn't have met you.' I turned and his mouth was right there. He kissed me. It was soft but lit a fire inside me. His hand went behind my neck to hold me to him and I totally lost myself in the taste and feel of him.

He pulled away, too quickly, and led me to his room. His arm was around my waist and his fingers gently rubbed my side, sending tingles through me in waves.

Everyone had flopped down on the bed, on the large black leather bean bag or on the floor. Wax gave a hard look at Josh and he moved his legs so I could sit on the bed. Then he sat on the floor, leaning against the wall opposite me. His eyes looked into mine, turning my insides to liquid. I wished I knew what he was thinking.

'What the hell was all that?' Ollie said.

I dragged my eyes from Wax and stared at him. He looked in shock. They all did.

Tallulah started crying. 'So all this is – our lives here – is just because of him.'

Ollie pulled her into his lap, kissed her head and stroked her hair. 'I don't think we're in the real world. Wax can see us,' he said, nodding at his brother. 'But it's more like he has us trapped in some fake loop or dimension,' he said to everyone over her head. 'Think about it. Wax is the only real, live person we interact with.'

He was right.

Tallulah began to sob.

I felt sorry for her. Their existence had no higher meaning than his will for them to be there; it was pointless. I guess they'd all harboured some romanticised notion that they were here for some preordained reason for something. Yesterday they didn't seem to care, now it felt like they'd lost something.

Wax knocked the top off one of his beers and passed one to me, then to his brother and anyone else who wanted one. He looked genuinely sorry. I thought how terribly he'd been used too. His uncle had obviously discovered his psychic gift and unashamedly used it to monitor if what he was doing was working. Then, at the same time, making everyone think he was mad, making him a social leper just to keep him where he wanted him. No wonder he got angry. 'So let me get this straight,' I said, somehow knowing that Wax wouldn't bear me feeling sorry for him. 'He's done all this to get us here to start the curse … Why?' I looked around at everyone for the answer and was met with silence. 'Is he trying to break the curse or use it for something else?'

Wax had an expression on his face I'd never seen before. It was part smile, part amazement. 'She's right. We need to figure this out as, you can bet, he doesn't give a shit about any of us.' He finished by looking me deeply in the eyes. The look smouldered, making me wish I could take the cardigan off that covered my ridiculous dress. I looked down, suddenly remembering I had it on. It had been a long night.

Wax chuckled as if he'd read my mind, while the others looked at each other, puzzled. He got to his feet and went to one of his drawers. He pulled out some sweats and a plain white t-shirt, then passed them to me.

I took them hesitantly, wanting to put them to my nose, but realising how weird that would look. 'Can you show me the bathroom up here?' I said, suddenly hoarse.

Joe was nearest the door and went to get up. 'Sit down,' Wax ordered. He got up and helped me off the bed. He glared at Joe as we left and it didn't bother me nearly as much as it should have. 'Are you normally so rough on them?' I said as soon as we got out in the hall.

Wax was holding my elbow while I made slow progress along the landing. 'I have no interaction with them at all,' he said with a shrug. 'Except for my brother. He's always with that annoying girl and I have to continually tell them to shut up.' When I took a sideways glance at him, I caught the corners of his mouth twitch into a smile as he realised how moody he was sounding.

We got to a room right at the end and he pushed the door open. 'I'll wait here … unless you want me to come in?' he said with a wicked grin.

I rolled my eyes and turned and went inside, but my butterflies somersaulted at how good-looking he was. The smile that was so rare made him even more so.

The bathroom was large and plain, but not dilapidated like at my aunt's place. Then the reason hit me. Everyone in it was dead. It was frozen and empty, where this one still held the living. Wax's uncle kept up the household staff, bought TVs and fridges and renewed the decor. That was why this room had a modern white bathroom suite, gleaming tiles, chrome taps and a shower. I wished I could use it, but Wax was outside and I didn't want the uncle to wonder who was in here. I wriggled out of the dress and folded it with a smile. I guess it did make an impression.

I pulled the white t-shirt on over my head and the clean linen smell was edged with him. It totally surrounded me and I loved the feeling. I pulled on the grey sweatpants that went over my plaster cast easily and bunched at my ankles. He had to be almost a foot taller than me.

I came out eventually and his eyes glazed over for a second. Then he nodded. 'That t-shirt looks better on you. It's a shame the others are here because you could lose the sweats.'

Before I could register what he'd said and blast red, he'd picked up my hands. I thought it was to take me back to his room, but he used his weight to step me back into the bathroom. We were kissing again and it felt more urgent than before. He groaned, hands in my hair and pushing his fingers into the skin on my back.

I couldn't believe how I responded to him. Before coming here I'd barely kissed anyone and here I was, in a strange boy's bathroom, wanting to rip his clothes off.

He pushed me up against the basin and his hands gripped either side of it, trapping me against his body. Before I knew it, my legs were clamped around his waist and I was moving against the fabric separating us, running totally on instinct. Then, just as I was about to pull off my top, his incendiary kiss died against my lips.

He slowed until he stopped. I looked up at his face and his eyes were on something behind me. Except I knew all that was there was the basin and the mirror.

That last word in my head made me unlink my legs and slide them down to the floor. I turned, slowly, to look at what Wax could see.

The face that gazed back at us in the mirror.

CHAPTER 15

*T*he face in the mirror was that of a woman. A young woman with blonde curls framing a pretty face, wearing a faded yellow bonnet. She was clearly scared, her hands pressed to the glass and her mouth moving rapidly. It was like she was trapped in a glass box.

I looked up at Wax behind me and he seemed frozen to the image in front of him. 'Who is it?' I said to shake him out of it, because I had a good idea who it was. The similarities to the portrait were undeniable.

Then she seemed to see him and stopped moving. Her lips began to move like the TV with the sound turned off. I looked up at him again to see what was going on. He appeared to be following what she was saying because he answered, 'Don't go to the doorway or he'll have you.' I was amazed they were communicating.

Another volley of animated conversation followed until she was suddenly pulled backwards by an unseen force. It happened with a scream so loud, I had to cover my ears with my hands. I could only gape in horror as she shrunk in size the further away she got, the image faded to grey and she disappeared completely.

After a moment of shock, I looked up at Wax who smacked his hands on the wall, rested his forehead against the glass and closed his eyes.

'What just happened?'

He straightened, picked up my hands and searched my face. 'It was Lila. She kept saying she's stuck in the Inside Out. I have no idea what that is, but I guess it's a plane that runs parallel to this one. She said the Waxley-Black brothers imprisoned her there and the only way out is a door into my uncle's basement.'

'You're not suggesting we go back down there?' I said, feeling acid in my stomach at the thought of facing his uncle again.

Wax started to move towards the door. 'No, not yet. We should wait until he sleeps again. Then we need to get in there and find Ainsley's journal.'

My eyebrows rose at that.

'Lila said my uncle has it and it will explain everything.' He opened the bathroom door and I followed, limping as quickly as I could behind him, back to his bedroom. All the while, I couldn't help the pain I felt in my chest. I knew it was jealousy at the way he said Lila's name, as if he knew her. Nevertheless, I couldn't help feeling something wasn't right; I just didn't know what it was yet. Lila was beautiful and Wax was trying to help her, but something felt off.

We got back and Wax told the others what happened. They all became animated with excitement, offering theories of what we should do to help. It all went over my head as I studied Wax. Thankfully, his tolerance of anyone was short and he soon told them all to clear off to Ollie's room to give him some peace.

I went to turn and walk out with them.

'Not you,' he said, bobbing his head in the direction of his bed to rest on.

I did as I was told, though I was still uneasy. I had to go over in my head again and again the evidence I'd found that Lila was murdered, so I felt sympathy for her. It made sense that she needed help, but I couldn't shake off the feeling that Wax was walking into some kind of trap.

Tallulah gripped my arm as she walked past and widened her eyes. 'We're just next door if you need us,' she said, flicking her eyes at Wax. She was still wary of him. Maybe I should be too.

We were now alone and Wax was pacing. 'We'll wait an hour after my uncle goes to sleep tonight and then we'll go back into that room.'

I sat down heavily on the bed and watched him walking up and down in the space at the foot of it. 'Won't he rig something up now so he knows if you've been in there?' Then I thought about the speed with which he caught us. 'He may have done that already.'

He shrugged moodily. 'Probably. We'll have to be quick. You saw how scared she was. I can't leave her to that prick. You don't know what he's like, Becks.'

His eyes looked desolate when he paused his pacing to look at me. My heart sank a little more as there was no stopping him. She was the original damsel in distress. I sagged in defeat. I had to stop thinking like a needy little girl.

Wax must have read the exhaustion on my face. 'You should get some sleep while you can.' I turned my head and looked at the inviting soft quilt. Then at the window. It was getting light. When I looked back at him, he was already shaking his head. 'I don't sleep ... not without one of those,' he said, nodding towards a small brown bottle on the nightstand.

I totally got why he didn't want to take them. His uncle

had probably got them for him and God only knew what was in them.

Then an idea came to me before I got too comfortable. 'Maybe we would be better off searching your uncle's bedroom while he's occupied. He might have left something there.'

Wax stopped and stared at me like he was seeing me for the first time. My insides melted at the smouldering look he gave me. He was in front of me in a single stride and pulled me up into his arms. He kissed me for one overwhelming, combustible moment and then it was over. 'Come on.' He led me by the hand, back out to the hallway and down to the end to his uncle's bedroom.

The room was old fashioned and dark. Black velvet curtains didn't let in a single bit of the fast-approaching daylight. He swore and flicked on the light, firing a black crystal chandelier into life. He found a lamp by the bed and switched the overhead light off again. I'm not sure who would have seen, anyway. 'Search everywhere, but be careful to leave it as you found it.'

I started to pull open the drawers of a tallboy chest. 'What are we looking for, exactly?' I asked.

'Anything,' he whispered back.

So we systematically went through the room. The huge black wardrobes, the many drawers in chests, the bedside tables, even under the muted blue and grey Persian rug. We worked as quickly and as quietly as we could, careful to return everything to the way it was before.

After twenty minutes we found nothing.

Wax shook his head as I looked at the bed. He'd already pulled up and looked under the mattress. It was a bit too obvious. Maybe not if it was his bedtime reading. I pulled back the quilt and looked under the pillows. At first I thought there was nothing there until my hand touched something in the pillow case. It was small, no bigger than a wallet. I tipped the pillow upside down and out fell a small leather-bound notebook. I held it up for Wax to see.

His eyes widened in amazement. I don't think he expected to find anything at all. 'Put the bed back,' he said, grinning. 'We'll look at it in my room, just in case, and put it back later.'

Wax turned off the lamp and we rushed back to his room as fast as my leg would go. My heart was pumping hard, like I was being chased. When we got there, Wax closed the door and we rested with our backs against it and laughed. We were excited and out of breath as if we'd just got away with a robbery. I looked up into his eyes, alive and happy, looking down into mine. I wanted to kiss him, but he sprang off the door and went over to the bed, holding back the quilt. I smiled and accepted his invitation. I limped over and he helped me in and got in next to me. My body immediately came alive feeling his next to mine.

However, his mind was on the little notebook. He switched on the torch on his phone and cracked open the little leather book that looked like it was at least a hundred years old.

It was full of handwritten notations and numbers. Page after page of diagrams, equations and symbols. I had no clue what any of it meant. 'What is it?' I asked, disappointed. It seemed completely unreadable.

I checked out Wax's profile while he concentrated, taking in every single thing. 'I'm not sure, but I think it's some kind of spell. And it was written down by Ainsley.'

'Ainsley,' I repeated flatly. We had so little information about him, it was as though he hadn't existed when I started digging into all this. I just imagined him the poor wronged husband in the background. This was huge. 'So was he some kind of magician?' I asked?

Wax looked troubled. 'Worse than that, I think. This is some serious shit right here,' he said, lifting the book in his hands.

Unease was creeping up my spine as I said, 'What's it for?'

Wax was going through the pages again, muttering as he read. 'I think this is the summoning spell my uncle is using in the basement … but something is missing.' He stopped and pointed at a page. 'You see here?'

I looked at the circular symbol with a straight line coming out of it. I had no idea what it meant.

'Remember the circle with the pentagon inside it on the floor?'

I waited, frowning, still not able to see how it was connected to the symbol.

'There was something missing at one of the points.'

I remembered, but it hadn't registered much with me at the time.

'It should be this,' he said, jabbing the page with his finger. 'A mirror.'

My mind instantly went back to the face of the woman in the bathroom mirror. *Lila.*

Wax nodded as if he'd read my mind. 'I think my uncle is trying to bring Lila back.'

We stared at each other after he'd finished speaking, absorbing the enormity of what we'd just discovered. The moment was so heavy in the end that I had to swallow. 'Why though?' I said eventually, with barely any voice.

He shrugged and sighed deeply. 'Let's list what we already know.' He got out of bed and went over to his desk and grabbed a pad and pencil. Then he slid back in, making my mind wander to his long legs and whether he was tattooed under his jeans. 'Think … everything,' he said, completely oblivious to my one-track mind.

I looked around the room and tried to recall everything

I'd learned since I got there. I was shocked at how long ago that felt. 'The round house,' I said. It had been the focus of it all right from the beginning. 'I'm not sure why, but that's important.'

'OK,' Wax said, scribbling it down. 'It's a start.'

'No,' I said, labouring my point. 'It's pivotal to something. I don't know how I know, but I do.'

Wax searched my eyes for a long moment before he nodded.

'You just have to trust me on this. There's been roses left there for me to find, love letters left there for Lila from Jedediah. The one that changed tone completely. It wasn't just a meeting place. Someone is calling someone now … in this time. Maybe your uncle … I don't know. But whoever it was, it was enough to lure me. That's how I came to look like this,' I said with a wry smile and, remembering my scratched-up face, my hands came up.

He exhaled, nodded and wrote it down. 'What else?'

'The ghost that first called me a Shade was female. It led me to the secret room filled with Lila's stuff.'

Wax scribbled that down. 'Is that everything?'

I thought about it. That wasn't all. There had been something else that night – a darker force. Angry. Trying to get me out of there. 'No, there was definitely something male there. I felt him in the bathroom. He almost drowned me.' As I said it, I still wondered guiltily whether I'd just fallen asleep and slipped under the waterline. However, something deep down told me it was the same presence who'd knocked me down in the secret room.

Wax wrote it all down. He read it all back and then added, 'And there was the locket. We need to work out which of the brothers that was. Where the mine fits in. Nothing makes sense.'

He was right. My theory of a jealous husband-to-be

killing Lila in a fit of rage and hiding her stuff and probably the body, wasn't enough anymore.

I studied Wax, who was racking his brains too. 'In the mirror, she seemed scared. Did she give you any clue why?'

He shook his head sadly and put the pad down with the pencil on the nightstand, then pulled me back with him to lie down. I felt strangely comfortable with my head on his shoulder and my hand in his on his chest. It was such an adult pose. One I'd never done before; only seen on the films.

His heart was beating against my hand and his body heat burned through his shirt. I still couldn't believe we'd gone from boy and girl next door to this. Yesterday morning I was fit to punch out his lights for always being so cold. And now we were this. Strangely, my being dead didn't come into it.

His other arm was behind his head and he was looking up at the ceiling. I wondered if he was thinking about me or the mystery of Lila. I hoped, but I wasn't that confident it was me.

'Whatever Ainsley was dabbling with, my uncle must have discovered it and is doing the same,' Wax said, making my heart sink a little. 'The question is why? What are they after?'

I threw off my melancholy and put it down to overtiredness. He wasn't going to find a whiny, immature little girl attractive. 'And why do they need Lila to do it?' I added, trying to hide the slight wobble in my voice.

He turned his head to look directly into my eyes with real respect. I was right and he knew it. Ainsley wrote the spell to summon her back then and his uncle was carrying on his work now. 'I think we need to find out what the Blackwood curse actually is,' I said.

Wax didn't answer, but turned onto his side to face me. I became acutely aware of just how tall he was in comparison to me. He seemed barely contained by the bed.

He seemed to sense my overwhelm and moved back a little, then picked up my hand and kissed it. I fell in love with him a little more right then.

'I think you should go back to your aunt's for your own safety,' he said in a husky whisper. As if something had shifted in him too.

Suddenly, leaving him became a terrifying prospect that made no sense. I barely knew him twenty-four hours ago. My Aunt, Gerty and Bert were there, but they seemed so distant, so far away from me now. Wax had been the only person that had gotten through my guard since I arrived, and I couldn't bear to leave that. 'I don't think it matters now, does it? Like you said before, I'm a Shade. I can do what I want.'

It felt like he knew. Like he saw everything I felt, because he leaned forward and kissed me gently. First rubbing the soft cushion of his lips against mine and then opening them with his tongue. 'Not just that,' he whispered against my lips. 'I don't trust what my uncle is up to and he's dangerous,' he said, averting his eyes.

I didn't want to push him. My heart broke for him. I could just imagine what a bully his uncle could be to a young boy. I pulled his face round by the chin to look at me again. 'He can't do anything to me, I'm dead, remember?' I said with a grin.

His smile transformed his face and he rolled on top of me, robbing me of breath with his weight. He kissed me again and suspended his weight to look into my eyes. 'You might not be entirely safe with me,' he said with a glint of mischief.

His words lit something deep in my belly and my heart literally fluttered out of my ribcage.

He laughed and rolled off as if he'd embarrassed himself. I hated that he felt that and immediately hugged him to me again. 'Let's get a few hours' sleep, shall we?' I whispered.

I felt him relax around me and nod. We said nothing after that. His breathing slowed until it was a soft, even breeze in my hair and I felt myself drifting off too. I felt the most warmth and love I'd felt in a very long while.

I WAS RELAXING in a bath filled with bubbles right up to my chin. Wax was pacing, tall and brooding, next to me. 'How could you?' he said angrily. 'Make up your damn mind! I can't wait for you much longer. It's me or him; do you understand?'

I was shocked and terrified that I'd made him so angry and held out my arms to him. He moved into them and then he was right there, kissing me deeply. His taste was such a familiar homecoming. Except he began to feel different. It wasn't Wax. He felt thinner. Smaller. His clothes were wrong under my hands. They were rough and old fashioned and the tattoos weren't there at his neck.

Then, in a moment of clarity, I knew it wasn't me either. I was Lila and the room was the bathroom at my aunt's. The pressure of the kiss pushed me below the surface. It went on and on, until I needed to breathe. But I couldn't. He wouldn't let me up for air.

I struggled, hit his back with my closed fist and scratched his face. I could feel the water seeping into my lungs. I tried to cough, but it was useless. Airless, I mouthed, *Jed ... Jed.*

'BECKS ... BECKS.'

I was fighting, hot and sweaty. My whole body was shaking. When I finally blinked open my eyes, I saw Wax's concerned face. He was holding my wrists when he pulled me into his arms in relief. 'You OK?' he said, holding me tightly. 'You were having one hell of a nightmare.'

I was still gasping for air next to his neck. My mind was tumbling and confused and my heart was still thrashing with fright. His smell and the tattoos going right up to his hairline comforted me. 'It was terrible,' I said, eventually.

My heart gradually slowed and I pulled away to give him the bones of what happened. 'It was exactly like the dream I had before. We were kissing, then I was under the water … I couldn't breathe.' I looked directly into Wax's eyes. 'Except somehow I just know it wasn't me and it wasn't you.'

He relaxed back and reached for a glass of water. Passing it to me, he said, 'Here.' Then he watched me drink. 'Do you think, somehow, you're dreaming her memories?'

I shrugged. I was still confused. 'Yeah … maybe.' I definitely felt it was how Lila died. But it didn't fit with what I thought I knew.

Wax searched my face, puzzled.

'It was Jedediah, Wax. The guy that drowned Lila was Jed, not Ainsley.'

He sat still for a whole minute, absorbing my words, until a look of resolve came over him.

'What?' I had to say eventually, unease already creeping up my spine.

'Tonight, we're going back and getting Lila out ourselves.'

CHAPTER 16

*I*t was a strange, bewildering day.

There were no worried phone calls to find out where I was, or why I hadn't come home. No one to ask if I'd been mugged or murdered in a ditch somewhere. It gradually sank in that, to everyone in the regular world, I wasn't there any more.

My parents had said their goodbyes and I was stuck in limbo-land; in bed with my hot, very red-blooded, boyfriend.

Boyfriend. I kept saying it over and over in my head to see how it sounded. And it sounded weird, like I wasn't worthy, or didn't qualify, or something. There was no doubt it was a tricky situation to navigate. Especially when Wax pulled me into his body heat or rolled almost on top of me several times during his sleep.

I couldn't help watching him. He looked so relaxed with his face close to me on my pillow. Awake, he was always so intense. I wanted to trace the lines that always furrowed his brow.

His eyes moved under his eyelids and he blinked awake. 'Hey,' he said, croakily, smiling. 'I slept.'

The words were said with such surprise that it made my heart ache and wonder if it was me being there that had helped him fall asleep? 'You did,' I said, smiling back.

He leaned in and kissed me gently on the mouth. I melted immediately into it. Everything he did was with such fluid, sexy ease, how could I not? It was all so new – and I didn't just mean the dead thing.

He hovered over me and looked deeply into my eyes, as if he was looking for something there. 'I know it's weird, but we'll work it out, OK?'

I smiled weakly and wondered how he managed to always know how I felt. 'I'm scared,' came out on a breath before I could stop myself. And I was. Of everything. Scared of being dead and being conscious. Of what it meant. Scared it was temporary. Scared that it wasn't. But, more than all that, I was scared of the overwhelming, very physical emotion I was beginning to feel for Wax. And despite his obvious experience in this kind of stuff, he was fragile and damaged and very emotionally cut-off. It felt a very big responsibility for me to carry – someone who had no clue about anything.

I was also terrified of his uncle and what he'd do to Wax or any of us if we were caught. I was confused about Lila and whether she was up to something. Then there was the murderous ghost that still walked the corridors of my aunt's house. Something wasn't right; it wasn't fitting together.

I was scared of it all and the only person in this world who could protect me was eroding my barriers little by little until I was completely at his mercy. That was what scared me the most of all.

'I'll look after you,' Wax whispered, then brushed his lips against mine. It brought me out of my panic, grounding me with that one tantalising point where we connected. Maybe he read it in my eyes, or I was that obvious. Either way, it was sweet. 'Like you do everyone,' I said with a weak smile.

He frowned and lifted off me a little. 'No. Not like everyone. You're more than that to me.'

For a moment I felt stricken that I'd hurt his feelings, but he closed the distance and kissed me with the most powerful, heartfelt kiss of my life. It felt like an extension of everything in him pouring into me. My heart nearly burst out of my chest, it hurt so much. I think it was that exact moment that I fell for Wax. Completely. Totally. Utterly. I tumbled headlong into the abyss with him and there was no clawing my way back out.

When, at last, he pulled out of the kiss my eyes fluttered open and I hoped he felt the same. But all he said was, 'It's time.' I would have followed him anywhere.

He lifted off me and I swung my bad leg over the side of the bed and dragged my fingers through my hair. 'You sure you want to face him tonight?' I said.

He pointed at his clock. 19.30. 'I have to stick with routine. I'll have dinner with him, then, when he goes to bed, we'll get into that room and set Lila free.'

'What if he gets up or we set off an alarm or something?' My heart jumped in fear at just the thought of meeting him again. 'What if he comes in here?'

Wax reached over and shook the bottle of pills next to his bed. 'I'll be putting these in his port … it's not the first time,' he said with a grin. 'Don't worry. He can't see you and you'll be with me.'

I looked into his face, filled with confidence, cute dimples and rosy cheeks and didn't know whether to be hurt or happy about what he'd just said. I knew what he meant, but it made me feel kind of empty.

'Shower?' he said, simply.

He laughed at what must have been the terror on my face.

Whatever it was, it worked because all sappy thoughts evaporated as I took in his huge grin. He was already pulling me to my feet and leading me towards the door. 'It has to be quick. It's better not to show up at all than be late with my uncle. He eats at eight.'

Wax seemed to enjoy teasing me – especially about sex. I guess he did always smooth it over afterwards, though. He led me by the hand out of his room, just as Ollie was leaving his.

Ollie looked straight at our joined hands and smiled, with a hint of concern, at his brother. Wax's expression was blank and clearly dared him to say one word.

'Where are you going?' Ollie asked, taking the safer approach, and I breathed a little easier.

'Nowhere. Listen, I need you to make sure everyone stays up here, OK? I need to take care of something with Becks.'

Ollie looked disappointed and I could tell he wanted to protest, but Wax put up a hand. 'I can't have you there. Not tonight.' A long look passed between them where Ollie clearly made up his mind not to argue. 'I'll come and find you as soon as it's over.'

Ollie looked at me to check I was OK with it and I nodded with a wry smile that totally said that I wasn't. Then Tallulah went to come out of the room and Ollie turned and herded her back in with a final, 'Be careful.'

Wax pulled me along to the bathroom and went straight to the shower and turned it on. The room soon felt balmy with steam. 'You said you were *dying* for a shower.' He grinned at his own silly pun and pulled his black t-shirt over his head.

I was already sweating in the clothes he'd loaned me, not able to help myself gazing at his body with every square inch covered in ink. There were geometric lines, Celtic symbols, Sanskrit verse, eagle's wings and creeping vines. I wondered what it all meant. He watched me watching him and popped the button on his jeans. Then he pushed them down and kicked them off, till he was left in just his black body-hugging shorts.

As I suspected, the ink travelled the length of his legs, even venturing onto his feet. 'So many,' I whispered.

He kicked his clothes into a heap and stepped closer in one move. My breathing went out of rhythm, as if I'd forgotten how to do it. Along with the steam, I felt a little lightheaded.

'Tattoo parlours stay open all night,' he said by way of explanation that didn't really explain anything at all. He was looking down between us and his hands were already picking up the hem of my – his – white t-shirt. He paused and looked into my eyes for permission.

I don't know what came over me. I felt quite unlike myself. I didn't want to be scared. I wanted to be carefree like the characters in the films. Except then I remembered that Wax was a hot, dangerous English boy I barely knew, all too ready to show me everything and any semblance of confidence drained away. Terrified, I swallowed hard and nodded.

He surprised me by kissing me then. The top came up, grazing my face without me paying too much attention. Then it was gone. He put his mouth next to my ear. 'We're just showering … but soon.'

He pulled away and stepped under the water. Part of me felt strangely bereft and the rest relieved. We didn't have time and he was slowing things down between us; I should feel grateful. 'Get rid of those,' he said, looking back at me and dropping his eyes to the track pants.

I nodded and pushed them down, wobbling as I tried to get them over my plaster. Dripping arms held me and pushed me back to the bath where I could perch and remove them easily. His face was there and then it was gone, returned to the shower. I couldn't help remembering his wet skin so close to me.

I limped closer to the shower in just my bra and panties. The cubicle wasn't that big so it would be a squeeze. He turned and put his head back in the spray and his eyes never left mine. I knew what it meant. It was a question: would I keep my underwear on or take it off? His had gone. I felt my cheeks prickle and opted quickly for bra off, knickers on. The thought of getting them off sexily over my plaster was just too fraught with embarrassment. As it was, I'd have to stand weirdly to keep it dry.

Wax simply turned, giving me his back for privacy and began to soap his body. I was grateful. He passed the soap behind him, without looking, and I lathered it in my hands. I marvelled at the ink all over his body. He wasn't that old to have all this done. He literally must have got them all the time.

I washed and rinsed off and Wax turned back to face me. It was astonishing how much power he had in that look. It turned up my pulse like a dial. His hair was flattened to his face and he pushed it back with his hands so it stuck out in all directions. It didn't matter; he was incredibly good-looking.

He smiled like I'd given something away, and, just when I wanted to shove him to stop teasing me, there was a knock at the door.

'Dinner!' an unfamiliar voice said. 'Mr Waxley-Black warns you not to keep him waiting.'

Wax had watched me the whole time, but now looked regretful. His eyes dropped to my lips and then back to my eyes. 'You're safe … for now,' he finished with a grin.

Wax walked me back with a towel wrapped tantalisingly low on his hips. Me, not so much. I hobbled with mine clutched to my chest in case it fell. When we reached his room, he threw me another white t-shirt. 'Be quick,' he said.

I tugged the sweatpants back on and watched as he pushed his legs into black skinny jeans and a grey t-shirt, leaving his feet bare. 'Come on,' he said, taking my hand.

My first sleep and shower with a boy was over.

THE DINING ROOM reminded me of one of those films where the mega-rich family eat from opposite ends of an extremely long dining table. This room was dark green and tastefully decorated in the style of the period in which the house was built: dark wood, china in cabinets and chandeliers hanging above the table. Two places were laid at one end, reminding me, brutally, that I wasn't there. I continually forgot and wondered if that would ever change.

Wax's uncle was already seated and folded up a news-paper when he saw him. Three cloche-covered dishes were already in front of him.

Wax pulled out his chair and sat at the place set next to his uncle. He nodded towards the armchair next to the wall, opposite him, as I was frozen to the spot. I sat nervously, still wary of what his uncle and maid could sense or see.

'How's the experiment going?' Wax asked, lifting a cloche and spooning out what looked like mashed potato, then some sort of casserole, onto his plate.

My stomach rumbled so loudly that I clutched it with my hands. It smelled delicious. I prayed nobody heard.

'Well,' his uncle said, pouring some red wine. 'There's just one small ingredient missing.'

I suddenly felt chilled at what that might be. His uncle was stern and scary and reminded me of an old-fashioned school master. He was a tall, harsh-looking man, without any real warmth in him at all. I wondered how on earth Wax would spike his drink. He didn't seem to miss a thing.

Wax didn't seem nervous. He continued to eat slowly.

'You have something of mine, I believe?' His uncle held out his hand without even looking at him.

Wax stopped chewing and froze.

So did I. I couldn't believe we'd been busted so quickly.

Wax reached into his back pocket and slapped the little book in his hand.

'Thank you,' his uncle said, matter-of-factly, and continued eating.

Wax was left staring at his plate. 'What is it?'

'You know what it is.'

Wax rolled his eyes, losing patience. 'OK, why? What are you even trying to do? Who's Ainsley? What's all this about?' He dropped his silverware down on his plate with a loud clink and sat back in his chair.

His uncle, knowing that the meal was very definitely over, did the same, a lot more softly. He sipped his wine, apparently amused, making me want to smack the smug look straight off his face.

He looked at Wax as if he was weighing him up; deciding whether or not to tell him. All I could hear was his finger-nails tapping on his glass and a loud clock on the mantle-piece. 'You've heard of the Blackwood curse, no doubt?'

Wax bobbed his head. He wanted to draw him out in conversation. 'A bit.'

'A few generations ago, there were two Waxley-Black brothers: Ainsley and Jedediah. There was a relative from the Blackwood house on the other side of the woods called Lucinda.'

Wax's eyes went straight to mine and I mouthed, *Lucinda?*

His uncle narrowed his as if he'd caught his surprise. 'What is it?'

For a horrible moment I thought Wax had given me away.

'Nothing … I thought I heard something. Go on,' Wax said, turning to him again.

My breathing returned slowly to normal. I ached for him to ask who the hell Lucinda was and how Lila fitted in, but knew he couldn't without tipping our hand, so all we could do was listen, dumbly.

'Anyway. Where was I?' his uncle said. 'Lucinda was promised to Jedediah, the oldest, set to inherit the estate, as you would expect. She had a substantial dowry and would replenish the fortunes of both houses. But both brothers were wasting their time dallying with the penniless Black-wood daughter of dubious birth. Lucinda's father had to threaten to take his daughter out of the equation to put a stop to it. They had to avoid the scandal at all costs and she went ahead and married Jedediah in the end, I believe.'

So Jed was definitely the oldest. I wondered why we had never heard of Lucinda before. Although my aunt had mentioned how the parents of Jed's intended had got involved in his affair with Lila. It made me wonder if they were responsible for her disappearance. Something wasn't adding up. There had been no announcements in the papers that year.

'What happened to Ainsley?' Wax asked.

'Oh, he threw himself into his career … an army man. Often the fate for second sons.' He sneered at that. I'd put money on Wax's father being the eldest of the two of them.

Wax was doing really well, faking conversational calm, when I knew he wanted answers as much as I did and not able to give away what he knew. 'What did Jed do – apart from running the estate, I mean?' he said, daring to fish a bit more and picking at his dinner again.

'Oh, investments mainly. And, of course, the mine.'

Wax clinked his knife loudly on his plate as he almost dropped it.

'Something wrong?' his uncle asked. He was watching him closely.

I was already on the edge of my seat, heart banging in my chest, ready to get up.

'Nothing,' Wax said, shaking his head and looking him confidently in the eye. 'What happened to it?'

His uncle shrugged and poured himself another glass. 'Get the port,' he said, pointing to the sideboard next to me.

Wax got up, wandered over to me and raised his eyebrows in the universal language of 'what the hell is going on?' He checked over his shoulder and his uncle was still droning on about the mine and how he believed it was on the edges of their land, which, by the sound of it, was quite substantial. It had run out of tin and been left to dilapidate.

It gave Wax time to take out a small wrap from his pocket and quickly tip the contents into the bottle. He held it up to his eyeline to see how much was there and circled it around like a chemistry flask. 'Is tin worth anything?' he asked, pouring a large measure into the glass and wandering back with it. Another discrepancy. We'd been under the impression it was silver.

He put it down directly in front of his uncle. 'It was a good income for the family back then. Now, it isn't worth the expense of digging it out – not with something infinitely more priceless than precious metal.'

Wax's eyes went immediately to mine and I shrugged. I had no clue what he meant. 'Did the brothers get on?' Wax asked, in an attempt to smooth over his surprise.

Oblivious, his uncle shrugged. 'As good as any, I suppose.'

'So where did the curse come into it?'

His uncle looked thoughtful for a moment and turned in his chair to face him. I wished I could get a closer look at his face. 'Have you ever noticed that in each generation since, there have always been two Waxley-Black brothers and one Blackwood daughter?'

I certainly didn't and I was sure Wax didn't either. We hadn't bothered to look into the generations in between.

'Well, there were,' Wax's uncle said, very satisfied with himself. 'Every generation to fight for some stupid girl every time.'

It made no sense, and I could tell Wax was thinking the same thing.

'But there aren't two this time … not anymore,' Wax said darkly, his whole demeanour changed.

Ollie was so real to me that I kind of forgot that Wax had a very different life with him when he was alive. He must have been devastated when he died.

His uncle conceded his point with a bob of his head. Wax was losing patience fast and pushed his plate away from him. 'And, anyway, what's any of this got to do with the mine or what you're doing in the cellar?'

Uncle gave a blast of air from his nostrils in amusement and threw back the contents of his glass in one go. 'There is something else in that mine. Something the brothers knew about all that time ago. And that spell is the secret to getting it.'

Wax was clearly waiting for him to tell him what it was. When it didn't come, he blurted, 'Who is Lila?'

Her name had been conspicuously missing until that point even though I instinctively knew it had been her the brothers had been fighting over. The amusement immediately dropped from Wax's uncle's face, then came back as fake as it was before. Without looking him directly in the eye, he asked, 'You've spoken to her? Is she here?' His eagerness for the answer was evident even from where I was sitting.

Wax was studying his face closely and I could tell he was as confused as I was. Except, I guess, he knew his uncle better than I did. 'What do you want with her?'

His uncle turned his head to glare at him, his face now implacable and hard. 'Listen to me, boy. If this spirit has come to you, and I suspect that she has, then run. Run as fast as you can, because she is bad news. She was trouble when she was alive and can be nothing but trouble now she's dead.'

I had a thousand questions and I'm sure Wax did too. He was the bad guy and even he was warning us against Lila. I believed what he was saying, but something was off. Wax, I could tell, wasn't sure. He had spoken to her and was evidently weighing what he knew in his mind. To him, she needed saving. I didn't know Wax's uncle and I certainly didn't like him, but I was sure he was telling the truth. It was something in his smugness.

In the end, I had to stand up and shout, 'No!'

The candle in the middle of the table went out and the salt cellar fell over. Wax looked over at me, amazed by my outburst.

His uncle looked around him, immediately alert. 'Is she here now?'

'Don't listen to him, Wax. There is something not right.'

'No,' Wax said, turning to his uncle again and completely ignoring me. 'I'm bombarded with nuisances all the time, remember?' he said, flashing me an impatient look.

I sat back into my chair flattened, bewildered that he wouldn't listen.

His uncle stood up, taking the bottle of port with him, and swayed a little. 'I'm off to bed.' His words seemed a little slurred. 'I'll leave you lovebirds to it.'

That did it; I knew he knew more than he was letting on. The pills were working and he'd let something slip. He walked, a little unsteadily, towards the door, mumbling away to himself. I was already on my feet.

'Hang on, I'll help you,' Wax said, moving quickly to get under his arm. He looked over his shoulder and mouthed, 'Stay put.'

I scowled. I guessed he wanted to make sure his uncle got safely tucked up in bed.

By the time I'd drifted out to the kitchen, Wax had come back with a handheld mirror in his hand.

'Did you hear him?' I asked as he walked past me and went straight to the pantry.

'Come on,' he said, completely ignoring my question.

I caught up and we went through the musty pantry to the cellar. 'Aren't we going to talk about what your uncle just said?' I tried again.

Wax was already opening the cellar door and turning on the light. 'What's there to talk about? You don't believe his shit, do you?' He turned to glare at me and I almost bumped into him. 'It's what all this has been about, bringing her here to capture her. You just don't get it.'

The trouble was, as I limped down the stairs behind him, in a weird way, I did get it.

'Think about it, though, Wax. Why does he want to capture her?' I knew his uncle was an asshole and Wax saw the worst side of that, but I just didn't feel good about this. His emotions were ruling him and he was missing something crucial.

When we reached the bottom, Wax went straight to the bottle lever, pushed it and the panel moved across; like it did before. Everything looked just as we'd left it; candles lit on the altar and pentagon with artifacts on the floor.

Wax put the mirror down at the point of the pentagon with no relic. 'Right!' he said, backing off to stand next to me. 'I just need to say the incantation.'

179

I felt a strange sense of relief when I remembered his uncle had taken the book, thinking it would buy me some time to convince him against this.

Instead, he smiled spitefully and pointed at his temple. 'Good job I memorized it. Photographic memory,' he said.

'Great,' I said, under my breath, and looked around for somewhere to sit.

'No, come here,' he said, his tone softer. He picked up my hand. 'I want you with me in case anything happens.'

It warmed me a little and I gave his hand a squeeze. Then I looked down at the pentagon nervously. I was sure we were dabbling in things we didn't understand.

Wax began to chant words that sounded like a priest, except I didn't think it was Latin. It sounded like nothing I'd ever heard before. He said it over and over and nothing happened.

Then I did start to feel strange; a little lightheaded. The light in the room had got unusually bright. Then it went dark and I let out a scream that came out of me before I could stop it. My chest hurt and I had trouble breathing.

I began to gasp for air.

'Becks … Becks.' I could hear Wax, but he sounded further and further away.

The pain and breathlessness gradually subsided and I looked up at the only source of light. It was circular and directly above me, so close I could touch the glass. I smacked my hands against it. I saw Wax's face look down at me through it. 'No! No!' he shouted.

Then I realised where I was. I was the one trapped behind the mirror.

CHAPTER 17

'*B*ecks! Becks!' Wax's eyes were pleading.

'Wax!' I screamed back, clawing at the glass. Then hissed with pain as my nails snapped scraping the underside of the mirror. Then, with one final, 'Becks!' he disappeared as if he was pulled away.

I collapsed to the floor, wailing his name. My bloodied fingers stung against the dusty floor, proving it was real. I couldn't even kid myself it was one of my dreams. We'd been cruelly tricked. It refuelled my tears and I folded into a ball. I'm not sure how long I lay there. Time lost all meaning as I sobbed into my hands. In the end I guessed I'd simply cried myself out. The grime, blood and salt felt tight on my face where it had dried in smears.

I sat up and looked around me. It wasn't completely dark. The round mirror above me acted like a skylight to the room and cast a grey light. I began to recognise the things around me. It was an exact replica of the basement above me, but a greyed-out, mirror image. The way the world sometimes looks when you wake up in the night and you aren't fully awake.

I clambered to my feet, a little shakily as my knees had been bent for so long. My cast had gone. That threw me for a moment. That maybe it was a dream, nightmare or simply a spell. I knew I was dead, so, I guess, anything was possible. What was immediately apparent was that, here, I was a different representation of myself than the plane Wax existed on. Getting back to him felt more urgent than ever now. Before I disappeared or was taken from him completely.

There was no pentagon on the floor and the altar was simply a bare piece of furniture. I went closer as there appeared to be no objects on it at all. It made a kind of sense. They were the tools of magic that got me here; they wouldn't exist on this side.

Just then, as I had the thought, the room flooded in yellow light and I had to bring my forearm up to shield my eyes. I let my guard down slowly as I got used to the light and slowly edged closer to the altar. I could see that the back of it was glass – *no, a mirror* – from a big, carved dresser. On the other side, I hadn't noticed it before as it had been behind the altar candles and covered by a cloth.

I ventured closer as I could hear voices. My nose was almost touching the glass. I was viewing the outside world – the one with Wax – as if from the inside of a TV. The sound was low and muffled, like they were talking into a bottle, but people came into view and I could just make out what they were saying.

'Get her out!' Wax was shouting, menacingly, down at someone.

A girl was standing in front of him in a light-grey, full skirted, Victorian dress. *Lila.*

'I cannot,' she said back to him. 'Only another Blackwood can do that. With the spell you just created, with one foot in this world and one in the next. That is the curse of our families, I fear,' she said, regretfully.

Even from where I stood, she seemed over the top and dramatic and not sincere at

all.

'A life for a life, or afterlife, as in this case,' a male voice said. When he came into view, I could see that Wax's uncle had joined them. He'd been standing next to the altar and still held the covering from the mirror in his hand. 'Don't be rude, Bret. Say thank you and goodbye to your young friend here. She has made a huge sacrifice today. Thanks to her, Lila is free of her prison and we can all go on with our lives.' Then I knew; he'd removed the covering deliberately, so I could be part of the conversation. How I hated him.

Wax immediately turned to see what he meant and looked straight at me. His whole body seemed to sag in a mixture of relief and misery and he ran and put his hands to the glass.

I did the same on my side and looked intently into his bloodshot eyes.

'I'm so sorry,' he said, then he scratched at the edges of the frame for a latch or a handle to find his way in.

It was useless. Even I could see that. I started to cry. 'Wax!' I wailed.

Wax stopped scraping at the glass and his hands dropped to his sides. Tears were escaping from his eyes too. 'I'll get you out. I promise.'

Wax's uncle came and stood next to his shoulder, put an arm around him and smiled directly at me. It seemed he could see me now. 'Quite impossible, I'm afraid. She was the last of the line of living Blackwoods.' He picked up a broom and began sweeping away the white powder that made up the pentagon on the floor, knowing I could never remember how to recreate it. 'It would take Blackwood blood to do that.'

How I loathed him then.

Wax looked as stunned and broadsided as I was, but I could see the anger building inside him and I knew what was coming. He was clenching his jaw, balling his fists and hunching his shoulders as if readying for battle.

'Steady now, Bret. Calm yourself.' His uncle sounded a little more nervous than I'd seen so far. He was circling around to protect Lila, who was backing away. He whispered something to her over his shoulder and she disappeared from view. I guessed she'd run to safety or to get help.

'Wax!' I called. 'Stop! Don't give him the satisfaction.'

'Listen to your little girlfriend there.' Smug amusement was now back in his voice.

'Please, Wax.'

Wax was shaking his head as if he was arguing in his own mind. Maybe he was hearing other voices taunting or goading him on. He took a threatening step towards his uncle, who put up his hands defensively. 'Come on, boy. You hardly know her. The spell worked. You are free now to go on with your life.'

I thought about what his uncle was saying. Wax could be free if he wanted. It was an opportunity for him to escape.

'It makes no sense. Becks isn't alive,' Wax said, desperately. 'I know that because I can see her. Isn't that the whole reason the spell worked?'

His uncle smiled mischievously and held his arms open wide. Lila came back into view and glided effortlessly into them, followed quickly by four burly men and the nurse. The ones used to control Wax's violent episodes.

'Oh no!' I cried in frustration, banging on the glass.

'Lila,' his uncle said, gazing into the young girl's eyes.

'Ainsley!' she said back and then they kissed.

I had no idea what was going on. It was like a slow-motion car crash as I watched the horror spread on Wax's face, the grotesque kiss and the hired hands closing in to get a hold of him. A strange understanding crept up my spine. Wax's uncle wasn't just named after the dead Waxley-Black brother; somehow he had a connection to him.

Wax was backing up but had drawn the same conclusion as me, because he was shouting, 'How? How is this happening?'

His uncle pulled Lila into his chest and smiled benignly as the nurse held up a huge syringe. She flicked it with her finger to remove any bubbles and squeezed a little of the liquid out. Then the men closed in.

'Run, Wax!' I screamed. I began to cry as he turned his back towards me, protecting me from the menace coming towards him. 'Go … I'm the safe one,' I trailed off before I called him a fool.

They were quickly upon him and the nurse efficiently stabbed his neck with the needle. All I could do was scream at the top of my lungs, over and over, as I watched him collapse and the men carry him away by his arms and legs. I whimpered 'Wax' helplessly, as they carried him out of view. I knew they were taking him back to the bed I'd seen him in that first day and that they would never let him be free.

The uncle picked up some of the artifacts left on the floor. 'Jed will be here in the morning. His father will calm him.'

I couldn't believe what I was hearing. Both sons had the same name as their ancestors.

'What about her?' Lila said, nodding her head in my direction.

Ainsley came towards me, smiling, and picked up the cloth that normally covered the glass. 'Cover the mirrors,' he said, laughing. She joined him as if it was an in-joke. Then, as my world went dark, I heard the thump and crank of the mechanism. The wall was closing. I wanted to shout out not to leave me alone, but I knew it was useless.

'Don't worry, she's trapped. Once the malevolent ones discover her, she won't survive for long.'

I sank to the floor and cried; great gut-wrenching sobs. I had fallen down a well, without a hope in hell of anyone ever finding me. I had no idea what was happening to Wax now that they had what they wanted. They could be killing him for all I knew. I had to help him before Jed came in the morning. *Jed? What was going on here?*

I sniffed back the tears, stood and turned a slow circle. I was in a blue-grey version of the cellar. The partition was open – or wasn't there on this side. There was no red button that I could see, so it pointed to it not being an exact representation of what was on the other side. I thought about it as I climbed the steps. This world was so dark and gloomy.

I screamed as a rat scurried across the next step just as I almost trod on it.

I stood, shaking, holding the rail, getting my breath back and dragging my grimy forearm across my brow. I was sweating, my clothes were sticking to me, so I pulled my top away from my skin to let in air. Then I edged slowly up the steps one by one; straining my ears for the slightest sound, dreading what was on the other side of the pantry door.

The shelves were different. Tins and packets of cereal were replaced by jars and wooden vegetable racks lined with paper. A cold sensation seeped into my body as I grasped the doorknob to the kitchen and slowly opened it. I peered cautiously inside. The modern chrome and wood finish were gone, replaced by a huge range and long wooden table. Pots of varying sizes hung from the ceiling above it and flagstones covered the floor. I couldn't be sure, but it seemed I was standing in the kitchen of a hundred and fifty years ago. Except everything was muted and grey, like the warmth had been sucked out of it and a dry mist hung in the air.

I tried to rationalise it as best I could. I was stuck in a spell, designed as a prison, that was constructed in Victorian times. That was why it didn't match the other side of the mirror. It was a reflection of the house back when Lila was alive.

I shuddered with a mixture of fear and cold and moved out into the hallway.

Laughter and then a scream pierced the air through the house. I flattened myself against the wall, heart pumping as my eyes adjusted to the change in the light. I swallowed and inched along the wall to the foot of the stairs. I had to make my way to Wax's room to find him. If he was there on the other side, the chances were I could reach him from here too.

Nothing much had changed in the hall. Except the light from the stained-glass windows only shone blue and the portrait at the end was a smirking likeness of a man with a striking resemblance to Wax's uncle. I hadn't noticed it in the modern house. I simply couldn't believe he was there, still affecting lives today. The one next to it was softer, kinder. *Jed.*

I went along the dark landing until I came to Wax's door. I turned the knob and pushed it wide open and another door took its place. I did the same, again and again, over and over and there was always another door to bar my way.

I fell against it as hopeless tears streaked down my face. This had all the hallmarks of a terrible nightmare. I could have taken heart from that if only it was likely to wake me up.

There was another shriek and I stood still, holding my breath. I was terrified of making a sound. It sounded like it came from the next door.

Tallulah? My heart thumped at the possibility that the others could be behind that door. I retraced my steps and turned the handle slowly.

The room was cold and empty. The modern furnishings of a teenage boy had gone and were replaced by a modest wooden bed and heavy dark furniture. A china basin and pitcher stood on a sideboard where his desk should be. It was blue-grey like all the others, but an orange light began to grow in the glass above the dressing table.

A mirror they'd forgotten to cover. The idea came to me like a bolt of lightning. It became brighter and brighter, but, strangely, threw no light into the room.

I edged closer until I could put out my hand and touch the surface.

Another shriek of laughter made me snatch back my hand. There was definitely boys' voices and chatter. My heart sped up. They were all still in Ollie's room.

I put out my hand again and touched the glass with the tips of my fingers. The light flashed white and the glass felt so hot that I couldn't bear it for long. Then it settled to a warm glow and I cautiously moved my face closer to the glass.

I could see them all lounging and laughing. Some were sitting on the floor, Joe was on a beanbag. Archie was munching chips. Ollie was play-fighting with Tallulah on the bed, setting off her peals of laughter when he tickled her or bit her neck. It was such an unremarkable scene, but it warmed my heart so much it ached when I compared it to the cold and the blue of where I was. 'Guys! Guys!' I whispered as loudly as I dared. I still wasn't sure if I was alone in this place. Then I knocked my knuckles against the glass. 'Hey! It's me. Can you hear me? It's Beccah!'

'Shh!' Josh said. 'Did you hear that?'

'Hear what?' Ollie said, freezing mid-hover over Tallulah, to listen. 'I can't hear anything.'

'Ollie! It's me, Beccah.'

'Beccah?' Ollie said, looking around him, confused.

Every part of me wilted in relief as I thanked God they could hear me. 'I'm here. Over here.'

They were all looking around them, trying to home in on the direction of my voice.

'Here!'

They all got it at the same time and looked directly at the mirror.

'Shit!' Tallulah said, finally sitting up.

Ollie scrambled off the bed and came closer to peer right at me. One by one the others came and joined him. Tallulah pushed in front by crawling through on her knees. 'How did you get in there?' she said, her expression so childlike it almost made me laugh.

I'd never been so glad to see her or anybody in my life as I quickly spewed out the lead up to what had happened.

'But why, I don't get it?' Ollie said, looking confused and concerned.

'Your uncle wanted Lila out all along.' I suddenly became aware of where I was and looked all around me, nervously. I wasn't sure how long I had or if I'd be disturbed. 'Now I'm the one who's trapped and Wax has been drugged and I can't get into his room,' I said, looking back at him, desperately.

Ollie frowned while he thought through what I'd said. 'Mirrors,' he said, with a slow nod. 'If I understand it right, your only contact with our world is through mirrors. Wax doesn't have any mirrors.'

Oh my God. He was right. I hadn't noticed.

'It's a common way for spirits to come through. They act like portals. Wax hates them.'

It made so much sense, but didn't help me at all.

Then he grinned.

'What?' I said, seeing the lightbulb go on in his eyes.

'But you know what Wax has got?'

I shook my head.

'An impressive bank of state-of-the-art computer screens.'

He was right, but my half-hearted smile faded. I didn't understand what difference that made. 'I still can't get into that room. It's closed to me.'

Ollie thought about it, then switched his attention onto something out of view. His fingers clicked away on something I quickly guessed was a keyboard. He pulled his laptop closer. 'But you can in here,' he said absently.

His hands worked lightning fast.

Then a deep moan echoed behind me. 'Shaaaade.'

I turned my head and screamed.

A WARM TRICKLE ran down my leg as I stood staring at the apparition. It was pale and translucent, but I could clearly see the female clothes of the mid 1800s and the ringlets in her hair. At a certain angle, she could have been drawn from chalk. *A hostile one,* I remembered from Wax's descriptions of ghosts.

Everything shrieked for me to run, but I could barely breathe. I'd heard people say on TV that they froze in fear and I'd never truly understood what it meant until that point. But I was. Absolutely and completely paralyzed by terror.

Then I heard it. A rumble like thunder. And the word, 'Lucinda?'

It felt like it shook the room, it was shouted in such anger.

'This way.' Before I knew what was happening, my legs were moving and I was running along the landing to the servants' staircase, next to Wax's uncle's room, and straight down to the kitchen.

'Faster,' the ghost hissed over her shoulder. 'He is almost upon us.'

Somehow my legs pounded the floor after her, blindly, even though my eyes were wide and my nostrils filled with the bitter smell of sheer terror. Air rasped my throat as it occurred to me I had no idea where I was going or what I was running from. Even so, my eyes stayed fixed on it. The apparition could move remarkably fast.

Then I took one look over my shoulder and the world went to slow motion. Bone-white hands reached for me from a swirl of black robes and an evil grin flashed from gnashing white teeth, just visible from a hood almost completely covering its face.

Before I could let out a scream at the grab of his hand, I was yanked sideways, into a closet beneath the staircase that took us into a long tunnel. One I had no idea was there and I was sure Wax didn't either. I took a moment to recover, then continued to run, making the blue-flamed torches dotted in the walls flicker. Whatever it was had almost had me.

My head was now pounding and my throat was sore from stale air hacking through my lungs. It was no good, I couldn't continue the pace and slowed back down to a walk.

'Not long now,' the ghost said.

The ceiling to the tunnel became lower and smoother and a door came into sight. It opened into a closet the other end and then into the maroon hallway I recognised as my aunt's place. At least I now knew how my ghostly visitors were getting in and out of the house.

As I got my bearings, I began to catch my breath. Then it dawned on me that my aunt's hallway was not in the suffocating, monochrome grey of Wax's house. I was about to relax in relief when I remembered the ghost, hovering a little way off, watching me. 'This house is frozen in time. Nothing here changes,' she said, wistfully. Her voice rang like wind chimes on the air, up to the vaulted ceiling. It made me wonder if she was on this plane at all.

'Who are you?' I said eventually. I guessed if she was going to do me harm, she would have done it by then. I frowned at the blind stupidity that had made me follow her like that. I guessed panic would do that to a person.

'Lucinda Trevelyan, of the Devonshire Trevelyans,' she said and bobbed a curtsey.

I realised that her silence meant she was waiting for a response. 'Oh … Rebecca Whitely,' I said, with a little bow of my head and not even attempting a curtsey.

She nodded knowingly. 'Wise. To change one's name to the furthest possible from Blackwood.'

It startled me. It hadn't occurred to me that my mother may have consciously thought that. I wondered for the first time how much my parents knew. 'You're not a Blackwood,' I said. It explained why she wasn't in the line-up of portraits.

She pointed behind me at the secret passage door. 'It should hold him at bay for a while. There is a charm barrier here that a Waxley-Black may not pass.'

My mind whirled with the information I knew, trying to test what she was saying, but she was right. The angry one never came out of the secret passages. Then my mind shot to the round house. Maybe the ban existed when they were alive and was why they met in there. 'Who?' I said. My blood rushing in fear at the terrifying thing I'd only just escaped. 'Who is chasing us?'

'Jedediah,' she said, simply. As if it was the most obvious thing in the world. She began to glide her way down the hallway.

I followed her, in shock, forgetting what she was in my eager search for information. From what I'd seen, he didn't look human at all. None of it tallied with what I thought I already knew. 'But I thought he and Ainsley were still alive?' It was ridiculous, of course. But after everything Wax's uncle had explained, it certainly pointed to that.

She led me into my aunt's drawing room. The one where we'd met on my first day. She would be long tucked up in bed. The room was as I remembered it, except the fire had burned itself out.

She sat in my aunt's armchair and I sat stiffly in the other. *I was dead and sitting with a ghost.* I guess my fear was subsiding because of the sheer absurdity of the situation. She wasn't going to hurt me, so I may as well get some information. 'Can you tell me why Jedediah is out to get me?'

She began to pour the remnants of the tea left in my aunt's flask. 'It's barely warm, but better than nothing, dear.' She passed me a cup. 'You're American, aren't you? I had so wished to travel to that part of the world.'

I took the cup, a little exasperated. 'Yes, I am … Are you going to tell me what's going on, please? I need to get back to my friends.'

She nodded and let out a deep sigh, as if what she had to say was inevitable. 'Ah yes, the poor Waxley-Black boy, ill-used for a very long time. And so the cycle begins again.'

I put my cup down roughly, spilling the tea over the sides and onto the small table. 'What cycle?' I was sick of hearing riddles and half-truths from everyone. As I went to get up, she put out a hand to stop and gave me a look that said she'd stall no longer.

'You feel so real,' she said on a breath.

I sat back down and stared at her, waiting, only taking my eyes from her at a noise I thought I heard from the hallway. If it was the angry ghost of Jed, it wasn't going to give up that easily. 'Do you know why they trapped me?' I said, focusing on her again.

She nodded sadly and looked at her fingers in her lap. 'I'm afraid I do. It's to live again and for what is in the mine – The Elixir of Life.'

My mind went into freefall. Back to Wax's uncle's comment at dinner: *Infinitely more priceless than precious metal. The mine. Of course*. We knew there had to be more to it.

Then she looked directly at me and shook her head. 'I swear, I had no idea at first. No one did. It had to be someone with a foot in both worlds and a Blackwood. You were Heaven-sent, to them.'

Her eyes went to the middle distance, so I held back my questions in the hope she'd continue on with her ramble of memories and tell me something useful.

'I came here as a young girl, betrothed to Jedediah Waxley-Black. He was set to inherit the estate. I was a Black-wood cousin with a good dowry and he would become a viscount one day. It was a good marriage for a girl of my standing.' She sounded regretful.

'And Jed was the oldest?' I said, needing to clarify that to make sense of it all.

'Yes … by one year. Ainsley, as second son, had to make his own fortune.'

I was more confused by the minute. She was speaking with affection for Jed. Another clang from behind me was a timely reminder of the terrifying reaper who'd almost had me. He seemed the furthest thing from the gentleman Lucinda was describing.

'I came here for one idyllic summer on my betrothal. The house was alive and beautiful then. There were flowers and trees and the master of the house entertained. I was young, full of hope and in love. Jed was a handsome, serious, boy. His younger brother was stronger and more confident than he was. Of course, that was far easier for the one who didn't have the weight of responsibility.'

I saw immediately, the picture she was painting. I'd seen it in the weird pang of nostalgia I'd felt when I'd first glimpsed the round house. It was as though I was back there again …

'WHAT ARE YOU DOING IN HERE?'

I was sitting on the love seat in the orangery and the Victorian man in front of me was devastatingly handsome. His dark eyes flashed and he angrily swept a hand up through the dark curls framing his face. *It was Jedediah.* The family resemblance was uncanny. He looked so much like Ollie.

'But you've ignored me all afternoon. I just thought …'

I looked around me and guessed immediately that I was invisible and it was Lucinda Jed saw sitting there. How lovely she looked alive, with her peaches and cream skin and blond curls, only just contained in the straw bonnet she wore.

Then he surprised me by coming closer and falling to one knee in front of her. *'Please believe me when I say it is not safe for you here. Allow me to do what I need to do and then I promise you, all will be clear.'*

·   ·   ·

It was a bewildering vision and, before I could question it too deeply, I was back in the room. Lucinda was still talking about what a good man Jedediah was.

'I remember his portrait,' I said, recalling the gloomy faces on Wax's staircase. It seemed nothing like the earnest passion I'd seen in the memory of Jedediah and even harder to make the leap to the thing that lurked in the halls.

My eyes continually strayed to the doorknob, expecting it to turn, but all I could hear was a curious scraping of wood against a bare floor. My breathing went shallow and I looked at Lucinda to gauge her reaction; she seemed completely unaffected.

'Jed was my great love,' she was saying, wistfully.

I sat staring at her, trying to work it all out. She had come to marry the eldest son, Jed, and evidently fallen for him, so everything should have worked out. But her demeanour suggested otherwise. 'Did he not love you?' My heart began to sink as I was already guessing the answer to that. 'And Ainsley, who did he love?' I said, cautiously.

'Lila,' she said, simply, on an exhale. As if there was nothing more inevitable in the world. 'She ensnared them both.' Her face darkened. 'Nothing but a jumped-up lady's maid. A brat sired by the lord of this house, with a servant, and she had both Waxley-Black boys eating out of the palm of her hand like a pair of sparrows.'

I compared what she said with what I already knew. The rumours and the legend were starting to make sense.

'Ainsley was earmarked for the military as a second son and greatly resented that his brother got everything by simple timing of birth.'

'And Jed?' I said, looking at the door again; the noises were getting closer.

'He was a kind and sensitive soul who spoke of books and

poetry. He was devoted to his brother, but there were never two brothers born more poles apart.'

A bang against a wall made me jump.

She didn't appear to hear and took on a far-off look again. 'His father envisioned a strong, lusty son to take over the estate.'

'What happened?'

'When Jed's affection for Lila came to light, my father offered to put up the capital to open the mine. It was offered with one condition; that it was given to the new couple as a wedding present if he married me without any scandal. Jed's father seized the opportunity to pay his debts. But the condition came with a strict caveat; that Jed cease all connection with Lila, otherwise my father would see to it that all his loans were called in, driving the family into financial ruin.

'I'm not sure what deliberations were made, but Jed accepted. He even offered Ainsley a percentage feeling keenly, as he always did, the inequality of their station. However, soon after, Lord Waxley-Black conveniently became bedridden and then Lila saw to all our futures, one by one.'

I watched as Lucinda gripped the arms of her chair to contain her anger. She'd been wronged. They all had. It seemed everyone had fallen prey to Lila's ambitions. 'So, what happened? All the while I spoke, I felt the angry spirit of Jedediah was getting closer by the minute. 'What happened with the mine?' There was a loud beating on the door. I moved to the edge of my seat, anxious to move on. I knew we didn't have much time. 'How can Jed and Ainsley still be alive?' As I said the ridiculous words, I wanted to run. Jed was now in the hall and trying to get into the room.

'They are not alive,' she said, looking me in the eye. 'And neither do they rest in peace.'

I was on my feet. Pleading with my eyes for us to move

and looking at the door as splinters flew out from the centre of it. I could barely speak as I forced out the words, 'So Wax's uncle … isn't Ainsley?' I said, breathlessly. I had to find out. This may be the only opportunity I got. My thoughts were all over the place, wanting to run and needing to find out where that left Wax.

'In body, no. He's but a namesake. But the spirit of Ainsley is strong and attempts to possess him at every opportunity.'

Then, just as a hole smashed through the door, the answer hit me. 'The ghost of Ainsley wants to become him.'

Lucinda nodded solemnly. 'To win Lila and get the mine. Brother is still very much against brother.'

CHAPTER 19

*J*ust when I thought we'd surely have to run, everything seemed to die down and go quiet. I sunk stiffly back down into my chair, every sinew in my body on high alert. My head hurt and I had no spit to swallow.

'Do not fear. Jed is naught but anger and bluster,' she said, dismissing everything with wave of her hand. Then her face took on a faraway look. 'Lila spelled this house to ward off Waxley-Blacks many years ago, but Jed was always nothing but sweet and attentive to me. And yet Lila beguiled both Jed and Ainsley.' Her face darkened as the anger built inside her again. 'As she did any man she came into contact with.'

Her anger seemed to ebb and flow like the tide and she calmed down again. I could barely keep up with her. 'However, not every man came with a title and a mine containing the waters of youth,' Lucina said, her look blackening again. 'Jed would leave notes here, in the orangery, where she would find them and they would meet in secret.'

'That was before you were married though, right? Jed was free.'

She conceded with a nod of her head. 'When I look back, I wonder whether it was why Jed's father sought our marriage arrangement in the first place. I came as a young, naive, girl oblivious to what was going on here. Instead of breaking off, they continued to meet in secret.

Intrigued, and a little more confident that Jed was not going to burst into the room, I nodded, eager for her to continue her story. 'And you found out and intercepted the notes?'

'When I could … they became so clever, you see,' she said, totally immersed in her memories. 'I even approached Ainsley and he tried talking some sense into him. I thought he was so noble.' Then she looked directly at me with such a murderous look that it made me move back in my chair. 'Until I discovered that he was in love with her himself.'

'What happened?' I said, my heart pumping in anticipation for the answer.

She averted her eyes as if she was ashamed of what she was about to say. 'I engineered it so that Jed came upon them. It was the only way either of them would listen.'

'So Jed killed Ainsley,' I said to myself.

'No. No one died. Not then. They argued, of course, and Jed saw her for what she really was: an enchantress. A witch who'd seduced them both and that all she really wanted was his title and what was hidden deep within the mine. She was turning the brothers against each other, making Ainsley believe, as his business partner and heir, that the title and the mine could be his.'

'Did Jed know about the Elixir of Life?' I asked.

She shook her head. 'At least I don't think so. I mean, he knew there wasn't any silver in the mine, only tin.'

'What happened to everyone?' With them all still walking these corridors, I knew it couldn't have ended well.

'Lila and Ainsley began to spend a lot more time together

now they were out in the open. With Jed out of the question, she threw in her lot with Ainsley. She had her eye firmly set on the prize and would get it one way or another. She began teaching him her witchcraft for something they were cooking up together. Jed still had a great regard for his brother and tried to warn him, over and over, but Ainsley ignored him, accusing him of jealousy and they continued on with their so-called science experiments.

'Science experiments?' I repeated, my mind going straight to the cellar in Wax's house.

'That's what Ainsley called them. But I wasn't fooled. They were meddling in the black arts. Later it became clear that they were looking for a way to cheat death. Lila wanted to remain young for ever and Ainsley was her unwitting fool who would help her achieve it. Their father would have put a stop to it, but he remained on his sick bed, and so Ainsley went on unchecked.'

It reminded me frighteningly of the parallels with Wax, the cellar and what was going on there now.

'One night, I overheard them talking. She was trying to convince Ainsley to marry her and kill Jed so everything could be theirs. I told Jed and, thankfully, because of what he already he knew, he believed me. And so he played along, but came earlier than the appointed time. The maid had just set her bath and when he came upon her, she was there, defiant and unafraid. He said to me even then he faltered, and she almost won him around. But for the good of all concerned and the heavy cost to his soul, he held her beneath the water and killed her.'

I closed my eyes. The image, all too vivid in my mind. I'd dreamed it a hundred times – the kiss in the bath – the intensity. Pushing her under the waterline until she had nowhere left to breathe. It left me gasping, just thinking of it.

Then it didn't make sense. 'But if she died, how did she end up here?'

Lucina was already shaking her head. 'The house was already hexed with her own insurance policy. Instead of dying, her spirit came here. Then, from that moment, the

Blackwood curse began. Blackwoods and Waxley-Blacks, drawn together in every generation, until the one came that would help to set her free.'

'Me,' I whispered. I still didn't understand what made me special.

'Jed was inconsolable after that. His brother was totally changed to him. His father died and Jed and I married quietly in a small chapel. We eventually had two children. Two boys,' she said, wistfully.

'Wait. I thought that you and Jed must have been …' I left off the murdered part. I naturally assumed because they were here that it meant they'd met a violent end.

'Jed found out the real reason Ainsley and Lila were so interested in the mine and he became determined that Ainsley should have no part of it. He began by blowing up the tunnels and encouraged the rumours of the Blackwood curse. I don't think he ever knew about the contact Ainsley had with Lila through the mirrors while he lived and how they plotted to be together again.'

Now it made sense. Wax's uncle had continued Ainsley's mission to get into the mine. Lila had helped him design the spell that made the Shades come, until they finally found and trapped me: the last in the Blackwood line. Wax's psychic gift had been perfect to help them. 'But why now. Why me?' I asked, as a groan and something scraped across the floor in the hallway. The malevolent spirit of Jedediah was on the move again and our time was running out. Even Lucinda became aware this time and was checking over her shoulder at the door. I hoped Lila's protection spell, or whatever it was, held him out.

'They needed a Blackwood with a foot in both worlds. One neither alive nor dead, to act as a bridge for her to cross and take her place. They waited over a hundred years. Have you any idea how rare that makes you?'

I didn't, but there it was at last; the reason for it all. Lila was trapped and continued to use a Waxley-Black to get what she wanted. Except now she had Wax in her sights and I wasn't going to allow that to happen.

It appeared that it was a lot easier to trap someone behind the mirrors than get them out. The real spell was in order for Lila to escape – to live again in the flesh. And what was in the mine must somehow be for Ainsley – the original one.

A much louder bang made us both jump and turn our heads at the same time.

'He's broken through,' Lucinda whispered.

The look on her face made my blood freeze in my veins. 'What do you mean? I thought the spell was an impassable barrier?' My heart was now racing as Lucinda was on her feet.

'A barrier, yes. He's had no reason to break through it before.'

I looked fearfully at the door as the only way out, while Lucinda ran to the furthest corner of the room.

I stood for a second, bewildered, then ran blindly after her. She began to frantically run her hands across the wall as if feeling for something hidden, until she pushed a wooden panel and a small door opened for us. We squeezed into a small passage, Lucinda keeping hold of the door and clicking it shut behind us. My mouth was dry and the sound of my breath deafening as we crouched in the dark. I had to put my hand over my mouth to quieten my gasps for air as a voice bellowed from the room we'd just left. 'LUCINDA!'

I looked at Lucinda to gauge her fear, who seemed more real than ever in the darkness. Her chest was rising and falling as hard as mine and she was listening just as keenly to the heavy footfalls on the floor beyond the little door that separated us. She offered no comfort; she was scared. My eyes strained against the dark and fixed on the thin strip of light around it.

We waited.

My heart drummed the walls of my chest and was so loud it was all I could hear in my ears and the sweat that pooled in the centre of my back sent a cold chill trickling down my spine. I don't think I'd ever been so scared. It was a whole other level of fear.

Then, at last, we heard the heavy march of his steps as he finally assumed she wasn't there and left. I went to reach out my arm, but Lucinda pushed it back down again. I don't know who was more shocked that we could feel the other. She flickered more translucent for a moment. Then, before I could check myself, the words left my mouth, 'What happened to you? Why are you here?'

She relaxed back against the wall and sank down onto her haunches. I joined her and waited. 'I guess I was just a loose end that they wanted tidying. I was smothered in my sleep.'

I looked at the flimsy door and heard Jed bellowing somewhere else in the house. 'Ainsley,' she said, without me needing to ask.

'But why? He had everything.'

'Not the mine. Jed refused to work it or give it to him, either.'

Then the shriek of the angry ghost of Jed sent the final piece crashing down into place. 'He killed his own brother.'

She nodded her head, sadly. 'A shooting accident.' My heart stalled with sympathy when I remembered their small, vulnerable sons, but she was way ahead of me and shrugged.

'Strangely, he needed them. Their wardship was enough. The Waxley-Black name had to be assured to bring Lila back from the mirrors.'

I put my head back against the dusty wall and let it all sink in. The small space was hot and I was beginning to sweat heat instead of fear. The enormity and far-reaching effects of it all was astounding. Everything they'd done and the whole one hundred and fifty years in between had been leading up to this very day. My doom was here, sitting in this dingy secret passageway, waiting for an angry ghost to cease my existence completely. I fought back the urge to cry. 'I'm not even English. I live halfway across the world,' I began to babble to myself. 'How could they know I would even have an accident?'

Lucinda was studying my face, as if it was the first time she'd had the chance to have a really good look at it. 'You know Lila was in the sleep from which no body wakes when her spell brought her here. Her body remained breathing and warm, but her spirit had already left it.'

She was looking at me intently, as if there was some major point I seemed to be missing.

'You are a Shade, but not like the others.'

Then sudden comprehension stopped my breathing. My heart stopped and I blinked at her for several seconds. Her words from earlier echoed: *A foot in both worlds.* She was trying to tell me somewhere, somehow, I was alive. *In a coma.*

My heart and mind raced with the million possibilities that it brought with it: seeing my parents. Waking up. Having a chance at life again. Wax. Yes. I could come here and meet Wax as the real me. He could have a life. I could have a life. We could have a life together. Then I noticed Lucinda watching me regretfully and I knew it wouldn't be as easy as that.

'All the while you are here, you will never wake.'

My mind went to my parents standing over my bedside as they'd done with Pete. Except it would be months, or maybe even years. Until, eventually, they would nod and have my monitors and life support machines switched off. And I realised what she was saying. I didn't have forever. In fact, after all these months, I probably didn't have that long at all. My mind went straight to Wax, drugged and manipulated by his uncle. He'd served his purpose too.

My eyes flashed to Lucinda's when I got it.

'The boy. The Waxley-Black son. My living blood relative. He is in great danger,' Lucinda said, steadily, as if it was imperative I understood.

My heart beat wilder at the realisation. 'You! It's you who protects him.'

Something sounded a little way off, as if to protest at what I was saying. 'From Jed,' I whispered, straining to locate the direction of the noise in the house.

Then I heard a shuffle to my left and I turned my head to where the passage went off into darkness. I could just make out the silver outline of a huge man. My stomach fell into my bowel as I took in the holes in his skull meant for eyes. It was the angel of death himself.

I struggled to stand, to scream, but my motor skills had gone. I couldn't kick or run and my scream came out as empty air.

He didn't move. He hovered there and Lucinda whispered behind me, 'No, Jed protects us all.'

I stood, shocked rigid, knowing there was nowhere left to run. The ghostly apparition appeared to move and swirl, even though he was standing still. It was as though his black robes were alive with roaming snakes. However, he was less corporeal than even Lucinda. I could see the corridor disappearing off behind him. His eyes were hidden beneath a deep hood and his mouth was a thin slash across his pale chin. It was clear to me that he was a very different entity entirely. I wondered if he was one of those malevolent ones Wax had spoken of. He looked right through me, to Lucinda. Then, as if he was satisfied I was a friend and she was OK, he receded into the blackness, until he was gone completely.

I turned to Lucinda, still numb, hoping for more of an explanation, but she was becoming dimmer too. Suddenly the thought of being totally alone scared me far more than any spirit. 'Don't go … don't leave me,' I said, reaching my hand through dust motes.

I started to cry.

'Protect my youngest ancestor and undo the curse,'

floated on the air. I looked frantically around me to catch where her voice came from, but there was nothing of her left. 'Go back to the Shades and, remember, Jed and I will do all we can to help you.'

I had no more time to process what she said. She was gone. The light from her form was soon replaced with a creeping blackness that seeped into the room like a damp mist.

I sank to the floor and cried heartbroken, hopeless tears, right from the depths of me. A great outpouring of emotion that I didn't know I had left after Pete had died. Sitting in the dust of a hundred years, my sobs subsided and things started to come together with a weird kind of clarity. As if I gradually accepted what couldn't be changed. I came to understand that it was that realisation that made me strong.

Pete had died while I'd been on life support in the hospital. I'd wandered around in my old life trying to fit into a world that couldn't see me. That was why no one took any notice of me at home or at school. Then Ainsley's spell had pulled me to England, while my muddled mind rationalised the journey. I was summoned to this house to free Lila. Lucinda and Jed were wronged, malevolent spirits that needed closure. Someone needed to break the Blackwood curse to stop Lila and Ainsley and to free all concerned, once and for all.

I knew now that was me. My purpose here. I was neither alive nor dead. I was literally the only person who could do it. Lila was behind everything, for sure, and the real danger. Now she was alive and free to go anywhere and do anything. She was with Wax – my Wax. I had to get back to the others and tell them all I'd learned.

I got up, clicked open the door to my aunt's sitting room and retraced my steps to the long tunnel back to Wax's place. Strangely, after meeting the spirit of Jed, I was no longer afraid. He had to be the scariest of all the ghosts and, according to Lucinda, they were on my side.

For the first time since I'd been there, I had something to do. I had something to live for. I would beat this thing, get back to my body and live.

THE TUNNEL SEEMED a lot further going back than it had been coming, but, eventually, I came out in the greyed-out version of Wax's hallway. After the colour of my aunt's, it still came as a shock that I was a prisoner of the Inside Out.

I went up the stairs to Ollie's room and straight to the mirror above his dressing table. At first I panicked that there was nothing there but my own reflection. Then, after an agonising minute of despair, it began to cloud over. Colour replaced the grey and a moving canvas of Ollie's room appeared in front of me. 'Psst! Guys!' I whispered.

One by one they looked around and asked if anyone had heard something. Then Sam pointed and they all rushed over to the mirror. The sense of relief – that they could see me – left me overwhelmed with emotion and out of breath for a moment.

'Thank God you're back,' Ollie said.

'You've been ages. What happened?' Tallulah asked, pushing in front of everyone else – again.

'I'll tell you everything. Is Wax awake?'

Ollie shook his head and looked concerned. It *was* worrying. It was a long time to be out cold. 'No, I think they tranqued him up enough to fell an elephant this time. They know how pissed he's going to be when he wakes; that's why they've called back my parents.'

I absorbed that. They were an added dimension I hadn't thought about. I wondered what kind of people would leave an impressionable young man with the likes of Ainsley and whether they would be of any help. Somehow I didn't think I'd like them very much. Butterflies kicked in my stomach that Wax would be furious because of me and I secretly liked it.

I relayed what had happened with Lucinda and Jed and what she'd said. It left many of them shaking their heads in disbelief. None of them argued the truth of it, though. It was a pretty evil thing to do to a bunch of kids just to satisfy your own selfish ends.

'So the big bad one is Jed, my great, great, great…' Ollie said, giving up after three. 'And really a good guy?' he said, trying to look past me as if he wasn't convinced and Jed was going to pounce out of the mirror at him at any minute.

'So Lucinda says. She sent me back here and told me they were both on my side.'

'What happens if it works?' Tallulah said, stilling his arm on the keypad.

He searched her eyes, puzzled for a moment.

'You know, if we're all freed, do we just die? I mean, do we want that?'

She was right. I'd been so selfish being wrapped up in myself and my own predicament that I hadn't given a single thought to what would happen to my friends.

Ollie understood immediately and pulled her into a hug and spoke into her hair. 'Don't worry. Whether we stay or cross over, I won't let you do it alone.' He pulled apart and held the sides of her face. 'OK?'

Tears were making the top of her cheeks shiny, but she smiled back at him and nodded with a sniff.

I took the opportunity to quickly wipe them from my own eyes.

'And that goes for everyone,' Ollie said, looking at each of them in turn.

They all nodded, me included. Archie put a hand on his

shoulder and gave it a squeeze and brought a lump to my throat all over again. Seeing the warmth in such a cold world, from people who should have left it, made it impossible not to cry. Then Ollie looked directly at me. 'I've been working on a static link from my laptop to Wax's,' he said, pulling his laptop closer again.

Everyone huddled in, glad of the distraction. I was growing to love these new friends I'd made. Too bad a girl had to almost die to get some.

'I don't think it'll work on the ordinary web as we're not part of the worldly plane – particularly you, Becks. You're somewhere else entirely,' Ollie said.

I was desperately trying to keep up. Tech was certainly not my major at school.

'I've kind of borrowed the technique Wax used to talk to you, secretly, before.'

Heat went straight to my cheeks. I looked nervously into each of their faces and no one seemed surprised. Everyone seemed to accept me connected with Wax; without question, now. I liked it and schooled my features to look interested in the tech know-how.

'How did he do that?' Josh said, speaking for everyone. 'He must be like some super hacker or something.'

Ollie's fingers worked lightning fast across the touch keyboard. 'He must have gone in through the Dark Web. There!' he said, with a louder tap on the Enter tab. 'I'm in!'

I watched his eyes moving up and down and knew he was scrolling fast. The others were glued to what he was doing too. It was frustrating being this side of the glass.

'There's this one paranormal site called White Noise,' he said, thinking aloud. 'Wax told me about it once. There!' He straightened up and looked at Tallulah. 'Check your Fitbit.'

Tallulah frowned, then looked at the band on her wrist. She touched the side and then looked back at Ollie, confused.

Ollie tipped his head to me. 'The rest is up to you.'

I looked blank, not sure what he wanted me to do.

He looked around him as if searching for inspiration, then back at me intently. 'Think about what you do when you want to be seen in a mirror.'

I hadn't done much of it, but I concentrated on what actually happened. It wasn't so much about being seen, but seeing through, like through a window. When I'd come back from speaking to Lucinda this had been just an ordinary mirror. In the end I'd waved my arm and the answer came to me. 'I just willed it.'

'Can you do that with Tallulah's watch? Remember, you've not actually gone anywhere. In reality you're in a hospital bed in California. It should be a small hop from a mirror to a watch.'

I stared at him, gobsmacked. He was so right. All this was in my head. I had to keep telling myself that.

'I mean it is genius tech work on my part,' Ollie said, half-laughing. Tallulah gave him a light shove in the shoulder. 'Just imagine the broadband light as tunnels or something.'

I closed my eyes and gave it a go. I concentrated and held my breath. When I peeked through my eyelashes, everyone was pulling a pained face just watching me. I let out a blast of air and sagged. 'It's no good.'

Ollie seemed a little frustrated with me, then he looked down at his laptop. 'Maybe we're trying to run before we can walk.' He looked up and turned his laptop to face me. It looked speckled with static. 'Try the laptop first. It's closer and bigger and might be easier for you.'

I saw what he meant, but I still wasn't sure.

'Concentrate,' Ollie said. 'I don't want to hurry you, but I want to close the link to the site. It's built for hackers interested in the supernatural. I don't want to even think about the type of viruses circulating in there.'

That was enough to get me to focus and try again. This time, I visualised the static on the screen and my moving out through the mirror and through the circuitry to reach it. I was suddenly sucked through. Moving in a white-knuckle ride through a tangle of fibres – each one narrower than the last. I couldn't breathe. The light got brighter, until I couldn't stand it any longer. My head began to split with the pain until I fell in a heap on the floor.

'Where is she?' I heard someone say.

I slowly opened my eyes. I'd replaced a grey box for a black one. Sheer black windowless walls hemmed me in on every side. Except this one had a small square of glass in front of me – the laptop screen. I'd done it.

'There she is!' Tallulah squealed.

They all congratulated Ollie and grinned back at me. Ollie most of all. 'Am I out, have you broken the spell?'

Ollie's smile was a little sad when he shook his head. 'Think of it more like we've added a little extension to the boundary of it. But you did it,' he said, more brightly.

I smiled back more enthusiastically than I felt.

'Now you've done that, it should be a short hop to our phones or Tallulah's watch. You should be able to get into anything with a circuit board now. So cool.' His eyes were wide with excitement. 'The only thing to remember is the device has to be switched on and, better still, have Wi-Fi.'

I nodded, bewildered. I saw the genius of it, I did, but my world had been pulled out from under me so many times since I got here that I didn't know what was real or not anymore.

'Trust me,' Ollie said, and, for a moment, he looked star-tlingly like Wax, reminding me of the danger he was in too.

I rolled my eyes. 'If you lose me in cyberspace, I'll haunt you like you wouldn't believe.'

He grinned, letting my lame threat roll straight off him.

'I'm linked to everyone here through my laptop: Messenger, email, social media. All you have to do is go wherever you wanna go from here. Like a bus terminal,' he said, picking me up in his laptop and giving it a little shake.

'OK, OK, you're making me dizzy,' I said.

What he said made perfect sense. If I remembered I had no physical body, then, in theory, I should be able to go anywhere I wanted within the confines of the spell. 'So your laptop is like an anchor?'

'Exactly!' Ollie said. 'From here you can go anywhere. And now you're away from that Dark Website, we should be pretty confident that you're alone in there, so it's safer too.'

I wish I felt happier about that but, somehow, what he said didn't feel that comforting. The idea that I wasn't the only one occupying this space hadn't occurred to me until then. It was a brilliant plan though. 'Is Wax awake?' I asked, the desire to see him suddenly gripping me.

Ollie disappeared out of shot for a moment, then shook his head. 'We'll have to wait. He's still out.'

WAX HAD BEEN out for two days straight. It was so long that Ollie had to check he was still breathing a few times. I was now easily tagging along in Tallulah's watch.

In reality, I was in a bare black room, but I was seldom there, so I kind of forgot about it. If I really dug deep and thought about it, I had to acknowledge that I was in a coma in a hospital bed and not there at all, which kind of blew my mind. So I pushed it aside and lived in the moment with a slight pang at the irony.

In the end, Ollie put me on FaceTime and got me to call out Wax's name. 'He hears voices all the time,' I reminded Ollie. I would have thought he'd learned to tune them out by now.

'It's you, though. Keep trying,' Ollie said. 'I'm starting to get worried.'

That was enough. 'Wax ... wake up,' I said, over and over, with Ollie pushing his phone right up into his brother's face.

Nothing seemed to be working and I was getting really worried.

Ollie bent down to his brother's ear. 'Wakey-wakey. Your girlfriend's here and she wants to snog you,' he sang.

He looked at me with a wicked grin. 'Never underestimate the ability of a little brother to drive their older sibling to violence.' He laughed again as an idea came to him. 'I'm going to download a film from that really unsafe, virus-ridden pirate site onto your computer ... I'm doing it ... right now,' he said in the same sing-songy voice.

I had to giggle. I'm sure there was a real element of danger to that if Wax had been awake.

There was a small flicker in his long black lashes.

'Wax!' I said, hitching a breath at the same time. His eyes rolled under his eyelids and he moaned and rolled onto his back. Then he opened his eyes and looked up to the ceiling. It took him a moment to get his bearings and remember what had happened before he was knocked out. 'Wax?' I said, more softly.

Then, as if he suddenly realised he was being watched, he turned his head sharply to the gallery of onlookers standing next to his bed. 'What are you all doing in my room?' he said, gruffly.

Ollie's answer was to hold out his phone. I knew the exact moment when its significance hit Wax, because his face looked pained and he sat up. His hand went to his head as if he'd done it too quickly. Then he searched my face as if he was looking for injuries and then straight into my eyes, unable to speak.

'You've been out for days,' Ollie said, breaking the awkward silence.

'What happened?' Wax demanded, in a cracked voice, bobbing his head towards me in the phone. 'Where is she?' He must have had a major headache because he was squinting and putting his hand up to shield his eyes from the head-splitting light.

'I'm not sure what they did to her, but she was only visible in the mirrors of the house, so I rigged a catapult system, through the White Noise site, to put her in there. I figured it was safer.'

Wax closed his eyes for a moment. It was so long that I worried that he was unwell. Then he narrowed them at Ollie so I wasn't sure if he was angry or not, but he eventually nodded. 'Clever,' he said, simply, and clicked his fingers for him to hand me to him on his phone. 'We need to get her onto my closed IP network. She'll be safer there.'

'Ollie was careful, Wax. She's not just yours, you know,' Tallulah said, moodily.

Wax threw her a dirty look and Ollie reached for her hand with a look that said: be quiet. 'Any hacker or sociopath, dead or alive, could have followed her here,' Wax reminded her.

It was enough to make me swallow hard. I couldn't see poor Tallulah's face to reassure her as he'd gotten up off the bed and taken me with him. 'Don't be hard on them, Wax,' I said, speaking up for the first time. My voice sounded tinny, like I was on a transistor radio with slightly bad reception.

The next time I could see anything, Wax had changed his clothes. He propped me up, facing him on his desk, while his fingers worked their magic on his keyboard. Even with dark circles under bloodshot eyes, he was startlingly handsome.

'Thanks,' he said, turning his head, I guessed, to Olly, just out of view. There was a private moment of nothing, where they communicated with their eyes. Then Wax cut through it with; 'Get out … all of you,' and the room was silent.

I watched his face, serious, brows furrowed and concentrating on what he was doing. 'They worked hard and did a good thing, Wax,' I said.

His eyes flashed to me and he went back to his work without breaking stride in what his fingers were doing.

'It was brilliant thinking,' he said, simply.

I wanted to shake him that he showed so little of that to Ollie, who adored and looked up to him.

'I just had to make you safe and be alone with you.'

My next words in Ollie's defence died on my lips to be replaced by toe-curling heat. My stomach fluttered as it flowed right up through me. 'Would it hurt you to tell him from time to time?' I said as soon as I was able.

'His head will swell and it's big enough as it is.' He smiled genuinely then. As if he knew he was being pig-headed. 'Right! There!' he said with a louder tap to the Enter button. 'That should do it.'

For a moment, nothing happened. I sat and waited for Wax to say whatever it was I knew he wanted to say, but something went past me so fast it knocked me off my stool. I didn't even get chance to see it, only that it was huge and black and the world dropped out from under me. I don't remember ever screaming like that since I was dropped several stories at a theme park.

I landed in a heap and lay still while I assessed myself for injuries. After wiggling my fingers and toes, I slowly sat up.

'Sorry. It's a crude world-building program I've been working on,' Wax explained.

I looked down at my hands. They looked real enough. Then I looked round and saw that the black cube had been replaced by a very angular version of Wax's room. It was a strange, dizzying feeling because it wasn't real and, at the same time, it wasn't the Inside Out. It was more something an architect or a set builder would draw.

Suddenly, I was utterly bewildered and wanted to get out. I looked back at Wax and was at the same level as him.

'You're on my main screen now,' he said. 'I'm sorry it's not better. You're still in the spell, but this should keep you safe and at least off the Dark Website.'

I did have a clearer view of his room now I was bigger.

He got up to retrieve his own phone from the nightstand and switched it on. 'And with this, you aren't dependent on mirrors.'

I tried to smile and not dampen his enthusiasm. It was a brilliant idea of Ollie's, but, right then, it all seemed just too much to bear. Tears came no matter how hard I fought them off. In the end I had to turn around so Wax could only see the back of my head.

'Hey, please don't cry. If you want to get out of the program all you have to do is hit the Escape key, OK?'

I turned back round, sniffed and looked down. He'd even built my own keyboard into the program. That only made me cry all over again.

'There are other spirits I had to protect you from,' Wax said. When I looked at him, he looked filled with anguish for me. I felt bad then. None of this was his fault, so I sniffed back the tears and nodded.

'I'll get you out, I promise,' he said.

I nodded again, feeling like a small child placated with the promise of a treat.

'Tell me what happened,' he said.

I knew it was mainly to distract me, but I could see he was ashamed too. 'You couldn't have done anything, Wax. It happened so fast.'

He smiled, but wasn't convinced. 'I should have seen it coming.'

'I met Lucinda and the original Jedediah,' I said, switching his distraction tactic on him. 'They know what's going on here.'

His eyes widened in surprise and he sat back down in his chair. As I told him everything that had happened when I got trapped and followed Lucinda, I watched the range of emotions cross his face. He listened intensely to my every word, and I saw sadness, concern, amazement and admiration. I never knew something as simple could have such an effect on me. It made me warm inside and gave me the confidence to fight the world.

'So they've been trying to warn and protect you all along,' Wax said, shaking his head. 'I just assumed they were malevolent spirits.'

'Well, they're definitely angry, but I'm not sure what good they can do. You're the only one who can physically do anything.'

Wax looked troubled after I said that, and I could have kicked myself. I didn't mean that he was in any way weak. Far from it. Nevertheless, I could see his mind veering off in that direction. Then his hands went back to the keyboard as if an idea had occurred to him. 'I'm going to put you back on my phone and go downstairs. I'm starving.'

'Wait! Wax.' I was instantly filled with panic. We needed to talk this through. Honestly, I was terrified of seeing Lila again.

'I want to find out their plans now she's out.' He put an earpiece in his ear. 'I can still hear you, OK? But no one else will.'

Before I could say anything else, the world went black as I was jostled around in a pocket as he went downstairs.

CHAPTER 21

The kitchen was another room with no mirrors or circuitry, so I was glad of Wax's phone. Despite how terrified I was, I didn't want to miss a second of his conversation with that woman.

I was frustrated that he put me down flat on the counter and all I got was a view of the tiny ceiling lights. 'Hey!' I called out. All I could hear was him riffling through cupboards and then pouring what sounded like cereal in a bowl. Then another door opening and the slurp of liquid poured. *Milk.* A glass clinked and some more liquid followed. I knew he must be famished after two days out, but this was ridiculous. 'Can't you just stand me up against something, at least?' I said. 'Testing, testing.'

I could literally hear the grin in his voice. 'Try the cupboards.'

After I scowled at him for enjoying this, I looked around me for the first time. It was another representation of the room I was in. This time the kitchen. I began opening cupboards and saw he had designed boxes and tins of food into the program as well. It was marvellous detail. I reached for a box of Cinnamon Crunchies and retrieved an equally realistic glass bottle of milk from the fridge and sat at the counter. It actually tasted good. I guess I hadn't eaten for two days either. 'Come on, don't be an ass,' I said between mouthfuls.

My world rolled again like the bowels of a ship and Wax came into view. He'd propped me up to face him on the counter. 'Finally,' I grumbled.

He threw down a loaf of bread as a shield and simply grinned. My traitorous heart fluttered at the show of dimples instead of getting angry like it rightly should. I gave in, it was hopeless.

'Bret!' A male voice said from behind me. 'You're up.'

A tall man I didn't recognise came around to Wax's side of the counter and hugged him tightly, sighing loudly and smacking his back with a dull thud. 'Dad? What are you doing here?'

His dad put him away from him and took him in. 'I came as soon as your uncle called me to say you were ill. Let me look at you. My word … you're a man,' he said, shaking his head.

I wanted to shout out the truth, but I daren't until I knew what kind of man Wax's father was. He seemed nice enough and Wax seemed comfortable with him. Much more than with his uncle, anyway.

'Nothing to do but grow around here.'

His father laughed. 'And computer coding. I saw the impressive set-up you have. That's quite a sought-after skill in the city.'

Wax shrugged. I shouted, 'Fat chance of that with Uncle Ainsley drugging him at every turn!' into his earpiece.

Wax didn't react, but his mouth hardened in a way that sobered me, instantly. Something told me that he wasn't playing here. He gestured for his father to sit at a stool on the edge of the counter. I could just about see him.

Wax got out a bowl and pushed the cereal towards his father. He smiled and Wax sat and continued eating with a flash of his eyes my way, warning me off.

I sat glumly, sufficiently scolded. It was easy to see who the guy was. He was tall and dark like Wax. Same eyes and similar frame. Except he had a little grey at his temples and wore his hair shorter than Wax. I put him in his forties. He was stylish though. His clothes were more *GQ* than Jules Verne, like his uncle. They seemed poles apart.

I had to keep reminding myself that this wasn't the original Jed. He was the ghost at my aunt's. His only crime that I could see other than sharing a name, was leaving Wax alone with his uncle. And that wasn't really a crime. Instead, I had to content myself with watching their reunion.

'How have you been?' Wax asked, raising his eyes cautiously to his father.

I was mildly exasperated with his question, thinking, surely, it should be the other way around.

His father nodded. 'Well … Physically. We travelled. I'm sorry we let you down, Bret. We just needed to get away … to forget, you know?'

He looked at Wax with devastated eyes and Wax mirrored them. I looked between them trying to catch up with what was going on and then I realised, like a massive thump on the head. *Ollie*. They'd lost Ollie and his parents stayed away in order to come to terms with their loss. I hadn't thought of it because I saw him all the time. For his father, he'd left their life completely eighteen months ago.

'We've been to India and Tibet,' a strange female voice said from behind him. A beautiful, tall brunette put a hand on his father's shoulder and kissed his cheek. She had a kind face, Ollie's warm brown eyes and similar, high cheekbones to Wax. *His mother.*

'It was marvellous. Such a spiritual place.' She moved away and I heard her fill the kettle. I shrank back, afraid I'd be seen. A stool scraped and she sat between Wax and his father, nursing a steaming cup. She put up a hand and ran it through the unruly tendrils of Wax's hair. 'Could do with a cut,' she said.

He smiled a little and moved his hair out of range of her hand. It saddened me because the easy atmosphere with his father had shifted. Wax had clammed up with his mother asking inane questions about what was going on in the village and the weather. I noticed his father was closed off too.

I found myself disliking her instantly.

She started to go on about their travels and all they'd seen and I found myself getting angrier by the minute. 'If you don't ask them, Wax, I swear I'll dial up and call them myself,' I said in his earpiece.

I saw the tiniest twitch to the corners of his mouth as he tried not to smile. He put down his spoon and pushed his bowl away from him. Then he picked up his glass of orange juice, as if he was going to take a sip. His mother was still droning on. I'd long tuned out.

'Did you know?' Wax said, cutting right across her.

'Know what?' his mother said, suddenly stopping the constant flow from her mouth. She looked at his father as if he might shed some light.

'Stop lying, please.' Wax's voice sounded calm and level, but I could see the tension in his jaw and I started to worry that maybe his mother didn't know him that well at all. 'I am asking you a reasonable question.' His hands clenched and I could see his knuckles go white. 'Did you know what Ainsley has been doing here?'

They didn't answer right away.

Wax slammed down his glass on the counter, making a tidal wave of juice.

His mother jumped in fright and his father immediately stood to put himself between them.

'Well clearly you know something because you were both back here at the drop of a hat, when I haven't seen you in six bloody months!'

'Darling,' his mother said, trying to come closer to soothe him, but his father wouldn't allow it. It proved they knew what Wax could be like.

'Stop the bullshit!' Wax shouted, and, for a terrifying moment, I thought Wax would explode, but he held onto it and I hoped and prayed that he did it for me. They had no idea the effort it took him, but I did and I was so proud of him at that moment.

His mother said something to his father that I didn't quite catch. He shook his head. 'No, don't call him.'

Oh my God. I seethed for Wax. She was actually suggesting they call his uncle. Sedation seemed their answer for everything. At least his father seemed against it. 'He's just angry,' his father said.

'Do. You. Know. What. Ainsley's. Been. Doing?' Wax repeated, stepping into his father menacingly. 'Do you know about the spell in the basement? The dead people he's been calling for me to see?'

His father shook his head bitterly. 'It's for Ollie. He thinks he's helping.'

His mother started to cry and buried her face in her hands against his father's back, but I was glad Wax didn't relent. Instead, he shook his head angrily. 'Ollie? Ollie's here. It's not because of bloody Ollie,' he said, half laughing that his parents were that stupid.

His mother stopped crying and his father looked rattled

for the first time. He put his arm around her and they faced him together, suddenly listening.

Wax nodded, dumbfounded, at them. 'Yeah, every goddamn spirit for miles around can't rest because he's been calling them here. He doesn't give two shits about your son. Either of them,' he added. 'So I'll ask you for the last time, did you know?' he ended raising his volume to a shout that made his father blink.

To his credit, his father tried to calm him down. He put up his hands defensively and shook his head. 'Listen, I swear we had no idea it had got that bad. Well, I knew what he was trying to do, but I didn't know the extent of it. And he was here and you were ill …'

He was rambling and Wax was becoming impatient.

'We were looking for answers to heal you,' his mother chimed in.

'Heal me,' Wax repeated, flabbergasted with disbelief.

'It's true, Bret,' his father said, putting a gentling hand on his chest. 'We just thought if we could heal you – find you a cure – you could at least get some relief. And Ainsley agreed to stay here with you to help while we did that.'

I thought Wax would combust.

'Stay calm, baby … Wax … don't react. He doesn't know. You have your answer. Remember your question. They didn't really know,' I said, trying to talk him down. I could see him balling his fists and stretching out his fingers over and over while he took in what I said. 'Stay calm, you'll only play into Ainsley's story if you blow up. They'll tranq you in a heartbeat and you won't be able to do anything.'

I could see how desperately he was trying to get a hold on his temper. He was breathing deeply and slowly. 'There is nothing wrong with me,' he said eventually.

'I know there isn't,' his father said, placating him.

'We know,' his mother said as well, making me want to slap her to let him speak, myself.

Then the moment that Wax so badly needed, for a real heart to heart, was obliterated when Ainsley sauntered into the room with a much more modern-looking Lila on his arm.

Her eyes went directly to me and Ainsley said, 'Ah, the family is all together.'

*M*y heart almost stopped at being discovered by the most dangerous person in the room. *The apex predator.* Funny, how I should be reminded of that. I swallowed and waited for her to expose me.

But she didn't.

Wax had his eye on his uncle, fooled as all men were around this woman. But I knew the real culprit, the instigator of all that was bad around here, and it was all in that one, knowing look. She knew that I knew and, rather than pick a fight, she enjoyed it. Instead of being rattled, that slow smile I'd glimpsed in the painting spread over her face as if life was just about to get interesting.

She terrified me.

I was forced to tune back into the conversation. Wax's father was on his feet accusing his uncle. They looked so alike right then. 'Bret says Ollie is here and you never said a word.' Wax's father was furious and his mother renewed her tears.

Ainsley turned his head to Wax, contemptuously, 'That is because your son saw fit to keep that from me.'

The conversation was descending into chaos. Wax's mother was wailing, 'My son … my poor son.' It was clear there was no love lost between this Jed and Ainsley.

'He's in his room with all his friends,' Wax said impatiently, to shut his mother up. I hitched a breath at how rash that was and the look he flashed me was more a flinch and I knew he regretted saying it instantly.

His mother ran from the room.

'Stay calm, Wax, stay calm.'

But he was on a roll now and continued on. 'He hasn't been looking for Ollie, he's been looking for a Blackwood daughter.'

I didn't know whether to be thrilled or terrified. I felt both, and proud of Wax for having the courage to confront his uncle. Maybe we'd finally get some help in his father to fight him. 'A Blackwood daughter,' Wax's father repeated. As frustrated as I was, it was a comfort to know that Wax's parents appeared to be in the dark about it all.

But Ainsley was clever, and, even more so, Lila. 'You see, this is what I have to deal with,' he said, immediately deflecting the comment.

'Don't listen to him,' Wax continued. It's what he's been after all along. He wants the mine for the Elixir of Life.'

I wanted to slow Wax down, so his father could keep up. For a moment, Ainsley and Lila looked at each other, rattled. Wax's father looked at him, worried and bewildered. He was losing him. I wanted to warn Wax, but Lila seized the opportunity to cut in. She put a hand on Ainsley's chest to hold him back. She had read the indecision and doubt on Wax's father's face as well as I did. 'Let's remain calm, shall we? Why don't you take Jed to the study and I'll send you some tea. I'll get the housekeeper to see to some nice breakfast for us all.'

Wax was completely broadsided by her perfectly reasonable response and an awful bewildered, lost look was entering his eyes. 'Go. Leave, right now!' I shouted into his earpiece. I wanted to make him move to snap him out of it.

But when he turned to me and I thought he'd come and pick me up off the side, she put out a hand to stop him. Ainsley was already leading his father from the room. 'Please stay. Wax, isn't it? I fear we got off on the wrong foot and I wanted to say thank you.' The look she gave me over her shoulder was nothing short of triumphant.

How I hated her right then. She was showing me her power over her pawns and all I could say was, 'Wax. Don't listen to her. She's evil,' and I knew he couldn't resist hearing what she had to say.

She was dressed in fitted jeans, but her shirt was still frilly and Victorianesque. She wore her blonde hair up with curls escaping around her face. She was like a doll, dainty and beautiful, and that was all part of her power to lure people in. She took a provocative step closer to Wax.

'Wax,' I said, but it came out more of a whimper. He didn't move back or even answer or look my way. 'Don't listen to her. Look at me, Wax. Let's go. Your mum is with Ollie. God knows what's happening,' I threw in, in a vain hope of shaking him out of it.

But his eyes remained riveted to hers and she took another step into his personal space and looked deeply into his. My stomach turned to acid as she inveigled herself into his mind and he wasn't defending himself or pushing her away.

She reached up a delicate hand to the side of his face.

'Wax! Listen to me. Wax!' I pleaded.

'Thank you, Wax,' she said, softly. Seductively. 'For getting me out of that place.' Then she gently guided him down to kiss him on the cheek.

I smacked the screen and tears brimmed in my eyes. I couldn't help it. I'd never felt so helpless in my life.

I was forced to watch as Wax didn't push her away. He remained stiff and confused and she planted the gentlest of kisses at the corner of his mouth. It was a masterclass in seduction. 'You and your friends must be careful of Ainsley. He trapped me there in the first place to teach me a lesson.'

'No, Wax, don't listen. It was to save her. To bring her back later. They cooked it up together. Remember?'

'Then you need to get away. Tell my father,' Wax said.

She looked at him sadly as if it were only that simple. 'He needs me. If I don't do what he says, he'll get rid of me, and to a far worse place than the mirrors.'

I saw it in the tilt of her head, the lowering of her eyelashes, that she had him in the palm of her hand.

'Come on, Wax. Please. Don't buy this line of bullshit.' It was like he was paralyzed.

I don't know whether she heard me or had known about the earpiece all along, but she put her mouth right next to it to whisper, 'I can help you beat him.'

'What about my friend? She's trapped now.'

'Finally,' I said, in relief, but as soon I said it, I knew he either couldn't hear me or wasn't listening. Then I saw the earpiece resting on his shoulder. She had pulled it from his ear. I also hadn't missed that he'd called me his friend and not his girlfriend either. A weight the size of a medicine ball settled in my chest cavity.

She smiled sympathetically and led him back to a stool to sit down. 'What Ainsley has done is unforgivable, but the curse must be satisfied one way or another. If you help me, I promise, I'll help you to get her out.'

'Don't listen to her!' I shouted, but I knew it was useless. I wasn't even sure if he could hear that he would listen. She had him, just like she had his grandfather and uncle – with too many greats to count – before him. The very thing that had destroyed and cursed the two families in the first place. Only one good thing had come from this, whatever hocus-pocus she used; it had shown me that it very definitely did not work on women.

She reached out her dainty hand and smoothed the furrows along his brow. 'Don't worry. I'll take care of everything. You'll never be alone here again,' she said flashing me a spiteful look. Then, with a flick of her hand, my world span and I landed in a heap on the floor. By the time I scrambled to my feet and went back to the screen, I was back in Ollie's room and his mother was sitting on the end of the bed, crying.

Ollie was sitting helplessly next to her with the others clustered around them, equally unsure what to do. For once, even Tallulah looked lost for words. Ollie instinctively knew I was there and his eyes tracked sadly to me. His mother couldn't see or hear any of them. To her, she was sitting in an empty room.

Ollie shook his head, proving I was right, and his mother continued to cry into her tissue.

Then an idea came to me. It was wild and out there, but I was all out of options. Lila was downstairs, all but making out with my boyfriend and making fools out of us all. 'Hey! Hey! Is that you, Mrs Waxley-Black?' She stopped crying, sniffed, and looked around her. 'Mrs Waxley-Black! The computer screen on Ollie's dressing table.'

She looked a little startled in the direction of my voice and slowly stood up. My hunch had worked. I thanked God for Ollie's tech genius. It would be a lot easier for his mother to take than speaking to an apparition in a mirror. My voice could be heard electronically, on the static airwaves and it appeared she could see me too as she looked right at me. 'Hi!' I said. 'You're Ollie's mom?'

She stopped crying completely and eased into the chair opposite me at Ollie's desk. 'Hello,' she said, dabbing under her eyes with her tissue. They were red and smudged black from crying. She tried to smile a little.

Seeing her like this reminded me of my own mother and any hostility I'd felt towards her earlier disappeared. 'Hi,' I said again. 'You don't know me, but my name is Beccah and I'm a friend of Ollie's.'

Her face began to crumple again, but I didn't have time to let that happen. 'No, no, don't, please. I just wanted you to know he's right here.'

She looked beyond me through the screen and it was clear she didn't understand what I meant at all. I had to take a chance that I wouldn't completely freak her out. 'No, not here with me, but right there with you.'

For a moment her face clouded as if I was playing some kind of cruel joke. 'He's next to your right shoulder and Tallulah and all his friends are right there with him,' I said, saying a quick prayer that she didn't close me down before she heard me out.

She frowned, unsure what I was saying. 'You're a clair-voyant?' She turned her head and looked straight through him. 'He's here?'

I didn't correct her with what I was. Instead, I kept to the point. 'Yes! Close enough to touch.'

Ollie put both his arms around his mother's neck and hugged her. She must have felt something as she closed her eyes. 'I can smell him,' she said on a breath.

'He's hugging you right now.'

She blinked away more tears, but didn't argue as if she was processing it all. I guess she was good with weird; traipsing around India and Tibet trying to make sense of it all.

'He's there, I promise you.'

'Is he OK?' she asked, turning to me again. 'Can you ask him if he's happy?'

'He can hear you. He's reaching for your hand.'

She held up a hand as if it was an alien thing on the end of her arm. He held it, but it was clear she couldn't feel him at all.

'He says he's fine but that you need to look out for Wax. He has his friends and he's happy, but Wax is alone and you all need to be careful of Lila and Ainsley. She's a Blackwood and dangerous.'

She looked stricken for a moment as if I'd deeply shocked her. 'A Blackwood? Ainsley?' She said it as if it was highly unlikely. 'I'm not sure what I can do.'

'The thing is,' I began, not sure exactly how to say what I needed to say, without it sounding ridiculous. 'I'm not sure what she does, exactly, but she has her claws into Ainsley and she'll do the same with your husband and Wax too. It's what she does. We need to protect them and keep them safe.'

She looked down at her hands, holding her tissue, in her lap. I could tell she was warring with what to believe. She picked up a long pendant hanging around her neck and ran her fingers over the smooth green stone. 'We searched for a very long time for answers about my son. What happened. The meaning of it all. And to think he was here all the time.'

I felt desperately sorry for her and was reminded again of my own mother and what she must be still going through. 'He didn't move on, because Ainsley hasn't allowed him to. He was trying to free Lila,' I said, trying to keep the desperation and hatred out of my voice and not spook her.

She shifted in her chair uncomfortably, still not convinced. 'Can you ask Ollie something for me please?' she said, still not getting that he could hear quite clearly what she was saying.

'Go ahead,' I said, looking straight at Ollie.

'Can you ask him if he still remembers the little notes I put in his lunchbox when he first started school? He didn't want to go, you see, and he said they helped him through the day.' It was clever of her to pose a question only Ollie would know.

Ollie didn't hesitate. 'Tell her, I do, and I will never forget them: *I love you to the moon and back and, if by chance, you get home before me, put the kettle on, I'm coming soon.*'

It was a heartbreakingly charming message; just a silly saying they probably said between them again and again; that she'd always be there for him or never far. I repeated the message and she dissolved into sobs, burying her face in her hands. 'Thank you,' she said. I'd passed her test and she was ready to believe whatever I told her. I relayed it all.

'What does Lila want?' she said eventually, through gritted teeth.

'The Elixir of Life. We think it's in the mine.'

She straightened in her chair and looked formidable. 'The mine is Bret's. It always goes to the eldest surviving son, never to be reopened, shared with a sibling or partner in any way.'

That explained a lot. Jedediah had seen to it that no other generation would make the same mistake he did by giving his brother shares in the mine.

'It also gives us a major piece of information,' Ollie's mother said, surprising us all. 'However Lila is managing to exist in the real world, it can't be permanent if she needs whatever's in the mine.'

She was right. Lila wasn't going to all this trouble for Ainsley's benefit. This was huge. It meant there must be a time limit and we'd have to work fast.

Ollie's mum was proving a lot stronger than I realised. She looked me directly in the eye with renewed determination. 'What do you need me to do?'

$\mathcal{I}$t was a relief that Wax wasn't the only live person who could see me, but scary too. If Wax's mum could then it probably meant anybody could and that put me in a vulnerable position. I still didn't know what Lila was. At least when I was ghosting, no one knew where I was.

Wax's mum introduced herself properly as Olivia, which figured; Ollie must be short for Oliver and named after her. I told her a white lie, that I was Ollie's friend from school. It was partly true and easier for her to believe, as she knew most of his friends who died around the same time. Although it encouraged more tears when I told her they were all there, with Ollie, in the room.

When she'd calmed down, we formulated a plan to monitor and report back on everyone in the house. 'You lay on thick the distraught, grieving mum, Olivia,' I said. 'Lila will continue to underestimate you. Her power and interest only seem to extend to the men. That should free you up to spy on anyone you want.'

'No stretch there then,' she said, with a wry sniff. 'I can do that.'

I decided I liked her. She was much stronger than she looked and would be a good ally.

After making sure everyone agreed and knew their job, Ollie sent me back to Wax's IP. It was still a mystery how Lila threw me out of it.

'You'll have the best chance of watching Wax. Just don't let Lila see you,' Ollie said. We'll try to flit between him and my uncle … Stay safe,' he finished.

I was alone, back in the sealed box on Wax's IP. I dialled his phone. Navigating the fibre optics was becoming easier. My mind thought of it as one of those find-the-quickest route puzzles. Once I knew it, it was always the same way. Although, when it just rang and rang, I couldn't tell if it was in the kitchen, but, with practice, I'm sure the GPS part would come.

In the end, Tallulah put me back on her Smartwatch and hung it out of a small breast pocket on the jeans jacket she borrowed constantly from Ollie. That way I could see straight ahead at what was going on.

We reached the kitchen and they were still there. Bile went straight to my mouth and my blood simmered. I couldn't believe it. Wax didn't seem at all worried about what had happened to me. They were seated together at the island, eating a nice breakfast, relaxed, in quiet conversation. Suddenly, the centre of my chest ached and felt empty, like someone had ripped out where my heart should be.

It took a full minute for him to notice any of us walk in. Lila immediately looked around her, 'We're not alone,' she whispered.

It was good to know that she only sensed but couldn't see exactly where we were. At least that's how it seemed. It did make sense. She could see me on devices that were in the real world, the same as any other living person could, but Tallulah's Smartwatch, just like my crutch, had followed her from death, and so it was as invisible as she was.

'What are you doing, Wax?' Ollie asked, as confused and as irritated by it as me.

Wax looked straight from Ollie to Tallulah and down to her watch, hanging at the front of her. 'It's OK, it's just my brother,' Wax said, ignoring the question.

The remainder of my heart was pulled from my chest. I couldn't believe what I was seeing.

Lila instantly relaxed and brightened. 'How charming. Tell him to join us.'

Ollie looked at Tallulah, clearly in as much shock as I was, and she returned a small nod. Then he went and sat on the stool opposite them. Everyone else hung back and observed, figuring the less they moved, the less likely Lila would know they were there. I wasn't so sure.

'You were saying,' Wax prompted.

I was in shock. I mean, I know things had moved fast for me to really know him, but I thought I knew him better than this. I saw his mouth move, but the words didn't matter. What I saw was the gentle touch to his knee. 'I was an outcast in my own family,' she was saying. 'Overlooked. Put aside. They would go to the other side of the country, to an insipid cousin, rather than see me worthy of the man I loved.' She sidled closer and put her hand over his and looked intently into his eyes. 'But the Waxley-Blacks … you … didn't see class or gender, or barriers at all. You were kind to me.'

Wax tilted his head to the side as if he found her puzzling and, instead of pushing her away, simply replied, 'These are different times and different people.'

My throat felt like I had an apple lodged in it. She was carefully weaving her spell around him like a spider. Wrapping him in a spiral of half-truths and deceptions so he couldn't move or escape before he knew what was happening to him. As they continued on in their easy conversation, it struck me and broke my heart the ease and confidence with which he spoke to her. No paranoia or quickness to anger that I'd witnessed first-hand. This was the Wax he was always meant to be and it hurt like hell because he was being it with her. 'I hate her,' I said to no one in particular.

'Me too,' Tallulah whispered from behind me and I loved her for it.

'So, say you can get that deep into the mine, what do you plan on doing with it? Why is it so important to you?' Wax was saying.

I pulled myself out of my quicksand of self-pity. I hadn't even realised they'd moved onto discussing the mine.

Lila seemed to know the exact moment I tuned in. Her eyes darted to exactly where we were before she spoke and my heart froze. She either had the most highly sensitive extrasensory perception or she'd lied and could see us perfectly, which was quite possible as she wasn't exactly alive herself.

She picked up Wax's hand and ran her fingers over the top of it. 'The spell that freed me from the mirrors has only one lunar cycle for physical representation.'

I ignored what she was doing as I raced to catch up with what that meant.

Wax narrowed his eyes. 'It has an expiry date? So, the spell will send you back?'

My mind stalled at the thought of her here with me. I willed Wax to ask the real question of what would happen to me, but he didn't. Instead, he looked at her intently and waited for her to answer.

Lila shook her head sadly, like something out of a soap opera.

I felt sick, not buying a second of it. Wax was absorbing it all.

'No, the cost of the month is to burn brightly with the living and then to cease to be. It was the price to break the curse that bound me. So you see how badly I need the elixir.'

Ollie looked as shocked as we were. 'Wax?' he said, trying to get his attention. When he couldn't get it, he looked anxiously over his shoulder at us. He'd drawn the same conclusion as I had. If the spell and the curse would be shattered, where did that leave me? Where did it leave any of us?

Wax didn't seem ruffled by it at all. 'And my uncle?' he asked.

Lila's eyes twinkled with mischief. 'He's very sweet and everything ...' She didn't finish her sentence but looked deeply into Wax's eyes and, still holding his hand, they shared a long moment of something. Something I wanted to scream and push out of my line of vision.

'Where will you go?' Wax said, in a voice suddenly gone hoarse.

'Oh, I have no idea. There are so many things I want to see in this century, far far away from here,' she said, wistfully. 'All ties will be gone and I'll be free to go anywhere and with whomever I want,' she finished with a coquettish smile straight at Wax.

I wanted to smash the screen. The inference was clear. She was dangling the carrot for Wax to go with her. No doubt, the same one she'd offered Jedediah, Ainsley and his uncle, before him.

I couldn't bear it and had to put my hand to my mouth to stifle a sob. It was the worst kind of torture. I was in a fishbowl, doomed to go round and round, only seeing through the glass, while the world, in full view, went on without me.

It was Ollie who spoke up. 'Ask her about the brothers back then: Jedediah and Ainsley. What happened to them?'

It was clever of Ollie to steer Wax's mind back to what we were all thinking ourselves. Wax repeated Ollie's question, though I strongly suspected that Lila had already heard it. Her posture stiffened very slightly. I would tell Ollie later. It made more sense to make her think she'd fooled us.

She immediately took on the damsel in distress persona. She was the consummate actress, it was clear. 'Jedediah murdered me, brutally, and refuses to leave these walls. Ainsley passed over and abandoned me.'

She took a handkerchief from her sleeve and delicately dabbed the corner of her eye.

It made me sick. It also occurred to me that Jedediah didn't have much of a choice. Lucinda had already told me he could go as far as the Blackwood house and no further and Ainsley had been noticeably absent.

Male laughter sounded loudly from behind us. Tallulah turned sharply and I saw Wax's father and uncle walk back into the kitchen a lot more jovially than when they'd gone out.

'Ah, you've got to know each other a little better, I see,' Wax's uncle said. 'Splendid.'

Olivia followed behind them, blowing her nose. We all moved out of the way so the newcomers could sit around the island with Wax and Lila.

'Did you see him?' Lila asked Olivia immediately, throwing a devilish look our way.

Lila was too arrogant to see the stiffness in Olivia's posture when she answered. Only I knew how she managed to hold it all together with sheer determination. 'I felt very close to him,' Olivia said and blew her nose again. 'It was a great comfort, thank you.'

Lila smiled with no real warmth. 'Many of these old houses are haunted.' Her eyes went directly to me. It was in that moment that I understood. It wasn't a poor poker face on her part, but a game. Everything was all a game where she enjoyed setting up scenarios and watching how the dominoes fell. A player, in every sense of the word.

She grinned as if she knew. Well, she could grin all she wanted. She was far too confident for her own good and we were growing in numbers. We had less than a month to get rid of her before she took the Elixir of Life. And we had to save ourselves.

CHAPTER 24

The next days were some of the darkest I'd ever known. Almost as dark as losing Pete. Like Lucina before me, I had nowhere to go to call my own and I was forced to watch helplessly as Lila took everything. When I say everything, I mean Wax.

On top of all that, I was becoming more and more convinced I wasn't alone. There was something dark and menacing with me in Wax's closed IP. At first, it felt like a growing anxiety tingling up my spine, something ominous. Ollie said it was anxiety because of the stress I was under. But I started to hear noises too. It sounded like something was being dragged across the floor and got louder the closer it got. Like something huge was being pulled across it.

It was all the more terrifying as there were no corridors that I could see, only boxes for the various devices in the loop of Wax's system. The only way to escape was to hop through the fibre optic cable and jump into a different device, which I had to do more and more frequently, only just escaping in the nick of time. It could no longer be put down to paranoia. I had to tell Ollie that I wasn't alone.

'Are you sure?' Because it's closed. There's only one place it could have come from if you're right and that's The Dark Web.'

'Yes, I'm sure,' I said, my heart already speeding up to run. The small hairs on the back of my neck were rising and my breathing began to come in shallow pants. It was getting closer again and I could hear the scrape ... scrape ... then, thump... THUMP. My eyes widened in fright. 'You have to get me out of here. Ollie!' I screamed.

Ollie's fingers worked frantically over the keys.

Tallulah screamed, 'Get her out!', panicking along with me.

But my eyes were fixed to something black and growing in the corner. It smelled of decaying meat and invaded the room, spiralling to the ceiling like bonfire smoke. It grew to twice my size, moving constantly, without any definite shape. It crept closer, menacing and looming over me, until I lost all feeling in my legs. My hands were ice and my stomach churned. 'It's here ...' I said, too quietly for anyone to really hear.

Ollie hissed, 'Shit!' from behind me and slammed the Enter button.

I was catapulted backwards, so fast I couldn't breathe. All I could see were javelin bars of light whizzing past me. It felt like a lifetime, but, in reality, it was probably no more than a couple of seconds, until I landed painfully with my arm caught underneath me. I blinked, finding it hard to focus after the bright fibre optic light. I recognised the familiar blue-grey light of the Inside Out. I was back in the hallway of the mirror spell.

Except before I could fully get my bearings, there was a second blast and a whoosh of air. Followed by something huge and black that landed with an earth-shaking thud next to me. I didn't wait to see what it was and scrambled to the far wall. Whatever it was had been expelled from Wax's IP too. As I turned to face it, my stomach sank into my bowel. The same monster I'd run from started to reform and grow in the centre of the room.

My fear was a visceral vice that gripped the sides of my head right down to my toes clawing in my shoes. I looked left and right for a place to run while I stumbled to my feet, but all that happened was I hopped indecisively in both directions, and my tongue rolled around my spitless mouth. Then, just as the creature wound its whisps of arms around me, I screamed and a wall of black robes appeared in front of me. It roared the loudest roar I'd ever heard and I flinched down to the skirting board, between a large urn and a chest. My jaw went slack as I gawped up in amazement. I recognised that roar immediately. *Jedediah* stood ferociously guarding me; huge, black and threatening. His white, soulless eyes fixing on the monster like spotlights.

I'd never thought I'd be so pleased to see the malevolent spirit, but I was. I crouched behind him. Lucinda said they were on my side and here Jed was, bigger and badder than whatever had followed me here. I could gradually relax enough to stand up.

The darkness was shrinking under his roar, snaking and snarling as Jed bore down on it, literally pushing it through the floor of the room. Then Lucinda appeared from nowhere and ran to me.

I was shaking uncontrollably.

'My dear,' she said, hugging me in her translucent arms that felt pretty real at that moment.

'Is it gone?' I said, still expecting it to appear and get me.

'It has … for now, at least.' The scent of violets surrounded me in a warm cloak. 'But it will be back.'

The spirit of Jedediah stopped roaring and gradually brought his arms down to his sides. He slowly turned to face me. I couldn't take my eyes off him. He still scared me, but I fought not to show it. I owed him my life. He wore a long black robe with a hood that had moved back to reveal his face. His skin was stretched and pale with dark pits for eye sockets, but, instead of eyes, light shone out as if power was escaping from the holes and was barely contained. He pulled the hood forward again so that it shrouded his face. It made me feel sad that he felt the need to cover it. I could still make out the shape of a strong, stubbled jaw remarkably like Wax's. He must have been a handsome man once. My heart broke at the family resemblance that nobody saw because he scared everyone off.

I guess it was the fall of adrenalin, the sense of relief, or simply my narrow escape, but I began to cry. Lucinda shot a warning look to Jedediah, who went to recede into the background. 'Please don't go,' I said, desperately.

'He doesn't want to scare you,' Lucinda explained.

'No,' I said, swallowing down my tears and trying to get a grip. 'I'm grateful to him. It's just the shock. They're all so strong and they have Wax.'

Lucinda looked at Jedediah, who slowly shook his head. 'He doesn't think so,' Lucinda said. 'Keep faith in the young master. Jed is watching over him.'

He bowed his head and disappeared into the wall. I felt oddly comforted, which was bizarre. He was no longer the big bad ghoul out to get me. 'We need to get back up to Ollie's room,' I said. 'They'll be worried about me.'

Lucinda inclined her head. 'I'll be close by.'

I ran back up the staircase with renewed energy, still relishing the lack of plaster on my leg. I flew into Ollie's room and stopped dead, right in front of the mirror of his dressing table. With a wave of my arm, I could already see there was a drama going on the other side.

Wax was in Ollie's room and they were arguing. 'What do you mean, something else was in there,' Wax shouted, pointing at Ollie's laptop.

'Something must have got past the Firewall and got in there with her,' Ollie explained, red in the face too.

'Where is she now?' Wax demanded.

'We don't know,' Tallulah and Ollie said together.

The others were behind them and the room looked pretty full.

'It's OK, guys. I'm in here,' I said and they all followed my voice to the mirror above the dressing table.

Wax pushed between them and sat down on the stool in front of the mirror, without even looking at me. 'I'm putting her back onto my system if it's out.'

I sagged in exasperation. They were talking like I wasn't even there.

'You don't know that,' Ollie said.

Wax's fingers continued to work nimbly over the keys.

'No!' I said, flatly. I wasn't about to jump to it now he'd decided to turn his attention to me. He finally looked me in the eye. 'I don't feel safe there. I'm too alone. I have my friends,' I said, pointing at the others, 'And I have Lucinda and Jed protecting me in here.'

I watched the split second flinch that registered the blow across his face, that he wasn't included on the list. 'I'll carry you with me at all times,' he said a little more gently. 'You'll be safe.' I could see he was hurt or angry because his cheeks were going pink.

'What, like you did in the kitchen, when you left me on the counter and allowed your new friend to cast me aside?'

'It's not like that,' he said, becoming angrier.

I saw Ollie pull Tallulah back and the others followed his

lead. They were expecting Wax to blow. I didn't care. I was at a safe distance and this felt a long time coming. 'What's it like then?'

I could see him breathing hard, trying to keep hold of his temper. His chest was rising and falling more quickly than it should. 'We were just talking. I'm befriending her to find out the best way of fighting my uncle so we can all be free.'

'Or you could be as gullible as all the other Waxley-Black men before you. Can't you see this is what she does? She uses the next man to get rid of the last.' I glared at him and for a moment he glared back, until he swept his arm across the table, knocking everything all over the floor.

'Your temper tantrums won't work with me, Wax,' I said, sounding more bored than I felt. He was pretty scary even from where I was sitting.

'You're impossible,' he shouted into the mirror.

'You're letting that manipulative bitch lead you around by the nose,' I shouted back.

His eyes widened and he drew back his fist and for a moment I thought he'd punch through the glass. But he paused and it was all I needed to try and calm him down. 'Think about it, Wax. She has a month to get the elixir to become real. That's her goal. So, what is she waiting for?'

He frowned. I was getting through to him because he was thinking about what I said.

'There must be something else she needs. Why isn't she up at that mine right now? Something doesn't add up. There's something missing. Something we don't know about.'

The anger drained out of him as if I'd pulled out a plug and he slumped back down into the chair. The others looked at each other in relief, as if I'd just talked down a roof jumper. 'Your uncle is being used but he can't be enough. Think! What else does she need?'

Wax shook his head, clearly confused. 'My uncle has been quiet. He's holed up in the basement, working on something with my father.'

'There's your answer. I bet whatever it is, it's for Lila. We need to get down there and see what it is.'

CHAPTER 25

I'd let myself get talked back into the phone. 'It's the safest way for us to stay together,' Wax said, still angry, I could tell. I decided to let it go and choose my victories, even though he was still pushing me around.

'It is the most portable way for you to be with us, Becks,' Ollie said more softly.

We were soon down in the kitchen again, waiting for an opportunity to get into the cellar. Wax's father and uncle came out like old buddies and his dad put his arm around his mom's waist a little unsteadily. He was smiling, cheeks rosy and drunk.

'You go ahead. I'll catch you up.' Wax put up a hand to his mom. I had to kick myself again, that he was the only one of us any of the living could see.

Ainsley locked eyes with Lila, stone-cold sober, and some silent communication passed between them. Wax's mom didn't lose the opportunity to kiss Wax on the cheek. 'Well, don't be long. I want to hear all about what you've been up to.'

Her eyes flashed to me on the screen, showing me she

was still playing her part and I was grateful for it. I needed all the help I could get right now. Wax's dad and uncle steered her from the room, leaving Wax with Lila again.

I wanted to throw something and rail at him. Every time they were alone, Lila got her claws deeper into him and he couldn't see it. We were missing our chance to get into the cellar.

Then he shocked me. As soon as they were all out of earshot, he leaned forward on his stool and whispered, 'What are they working on in the basement?'

For a single second, I thought Lila faltered. Like Wax had really caught her off guard. Then she just laughed and pointed a reproving finger at him. 'I can see you are the intelligence of the family and shouldn't be treated like a fool. Pay no mind to Ainsley.'

I simmered as she'd skilfully distanced herself from Ainsley's treatment of him and edged closer to him on his stool. Pushing herself provocatively between his knees and touching a delicate hand to his face. Then, to my horror, she wound her finger between the tousled strands of hair on his forehead, as some pathetic excuse to touch him.

'Wax … Wax?' My blood boiled that he didn't immediately push her away from him like the toxic thing she was. I covered my eyes, but, at the same time, I was compelled to watch; it was as if I had some kind of death wish.

'Particularly as we need each other,' she purred.

His eyes didn't falter from hers and he didn't look at me once. I could no longer speak. I was struck dumb; that he could do this right in front of me. Even though we needed the information, I would never do this to him. Not in a million years.

'What are they working on?' Wax said more quietly. 'They're down there too long to be just chatting over old times and they're not that close.'

'Oh my. You're worried. No need to be,' Lila said in a slightly mocking tone, edging ever closer to him, making him lose his train of thought. 'He's asking for your father's help in a simple locator spell. His travels in Tibet will help us design a divining rod.'

I wanted to process what she said, but I couldn't take my eyes off her mouth moving dangerously closer to Wax's. I swear I would have thrown something if my hand could have gripped something real. Instead, the lights flickered.

She looked around and smiled, knowingly.

Wax drew her straight back to the point. 'You don't know where the fountain is?' Wax's mind was clearly working as Lila's lips went to his and then began to kiss him along his jaw.

'No one does. Jedediah burned the map and destroyed the tunnels that led down from the surface.'

My heart was thrashing in my chest and bile reached my mouth as Wax rested his hands on her hips and didn't push her away. 'Where do I fit in?' he said, drawing her to face him. 'You must need me for a reason.' His actions were fluid and easy. Just like he was when he was with me. I couldn't bear it.

Tears were streaming down my face while she pecked him on the lips and whispered, 'Clever boy. I can see you will not be guided like the other Waxley-Black men.' Her arms snaked around his neck and she pushed closer between his legs.

'Oh pur-lease.' I felt sick, hating everything about her and him for playing into her hands so easily. She'd moved effortlessly from seduction to flattery and back again and he'd lapped up every mouthful. I'd complained about being clueless with the opposite sex. This woman was giving me a master class with my own boyfriend and he was letting her.

'I'm afraid, even if the tunnels were intact, we can't simply go there. Jedediah had been working on his own charms to secure it before his death.' She looked wistful for a moment, as if she really quite admired him for it. 'All Waxley-Blacks and Blackwoods are linked to the curse and therefore trapped in this realm. I saw to it myself. So you see, despite being free of the mirrors, until I drink from the waters, it seems I can't go outside the boundary of the spell.' She smiled at Wax ruefully. 'Jedediah saw to it that the mine simply wasn't in it.'

Clever Jed. She may have manipulated and turned the two brothers against each other, but Jed had seen through her eventually and managed to use her own curse against her. I had to applaud him for that. It seemed a lot more clever than where Wax was sitting right now.

'Can't Ainsley just go and get it?' Wax said.

She tipped her head as if he'd made a good point. Ainsley, his mother and father were all alive in the ordinary sense. 'You would have thought so, wouldn't you?' she said, bitterly. 'But no.' Her eyes took on a faraway look and she moved back to perch on her stool. 'When Jed discovered that Ainsley had helped preserve me in the spell, he was incensed and they fought.

Of course Jedediah tried, but he couldn't break my curse and he knew Ainsley would kill him for the mine in the end. So before he died, he left one very clever caveat to the Will. The mine was to be held in trust in each generation of Waxley-Blacks and could only be inherited by the one who broke the curse. That is you, Master Waxley-Black. Not your father, not your uncle, but you. You brought the Blackwood here and you enacted and broke the curse. The mine is yours.'

Wax looked down at her hand that had covered his own and frowned. 'Why didn't past generations simply sell it or get rid of it if they could never do anything with it?'

I was still reeling from the information and I knew he was grasping at straws, but he still made a good point. Surely someone would have offloaded it in the past.

'Foolish superstition. No one dared. All felt the weight of the curse so keenly they simply wanted to be freed. There had been no happiness between the two families and to lose the mine was to lose the opportunity,' she said, proudly, with her crafty, self-satisfied smile. 'Plus, everyone knew there was something of great value there. Greed made them hold onto it in the hope to one day obtain it.'

I guessed that would do the trick. The chance that someday someone in the family would be rich.

Wax was quiet, running things through his mind like I was. It was a lot to take on. We were the couple who had triggered the curse, except, this time around, I was the right person that fit the criteria to free Lila and Wax was the Waxley-Black now eligible to fully inherit the mine.

My mind went over and over it, but kept coming back to the same thing. Wax must never go there. All we had to do was stall until Lila's time was up and she would simply cease to exist like she should have done a hundred and fifty years ago.

I was nervous at Wax's hesitance. I knew he would have come to the same conclusions as me. *Was he looking for a way to beat Lila, or was he running through his options now he stood to inherit a fortune?* 'What if I refuse to help you?' he said, making me breathe a little easier.

She smiled regretfully and trailed a finger down the side of his cheek. I wanted to snap it off.

He smiled haplessly back. 'I don't exactly have much incentive to help my uncle, even if I wanted to help you.'

She put her head to the side, pursed her lips playfully and in a tiny, childlike voice said, 'But all I need is one tiny vial, filled from the waters of the spring that flows through that mine.' Her eyes narrowed and she became more shrewd. 'You can bring back what you will – bucketloads, should you so wish. You could sell it and make your fortune. Banish your uncle,' she said, with a flick of her hand. Then, more softly, 'Give it to your brother and friends that I know are still around you. You could set them free too.'

His eyes brightened and a light came on with every word she said. I saw it clearly. Who could refuse an offer like that? It was an answer to all his prayers. His parents would be happy again. They could live a normal and happy life. 'And Beccah?'

She smiled sweetly and pinched his cheek as if he should already know the answer to that one. 'She is the crux of the curse, Wax. In your heart you know she can never leave. You yourself put her there. She must hold the two worlds up. The spirit and the real. Without her, none of the blessings I mentioned can happen. Without her, everything else falls.'

She held out her arms with her palms up. 'Everything here. The halfway realms will collapse and she will simply die. Because she is neither one nor the other. To get her out would be to lose her for ever.'

Everything paled into insignificance after that. Wax was riveted to her every word. She had spelled it out so plainly. I was trapped and there was nothing anyone could do.

'You can have it all, Wax. Your brother back, riches and go anywhere you want.'

I DIDN'T WAIT for Wax to carry me back to his room. I was too upset. I transported myself back to his computer screens in order to be life-sized when I faced him. I felt diminished enough.

Wax found me as soon as he walked in. There was no sheepishness, just a look directly into my eyes.

I laughed derisively. 'So that's why she's been playing up to you.' I felt spiteful and wanted to wound him in any way I could. I wanted a reaction. Hurt. Anything that would possibly make him feel bad for me and hate her. It was petty, I knew, but I was betrayed and scared and, *what the hell*, jealous. I hated that I hardly knew him and he could make me feel like this. 'Only the one who broke the curse can enter the mine,' I mimicked with my poorest impression of her posh British accent.

Wax looked at me curiously and sat on the stool. 'And Ainsley has my father helping him make some sort of divining rod.'

'What even is that?' I said, guessing it was some kind of pointer.

'It's an ancient method to locate underground water or precious metals. It's usually two sticks or metal rods that move independently.' Wax crossed over his arms to demonstrate. 'They cross when they find something, so I believe.'

I stared at him, amazed that he was so matter-of-fact over all this. His eyes dropped away from me and I knew. This wasn't cut and dry for him. A ragged breath left me. Everything that had gone before had gone and I'd lost him. Not that I ever really had him, but still it hurt. I was dead and the stunning and beautiful Lila was there, promising him everything he could ever want. With a leaden heart I realised that I'd be selfish asking him not to.

Pity, pain, regret, guilt, crossed his face in a devastating millisecond of emotion. I recognised it and nodded without saying a word. I didn't even mention the notion of stalling the month. I didn't need to.

'I need to go and get it for Ollie and the others.' When he looked up he was desolate.

A lump formed so big in my throat I couldn't swallow it down. 'Of course you must.' I knew in that moment, that if the chance had arisen for Pete and me, I would probably have done the same. I just hoped Lila had given him all the facts and would allow him to give the precious liquid away. 'Can anyone else leave the house?'

He shook his head. 'Just homes, jobs. Things in the make-believe world of this spell.'

'Then she knows you have to bring it back here.' My anger had gone. I studied him sadly. 'I just hope she follows through on the plan.' I had my doubts she'd let him give it to anyone once she had what she wanted. It was all too easy.

Wax looked distraught, while I became oddly detached. He was being forced to drop me from his radar of worry in order to concentrate on his family. I got it, but it hurt. 'Maybe you need to talk to your father. He and Ainsley seem buddies at the moment?'

He nodded, distracted, as if there was more he wanted to say. 'Good idea.' Then he got up and, without a backward glance, strode from the room. I was left staring at the big empty space he'd left behind him.

It then hit me in one great tsunami of emotion. I couldn't bear it. I was so utterly alone. I was far from my parents, Pete had gone and my new friends were nowhere to be found. They would have to help Wax, anyway. I would never escape this prison. Lila was right. She hadn't even bothered to lie to Wax to keep him on her side. She was that confident that there was nothing anyone could do. I was the sacrifice, the pillar, that would hold everyone else up. Wax had seen that and accepted it, without argument, as fair exchange. Maybe it was time I did too.

I had no idea where that left me now. I wasn't alive, but I wasn't dead either. *Did I shrink away, or do I help them? But if I helped them, wouldn't they all leave the confines of the spell then and I'd be all alone?*

I thought of Tallulah and Ollie and their playful budding

relationship. Nicola and Archie and the others. I guess I had to give them a chance, even if there was none for me. I looked down at the computer-generated keypad that Wax had coded for me. He would be angry if I moved, but I think all this meant he'd kind of lost the right to tell me what to do.

Without further thought, I brought my finger down hard on the Escape key and landed hard in the grey of the Inside Out. The weight of the gloom hit me instantly in a heavy mist. For a moment I longed for sunshine, something I would no longer see. 'Lucinda?' came out in a strangled whisper. I couldn't lose myself to self-pity. I couldn't shout properly. I didn't know what else would come.

It wasn't Lucinda that answered.

A great moan made me swing around. Jedediah stood at the edge of the room, huge and looming, darker than ever. I knew he wouldn't hurt me, but the blackness in his soul permeated everything around him, giving me a feeling of dread. 'Hello, Jed,' I said, warily.

His movements were slow, but his arm came up and he pointed to the small door behind the staircase. The one that led down to the tunnel between the houses. 'You want me to go to my aunt's?'

He didn't answer. Instead, he moved in that direction, indicating for me to follow. I looked around in the hope I'd see Lucinda, but she was nowhere to be seen. I took a breath and followed the black hooded shape of Jedediah, like the harbinger of death, leading me off to hell.

The corridor gave way to rock, as I remembered from before, and we were in the dark tunnel, circular and rough, barely a man's height. Inadequate torches were placed at intervals on the wall, casting an eerie grey light every twelve feet or so. I wondered briefly who put them there, but dismissed it as part of the spell.

Jed glided on and I followed as fast as I could, so as not to be left behind. 'What is it, Jed? Where are you taking me?' I said more than a few times. When he didn't answer, I remembered that previously he'd spoken very little.

He came to a halt and pointed a bony finger at the rock wall. I didn't understand at first, until I took a closer look. The torches were father apart and the tunnel bent at this point. There was a fissure in the rock. It wasn't that big and you could easily miss it. No more than a few inches wide, but a slim person could squeeze their way through.

Jed was still pointing.

I was uncertain. He was definitely telling me to go that way. 'Where does it go?'

He didn't answer. My eyes went from his long white finger back to the gap in the wall.

I took a closer look. A breeze hit my face. There was definitely more beyond the wall. I looked back at Jed. His face was obscured, but I could see the stubble of his jawline, just visible from his hood. 'You want me to go this way?'

He slowly nodded. I was scared, but I started to think. My mind darted over everything I'd learned. The Inside Out had been originally designed to save Lila from death and extended between the two houses. Jed had turned it into a prison and it was him who'd linked the mine to the curse to stop them getting their hands on it. My breath caught in my throat. 'Is this a tunnel to the mine?'

Jed nodded slowly again.

This was huge. My mind raced over all the implications. I had to tell someone. I wasn't brave enough to go alone. I looked up to tell him I just wanted to get someone to go with me, but he'd gone. He'd completely disappeared.

I started back towards Wax's house at a jog. Jed had shown me that place for a reason. He was telling me something. Wax might be the only one who could go into the mine above ground, but someone else might be able to go in from down here.

Then a thought struck me. The Inside Out mirrored the real world. The tunnel must exist there too. That meant Wax could use the tunnel if he knew it was there, maybe even Ollie and the others too. Lila and Ainsley definitely didn't know about it, that was for sure.

I sped up my pace. I just had to find out how far Ainsley had got with Wax's dad. We needed to be ready to find the fountain.

CHAPTER 26

By the time I got back inside the house, it was after dark. Wax was gone.

'Don't worry,' Ollie said. 'This is typical behaviour. He just can't bear to be in the house with my uncle.'

I stared out of the mirror, miserably, not convinced. 'But I'm here,' came out a pathetic whimper. I coughed and pulled myself together. So what, if it was more proof we were over. I'd have to suck it up and remember we'd only known each other five minutes. Wax was just riddled with guilt and could no longer face me.

Ollie must have read the whole thing on my face. 'He's not very good at relationships,' he said, kindly.

I nodded and swallowed my disappointment, then caught them up with what had been said between Wax and Lila in the kitchen. I made sure I left out all the smoochy details, but there was a definite dimming of his eyes and more than one telling look to Tallulah as I spoke. Somehow, his reaction made it hurt so much worse.

I decided not to tell Ollie about Jed's tunnel just yet. It wasn't that I didn't trust him, it was that I wanted to hold it back from Wax and Ollie would undoubtedly tell him. Lila mustn't know about it at all costs.

'Wax cares a great deal for you, Becks,' Ollie said, cutting through my thoughts.

'That's true, Beccah. I've never seen him act like he does with you.'

Great. Now I had Tallulah's pity on top of everything else. It made me squirm in my seat. 'What happened to all of you?' I said, to change the subject.

Ollie instantly brightened. 'We spied on the cellar.'

All the unpleasantness was quickly forgotten. 'You did? Brilliant.'

They all nodded excitedly. 'They were drinking and messing around mainly, but they were doing something with a pair of metal rods.'

'Divining rods,' I said, absently. Then I told them what I knew about them. 'If only we could steal them. Then they couldn't use them.'

Ollie wasn't convinced. 'It would only delay them until they made more. And we can only touch objects in the confines of the spell, remember? The rods are in the real world where we don't exist. We're not poltergeists.'

I thought about what he said for a moment. Only Wax seemed to see clearly between the two worlds. 'None of you can?'

They all shook their heads slowly.

'Then I need to get down there after dinner to learn what I can.'

IT BLEW my mind when I tried to get my head around the complexity of the world in which I was thrown. I went from the mirrors to Wax's IP, then onto Tallulah's phone. There were three worlds right there. Then there were Ollie and the others, trapped in the dimension or loop of the spell that held the curse. That world lay neatly over the top or alongside the real world, where Wax, his uncle, father and mother and everyone else was. Lila was an anomaly. I suspected she saw through more than she let on.

That evening, while they were all busy eating, we all crept back down to the cellar with me on Tallulah's phone. She'd managed to rig up her phone case to a lanyard around her neck so I could see straight ahead.

Ollie showed me the two metal rods the shape of a large pair of Ls, nestled in velvet in a case the size that would carry a small instrument, like a flute. 'I think they have to be made from a certain metal, as a conductor,' Ollie explained.

'Of what?' I asked.

Ollie shrugged. 'Electric vibes, or something.'

Joe and Josh laughed at the non-sciencey explanation. Nevertheless, I took it all in. It was more than I knew and stealing them to delay what they were trying to do was the best plan I could come up with right then. 'See if you can pick them up,' I said to get them sensible again.

Each of their hands passed through. I was probably the only one who could have done it and I was trapped in here. It was useless. 'So they're ready?' I said to Ollie.

He shrugged again. 'Well, yeah. I think they say a blessing over them or something, then Wax will carry them up there.'

'It's so frustrating that Wax is the only one that can go,' Tallulah said.

I thought about that for a moment. Wax was going to go and there was no way of delaying them. A huge part of not telling everyone about Jed's tunnel was because I didn't want to face the fact that Wax would go no matter what. I guess a part of me wanted him to fight for me that way. But Wax's analytical brain had weighed all best possible outcomes and this was the one that benefited the most people. I was collateral damage.

I decided there and then that Ollie, Tallulah and the others had a much greater shot of getting what they needed from the fountain's waters if they went as well. So while we waited for Ainsley and Wax's father to come to the cellar, I admitted what I knew.

'That's brilliant! We can all go,' Tallulah said, throwing her arms around Ollie's neck.

'Remember, Wax has to go above ground so they don't know about the tunnel. Being the only one is what's keeping him alive at the moment.'

Ollie nodded in agreement. 'Yeah, and if Jed showed you the way in the Inside Out, I think you're meant to go in that way with him. Plus, I'm not sure you could even come through on a phone that deep underground.'

It made sense. I needed to follow Jed, but I also needed to stay in touch with the others.

Tallulah rummaged in her bag, eventually pulling out her gold, circular powder compact. 'Tah-dah!'

It took me a full minute to catch on with what she meant.

'Oh for God's sake,' she said, opening it and holding it out for us all to see. 'It has a small mirror I can fix onto the shoulder strap of my bag.'

It was brilliant.

'As long as you can spot it, you should be able to join up with us through this.'

'Not just an annoying face,' I said.

She rolled her eyes, but further conversation was cut short with the sound of the door at the top of the stairs. Everyone turned their heads in that direction and Ollie hissed, 'Shh!'

None of us could be seen, but it felt too open and everyone scurried to the edge of the room. Even I held my breath in my little black box. There was no pentagon on the floor. Just a workbench and tools, where they'd been working on the rods.

The wall slowly opened with the crank of the mechanism. I hated the sound; it filled me with dread. Then the two brothers walked in.

They were a similar build and height, except Wax's uncle was a little taller, skinnier and his hair had more grey. His dad was a little stockier with a much kinder face that always seemed sad. Even when he laughed it was tinged with regret. I guess losing a son would do that to a person.

My mind leapt to my own mum and dad, but there was no time to wallow and I put it from my mind.

'You think it will work?' Wax's dad said, walking up to the bench.

Ainsley reached up and took a dusty bottle from the huge wine rack. Then he took a gadget from his pocket and uncorked it. He found a couple of old glasses in the makeshift altar and passed Wax's dad a glass. He poured the red liquid with a loud glug. 'Between us, with what you learned in Tibet, and my grimoire, I see no reason why it shouldn't.'

Wax's dad threw back his wine, then pulled up a stool and sat heavily down on it. He seemed so weary of everything. He came across as a man in over his head, who was going along simply because he was all out of options. Although, to be fair, I didn't know him and couldn't be sure. 'I wanted to thank you. For staying put and looking after Bret. You have your own life to live. I'm grateful.'

Ainsley refilled his glass and shook his head. 'Don't mention it. They are my nephews too, remember. Without it, we wouldn't be where we are today.' He held up his glass. 'Let's make a toast. We're on the brink of something monumental, you and I. A cure for death itself.' He reached forward and they clinked glasses. 'Wax has a great gift, Jed. We've always known it. Ollie is here with us; we just can't see him. Once he has drunk from the waters, we'll have him back. You'll see. Lila will be cured and we'll make some real money. Rich beyond our wildest dreams.'

It was hard to tell if Wax's dad was excited or not. His emotions were very closed. I guess that was where Wax got it from. 'So they're ready?' he asked.

Ainsley nodded with a grin. 'You just need to bless them with the words from your Shaman, and we're good to go.'

I watched in wonder as Wax's dad held out his hands over the open case containing the rods and closed his eyes. I couldn't hear what he was saying as it was only a mumble. Then Ainsley followed, doing something similar. Some dark magic, I guessed. It was completely weird seeing two grown men act in this way. My whole life had turned into a stoner's dream. A very dangerous dream.

I shuddered, suddenly cold. I had to trust that Wax was strong enough to see us all through.

'Another?' Ainsley said, holding up the bottle of wine.

'I need to spend tonight with my wife.'

'Of course,' Ainsley said, putting an arm around his brother's shoulder. 'Big day tomorrow.' He walked out with him, smacking the button on the wall as he went. The wall slowly closed and he turned and surveyed the room. It left me wondering if he knew we were there.

Everyone eased through the gap before we were trapped. 'Well, that was no help at all,' Tallulah said as soon as the door at the top of the steps clicked shut.

I couldn't help agreeing. It was a good job we had our own plan.

'We just have to let Wax do his stuff,' Ollie said, with a lot more optimism than I felt.

We went back to Ollie's room to wait for Wax to come back and what mood he'd be in.

WHILE WE WAITED, we went over the plan. 'I don't want you to say anything to Wax,' I said seriously to Ollie and he worked to set me up on his computer screen.

He frowned and shook his head. 'I dunno. I'm not happy about keeping anything from him.'

'I thought we'd all agreed.' My blood pumped in panic. 'You can't, Ollie. Promise me. For it to work, he needs to think he's on his own. They won't believe him otherwise. You must walk the tunnels and surprise him there so they don't suspect a thing.

'How will we find him?' Tallulah said, looking terrified. 'You don't even know the way.'

'I'll have to go in the Inside Out.' I prayed silently that Jed planned on leading me. 'Just be ready with your mirror,' I said, pointing at her bag.

She immediately pulled out her compact and tapped it. 'Got it,' she said.

'Just don't put it down and forget it,' I said, dying at the thought.

She rolled her eyes.

'What other things are likely to be in the tunnels with us?' Sam said, looking really scared. She was the one of my friends I knew the least. I guessed she'd been through a lot too, not knowing how she died. If we got through this, I vowed to help her find out.

My mind went to the scary black entity that came from the Dark Web, but I didn't mention that. 'Just Jed and Lucinda.' I hoped. 'Jed's the unpredictable one and he will be with me.'

She nodded, still looking uneasy. Ollie pulled her into a

hug. 'We'll all be together to face whatever it is, OK?' he said, kissing the top of her head. It struck me what a lovely guy he was.

'You need to join up with Wax as soon as you can. Once he has the water from the fountain, Lila can't be trusted.'

'Who can't be trusted?' came from directly behind them. *Wax.*

Everyone jumped and turned to face the door. I wished I could see, but they formed a wall in front of me. It didn't matter, I'd know that pissed voice anywhere. Whether he was pissed drunk or pissed angry remained to be seen. Probably both. 'Clear off, all of you,' he said loudly.

'It's my bloody room, mate,' Ollie said, raising his voice to match his brother. I'd never heard Ollie angry. I quite admired him for it, but I couldn't help thinking he was a little crazy to antagonise him in his current mood.

'Well, send her to me then.'

Josh and Joe parted and I had a clear view of Wax pointing at me on Ollie's laptop screen.

Ollie looked at me, unsure.

'It's OK,' I said quietly. 'I'll be safe in there.' It struck me then how absurd that was coming from the dead girl who was just static in a computer server. Ollie seemed to accept it though and began to click his fingers over the keyboard.

Wax slammed the door on his way out.

'He's good with you, but don't bait him, OK?' He held my eyes until I nodded. 'You think you know him, but you don't. Not properly.'

I nodded again. He was right. The next thing I knew, I was lightheaded in a heap in the black room of Wax's IP. As my eyes came back into focus, Wax's program of pixelated furniture loaded and built around me. I got up on my feet and went and sat at the desk where Wax sat brooding in front of me. He was wearing a black t-shirt with words

'Craic Whore' written in the italic coke lettering. His leather jacket had been thrown down on the bed.

We glared at each other, both waiting for the other to speak. I was determined not to give in first. Instead, I took in the redness of his eyes and the stiffness in his jaw.

'You're impossible,' he said, eventually.

'You're drunk,' I said, trying to rein it in and remember Ollie's warning. The last thing we needed was Wax tranquilised and asleep.

I considered that for a moment. If he was unconscious, then he couldn't go. What would Lila do about that? Then I shuddered. There was no telling what Lila would do out of spite. She knew what she was doing to hurt me with Wax. Plus, we needed to bring this to a close. We'd all been dancing to Lila's tune for long enough.

So, despite how annoying he was being, I didn't trust her not to hurt him or my friends. Even when he smirked. 'How else would I deal with all the nagging voices?' He widened his eyes and opened and closed his fingers next to his ears like a pair of beaks. It was clearly meant as a barb, but it made me laugh. I couldn't help it.

He scowled in confusion; it wasn't the reaction he was expecting.

'Shouldn't you be busy trashing the place or something?' I said casually, looking at my nails. 'Bad boy rep and all.'

He narrowed his eyes, knowing I was mocking him and I did shift uncomfortably at that. He was intimidating when you were on the receiving end of that look. He pointed a reproving finger at me. 'Be very careful, otherwise I'll have to code you back into the ridiculous maid's outfit again.'

My eyes widened at his sudden change of mood to playful and then our faces dropped at exactly the same time. It was the moment when we both remembered that I was never going to get out of this place to wear any silly outfit. To save his brother he would have to get close to Lila and sacrifice me to this place.

It was very telling. It meant that, deep down, I knew he was using her as much as she was using him. It still hurt, though. In our whirlwind couple of days, I'd fallen for the arrogant, grumpy, antisocial boy sitting in front of me. Dead or alive, he'd made me feel more of anything than I had in a very long time. It was devastating that it had to end.

He looked down at his hands sadly, as if he'd gone through a similar thought process in his head.

'I'll be OK,' I said, a huge lump forming in my throat; big enough for both of us. 'I get it, I do. Just don't fall under her spell, OK? Don't trust her. Whatever she promises you, she's in it for herself.'

His look was black and scary when his bloodshot eyes went back to mine. The muscles tensed in his jaw and all signs of drunkenness were gone. Then he just looked lost and alone. 'I swear, if there was any other way.'

'I know.' I smiled sadly, knowing he meant every word. 'I guess I'll always be here when you visit.'

By his frown I could tell the implications of his freedom were just hitting him. He'd be out of here so fast all anyone would see was dust. He'd been trapped for so long, I couldn't blame him. 'I'm not giving up on you,' he said, suddenly. His look hardened with new resolve.

I appreciated the thought, but it was useless and I didn't have any emotion left in the tank to waste on false hope. 'You need to get in her good books … go,' I said, with a flick of my hand. I was already turning away and didn't want to see the look on his face. As I hit the shutdown button, I could hear him calling. 'Becks, wait! … Becks!' Then the screen cut off to a small dot.

Everything in my world was quiet, except for the electronic hum of the server that I realised was permanently on in here. My sobs came thick and fast; going on and on, racking my whole body. I wanted to isolate and feel sorry for myself as I'd done so many times over the last months. There was no point in spending time with anyone, because they'd all soon be gone. I dragged myself to the pixelated bed, flopped face down onto it and spent a lonely night, where crying was the drug that sent me off to sleep.

It was Ollie who shook me awake. 'We're setting off, Becks.' He was peering in, too close to the phone screen.

They must have moved me while I slept. I hated it when they did that without my knowledge. 'OK,' I said, groggily.

'I want to chuck you out so you're in the Inside Out, ready to go.'

It made sense. 'Can you take me down with you first? I want to make sure Wax's head's in the right place before he sets off.'

Ollie nodded. 'As soon as he leaves, you go to your tunnel and we'll go to ours.'

I agreed and we went together down into the hallway. It seemed full of people, when in fact there were really only four. Wax's mom was fussing over him and his father, handing him a torch and telling him to be careful.

Wax looked awful. I guessed his hangover had hit without him having slept. His hair was pushed flat under his beanie, his skin pale and his eyes dark. Lila hooked her arm through his and pulled him down to whisper something in his ear. He nodded and their interaction made my stomach churn.

Ainsley came forward and passed him the long, flat case that I knew contained the dousing rods. 'Use them just like I showed you,' his dad was saying. 'Loose, letting the rods do the work.'

Wax nodded, looking like he was battling not to be sick.

'Follow where they point until they cross.'

Ainsley took out another black flat device, turned a knob

and passed it to him. A walkie-talkie. 'Keep in touch. Channel two.'

Wax put it into an old black rucksack, along with the rods, and pulled on a black bomber jacket. He reminded me of a Special Ops guy. Then, while his dad was given the same drill and pulled on a similar jacket, Wax looked over at us. We were all congregated on the stairs. My heart leapt as he was obviously searching, until he found me on Ollie's phone. 'Bye, then,' he said, sounding like he was saying it to no one in particular, but I knew he was saying to me.

I mouthed the words *be careful*.

'Come on, I'll drive. 'I've got the ropes, shovels and everything, already loaded in my car.'

Wax took one last look and strode out the front doors with his father.

We stood directly behind Olivia, Lila and Ainsley, seeing them off. The shiny black Range Rover crunched away on the shingle. Olivia dabbed her eyes and blew her nose. She turned and ran back up the stairs, not realising she'd run right through her other son.

Ollie went to move away, but I called, 'Wait!'

Ainsley swung the doors shut and pulled Lila into his arms. Right after her being all over Wax. He kissed her passionately and she responded. It made me feel sick. He seemed old enough to be her dad. 'The day has finally come,' he said, breathlessly, releasing her mouth and pulling her into his body. He pulled apart to look her in the eyes. 'As soon as the boy comes back, we're away from here. Have you packed?'

She nodded. Then my heart stopped as she turned to look straight at us at the foot of the stairs. I still wasn't sure if she saw us or just sensed. Either way, she knew we were there.

'Our guests?' Ainsley said, turning to look in the same direction.

'Will the waters really give them life?' Ainsley asked. 'It will cause ripples in the community if they're suddenly back from the dead.'

Lila shrugged and her look turned spiteful. 'It doesn't matter, because they won't be getting any. The fountain must remain a secret if we're to be rich.'

'What about Bret? We can barely handle him and I walk a fine line with his parents as it is.'

She smiled sweetly at him and cupped the side of his face. 'We have his little girlfriend captive and, don't worry, he'll learn his place if he wants to stay out of the asylum. We can deal with his parents.'

Ainsley nodded, not looking totally convinced. 'It's a shame we need him as the only one who can get the waters.'

Lila tutted, turning on him sharply. 'I weary of all this, Ainsley. My Ainsley would have sorted it like this!' she said, clicking her fingers next to his face. 'I wouldn't need to explain trivial things. He would know that your brother and his wife will simply go on their travels and never return.' She roughly pulled out of his arms and flounced off down the corridor. 'Pack! You useless buffoon! Must I do everything.'

While Ainsley stood, baffled at her outburst, wondering what on earth he'd done, I whispered, 'Let's go.' We'd all heard enough to know I was right about Lila. All our lives were at stake.

CHAPTER 27

*I*n a moment I was back in the grey of the Inside Out, staring back at my friends through Ollie's bedroom mirror. The only plus side being that it felt less claustrophobic. 'So you know exactly where to go.'

They all looked at Ollie. 'Through the servants' corridor under the stairs, to the door on the far side that leads to another corridor, that leads into the tunnel between our two houses. Move along it about a hundred yards to where there's a slight bend and there's a gap in the rock on the left,' Ollie recited.

I let out a breath and nodded. 'We can do this,' I said, taking in each one of their faces. It was amazing how deeply I felt about them all and I didn't even know them a few days ago.

'We need to get going, sappy,' Ollie said with a grin.

He was so damn likable, even when he was making fun of me. 'OK, go!' I said, swallowing the lump in my throat with pride. They'd all dressed in something black of Ollie's and trooped out like a line of coalminers. All they needed was soot on their cheeks. How I wished I could go with them in the real sense.

My job was much lonelier and dangerous. I'd be traveling with the vengeful ghost of Jedediah Waxley-Black.

I left the mirror and navigated the house, bathed in the eerie grey light, in exactly the same path I'd sent the others. It was hard to believe we were occupying the same space in different dimensions.

Jedediah was a dark and foreboding figure waiting for me at the fissure in the tunnel. His head was down and the dark hood covered the scary lamps he had for eyes. I came to a stop as near to him as I dared. 'I'm ready,' I said.

Without looking up, he lifted an arm and pointed a bony finger at the gap in the wall. I guess that meant I was going first.

I squeezed through sideways, amazed at just how tight it was and how anyone bigger could possibly make it. However, Jed was already on the other side when I got there, proving he was even less corporeal than me and had very few boundaries. It brought me up sharp and I had to hold my chest to steady my heart. I still wasn't used to the rules of all the various types of beings.

 He didn't speak, he just turned and glided along what was a narrow ledge lit by a strange light from candles set in the jagged wall. Great lumps of rock loomed and leaned on each other, forming a roof, and to our right fell off a sheer drop that I was too scared to look down in case I lost my balance. While Jed appeared to float, I climbed natural steps upward and shimmied slowly down slippery slopes on my butt. The grey from the candles became further apart, until I was sure the only light came from the projection of Jed's eyes. I had no phone with me to use as a torch, so I was forced to stick closely behind him. Strangely, my fear of falling was greater than my fear of him. Although it did make me wonder just how powerful Jed was.

It felt like we'd been walking for hours. I hoped the others were making good progress. I thought about Tallulah's mirror and began to look for shiny objects as I walked along. I hoped she remembered to take it out of her bag. She was so ditzy at times.

Jed pushed on, strong and determined, downwards, to what felt like the bowels of the earth until we came out into a large, circular, perfectly lit cave. It had to be about thirty feet across and a similar height, with great rock shards jutting over our heads.

I hoped it was safe. If not for me then for the others. Jed slowed and turned and I realised we must have reached our destination. I could hear a light tinkle of water and looked at Jed and frowned. There was no great pool or the waterfall that I was expecting.

He put out his bony hand to a collection of small rocks where the light grey was marbled with black. It was hard to tell colour in this place. I edged closer, not sure what I'd find. The tinkle got louder until I peered between the rocks to find a pool no bigger than a kitchen sink. It had a tiny trickle from a narrow channel running into it and another where it flowed away back between the rocks. It was perfectly hidden and contained. 'That's it?' I said, standing up straight and facing Jed again. It was hard to believe that it was what all the fuss was about. So many people had died or had their lives ruined over generations for this.

Jed stood, unmoving, with his head lowered. It was how he always seemed to rest. In a state of waiting. However, today he seemed more sad than usual, as if even he saw the futility of it all. Perhaps he was remembering that his brother had betrayed him for it with little or no remorse. 'We have to find the mirror,' I said, cutting through the unbearable silence.

There was nothing in the cave, so they hadn't made it that far on the other side. Jed understood and moved towards the way we came. We retraced our steps to an area where the path forked. It would have led them in the wrong direction or at least made them stop, not knowing what to do. If they had sense, it was here they would wait.

I was right. I loved Tallulah right then and vowed to tell her she wasn't as silly as she looked. I reached up for the small circular light propped up on the tiny ledge. I put my face up against it, the mists cleared and there they were; arguing over which direction to go. 'Guys! Guys!' I said, a little louder.

'Shh!' Ollie hissed. 'Listen.'

'Over here,' I said again, bringing all their heads around.

'Beccah!' Tallulah squealed.

Everyone gathered around and peered into the small circle of glass. I couldn't see them all, but they seemed safe and well. 'You made it,' I said, relieved. 'You must follow the right-hand fork. I could see the black outline of Jed looming behind them. They seemed to sense him and parted and he slowly shook his head. Then I got it. Things in the mirror were the other way around. 'Sorry, go left.' It was so confusing if you dwelt on it. 'I'll meet you there.'

In less than ten minutes, I was looking at them all again.

'I can't believe we're here,' Tallulah said, excitedly, as if they'd gone to the beach or something. 'Have you tried some yet?' she asked.

In all honesty, it hadn't crossed my mind, I'd been so worried about everyone else.

'God, I'd have my head in it like a horse in a trough,' she said.

Joe and Josh sniggered and she scowled at them.

'We don't know what it will do. Let's wait till Wax gets here safely first.' With the mention of his name, a sudden panic took hold of my heart. His journey was far more dangerous than ours, and he was, of course, alive and had something to lose. He would have arrived by car with his father and be trying to get through collapsed tunnels and mine shafts. Ruins that had been the same way for a hundred or so years. The structure would have long gone. At that moment, he seemed so far away. He was in the real world, not in the Inside Out or even in the curse plain. I hoped they overlapped as they did in the house because I wasn't sure whether even the Shades could manifest there.

I turned to look at Jed, who was already fading into the cave wall. 'Where are you going?' I said, alarmed. I was terrified of being trapped and alone.

He put up a hand, telling me to stay, then he blended into the wall. I was left with the only light coming from the compact. My hearing was on high alert for anything scurrying around my feet. I had to breathe to stop myself giving way to my fear.

'What's happening?' Ollie asked, reading the panic on my face.

'Jed's gone.' I knew I had to get a grip of my breathing so I didn't freak them all out. My eyes were slowly getting accustomed to the light. 'Sorry, it's so dark in here.'

'He's probably gone to get Wax,' Ollie said, kindly. 'Spirits are much stronger on the Earth plane than we are.'

I breathed a little easier, knowing he was probably right. Jed hadn't brought us all this way to leave us stranded. 'Can you see?'

Ollie nodded and looked around. 'There're candles and we've got our phones. No reception though.'

I did the same, taking the compact with me and using its

meagre light. I could hear the direction of the water. 'The fountain is a bit of an anti-climax,' I said, edging my way closer to it, careful not to fall. Dropping and smashing the mirror would be a catastrophe at this stage. 'Guess we should try the waters for ourselves, you know, to see what it does?'

Ollie shrugged. 'Tallulah just did.' He shook his head wearily as if he should have known she couldn't follow orders. 'She said she doesn't feel any different.'

'Well, I don't,' came from a little way off.

I chuckled to myself. Trust Tallulah to rush headlong into something. 'Tell her they are the ugly waters, the fountain of youth is over there,' I said, not able to keep the laughter out of my voice, as I pointed in the other direction.

Ollie laughed.

Tallulah shouted, 'Hey!'

I reached down to the fountain myself. The water felt ice cold, as you would imagine this far down. It was a natural spring, filtered through miles of rock. There didn't appear to be anything magical about it. Just ordinary-looking water that could have come from a bottle or a tap.

For a moment, I wondered if we could all have been part of an elaborate con. Well, Lila and Ainsley had gone to an awful lot of trouble to get it if it was.

I cupped my hands and brought some to my mouth and drank. It tasted sweet with a slightly metallic undertone. Kind of how I expected it to taste. Then I stood back up and waited. Tallulah was right. Nothing happened. 'Well, I'm still —' I went to say alive and amended it at the last minute to, 'here.' I frowned at the ridiculous irony.

All the others did the same, stooping, taking a drink and standing around waiting for something miraculous to happen. It didn't. Then we all looked at each other, wondering what was next.

A noise echoed on their side. They all turned to look. 'Wax!' Ollie said.

They all rushed over, but, in the excitement, they forgot to hold me up. I was blind and buffeted in the darkness. When they slowed, I was next to someone's blue-jeaned legs. Tallulah eventually held me up and clipped me over the strap of her bag. I could see Wax gazing at all of them and his father looking around, a little way back. 'I can't believe it. You're here. How did you get here?' Wax asked, a little alarmed. Then he noticed the compact. 'Becks?' His eyes went to Ollie, angrily.

'Don't be upset. Beccah came up with this plan so we weren't double-crossed. There's another tunnel that's also in the Inside Out. And how come Dad's here? … I didn't think anyone else could get in here apart from you,' he finished in the same accusatory tone.

Wax checked his father over his shoulder and shrugged moodily, then shot a glance at me as if I'd crashed a party he was at. 'We tested it and nothing happened. We guessed it was because the curse is broken and he's with me.'

Wax was treating me like I wasn't there. I told myself it was just because he was hurt that I hadn't included him. I had to suck it up and accept that, for the time being, he was on the other side.

His father came over. 'What is it? … Everything OK?' he said, helping Wax take off the heavy rucksack from his back.

'Nothing … usual voices,' Wax said, delving into the bag and taking out a small glass flask with a stopper. 'OK, take some while I fill this,' he said, throwing us a look and walking over to the group of rocks that held the fountain.

'Is it Ollie? He's here?' his dad said, whirling around in the vain hope of seeing something.

'Yes, he's here and he shouldn't be,' Wax said, crouching down and submerging the bottle.

'We've already tried it,' Tallulah said flippantly. 'I don't think it does anything. Not to us, anyway.

Wax paused and frowned.

His father came up to his shoulder. 'What is it?'

Wax didn't speak until the bottle was filled. He stood back up, corked it and slipped it in his bag. 'And this is definitely the place,' he said, talking to himself as if he was going over what he knew.

His father was following him expectantly. 'It must be,' he said with a shrug.

'The rods drew me in this direction and then we saw the light.'

I didn't say I knew it absolutely was the right place because Jed had guided us here himself. Wax was clearly feeling side-lined enough. The others were looking to him for the answers. His father was still searching around him. 'If you have it, let's go. I'm not sure how safe the roof is here.'

Wax swung the backpack over his shoulder. 'Wait. Before we go, there's something you should know. Ollie has already drunk the water and it hasn't worked.'

Wax's dad looked back at him, shocked. 'I don't get it. It has to. Ainsley said—'

Wax shook his head. 'He either doesn't know or he lied. Ollie's here, Dad, and if you can't see him then it hasn't worked.'

I felt desperately sorry for Wax's dad. He looked stricken. He'd done everything to help Ainsley in the hope of bringing back Ollie and it had all been for nothing. The dangers of the roof were forgotten and he went over to gaze down at the unimpressive waters of the fountain. It was clear he had no idea we were all there.

Wax reached over and pulled me off the strap of Tallulah's bag and held the compact out to his father. 'Except her. You might be able to see her through the glass.'

My heart thumped. I had no idea what on earth Wax was doing. I went closer to the glass and saw his father peering down at me. I knew the moment his eyes focused, as he jumped back in shock. I wasn't sure what the scientific explanation for it was, but his father definitely saw me. Maybe the glass was a conductor, I wasn't sure. I was somewhere else entirely to the others. Maybe the waters had helped in that. I didn't know for sure.

'It's Beccah. Rebecca Whitely,' Wax corrected. 'She's the Blackwood Lila trapped to get free.'

His dad looked from him to me, bewildered. 'Hi, Mr Waxley-Black,' I said, with a little wave as if Wax had just brought me home to do homework together or something. It felt weird.

Wax's dad continued to look from me to Wax and back again. 'But I don't understand.'

'This is what it's all really been about, Dad,' Wax said, tapping the mirror with his finger. Lila was trapped and Ainsley's made some kind of pact with her. I don't think they had any intention of bringing Ollie back.'

'It's true, sir. Lila has been dead well over a hundred years,' I said, hoping he could hear me.

He looked down at me with an expression that said he didn't know if he should be awake. 'And you?'

I nodded. 'Recently, though. Actually, about the same time as Ollie.'

'You know Ollie?' He put his hand to his mouth as he battled back tears. I felt desperately sorry for him. I guess grief made a person do mad things when they grasped at hope.

He walked away with his hand to his forehead, shaking his head and turned back again. 'I didn't know if it would work, if you want the truth of it. I suspected not, but—?'

I knew what it was to long to see someone that desperately. I felt it every day about Pete.

I was suddenly conscious that everyone had swung around to look at something.

Oh my God, Lila. Walking in and nudging Olivia along, with her hands tied behind her back and Ainsley holding a large shotgun behind her.

Wax went to take a step forward and Ainsley immediately held up his gun. 'Tut-tut!'

'How can you be here? Why did you need me?' Wax demanded, thrown and anxious for his mother.

We were all confused.

Lila clicked her fingers and pointed at Wax's rucksack. 'Give it to me,' she ordered.

Wax took it from his shoulder and slowly passed it to her outstretched hand.

'Why didn't you just come and get it yourselves?'

'We would have if we'd known about the tunnel,' Ainsley said. 'But we still needed you to get it. So we just followed the peanut gallery here.'

Lila grinned at the others, proving I was right and she could see them all along. She took out the glass bottle and held it up to the light. Then she uncorked and sniffed it and threw the contents straight down her throat. She closed her eyes and we all waited. The trickle from the fountain seemed deafeningly loud. Just when I thought the whole thing was a fraud, a blue light seemed to travel down her whole body in a halo, until it reached the floor and disappeared.

'What about me?' Ainsley said, shoving Olivia forward.

Lila threw the bottle at Wax, who made an excellent last-second catch. 'Fill it again,' she ordered.

For a moment, I thought he was going to refuse. Then he looked at his mother and knelt and did as he was told. He was clearly bewildered and trying to figure it all out. 'I don't understand. How does it work for you and not anyone else?' He stood back up and threw the bottle to Lila, equally aggressively.

She only just caught it and narrowed her eyes at him. I wanted to cheer. I guess the honeymoon was over, already. She uncorked it and passed it to Ainsley.

We had huddled together. Even Wax's father was standing with us. It said a lot. He was looking anxiously at his wife while Ainsley drank the contents of the bottle.

'It only works on the living,' Lila said with a smirk as if the answer should have been obvious. 'It prolongs life, heals and rejuvenates. It doesn't bring the dead back to life. In other words, it can't make life where there is none.'

Olivia let out a wail like a wounded animal. Wax's dad growled in anger and Wax put out a hand to stop him when he went to take an aggressive step towards them. They'd all been tricked.

Tallulah sniffed and Ollie put his arm around her. 'We're stuck being Shades for ever.'

I wanted to comfort her, but I couldn't take my eyes off the scene. Something was happening with Ainsley. He almost dropped the gun and shook his head as if he was dizzy.

Lila pushed Olivia roughly towards us while she went to Ainsley's aid. She grabbed the gun so he didn't drop it and held his shoulder with her free hand. 'Ainsley, is that you?'

I was confused, watching him stagger as if he was warring with himself. It was so bizarre, no one even thought to make a move on the gun. 'What's happening to me?' Ainsley wailed. His face was ugly and contorted with pain.

Then the truth, when it came, was as clear as the fountain waters. 'It's the old Ainsley,' I said, more to myself, but Wax heard and nodded. 'The original Ainsley is taking over his body. It's been the plan all along.'

Ainsley looked at Lila, startled, as if it was news to him, and then, with a final wail of 'Noooo!', he collapsed to the ground. He writhed and twitched, until eventually he stilled. No one knew if he was alive or dead. Then he slowly unfolded, blinked, rolled onto his side and shakily got to his feet. He held out his arms to Lila and she went straight to him and they kissed. 'Ainsley,' she whispered, but it seemed to amplify in the cave.

When he eventually looked over at us all, his features remained unchanged, but the way he stood and carried himself and the light behind his eyes seemed different. He was darker, crueller, somebody else. Wax's uncle had gone and his body had been filled by the spirit who had helped mastermind the curse that had ruined every one of our lives.

I had to admit that I was surprised how pleased and in love Lila appeared to be with him. I didn't think she had it in her. Still, there was no guarantee she'd stay that way when he'd outlived his usefulness.

Our group stayed riveted together, not taking our eyes from Ainsley, who took the gun from Lila and pointed at us again. He seemed harder, stronger and even more confident than Wax's uncle. He was the proven killer who'd murdered Jedediah. No doubt the very aphrodisiac that attracted Lila. He was as ruthless as her. It made me sick.

It was also clear he could see us all. Maybe it was something about death that meant it clung and gave them the ability. Lila stood triumphantly next to him, smirking, lording it over us like a queen.

It was then I understood how miserable and superfluous we all were. It was a stomach pitting moment when it dawned on me that everyone I'd grown to love could die. A great wave of emotion went out from my chest, like I wanted to scream and tear it out, with a gut wrenching, 'Nooooo,' I screamed. I was useless in the mirror. I was trapped in its airless confines. Suddenly it felt too claustro-phobic. I couldn't breathe. I wanted to reach out a hand to hold Tallulah's, but it I knew it was hopeless. Although something had changed. I felt light-headed and strange. I looked down at my arm and it was pale and chalky, just as I'd seen Lucinda's.

I looked up and I was there in the cave with everyone else.

Tallulah turned her head and looked down at my hand taking hers, then her eyes widened at me in shock. Without turning her head, she tugged on Ollie's arm next to her for him to look too. 'Beccah?' he said, like he couldn't believe it.

Everyone turned to look at me at the same time. I put up my hands as if I'd been caught doing something wrong. Except my eyes were distracted by them, powdery, pale and translucent. I was there, but I wasn't. I was somehow out of the mirrors but only partially. Maybe it was the fountain waters, or maybe my desperation had simply willed it, but I was there with my friends in spirit at least. My heart light-ened with a renewed strength and I stood straighter to face my enemies with them.

Wax had us all huddled behind him, shielding us with his father. Our fidgeting whispers, and the surprise in Lila's eyes, made him glance over his shoulder. Then, just as he was about to turn back and speak, his eyes found mine. There was only a brief moment of shock and then a wonderful split second of warmth where a strange understanding passed between us. It said, *There you are, you're here, with me, I'll protect you, I'm so sorry,* all in one moment of wonderful, smouldering communication.

Ainsley, however, wasn't waiting and cocked the gun, forcing Wax to turn back and focus on him again. We huddled tighter behind our wall of Wax and his father.

'How has she done this?' Ainsley said, in an angry, cheated

voice that sounded so different to Wax's uncle. 'I thought she was trapped?'

The smirk didn't leave Lila's face. 'Clever girl, she's just found a way to project an imprint, that's all. She's no more here than that tiresome sister-in-law of yours, Lucinda.' She tipped her head to me as if I'd impressed her in some way.

Ainsley renewed his grip on the gun and Wax shouted, 'Wait! and put up a hand defensively. 'You have what you came for. Just go. No one here will stop you. You can go anywhere now. Do anything.'

'Loose ends,' Ansley said, in a far more gravelly voice than we were used to. 'I have no use for my great great-great-great nephew, is it?' he said, intrigued, more to himself, as if he was trying it out for size. 'You're just an added complication.'

'Wait! Can you afford to take the chance!' I shouted, stepping out from the barrier of Wax's body. 'What if you still need him to get the waters?

Ainsley's eyes narrowed while he took a moment to consider what I said. 'It almost makes me miss my unfortunate brother, Jedediah.' The more he spoke, the more different he sounded and the smile he wore like a mask was more a grimace than anything kind. He smirked and pulled Lila closer with his free arm.

'The older boy must live … for a while, anyway,' Lila said.

Ainsley nodded. 'Just till we break Jedediah's hold on this place.'

I finally allowed myself to breathe. Although I didn't relax. I was still terrified. Ainsley was unpredictable and I wasn't exactly sure what I could affect in the physical world. My attention was drawn again as he rattled the gun pointing it again. 'We only need one of them.'

Olivia whimpered and Wax's dad pulled her into his chest so she wouldn't see what was coming. Josh straightened, Archie held Nicola and Joe did the same with Sam. Everyone knew someone was about to get hurt. 'No!' I shouted, holding onto Tallulah's hand and Wax's jacket so neither could move. Wax's dad tried to soothe Olivia with a jumble of words.

Then everything seemed to happen at once.

CHAPTER 28

*M*y hand had no grip and Wax and Ollie both pounced towards our captors and shouted. 'No!' Tallulah screamed. Everyone shouted at once in protest, sounding like there was a hundred of us in the acoustics of the cave. Emotion was so high, I was sure it could be heard on all three planes.

There was a great rumble and a loud groan like the depths of the earth were opening. The ground shook and dust and small rocks began to rain down from the roof. Everything began falling around us.

Then, just as suddenly as it came, the torches dimmed, the rumbling stopped and all that was left was the dark, fore-boding figure of Jedediah. The whites of his eyes cast their eerie light as he stood between us and them, fixing Ainsley and Lila with his terrifying glare. He was an awesome sight and although my adrenaline was pulsing through my nervous system, I wasn't nearly as afraid as I probably should be. I wanted to dance and shout, *How do you like me now, assholes*! in a victory chant.

But no one moved a muscle.

The quake had died down and all that sounded was the wind through the tunnels and the running of the water.

'Jedediah,' Ainsley stated, simply, as if he wasn't surprised to see him at all.

I needed to move so I had a clear view. Tallulah went to grab me, but her hand passed right though me. I apologised with a look and edged around the shield of Wax's body again. I wasn't going to miss this.

'Jed, oh Jed,' Lila said, making as if to take a step towards him. Ainsley put out a hand and immediately stopped her. For a moment, she looked between them, unsure, weighing her options.

Ainsley only had eyes for Jedediah. 'It's too late, Brother. You put up a brave fight, but you have lost. We have the Elixir of Life. I am no longer a spirit with no form. I have a live body that can be youthful again and Lila is free of the curse.'

Jedediah remained eerily still. With only some sort of cosmic wind buffeting the black of his robe, it made me convinced that he was no more really there than I was. That he was manifested by his sheer strength of will. He never spoke, he didn't need to. Arguments with Lila and Ainsley were said many years ago. Instead, he simply raised his arms and the cave began to shake.

This time, no one waited to watch. Seizing the opportunity, Wax's father grabbed Olivia and Wax and pulled them towards the way they came. For a moment, Wax hesitated.

'Go!' Ollie shouted. Shooing him out with his arms. 'We're OK. We'll meet you back there.' Then, just as the bigger rocks began to fall, with one final, agonising look at me, Wax allowed his father to pull him out into the tunnel.

The rest of us huddled in a natural alcove at the edge of the cave. It was strange, because we were all pretty much dead, anyway and yet we clung to that small glimmer of life, but it felt real enough. I couldn't even imagine what would happen if a boulder hit one of us. We clung together in a scrum to get as close to the wall as possible. Tallulah screamed and ducked, and, with an 'Oh my God', and with a loud crash like thunder, I got a clear view of a gigantic part of the ceiling fall directly on top of Ainsley, surely killing him outright. An arm and a foot just visible in a growing pool of blood. No one could survive that. Lila dithered, this way and that, until she ran back the way she came.

With both of them gone, the earth seemed to settle and the deafening rumble stopped. We slowly uncovered our eyes and tried to focus through the settling dust. Jedediah had gone but it was by no means over. 'Get out of here!' I shouted. We moved fast, picking our way through the rubble to the tunnel as quickly as we could. Another huge clap of thunder sounded behind us as the cave completely collapsed. We were all running for the safety of home, but I had no thought of that. Lila could not get away. Somehow I'd managed to merge my world with theirs, and I didn't know how long it would last. My head was splitting and instinct told me I couldn't hold myself there for much longer. I bit down the urge to rest and navigated the windy paths with my friends quickly, squeezing through the fissure, not stopping until we were in the tunnel between the two houses.

We caught our breath. Archie hugged Nicola, Ollie kissed Tallulah and Joe bent at the waist, spat and put his hands on his knees. Sam laughed in relief. It did feel like we'd pulled off a great escape.

I hovered a little apart, waiting for someone to bring up my altered state, but no one said a word. Instead; 'Which way?' Archie asked, hand firmly gripped in Nicola's.

I was going to say something when a moan brought our heads round in the direction of my aunt's house. *Jed.* And we were all soon off again. Except, this time, we were following the sound instead of running away from it. I knew he was calling us. He didn't want Lila to escape, any more than I did. We came to a sliding stop at the door to the house. My heart thrashed in my chest. Now we'd caught up with her, I had no idea what we'd do.

Lila grinned as if she knew and turned to go inside. However she pulled up abruptly.

Jedediah stood motionless, barring her way.

For a single moment, her composure faltered and fear flashed across her face. Then, just as quickly, she seemed to gather herself together. 'Jedediah, my love. It doesn't have to be like this. I forgive you. I understand. You should know that it's always been you.'

Then I got it. I remembered Lucinda telling me about the barrier spell stopping Waxley-Blacks entering the Black-wood house. Lila knew about it, probably because she herself put it there to stop Jedediah coming after her. It was the day Lucinda hid with me in the secret passage. Jed had searched for us until he finally broke through. The angry spirit was a master of finding loopholes, stretching curses to mines and shrinking spells to main rooms and not passageways. Lila didn't know that. She underestimated him just as she always had. Jedediah could get through and was more powerful than she could ever imagine. At the last moment, I held out my arms to stop my friends stepping forward. 'Wait! ... Watch.'

They did as they were told. Ollie looked at me, puzzled, but no one moved. Lila, full of the smugness I was expecting, grinned. She was already thinking she could skip round him and escape into the house. Except Jedediah moved to reveal Lucinda barring her way. Lila let out a single blast of laughter and rolled her eyes. 'Out of my way, you silly bitch. You couldn't stop me back then and you can't stop me now. I'm alive and this is my house. You're not even a Blackwood,' she spat, venomously.

She didn't even give Lucinda a chance to get out of the way before she stepped right through her like she didn't exist.

Then, before any of us knew what was happening, the evil blackness I recognised, whipped up lightning fast from the doorway, cloaking her in a whirlwind of black smoke. It billowed and engulfed her, smothering her screams. Her agonised face reappeared, the ceiling split with a single, blood-curdling shriek that stuttered and gurgled and the silky smoke shot into her mouth and suffocated her. She dropped to the floor in a convulsing heap and the smoke simply evaporated into the air. She eventually stopped twitching and her eyes, red with blood, stared vacantly into the distance with her skin ashen and lifeless. She was dead. We could all see it. It made me think of her own words: that the fountain waters only worked to prolong and rejuvenate life that was already there. It didn't give immortality. Here was the proof.

By the time we tore our eyes away, Jedediah and Lucinda had gone.

'Oh my God,' Tallulah said. 'What was that thing?' She comically picked up the compact still attached to the strap of her bag, looked at it and then directly at me for the answer. It was as if it had only just occurred to her that I wasn't in it. 'Did you see it?'

I grinned and nodded. I couldn't help myself. There was no one quite like Tallulah to bring a girl back to earth.

'Yeah,' Ollie said. 'It's like nothing I've ever seen.'

'I have,' I said more to myself. 'Well, I've sensed it.' I couldn't be absolutely sure, but I had a deep-seated feeling that it was the thing that had followed me into Wax's IP. 'I think it escaped from the Dark Web with me. I thought it had gone, but it must have escaped into the real world or the curse. I don't really know anymore.' And I didn't. I was here, but I wasn't. It was confusing.

'Bloody hell,' Archie said, pulling Nicola closer.

We all felt uneasy that it could now literally be anywhere.

'I think it's over,' Sam said, bringing us back to the present.

For now, I added in my head. But she was right. I was too tired to face anything else. A bone-deep fatigue swept through me. I looked down at my hand and it was barely there. I was slipping away and I had to fight with every ounce of my being to stay. I couldn't leave yet, until I knew Wax was safe.

We trudged back in the direction of the Waxley-Black house, subdued and in shock. I suppose everyone was exhausted and no one could fully believe it was over. I was too tired to put a dampener on it, but it wasn't over for me. Nor was it for Lucinda and Jedediah. The Shades were still Shades and we were all trapped on our separate planes – even though the lines had blurred a little today. Strangely it was Tallulah who eventually voiced it as we reached the house. 'It's not really over, is it?'

She was actually quite intuitive at times.

We piled into the hallway as Wax was helping his father bring his mother in through the front door. They all looked bedraggled and covered in dirt, but Olivia looked the most frail of all. Like an earthquake victim brought shakily from the rubble, which she kind of was.

They helped her into the sitting room and sat her down on the small sofa. Wax's father poured her a small glass of brandy and knocked one back himself. Seeing Olivia sink blissfully into the soft chair seemed to compound my own feelings of exhaustion. My eye was drawn to the mirror above the fireplace and it called to me like a crystal lake on a hot day. While my friends all had their attention on Olivia and congregated in a group on the expensive rug, I took a quiet step back from everyone else. I wanted Wax to notice me, but he was more concerned about his mother; finding a thick throw and tucking it in all around her knees. It was selfish of me, I knew, but I suddenly felt needy, not knowing my place anymore. My eyes strayed to the mirror again, like it was pulling me. Suddenly its power seemed far stronger than my will to stay. I was simply too tired. For a second, panic seized me that I wasn't there at all. I felt weird, like in the moments before you went to sleep. Perhaps they could no longer see or sense me. After all, everyone had taken the waters. We weren't exactly alive and no one knew how it would affect them.

I must have drifted as when I next opened my eyes, I was back in the greyness of the Inside Out. I went closer to the glowing glass and peered through the mirror above them.

None the wiser to my exit from the room, Wax's father shook his head and threw back another drink and held out his hand flat to show just how shaky he was.

'You OK?' Wax asked him, when he was satisfied his mother was comfortable.

'I don't know what to say to you,' his dad replied.

Olivia began to cry. 'To think we left you alone with that lunatic. He was unhinged,' she said.

Wax's dad let out a deep breath and nodded his agreement. 'You have to know we had no idea, Son.'

'I know,' Wax said. 'A lot of people were taken in by him.'

'There's nothing wrong with you, is there.' his father said as a statement. 'Can you ever forgive us?'

Wax let out a single blast of laughter. 'Except anger issues? No. And I guess I can. Things will change. It'll be easier for us all.'

'I'd better call 999 for Ainsley's body,' he said, wearily taking out his phone.

His mom cried harder and Wax put his arms around her. 'Don't cry. Why wouldn't you believe him? I was all over the place.' He kissed the top of his mother's head and she continued to dab her eyes.

'So what happens now? I guess we should just sell the place. Put the whole sorry mess behind us.'

Wax straightened up while he appeared to think about that. It struck me then that Wax was free. He looked over at the group that included Ollie and I couldn't tell if Wax could see them or not. Ollie stood silently, looking on, as if he didn't want to sway his decision either way. I guess he loved his brother very much and didn't want to tie him down any longer. Still, it was heart-breaking to watch. 'You can't,' Wax said, emphatically, as if he'd made up his mind.

I couldn't help the small leap in my heart. Hoping it was partly me that had helped him come to that decision. 'This house must always stay linked to the Blackwoods and owning it is the only way to be sure of that. Don't you under-stand? With the fountain and the curse, it can't fall into anyone else's hands.'

My heart broke for the enormous sacrifice he was making.

His father looked concerned and came and put his hand on his son's shoulder. 'I know the mine is yours, Son. I'm not trying to deprive you of any inheritance, but do you want it hanging around your neck like a great albatross? This is your chance to be young and start to live.' He gave his shoulder a squeeze. 'You could be free and have an ordinary life.'

Everything his father said was true. However, Wax turned and any doubt I had of what he could see evaporated as he looked directly at his brother. 'And I will, you can count on it. Ainsley took enough of my life, but I can do that without letting this place go. Ainsley has gone, but he's left a huge mess. Hundreds of Shades have been called and need my

296

help. They're frightened and alone and need guidance. I think I owe them that much.'

He still hadn't looked at me, but I was so proud of him then.

His father embraced him and smacked his back, 'The title will eventually be yours and I couldn't be prouder,' he said. 'Archibald Breton Waxley-Black, Viscount of Bondsborough.

'Oh my god,' Tallulah said, which cut through my shock.

I had no idea Wax was part of the peerage. He looked an unlikely candidate in his ragged, grey 'Shot Away' t-shirt and covered in tattoos. Even Ollie sniggered.

Olivia stood and joined in the hug. She looked into Wax's father's eyes and something passed between them. 'We'll move back here with you … if you want us to, that is,' she said, a little unsure. 'At least until you move on with your life.'

Wax hugged her to him and nodded. Hiding his emotion in her neck. 'It's all I've ever wanted, to be a family again.' He pulled apart, head hung low, exhausted and clearly relieved he didn't have to fight them anymore.

'Well, that's settled, then. I think I'll get your mother off to bed. I'll have to deal with the police when they get here, then we'll make a plan of action when we've had time to rest,' his father said, giving his shoulder a last squeeze. Then he helped Olivia out of her chair and headed for the door. 'Get some rest too. I want us to talk.'

I felt emotion rising in me too, watching Wax. He looked so vulnerable and young. As if conversations like this had happened so rarely in his life, he was bewildered at the thought of them. It did my heart good to think it would be a new era for him. For the first time, Wax had hope for the future.

The door closed and Wax came and stood in front of us all. His emotion had cleared and he just glared at us all one by one – particularly me in the mirror. 'So is someone going to tell me what you assholes have really been up to?'

After a beat of silence, everyone spoke at once.

'The tunnel was a last-minute opportunity to get around the curse. We couldn't ignore it,' Ollie said.

'And Beccah was safely in the Inside Out – well she was to begin with and Jedediah was on her side, anyway,' Tallulah threw in.

'He led us to the fountain, which was really his anyway,' Archie said.

Everyone pled their case until Wax had to put up his hands to shut us up. 'OK, OK, I think I got the gist of all that. You managed to save our arses. Thank you.' His eyes flicked to mine and, for a moment, I felt a tiny glimmer of hope that he still felt the same about me. Then it was gone when he turned to his brother, clicked his fingers and pointed at me. 'Send her back to my IP. I want a word with her … alone.'

My heart dropped into my stomach. I was scared. Really, this time. Tallulah giggled and grinned at me like a traitor.

CHAPTER 29

I stared into Wax's beautiful glacier-blue eyes. Eyes that now looked tired and not at all repentant. I wanted him to spill out apologies, begging me to forgive how he'd acted, but instead he was stern; as if he was waiting for something from me.

Suddenly, it all got too much. I hated that he made me feel this way. That it mattered that he was angry or thought of me at all. Tears prickled behind my eyes and I battled to get them to stay put. My face felt hot and I'm sure I came across angry. 'So what now? Your girlfriend is gone and all your plans are out of the window.'

Infuriatingly, he gave me no help to argue. In fact, he didn't bite at all. He just raised his eyebrows as if I'd surprised him.

I continued, regardless. 'What? You think we can pick up where we left off after you sold me out and smooched with a girl right in front of me?'

I could tell he was trying not to laugh. The corners of his mouth went to twitch and it was clearly taking effort to hold them in place. I wanted to hit him. I wanted to pull out my own hair and scream how much I hated him for what he did. 'It was like I didn't exist,' I said in the end, through gritted teeth to stop myself. 'The whole time she was out there with you, you only had time for her.' Now I'd started speaking, it was all coming out from the depths of me and I couldn't stop. Tears began to stream down my cheeks and all he did was stare back, astonished, and, in the end, sad. He let me rant on and that made me more wretched.

I went on about Pete and how alone I was until I'd met him and how he'd blown it, 'Because I'm stupid and you're sexy and have the whole quiet, brooding thing going on. But not anymore. No, sir. No way.'

He followed what I said, his eyebrows raising, then squinting, trying to follow and make sense of my tirade. At some parts he frowned, like he was sad or concerned. Others his mouth moved as if to smile and thought better of it, which was wise in my current, unhinged state. However, the thing that upset me most was that, through it all, he listened and didn't butt in once, when all I wanted was for him to wrap his arms around me and tell me it was OK. But he didn't because he couldn't. It was something he would never be able to do.

Then he said those three words that just stopped me dead.

'I love you.'

He didn't shout them, just said them matter of factly, as if the idea had just come to him right then.

I sat and stared at him as my chest heaved in and out with everything I'd just thrown at him. 'I'm dead, Wax,' I said, simply, without even voicing the whole 'I'm stuck in here thing'. 'And even if, by some miracle, we manage to break the curse, it would mean everyone would go. Ollie, Tallulah and the others might pass over. We would never see them again.'

We stared at each other another full minute while the

thought sunk in with both of us. 'The elixir only works on live people, Wax. Ainsley said it himself. It was the whole reason they had to get Lila out of here.' I thought about how we'd all taken a drink before Wax had got to the cave. How, deep down, we'd all hoped for a miracle. But it didn't come. Even my ability to manifest as a spirit in their world was temporary. 'They all drank it and they're still Shades, Wax,' I said, more gently.

Wax absorbed what I said without saying anything. I hated that I'd had to lay it on the line so brutally. Even his genius brain couldn't get them out of this one.

I relented a little. 'For what it's worth, I love you too,' I said eventually. 'Even though you don't deserve it.' I tried to recapture my anger of earlier, but it was replaced by an over-whelming hopelessness. I started to cry again. 'I can't be a spectator on everyone's lives, Wax. And I can't expect you to stay on your own, can I? I can't pretend I'm not trapped in here. It's worse than death.' I stared at him and he looked back at me, his own eyes glassy with emotion. 'Say something, please.'

He closed his eyes and, for once, I actually thought he'd accepted and agreed with something I said. 'I have an idea.'

I went to interrupt and talk over him, but his eyes held such sadness that I knew whatever it was was not going to solve a thing, well, not for him, anyway. 'Go on,' I said, scraping my tears away on my fingers. 'No more spells or computer systems or robots,' I threw in.

He smiled a little and shook his head. 'No robots.'

He bent down, rummaged in his bag by his feet and pulled out the glass bottle and put it on the desk between us. I recognised it right away. 'Elixir? But we already know that it won't work on me.'

He took a deep breath as if he was summoning the courage for something. 'Do you trust me?'

I studied him to gauge him for a moment. 'Smooching other girls in front of me, aside, you mean?'

He rolled his eyes and grinned. Then he got serious again. 'Shades sleep, right?'

I nodded, not sure I was going to like where he was going with this. 'Yes, but—'

'I think I can put you into sleep mode on my computer until I get you back – properly, I mean.'

I stared at him blankly. 'Why? What are you going to do?' All my accusations of earlier disappeared in my absolute panic that he was just going to leave me.

'You said you hate it there and I can make it easier. You can sleep until I find a way to get you out.'

'You're crazy,' I said, already thinking of excuses of why it was a terrible idea. 'It could take you years,' seemed the most obvious.

'You won't know or feel anything. The next thing you'll know is that you'll wake up with me.' He finished speaking and there was such a plea in his eyes and such an unsure smile that I couldn't ignore what he was saying.

It was too fantastic to ever come true, but he believed it and was offering me a way.

And I was tired. So tired of it all. Of being upset. Of being alone. 'Can I say goodbye to everyone first?' It came out before I had a chance to overthink it.

He closed his eyes and nodded. 'Of course.'

We both knew it was the best idea in a terrible situation. 'Then let's do it.'

'It's not as easy as that. We'll do it first thing in the morning when I've had time to think it through. I don't want to make any mistakes.'

I knew what it was; it was a plea for rest, to process what had happened. I had to remember this was hard on him too. He'd gone through some monumental changes today. The vulnerability in it made me love him all the more, if that was possible. It was so open and honest, I couldn't argue against it. I just nodded. He looked paler than usual. His eyes were low with exhaustion and a small vein pulsed just above his eye. 'You'll sleep, then?' I said, half joking, not convinced he would.

'I always sleep when you're here.' It broke my heart, because I knew that I couldn't. I'd be right here watching him fall asleep and long to be able to be right there in the bed with him.

He angled the monitor and got under the quilt, patting it down so he could still see me. We watched each other for what felt like hours, until his eyelids lowered and he eventually got dragged into sleep.

I WAS WIDE AWAKE. I guess it was the idea that I could be in suspended sleep for ever and if my parents turned off my life support back home, I'd cease to exist. I hadn't had the heart to remind Wax of that. I was going along with his plan for him as much as anything else.

My world was pixelated in Wax's IP but I'd never really examined me. My person. I felt real. To look at, everything was there: arms, legs, fingers and toes, but everything seemed a weird colour or out of focus. I laughed the same, cried the same, felt exactly the same as I was in the real world. Wax had designed a complete replica of his house like someone would a doll's house. Except I was living in this one.

With Wax sound asleep, I wondered over to the IP version of his bed and lay down. I felt the softness of the quilt and sunk into the deep, welcoming mattress. I came over with a soul-deep weariness that would take more than one night to go away. Maybe Wax's idea to sleep wasn't so bad. I was so tired of it all. It would feel good to let go and get carried by the stream for a change.

I sighed and turned over and let my mind wander for what felt like ages. Until the wonderful smell wound its way to my nostrils and the strong arm snaked over my waist and pulled me towards him.

Wax. I'd know his smell anywhere. The heady smell of clean soap and pure him. I turned into his chest and he gripped me tightly, his mouth burying in my hair and kissing the top of my head. 'Am I dreaming? Are you here in the program?'

'Does it matter?' he said, moving down to kiss me on the mouth.

Fleetingly, I thought of our first messages on the laptop and wondered if this was some kind of virtual meeting on the network, like that. But then his mouth found mine and I didn't care. His arms gripped me between my back and the bed and I opened my mouth and welcomed him. He tasted real, warm and wet and we rolled over until I was looking down at him. It was dark and I could just make out the pixe-lated angles of his face and the flaming wing tattoo by his ear. My whole body rested and felt all of his, warm and hard, against me. I couldn't see his eyes, but knew he was watching me as much as I was him.

He was right. It didn't matter if he'd come to me in a dream or some kind of chat room. We were together some-where and it felt as real and alive as if we were in his bed. 'I love you,' I whispered, figuring I was never going to get a better chance to say it.

'I love you,' he said right back.

I watched his lips say the words with my heart swelling to breaking point. He sat up with me in his lap, kissed gently down the side of my neck and I threw my head back, losing myself in the feel of him.

Then I understood, totally. Wax was giving me this one last perfect night of life, before he put me to sleep and it was as heart-breaking as it was perfect and beautiful. We would join together before we blew apart into a thousand shattered pieces.

I FORCED myself awake a few times to check he was there and he was. Wax slept the rest of the day and all through the night and I was right there with him. Then, at some point during the dawn, I must have dozed, because, with the creeping grey light, he was gone.

I went to the computer screen and the grey of his room looked no different to the Inside Out. It was so early. Except the rosy tint of dawn stole between a gap in the curtain to give away the real world. Wax's world that would forever be separate to mine. I imagined the dawn chorus of birds all competing in the garden for the loudest song. My world was so silent. Just the gentle mechanical hum of the computer system.

Wax was still in bed, his breathing moving the duvet gently. I remembered last night with a delicious ache in my lower abdomen. I blushed and my body warmed at the memory.

He'd woken while I was lost in thought. He lay there blinking, but his eyes were on me. He was paler in this light, but he looked happier and refreshed. 'Morning,' he said croakily, a crafty smile stealing across his face that instantly sent mine bursting red.

'It was real,' came out before I could stop it.

He sat up and put his feet out of the bed, onto the floor. He ran his fingers back through his messy hair and, still with his mischievous smile, said, 'Tech is a modern marvel.'

I put my hand to my mouth and laughed. He stood and

padded over to me, but when he looked down at me his head tilted to the side and he looked sad. He didn't say anything. He didn't have to. In the end he just said, 'I'll shower and get the others.'

I think it was the longest fifteen minutes of my life, particularly as I understood it was probably the last fifteen minutes of my life. The current one, anyway. There was one last place I had to go, that Wax would not understand.

Ollie had usually been the one to throw me out of the IP into the Inside Out, but today I concentrated like I never had before. Just like when I went from the IP to a phone device, I imagined the fibre optics and wires like tunnels, until I screwed my eyes shut and landed straight into the tunnel between the houses. I guessed that was the limit of the Waxley-Black Wi-Fi reach. As soon as I got my bearings and was confident that I'd actually done it, I ran the rest of the way to my aunt's.

There were people I needed to say goodbye to. People who'd been there for me when no one else had. I ran to the kitchen and couldn't get in. Of course, there were no mirrors. Then I ran to my aunt's sitting room. It was morning, she'd be taking her tea by now. I peered down from the huge mirror over the fireplace.

My heart leapt. Gerty was there pouring her tea, just like I guess she'd always had for years. 'Aunt! Gerty!' I shouted.

Gerty stood, looked around her.

'Over here. In the mirror.'

She came closer to the fireplace.

'I'm in here.'

'Who is it, Gerty?' my aunt said. 'If it's that girl and she's got herself into trouble, confine her to her room. Tell her, Gerty. American girls. So much more wild than English ones,' my aunt wittered on.

Gerty found me and smiled knowingly. 'It's alright, Sarah. I see her. She seems fine to me.'

I smiled. I knew instantly she understood. 'You found the Waxley-Black boy, I see.' She spoke severely, but there was kindness in her eyes.

'Yes, I've been with Tallulah,' I said. 'I wanted to thank you and let you know I won't be around for a while, you know, so my aunt doesn't worry.'

She nodded slowly. 'I'll pass that on.' She smiled and turned her attention back to my aunt, who was getting flustered with her blanket not being tucked in properly around her knees. I took one last look at them and went back to the hallway. There were two last people I needed to see.

I slowly walked up the staircase, taking in all the paintings. I remembered my plaster cast and how it made me slower examining each of the faces. Until I reached the last one at the top. Strangely, she didn't look quite so smug. 'Lucinda!' I called. Then I waited. I called three more times and was just about to give up when her outline came out of the wall from the secret passage. Of course. I should have known she would be somewhere there.

'I just wanted to thank you and say goodbye. For a while, anyway.'

She hovered closely, looking a little more 3D than usual. She still looked as if she'd been drawn with chalk, but seemed a little more fleshed out. I could clearly see the detail of her simple white blouse tucked into the small waist of her checked voluminous skirt. There was even a lace shawl around her shoulders and her pale hair was parted and pinned in tight curls around her nape. 'Thank you,' she corrected, smiling kindly. 'You helped us achieve something we never thought possible. Justice was finally served, thanks to you.'

It was then I became aware of him, hovering at the far

end of the dim corridor. Jedediah's darkness engulfed me all the way from there. I could make out the edges of his black robe because of the light coming from his downcast eyes. 'Well, I didn't want to disappear without a goodbye,' I said. I felt such a weight of sadness in my stomach whenever I saw them – particularly Jedediah. This was no existence for them both. It didn't feel much like justice to me. 'Look, Wax is trying to help me, and he seems to think he can find a way of bringing me back, so, if he does and it works, I promise to help you guys, OK?'

Lucinda smiled at Jed; he remained motionless. 'You have already done quite enough, but we wish you well and hope to one day see you again.'

I nodded. A weird lump appeared in my throat. I think it was because it was so non-committal, as if they hoped so, but thought it unlikely. They evaporated into the air leaving a cloud of sadness. I realised it was as much for me as it was for them because I was as hopeless as they were. Except, instead of roaming corridors, I was going to be in a deep sleep that my prince might never be able to wake me up from.

I wandered back to the tunnel, took a ragged breath and screwed my eyes shut. I imagined the nearest light socket and zoomed along the superhighway of wires back to his room. Then I concentrated myself back into Wax's IP.

I was just in time to see all my friends traipse into Wax's room. Ollie was holding Tallulah's hand. I was happy to see them and was now convinced they were definitely an item. 'Hey, wait! Can you feel each other now?' I mean I knew they could a little, but this was monumental. Tears were forming in my eyes and I had to get a grip before they fell and ruined my goodbye.

They were all grinning and nodding. Wax gave Ollie a

loud slap on the back to prove it. 'Yeah, they're getting more physical all the time.'

'We still ghost out sometimes though,' Ollie said with a shrug.

'We can do both,' Tallulah said, chirpily as if she'd found out she was double-jointed or something.

'Do you think you're all becoming alive?' I grasped my own mouth to stifle a sob. Maybe the elixir was working slowly on them and Lila just didn't know how it would affect them.

'No, I don't think so,' Archie said.

'I feel more solid though,' Nicola said and leaned in and kissed him on the mouth.

'It's like a miracle for us,' Sam said.

I looked at Wax for the answer and he just shrugged. 'I have no idea what's going on.'

'Can your mom and dad see them?'

Wax frowned. 'I dunno. Doubt it.'

'Call them Wax. For me. Let me see it before I go.'

He held my gaze for a minute and then nodded. I guess he didn't want to raise anyone's hopes and wanted to put off disappointment for as long as possible. He strode over to the door, pulled it open and called out through the gap. 'Mum! Dad! Can you come in here please?'

I got the impression they still weren't up as Olivia's voice came from upstairs. 'Coming. What is it?'

After a couple of minutes Olivia and Jed came in, still arranging their dressing gowns, hair ruffled from sleep. 'What is it?' Wax's father said. 'Is everything OK?'

Wax took a step back and Ollie took a step forward. Jed looked at Wax curiously. Nothing looked any different to me.

Then I saw it; the dawning of realisation on both Jed and Olivia's faces. They looked shocked, then their expression filled with joy as Ollie became real to them. They both rushed over and hugged him fiercely, Olivia planting noisy kisses on him the whole time. They were both crying and Wax stood by and watched, bemused. They eventually straightened, still not letting go of him and looked around. 'Tallulah,' Olivia said, holding out the palm of her hand to touch Tallulah's cheek. 'Archie, Nicola, Samantha, Josh, Joe. You're all here.'

It was clear the moment they couldn't hold their form because they both turned frantically as if to look where they went. They were, of course, standing in exactly the same place.

Wax came forward and held his mother. 'I thought … I thought he'd come back to us,' she sobbed into Wax's chest.

His father put a hand to his forehead, trying to get a hold on his emotions. He turned away and then turned back sharply. 'What's happening?'

Wax shook his head. 'Honestly, I don't know. Maybe Lila was right about the whole being alive thing. But being a Shade is a whole other thing entirely. They're not ghosts, they were conjured by Ainsley. So maybe they have something else. The ability to be both. It's hard to be sure at this stage.'

Olivia looked up at Wax as he held her to him. 'Are they still here?'

He nodded. 'Annoyingly so.'

His mother smiled. A couple of the others sniggered. It broke the tension.

'We'll talk later, OK. I'll explain everything,' he said directly to his father. Then he looked down at his mother again and spoke more softly. My heart warmed at the voice I realised he reserved only for her. 'There's someone else I need to speak to first.'

Olivia frowned as she pulled apart and, surprisingly, she looked straight at the computer screen and saw me. Recognition was clear on her face. 'Hi, Mrs Waxley-Black,' I said, with a little wave.

She came closer to the screen. 'This is the girl, Jed. The one who helped us all.'

Wax's father stood next to her and smiled, his eyes glassy and emotional. 'Thank you ... I mean it. For being there for my sons. Both of them.'

Olivia hugged into his side. I didn't know what to say. I saw the questions in their eyes, like, where was I, was I real and why wasn't I like the others? They were all there in a single moment, but, thankfully, Wax came to my rescue and herded them towards the door. 'Can you give us a minute alone, please? That means all of you,' he said over his shoulder at the others.

His father laughed. It was kind of funny and absurd. They all left, one by one, until just Tallulah and Ollie remained.

Wax rolled his eyes as if he'd had enough of the whole being sociable thing.

'So you're actually doing this?' Tallulah said.

I nodded, holding tears back, prickling my eyes.

'Can't you just stay ... for me?' she said. 'It's not so bad, is it?'

I laughed. 'I'm in a box, Tallulah.'

She laughed through her tears, begrudgingly. 'But you'll be back, right? We'll see

you again.'

'Wax is working on it,' I said more softly. I studied her pretty face, unusually bare from all the makeup as it was still early.

Wax was becoming impatient and sat down on his stool in front of her. She'd run out of time. 'It's not goodbye, just see you later, OK?'

Ollie put his arm around her shoulder and led her towards the door. The whole time, I was aware of Wax's

311

fingers clicking across the keys and Tallulah watching me over her shoulder until she was led out of sight and Ollie closed the door behind them.

My eyes went to Wax's. He'd finished whatever he was doing and his look was strong and direct. At least there was no lie, or flowering anything up in that look. I guess that was part of what I loved about him. 'I love you,' came out before I could even think about it.

He didn't answer. Not because he didn't feel it, but because he had to stay strong. I understood. 'When I put this program into sleep mode, it will power down and take you with it. You shouldn't feel a thing.'

My heart was pounding. It was like death, I guessed. But choosing to do it. There was never going to be a good time. I had to just do it. I took a breath, nodded and swallowed hard. 'I'll count back from three and when you wake up, it will be in the flesh. OK?'

I was terrified. I took a moment to map his face. The strain showed in the red around his eyes and the tightness of his jaw. I gave one stiff, final nod.

'Three ... two—'

'See you *soon*' died on my breath. Light zeroed to a single pinpoint and a high-pitched buzzing plummeted, as if a TV had died during a power outage.

CHAPTER 30

'*M*y baby … Oh my god, John, it's a miracle.'

I blinked rapidly and then squinted at the head-splittingly bright overhead light. My mouth was dry, my throat sore and I couldn't speak. Hands reached behind my head and guided me to a beaker tilted at my lips. I took a few loud gulps that were a little clumsy and water trickled down my chin and cheeks. Something soft immediately dabbed it away.

'Rebecca, darling, can you hear me?'

I turned towards the female voice next to me. 'Mom?' I croaked.

'Yes … yes, it's me. Tears were streaming down her cheeks. 'Dad's here too.'

Dad appeared at her shoulder. 'Hey, pumpkin. You had us all worried.'

My eyes slowly focused on his face, smiling down at me. He seemed older and greyer somehow. For a moment, I was confused and went to sit up, but gentle hands pushed me back down. 'You've been out a while. It'll take time before you can get up.'

'You broke your leg and you haven't walked since the accident. You've been in a coma, honey.'

Then the intersection, the side impact and Pete came back to me. Grief punched and gripped my heart and threatened to squeeze the life out of it. The terrible hurt was reflected back at me through both my parents' eyes and I knew it was true. Pete was gone, and, because I had been on the other side of the car, I'd managed to survive.

I went to turn away from them to curl up in a ball but my mother's hands stopped me. 'It wasn't your fault, darling. Some teenagers ran a red light.'

It didn't make hearing Pete was gone any easier and I began to cry. 'I'm sorry … so sorry.'

As my mother hugged me to her chest and her warm scent wrapped itself around me, I remembered a dream I'd had of Pete from when I slept. In it he'd told me it wasn't my fault and there was more I didn't know. Strangely, it made me feel slightly better. Like he hadn't left me completely alone. I stopped crying and looked into the devastated eyes of my parents. 'You never gave up on me in all that time.'

Both took it in turns to kiss me. 'Of course not. You're our girl,' my mom said.

A nurse came forward and changed my IV and took down my vitals for her chart. I watched her, but my mind was on a bizarre jumble of images. Voices and people were in them I didn't recognise. 'The doctor will be in to see you shortly,' the nurse said.

My eyes followed her to the door and to the tall boy standing there.

'Someone else never gave up on you,' my mom said.

I couldn't stop looking at him. I knew that boy. He was tall, with black hair and impossibly blue eyes and his pale skin was covered with tattoos. I looked at my parents, surprised they even let him in here.

I sifted through the many pictures I had in my head and he was in them all. Laughing, sometimes grumpy and always English. For a moment, I wondered if I'd seen him on TV and incorporated it into my dream.

'He came all the way from England to see you,' my dad said, as if it was an enormous feat. But I guess, just to see me, it was.

'He said you two had been talking online for a while.'

The boy approached the bed. He was very tall, towering over my parents. He was wearing a t-shirt with *A Tad Grungy* over the front of it and black skinny jeans. I could see his scary, cool tats running the length of his arms, right down to his fingers and even up the side of his neck. Boys my age had a few, but he showed serious commitment. There were even some small stars on his temple I could see when he was right beside my bed. And I knew that I knew them. That there were seven in a triangle. I'd seen them up close.

I looked at my parents and they didn't seem fazed by him at all. I blinked and stared back at him, at those remarkably familiar blue eyes. 'Vampire Boy?' came to me straight out of left field.

He grinned, transforming his face into the most beautiful thing I'd ever seen. 'Hello, Beccah,' he said, as if I'd done something truly remarkable. 'My name is Bret, but people call me Wax.'

My heart stopped beating in my chest as everything came back to me in one huge wave. I was vaguely aware of my parents moving away and mumbling something about getting some coffee. The memories engulfed me in a torrent, too fantastic and unbelievable to think they could possibly be true, but I had them, even though logic told me I'd been asleep for eighteen months.

I felt his warm hand take mine and it immediately grounded me. I could focus on the delicate arrows drawn down his fingers and the softness of his touch. He seemed as amazed as I was.

'Do you remember me?' he said.

I looked up at him and he seemed unsure. His accent was rich and British and I did remember it. I even knew the soft curls of his hair that came forward around his face and gently skimmed the collar of his shirt. I knew him. 'I don't understand. Have we met?'

'Not exactly,' he said, his eyes devilishly low.

'TAKE off will be in ten minutes. Please store your luggage neatly overhead,' the steward said over the speaker on the British Airways flight about to take off from LAX to London Heathrow.

Wax held my hand from the window seat next to me. My mom's came through the gap in the headrest and gave my shoulder a squeeze. They seemed to all sense that I still couldn't totally believe it. Me, my mom and my dad, all making a new start and moving to England, permanently. Wax had explained everything and I have to admit it took me a while to absorb it at first.

To my parents, Wax came from a small village that happened to be next to the house that would soon be ours. He'd brought papers from local lawyers, stating that, as the last surviving Blackwoods, the manor house was ours.

At first my dad wanted to sell it, but I begged him not to. Pete had gone and this was the new start we all needed. I knew, in my heart of hearts, if Pete were here, he'd be into it too. Wax was tempting enough, but something called me to the place.

Wax had helped me research the school system and I learned that there was a St Bart's and it had a great sixth form where I could repeat what I'd missed and the UK had some great colleges. So I was really doing this. Moving to a new country, lock stock and scary barrel, to meet the people I only thought existed in a dream.

We began to taxi down the runway and saw the buildings of LA drift slowly by. I knew I'd never see them again. It was a chapter in my life I wanted closed.

Wax gave my hand a squeeze as if I'd given my thoughts away. 'Not long now,' he said. 'Just a short sleep and we'll be there.' A sexy, slow smile spread over his face and his eyes twinkled with mischief. My heart sped up when I remembered the last time I'd heard him say that. It was in a dream of an unbelievable night together, where he'd given his promise, that, before I knew it, I'd wake and see him again.

He was the one that had seen the solicitor and got the Blackwood house transferred to my parents. Then he'd come halfway across the world, joked that he'd secretly fed me magic elixir taken from his family's mine and woken me up, just like he promised me he would.

He'd stayed for weeks, visiting me in hospital every day, encouraging me to walk again through endless physiotherapy. Never giving up until I was eventually jogging and showing him around the town. Every night the dreams came to me and he was in them all. I came to realise they were memories. They had to be, *didn't they?* How else would Wax know all about them?

'I know you, don't I? Really, I mean. Not just since I woke up?'

He was holding my hand across the armrest looking deeply into my eyes, so honest and intense and simply nodded.

I thought of him in all my dark, foreboding dreams, watching over me from the shadows. Others were with him; ghosts, spectres, grey light and gloom. But I wasn't scared. Strangely, despite the gloom and darkness, I felt a warmness from it all. How could I not? It was why I was sitting in the seat I was in today.

The plane rose and my spirits lifted. I was starting a new life where I'd see this intriguing boy every day. We settled back, the lights went off and I became sleepy. 'Tell me the story again about the rebel viscount who travelled the world to rescue his sleeping beauty with the potion he'd fought the wicked witch for.'

Wax narrowed his eyes on me, gauging whether he liked me making fun of him or not. He could be so stern at times. He let out a weary breath as if I'd worn him down. 'OK … well there was me … you know, your handsome, tall, dark and dangerous boyfriend.'

'Username Vampire Boy,' I added.

He gave me a nod. 'And I contacted a mysterious girl in my dream.'

'Me, Pearl White.'

He rolled his eyes. 'Are you going to let me tell you this story or not?'

I nodded, grinning. I'd made him tell me the story a hundred times, but it never got old. I'd never let him stop telling it.

'Well, there is my annoying younger brother, Ollie, and his even more annoying tagalong girlfriend, with the hideous laugh and all their annoying friends that I tolerate for your sake.'

I laughed out loud.

'You can laugh, but they never do a damn thing I say.' He turned to face me squarely and spoke more softly. 'But you'll like them. They're all waiting to see you, for real, in the flesh, for the first time …'

Protector
Lost Moon

Non-Fiction

My Migraine Story

CONTACT T

To receive your two 21st Century Sirens Novellas, and be the first to know anything relating to T's books, leave your details here:
https://mailchi.mp/d18c89c14f50/tstedmannovellas
And please don't forget to leave a review wherever you bought your book, I really appreciate the feedback.
Much love,
T
www.tstedman.com

https://www.facebook.com/TStedman1author/

https://twitter.com/AuthorTStedman

COMING NEXT IN 2021:

The first book in a new series: **Young Atleanteans**

And more in the **Night Shade series** ...
To learn more, visit:

www.stedman.com

Printed in Great Britain
by Amazon